THE PRAETORIAN
AND THE EMPEROR'S LIST

BY

ROD WARREN

TABLE OF CONTENTS

****

PREFACE

The year is A.D. 29* and Antonius Licinius is a precocious teenage boy living on his family's vineyard near the town of Aletium in the Italian southern province of Calabria. The small vineyard has been a family affair to produce and distribute the wine they make, owned by Antonius's father-Galerius. Galerius has not always been a wine-maker, however. Ten years previously, he was a Tribune in Rome's elite Praetorian Guard, serving under Emperor Augustus Caesar. He earned his way through the ranks of the army by being the most feared man on the battlefield. In numerous military campaigns, he was personally responsible for sending over 300 men to their deaths. When Augustus learned of Galerius's remarkable achievements in combat, he made him a Tribuni Augusticlavii in his newly formed Praetorian Guard. After Augustus died, the new emperor–Tiberius, assigned Galerius to be the head of his palace guard. Six years into Tiberius's rule, the emperor made a decision that greatly infuriated Galerius. Feeling he could no longer serve Tiberius; Galerius retired from the Guard and purchased the vineyard in Aletium, resuming the trade that his family once practiced. But Antonius has decided that winemaking is not for him. He longs to follow in his father's footsteps and become a member of the Praetorian Guard. Although Galerius hasn't encouraged him to pursue his dream, he has taught him how to use a gladius (short sword) and pilum (javelin) in case he was called upon to serve Rome as a soldier. Now Antonius is old enough to serve in Rome's military. He has decided to join the army where he hopes to distinguish himself enough to be considered for the Praetorian Guard like his father once was. Marcus, a friend who lives just over the hill, has a strained relationship with his father and desires to leave as well. He shares Antonius's dream about eventually becoming a Praetorian. Certain events are about to take place, however, that will give them the opportunity to realize their dream much sooner than they anticipate.

*The Roman date for A.D. 29 is actually 782 A.U.C., which was used by Roman historians, signifying the number of years since the founding of Rome. Since A.D. is more commonly recognized, the years will be described in that manner.

****

ACKNOWLEDGMENTS

To Shauna, my bright star, whose patience and
support made the writing of this book possible.

A special thanks to:
Editor/ writing coach, Fran Smeath
and English Professor Roger Ekins,
whose honest and insightful critiques made the story better.
Last but not least, all the credit for the inspiration goes to God.
****

Justice is defined by law;
Vengeance is defined by the unforgiving.
****

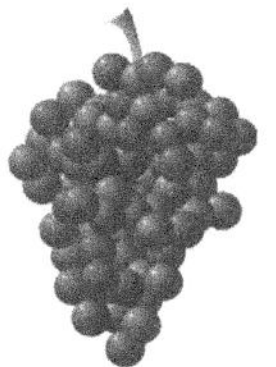

CHAPTER I-THE VINEYARD

Drusus shouted at the man he had just struck with his fist and knocked to the floor. "I know you've been secretly seeing my wife," he snarled. "It ends now or I will see to it your end will come!"

The man rose to his feet and wiped the blood from his mouth. Looking at Drusus with a tightened jaw, he said, "You may be the emperor's son, but you would be wise to watch how much you drink rather than watching your wife. Too much wine can be dangerous."

Ignoring the veiled threat, Drusus pointed to the door and shouted, "Leave my house, now!"

Feeling his temperature rising, the man looked around at the other dinner guests. Some of the women looked at their husbands while the men avoided his gaze and gave each other grim looks. The room was deathly quiet.

The man directed a menacing look toward Drusus then whirled about and departed with a snarl on his lips.

Drusus bowed unsteadily to his dinner guests and said, "My apologies for the incident. Please... eat, drink, enjoy yourselves. This is a party."

His wife Livilla, however, clenched her teeth and said, "I think the party's over for me," and stormed out.

Later that evening, the man Drusus struck made his way down dark stone steps, barely seeing where they led. His name was Lucius Sejanus and he was the head of Emperor Tiberius' Praetorian Guard. A torch, fortunately, gave him enough light to navigate and at the bottom, he entered a room lined with long wooden tables. Cages made of tightly woven metal strands sat on top. His curiosity aroused, he walked over to one cage and peered in. The tightly coiled black serpent lying inside suddenly spread its hood and gave out a warning hiss. Sejanus flinched and backed away. Quickly walking past the other cages, he approached the door on the other side of the room that was partially open exposing a shaft of light coming from inside. He slowly opened the door and saw a middle-aged man with dark hair graying at his temples, sitting at a table on the far side of the room. He seemed busy extracting liquid from a reddish-stemmed plant with white flowers. When the door creaked as it opened, he turned to see who the unexpected visitor was. "Who are you and what do you want?" he asked suspiciously.

"My name isn't important," replied Sejanus, who kept his face well hidden under his hooded cloak. "I'm looking for a man called Glycon?"

"Why do you want Glycon?" the man at the table asked with narrowed eyes.

"I was told he is well versed with poisons and I need his expertise," Sejanus replied.

The man at the table barely smiled and said. "I am Glycon. How can I assist you?"

Sejanus seated himself on a stool across from Glycon, gave him a cold stare and said, "I need a toxic potion that will simulate a natural death and work very quickly. Of course, no one else is to know about this. Do you have what I need? I will pay you handsomely."

Glycon rubbed his chin and lifted his head back. "I have what you need," he replied.

A short while later, Sejanus walked back up the stairs clutching a vial that contained a deadly brownish liquid. As he entered the dark street, he mumbled, "I have no choice; Drusus must die."

The next evening, Drusus glared at his wife Livilla from across the table after they had finished their supper. He had not spoken to her since the incident at the dinner party. She glared back at him, still angry from his outburst.

"I think you owe me an apology for the way you acted at the party. You embarrassed me in front of all our friends," she snapped.

"Why should I apologize to my whore wife for being unfaithful?" he countered.

She stood up and marched over to where he was sitting. Pointing her finger at him, she snarled, "You have no proof I've been unfaithful to you."

He stood up to face her and said, "I have no proof? What about those times when I'm away at the palace and you go shopping... without your maid I might add. According to my spy, you go to Sejanus's villa instead."

Realizing she has been caught in her own tangled web, she said through clenched teeth, "You had me spied upon?"

He smiled.

His smile was like rubbing salt in the wound.

Her reaction was swift. Swinging her hand quickly, she slapped him hard on his left cheek.

He reaction was equally as swift. He slapped her on her left cheek.

Tears formed in her eyes and she quickly spun around and strode away so as not to give him satisfaction that she was crying.

Drusus grabbed his goblet of wine and went into the great room of their villa and stared out the window, contemplating divorce.

Livilla walked back into the dining area with a vial containing a brownish liquid in her hand. Approaching the table, she uncorked the vial and poured a small amount into the silver wine pitcher Drusus had been drinking from, then left. It wasn't long before Drusus returned to the table and poured another goblet full of wine from the pitcher.

He drank deeply from it and was about to say something derogatory about her when suddenly, he felt a strange sensation. The bronze goblet slipped from his fingers and hit the white marble floor with a "Clang!" sending its reddish-purple contents in all directions. He clutched his throat and gasped for air.

Hearing the noise, Livilla returned to the dining area.

He gave her a wide-eyed look and opened his mouth to speak. Only a gurgling sound came out. Struggling to breathe, he staggered toward her as she backed away. As he reached out to her, he realized what was happening. Expelling a grunting moan as his heart stopped beating, he fell to the floor in a prone position. A small amount of wine mixed with spittle trickled from his mouth onto the white marble as his gaze went fixed.

Livilla smiled then quickly changed her expression to that of shock. "Arcadius!" she called out to her male servant.

****

Six years later, a blue chariot sped down a back road heading toward the town of Aletium, Italy. The nineteen-year-old strapping young man driving it almost failed to notice a clutch of chickens in the road as he rounded a corner. Unable to avoid them, he closed his eyes as feathers flew and the frightened poultry burst from the road in all directions. Cautiously opening his eyes when the obstacles had cleared, he continued, brushing feathers off his tunic and face. He shivered slightly as the cool breeze rushed through his curly dark brown hair and across his bare arms. Snapping the reins, he commanded his two light bay stallions to run faster as the royal blue chariot rumbled down the dirt road. He named them Mercury and Mars after the Roman gods. Mercury was the faster of the two steeds and Mars, the most temperamental, so the monikers fit them. Naming his horses after Roman gods might have appalled the religiously devout, but Antonius was a skeptic like his father, Galerius. His mother, Octavia, who was more of a "believer" in the traditional Roman religious customs and ideology, had come to tolerate her husband and son's views after many unsuccessful attempts to convince them otherwise.

A golden ball of fire began to rise from the hills behind him introducing a new day. As its rays stretched out to warm the city, the sleepy townspeople also began to arise. As he turned down another road, he hoped that his friends had already arrived at thehippodrome[1], and they could get started immediately. He had chores to do and didn't want to return home late and face his father's ire. Pulling up to the small track used for local chariot racing, he smiled as he noticed two other young men waiting at the gate in their chariots.

Since the hippodrome conducted the races on Saturday afternoons, Antonius and his friends would secretly run their chariots early on Saturday mornings. They did this to avoid the man they called the "smoother" who would come to the track just before midday and drag a flat rectangular frame of wood around the track to prepare it for the afternoon races. Usually, they wouldn't even have been allowed on the track, but one of the Saturday morning racers just happened to be the son of the hippodrome's lap keeper who had a key to the gate. Although Antonius was old enough to enter the official races in the afternoon, he lacked the entry fees. That's why he and his friends raced in the morning. They would all bet small wagers on themselves to win; "winner take all." Most of the time Antonius would be victorious, but saving money for the entry fees proved to be harder than winning the races.

"Where's Virulus?" Antonius asked, bringing his chariot to a halt.

One of the young men made a face and said, "Late again, as usual."

"I can't wait all day for him to arrive; I have chores waiting for me," Antonius barked.

"We all do," the other young man said.

At that moment, a red chariot came thundering down the road.

"Ah, finally," Antonius said, raising his eyebrows.

The young man in the red chariot reined his horses to a stop, covering Antonius and the others with road dust.

Antonius gave a couple of pretended coughs to show his disgust and said, "It is about time you arrived."

1-An arena used for chariot racing and other sporting events

Virulus shook his head and said, "Don't chastise me, Licinius; I saw you just pull up yourself."

"Well, I still arrived before you did," Antonius stated in a mocking tone.

"Yes, but you won't cross the finish line before I do," Virulus countered with an confident smile as his sister stepped off his chariot.

"You're not going to let my brother talk to you like that, are you Antonius?" the pretty eighteen-year-old girl challenged him as she glided over to the gate.

Antonius wrinkled his nose. "I'll get even on the track, Diana."

She smiled coyly and unlocked the gate, allowing the four chariots and their two-horse teams to enter.

"Same wager?" Antonius asked as they headed for the starting line.

"Same as always," Virulus replied. "Diana, you start us and determine the winner as usual."

She nodded and took her place at the side of the coarse sandy track. Taking out a small scarf from her tunic sleeve, she held it up and shouted, "Line up, charioteers!"

The four young men took their positions and waited for the signal.

When Diana was satisfied they had lined up evenly, she let go of the scarf and the race began.

As the four chariots rumbled down the track picking up speed, the young charioteers pressed their horses to take the lead. Not wanting her brother to win, Diana shouted encouragement to Antonius as they came around after the first lap. "Go faster, Antonius!"

After several laps, it was evident Antonius or Virulus was going to win. By the end of the sixth lap, Virulus was in the lead by half a chariot length with Antonius running close behind.

Giving Antonius a sneer, Virulus shouted, "You'll have to go faster than that to beat me, vineyard boy!"

"Just have your money ready at the end of the race!" Antonius shouted back.

As they rounded the last turn and headed down the straightaway, they were dead even. Just before reaching Diana, Antonius's horses surged slightly ahead of Virulus's horses.

"Antonius wins!" she shouted, waving her scarf as they passed.

Bringing his chariot to a stop, Antonius smiled and turned to Virulus, who rolled up beside him.

With a smirk, Virulus pointed his finger at Antonius and said, "I almost had you that time, Licinius."

"Yes, but almost doesn't win the race," Antonius replied sarcastically. "Pay up, losers," he said with a smile as he held out his hand.

Virulus and the others each begrudgingly slapped five bronze coins in his hand then all passed back through the gate they came in.

"When are you going to enter your chariot in the real races, Antonius?" Virulus asked.

"When I win enough from you snails to pay for the entry fees," Antonius responded.

Virulus chuckled. "You keep spending your winnings on things for your horses and chariot."

"I have to make sure it outruns yours," Antonius replied with a grin.

Virulus frowned then asked, "Why don't you get your father to pay the entry fees?"

Antonius grimaced and said, "I don't think my father would approve of me racing in the first place."

"Afraid of competing against men who will run you into the wall if you get in their way?" Virulus mocked.

Antonius smiled. "No, I'm afraid you'll cry when I don't give you a chance to win back all the money you've lost to me on Saturday mornings."

"Hah! Come, Diana, we must return home before Antonius becomes insufferable," Virulus said to his sister as she locked the gate.

With a sultry smile, Diana turned to Antonius and asked, "I'll be glad to help you spend your winnings this morning, Antonius."

With a pained expression, Antonius replied, "Alas, If I didn't have chores to do I would take you up on that, Diana." Having a second thought, he said, "Meet me here this afternoon before the first race and you can help me then."

Virulus guffawed. "Like I said, Licinius. You can't save your money. Come, Diana, we need to return home."

She continued to smile at Antonius as she backed away from him.

"I'm leaving!" Virulus shouted.

"All right, all right!" she scoffed as she hurried over and climbed onto her brother's chariot. Giving Antonius one last provocative look, she waved as Virulus rumbled away.

"Next Saturday morning!" Antonius shouted to the others, as he sped off.

Taking the familiar road to his home, he pushed his tired horses for all the energy they had left and hoped his father hadn't started his day yet. Arriving at the vineyard he called home, he pulled up to the stable and brought his chariot to a stop. It was then that he noticed his father standing there with his arms folded and a frown on his face.

Just shy of four cubits[2] tall, Galerius Licinius was a stocky man with broad shoulders and arms thick like anacondas. Although his mood was austere most of the time, he had a humorous side that would occasionally show itself, but not this morning.

Antonius smiled sheepishly at his father.

"You just couldn't wait to take your chariot out, could you?" Galerius said in a tone more sarcastic than reprimanding.

"I'm sorry, Father, but I figured I'd go for a run before you awoke. You're up early today."

Galerius shook his head slightly and said, "I didn't sleep that well, so I decided to get an early start. Where have you been?"

"Just into town," Antonius replied.

"I hope you didn't wake up the townspeople with all the noise I'm sure you made," Galerius said raising his eyebrows. He knew Aletium had the closest paved roads, and his son had a habit of frequenting them when the weather was good so that he could hear the clacking of his horses' hooves and chariot wheels on the cobbles.

"Oh no, I rode around the outskirts," Antonius replied with an innocent face.

Galerius gave his son a dubious look. "Next time you take your chariot out, at least, let someone know where you're going. Now rub down your horses, get something to eat and start on your chores."

"Yes, Father," Antonius replied, feeling relieved the reprimand was only minor this time. If it had been seven years earlier, however, Galerius probably would have beaten him for doing that.

****

A stern man, due to his long military career and the many battles he fought as a Roman soldier, Galerius started out as a strict disciplinarian with his children. But his attitude went through a metamorphosis one day thanks to Octavia. Antonius still remembered it vividly. He was eleven and bored, so he decided to take some of the old empty wine-blending jars up to the lake nearby and sling pebbles at them. He had broken a few when his father happened along.

"What are you doing?" Galerius shouted. After taking a moment to survey the destruction, he turned to Antonius, who was visibly shaken, and

---

2-A unit of length = 1.5 feet

declared, "For every jar you've broken, you'll feel the lash."

He then dragged Antonius by his arm to the stable and took one of the leather reins down from the stable wall. Doubling it up, he began to beat him. Octavia heard the commotion and came running out to see what was happening. By then, the welts on Antonius's legs were beginning to bleed. She bravely grabbed her husband's arm as he was about to strike his son once more and said, "My husband, why must you beat our son so?"

Galerius snapped back, "Because our son thinks we are so rich he can break all our wine jars to ease his boredom."

"I only broke a few that were old," Antonius sobbed.

At the risk of being struck herself, Octavia came between them. "Please, my husband. It is easier to replace a few jars than it is to replace a son's hatred for his father. There are better ways to make him see the error of what he has done."

Galerius glared at her for a tense moment then snorted and walked out into the vineyard to cool off.

Taking her whimpering son by the hand into the house, Octavia obtained some medicinal salve from her drawer of remedies and dressed his wounds. After regaining his composure somewhat, Antonius asked, "Why did Father have to beat me? They were old jars we never use anymore."

Taking his head and pressing it close to her breast, she replied, "My son, you must understand one thing. When a situation arises that is threatening or upsetting to your father, he reacts immediately and forcefully. This behavior is due mainly to his training as a soldier and has preserved him on many occasions. Now is a different time in his life, one he hasn't quite adjusted to yet. Reacting quickly and forcefully does not serve him well anymore. I will speak to him about it, but in the meantime, you should go back to the lake and pick up the jars you've broken." She held him out at arm's length and asked, "We don't want anyone to cut themselves while going swimming now, do we?"

"No, Mother," Antonius replied, wiping the tears from his dirty face.

A short while later, Galerius walked into the house, still upset but somewhat calmer. Octavia went to him and placed both of her hands on his broad shoulders. "My husband, please hear my words and do not be angry with me. As a soldier, you were trained to act quickly during the heat of battle. I'm sure this is why you are alive today. But you are no longer on the battlefield, and now just the opposite applies. You must think of the consequences your actions have before you act. They could mean the difference between your family fearing and despising you or giving you their love and respect. I tell you this because I don't want your son to grow up hating you."

Afraid of how he might react, she quickly kissed him on the cheek and left before he could respond. His reaction surprised her, however. A moment later, he came up behind her and wrapped his thick arms around her narrow waist and put his head on her shoulder. "I am fortunate to have a wife who knows how to tame the wild beast in a man."

She smiled. "Your son is at the lake picking up the jars he broke. Why don't you go and have a talk with him?"

He nodded then left to make amends with his son.

Being a man of action rather than words, Galerius preferred showing an apology over saying it. When he arrived at the lake, he silently began helping Antonius pick up the shattered pottery shards. He never mentioned the incident again.

Although his father was a reactor, fortunately for Antonius, his mother was a thinker. She believed it prudent to weigh the consequences before acting. Over time, she convinced Galerius that her way was a wiser choice. Consequently, after the broken jar incident, there were no more beatings and no more volatile outbursts. Galerius would still become angry occasionally when Antonius would disobey, but with Octavia's encouragement, he would take a moment before his anger escalated. The punishment for disobedience was usually more chores or a loss of privileges, but Galerius never used corporal punishment again. Antonius would get upset because of the occasional penance he would have to pay for his wrongdoings, but he never felt hatred toward his father or mother. He learned at an early age that all his actions had consequences, good or bad, depending upon what they were. He had come to accept that.

****

After recalling the broken jar incident, Antonius unhooked his horses and led them to the stable. Pretending he had just been the victor at Rome's great Circus, he removed their harnesses and exclaimed, "Mercury, Mars, you were magnificent! We won the victor's laurel and 100,000 sesterces[3]. I shall buy you both the best oats and have your stalls lined with gold."

Mercury snorted as if to indicate he had heard that promise before while Mars flicked his tail.

Quickly rubbing both horses down, Antonius put them in their respective

---

3-A sestercius was the largest bronze coin of this period; 4 bronze sesterces=1 silver denarius, 25 denari=1 gold aureus

stalls then hurried to the house to see if his mother had prepared the morning meal yet. Entering the triclinium[4], he saw his father and sister Augustina sitting at the large, oval walnut table. A plate of still warm pastries and another large plate of assorted seasonal fruit had already been placed on it. A cup filled with warm mulsum rested next to a small plate in front of each person's chair. The wine and honey beverage was a tasty staple for the Licinius family on the weekends. It was not as alcoholic as their regular wine, more like strong grape juice. Octavia knew how to make it just right, however, especially when it was slightly warmed during the colder weather.

Augustina brushed back her long, auburn hair and swallowed a sip as Antonius sat down. "Ah, Rome's most famous charioteer decided to grace us with his presence," she remarked sarcastically. "I heard you leave this morning as if the whole province didn't. You probably even made the gods wince with all the noise you made."

With a smirk, he replied, "If I did, it was because I was going so fast. Once again, the blue team was victorious." For dramatic effect, he raised both arms in the air.

"Yes, well the blue team had better get busy with his chores as soon as he's finished eating," Galerius interjected. He then stuffed a large bite of the apple-filled pastry in his mouth that Octavia had baked earlier.

"Ummm, that looks good. What are you eating, Father?" Antonius asked as he shoveled two of the pastries onto his plate.

Galerius looked at his son and made a face. "This? Oh, just a dried up old squash I found in the stable that was starting to rot." He smiled and took a sip of mulsum while Augustina rolled her eyes.

Walking in from the cucina[5], Octavia gave her husband a disapproving glance. "So... you are referring to my pastry as a dried up old squash? Is that what I heard?"

Looking like a guilty cat that had just done his business on the rug and been caught, Galerius replied, "No... I was telling Antonius that he's lucky I'm not making him eat a dried up old squash for being late." He then quickly gave his two children a look indicating that anything said to the contrary could mean extra chores.

"Well, if you don't like my cooking, I'll just have Augustina fix your meals from now on," Octavia said, pretending to be offended.

Augustina's eyebrows elevated noticeably while Antonius's brow fur-

---

4-*Dining room*
5-*Kitchen*

rowed.

"Augustina cook?" he exclaimed. "We'd starve to death before she put anything on the table we could eat."

Augustina slapped her brother on the arm and said, "I can cook. mother let me bake some bread the other day."

"Was that the loaf I used for sparring with Marcus?" Antonius said with an impish grin.

"No! You ate most of it, Antonius, so don't tell me you used it to spar with Marcus," she scoffed.

"Oh, that loaf. Yes, it wasn't bad, once I made it through the crust. I think I broke off two teeth when I first bit into it, though," Antonius remarked, looking at his sister peripherally for a reaction.

Augustina pursed her lips and a red hue spread over her face.

Octavia could see a battle was about to begin. Being the diplomat, she sat down on the bench between them and turned to Antonius. "I didn't notice you complaining about the texture when you ate half of it in one sitting, my son. Give your sister some credit. She will make someone a good wife someday."

"And very soon, I hope," Antonius replied, while Augustina gave him a death stare.

Octavia reached across the table to where she normally sat and pulled her cup of mulsum toward her. "What are your plans for the day, my husband?" she asked, as she took a sip of her drink.

Galerius looked at her with a mouth full of pastry and replied, "I think I'll ride down to Decastadium and check with the merchants we supply and see how low their stock is. We may have to make some deliveries. Then I want to see how well the grapes are doing. Antonius can help me with that."

"But I promised someone I'd meet them at the hippodrome this afternoon to watch the races," Antonius said.

With a full mouth, Galerius replied, "You will still have time if you finish your chores."

Octavia, demonstrably disgusted with her husband's eating habits, exclaimed, "Could you not stuff your mouth so full before you talk?"

Galerius looked at Octavia with his mouth still full and said, "Sorry."

Octavia shook her head.

"I think the world would be a much better place without men in it if you ask me," Augustina said, as she dished more fruit onto her plate.

"Are you including Marcus?" Antonius asked, knowing Augustina was quite fond of his friend who lived just over the hill.

Augustina smiled and raised her eyebrows slightly. "I would make Marcus the exception."

"I'll tell him you said that," Antonius said, getting up after devouring two of the pastries and finishing his drink.

"Don't you dare, Antonius!" Augustina warned, raising her voice.

Octavia put her arm around her daughter and muttered, "Augustina you know you can deny anything your brother says to Marcus. All you have to do is smile at the boy, and he will believe anything you tell him."

Augustina looked at Antonius and gave him an exagerated smirk that indicated Octavia was right. He shook his head and excused himself then hurried outside, determined to finish his chores before his father returned from his rounds. He had races to watch and a young lady to meet that was eagerly willing to help him spend his morning's racing spoils. It was going to be a good day.

****

CHAPTER II–THE NEIGHBORS

Over the hill from the vineyard, Marcus Flavius helped his father, Sergius, plant vegetables in their field. Unlike Antonius and Galerius, their relationship had deteriorated. For the past few years, Sergius had grown particularly surly toward Marcus, mainly because he felt his son had betrayed him.

It all began when Antonius and his family first moved into the vineyard. Antonius was only seven at the time and Augustina, two years younger. While Galerius was in town obtaining supplies, Octavia thought it would be a good opportunity to get acquainted with their neighbors. The only house close by was just over the hill from the vineyard, so Octavia gathered her children and walked up the hill. Arriving at the six-room farmhouse, Octavia nervously knocked on the door. Marcus's mother, Camilla, answered it.

"Yes?" Camilla asked, seeing the unknown woman with her two small children.

Octavia smiled. "Hello. My name is Octavia, and these are my children-Antonius and Augustina. We just moved into the vineyard down the hill."

"Oh! My son Marcus told me he saw some new people moving into the vineyard house. Please, come in," Camilla said, beckoning for them to enter.

Octavia stepped inside with her children in tow and said, "My husband is in town getting some supplies, so I thought I would see who our neighbors were and introduce ourselves."

"I'm glad you came," Camilla replied.

Hearing unfamiliar voices, Marcus and his siblings walked into the room and smiled at the strangers.

"These are my sons Marcus and Matthias and my daughter Priscilla. My husband, Sergius, is outside somewhere," Camilla related.

"Well, I don't want to keep you from anything, I just wanted to say hello," Octavia said.

Her words had barely escaped from her mouth when the door opened, and Sergius walked in. He looked at Camilla and said, "I saw someone come to the door and thought I had better see what they wanted."

Pointing to Octavia, Camilla said, "Sergius, this is Octavia and... I'm sorry, I forgot your children's names."

"Antonius and Augustina," Octavia told her again.

"Yes, I knew both their names started with 'A,'" Camilla said, blushing. "They just moved into the vineyard house."

Sergius eyed them suspiciously. "You're taking over the vineyard down the hill?"

"Yes," Octavia stated with a friendly smile.

"Won't you please sit down," Camilla offered.

"Thank you," Octavia said, sitting down on a small sofa with Antonius and Augustina.

Sergius sat down in a nearby chair while Camilla stood by his side.

"Where are you from?" Sergius asked.

"We moved here from Rome," Octavia replied.

"Rome," Sergius uttered as if it was a dirty word. "Are you plebeians or patricians[6]?"

Octavia hesitated. She sensed that Sergius might have a prejudice toward the upper class, since most of the people in the area didn't live in lavish accomodations, so she chose her words carefully. "My parents were patricians and my husband's parents were equestrians[7]. The separation of classes aren't that important to us, however."

Sergius nodded. "Have you owned other vineyards before?"

"My husband's family did when he was a boy. He left to join the army when he was of age and recently retired. He decided to buy a vineyard and take up making wine again. When he learned that this vineyard was for sale..."

"Your husband just retired from the army?" Sergius interrupted.

"Well, actually he was promoted into the Praetorian Guard, and..."

"Your husband was a Praetorian?" Sergius spat out the last word.

His tone and demeanor began to make Octavia feel uncomfortable.

"Yes... he was a tribune[8] in the Praetorian Guard."

Sergius's face twisted into a snarl. "Get out of my house!" he shouted.

Octavia turned to Camilla, who looked down in embarrassment.

"What have I said to offend you?" Octavia asked, puzzled by his outburst.

Sergius stood up and opened the door. "Your family is not welcome here! Now leave!" he said, his face turning crimson.

Octavia looked at Camilla again and noticed that although her head was still bowed, tears were falling from her eyes.

Gathering Antonius and Augustina, Octavia quickly left as the door slammed behind her.

6-Plebeians were the lower class of people from tradesmen down to the very poor, while patricians were the upper class including nobility and wealthy land owners

7-Patricians consisting of wealthy businessmen and high officials

8-Roman military officer who ranked above the Centurion

Turning to his children, Sergius roared, "You are not to associate with that family from the vineyard. Not any of them! Do you understand me?"

His children timidly nodded their heads.

As Octavia left the house, she felt confused and embarrassed by the unexplained confrontation. Hurrying back to her home, Antonius asked, "Why was the man so angry, Mother?"

"I don't know, Antonius," was all she could say.

When Galerius returned from town, she related the experience to him. His response was that the family over the hill probably hated Romans for whatever reason, and if they didn't want to be friendly, the Licinius family would find other friends. Octavia, however, was unwilling to sever a possible friendship so quickly and was curious to know why Camilla's initial warm welcome changed so abruptly to a cold banishment by her husband. She decided to try and catch Camilla alone and see if she would be willing to explain her husband's behavior. The opportunity came a few days later.

Octavia was in town to purchase food when she saw Camilla at a little vegetable stand she had set up to sell the extra produce grown on their farm. Octavia took a deep breath and approached her.

"Camilla, do you remember me? My husband purchased the vineyard just over the hill from your farm. My children and I came to visit you."

Camilla appeared somewhat embarrassed and quickly replied, "Oh, yes, I remember." She then hurriedly started to gather up her vegetables and load them into a nearby wagon, hoping to avoid another confrontation.

"I don't have time to talk, I must get back to the farm... it is getting late," Camilla said nervously, turning to leave. Before she could go, however, Octavia gently took hold of her arm. "Please, don't hurry off. I wanted to ask your forgiveness if something I said offended your husband. I was hoping you could tell me what it was that upset him so."

With a pained expression, Camilla turned and replied, "Actually, I should be asking your forgiveness for my husband's behavior. You see, something happened to him a long time ago involving Praetorians and a patrician. Ever since then, he has held hatred in his heart for them that he will probably take to his grave. It is not your fault; you just happened to represent the two things he despises the most. I really should be going now."

Octavia was persistent, however. "Before you go, I noticed you were selling your vegetables. They look delicious, and I just happened to be in town to get some food. Would you be willing to trade for some wine?"

Camilla hesitated, trying to decide if she was betraying her husband. In a halting voice, she said, "I... think that would be acceptable... as long as Sergius does not learn where the wine came from."

"I'll trade you a large amphora[9] of our best for what you can give me in vegetables. Come with me to my house and I'll get it for you. We can trade there if you're willing."

Camilla reluctantly agreed, and their secret friendship began.

After that, they would meet discreetly in town where they would trade goods with each other and talk. Occasionally, Camilla would wind up in Octavia's kitchen afterward teaching her how to cook. The lessons proved invaluable, much to the delight of Octavia's family. Galerius offered to hire a cook for the family, but Octavia didn't want servants and was determined to learn how to prepare meals herself. Her previous culinary experience had been limited to watching the cook in her villa prepare the food when she was growing up. Her first attempts at cooking for her family was nothing short of disasters. Most of her attempts were barely edible, and the bread she tried to bake had the consistency of a fireplace log. Camilla's lessons soon brought welcoming smiles to Octavia's hungry family during meal time.

As Marcus grew older, he became curious about the boy and girl, who lived in the vineyard over the hill and asked his father if he could play with them. But Sergius always forbade it. "They are in a different class and probably don't want to associate with us," he would say.

Marcus was crestfallen since he didn't have anyone living close by that was his age to associate with other than his siblings, and he wanted to be friends. But he knew he would suffer his father's wrath if he went against his wishes. He would occasionally go to his "special place" on the hill, where he watched as the vineyard boy and his father fought with wooden swords and threw spears at targets. What he wouldn't give to trade places with the boy.

One day, he was in the woods nearby practicing with his bow when Antonius happened by in his shiny blue chariot he had just received from Galerius. It was a present for his sollemnitas togae purae[10]. Seeing Marcus, Antonius reined his horses to a stop. "Ho, there!" he shouted. Turning his attention to the boy with his bow, he asked, "What are you doing there?"

Marcus looked at him and sarcastically replied, "Killing trees."

Antonius climbed down from his new chariot and noticed the large number of arrows protruding from a large cork oak tree. "It looks like you've

---

9 A tall ancient Greek or Roman jar with two handles and a narrow neck.

10-A rite of passage for a Roman boy into manhood, celebrated on his fourteenth birthday

already killed one."

Marcus nocked another arrow and pulled it back, pretending to ignore Antonius. He took careful aim then let it fly. It landed inside a little circle he had carved into the large tree.

"My name is Antonius. What is yours?"

"Marcus," the thirteen-year-old replied.

"Why don't you come over to my house and spar with me, Marcus? I have wooden swords," Antonius said, hoping to convince the blonde-haired boy.

"No, I would rather shoot my bow," Marcus replied, trying to hide the fact that he had never used a sword. He drew another arrow back but just before releasing it, Antonius said, "I'll give you a ride in my chariot."

The arrow went wild, and Marcus gave Antonius a disgruntled look.

Antonius raised his eyebrows. "It must be hard to kill a tree, eh?"

"Only when someone is bothering you," Marcus replied with a furrowed brow.

Antonius could have taken offense and rode off, but like his mother, he wasn't about to give up making a new friend. He pursed his lips and said, "If you teach me how to shoot a bow and arrow, I'll teach you how to use a gladius."

Marcus turned and gave him a puzzled look. "What's a gladius?"

"It's a sword Roman soldiers use," Antonius replied, giving Marcus a surprised look.

Marcus lifted up his head. "Oh, a gladius. I thought you said something else."

"Well, do you want to come over?" Antonius pressed.

Marcus turned and glanced back toward his house. "Look, we shouldn't even be talking to each other."

"Why not?" Antonius asked, as if Marcus' utterance made no sense.

"My father doesn't like patricians," Marcus said with rising cheeks.

Now Antonius' cheeks rose. "Who's a patrician?"

"You are," Marcus replied. "My father said that your mother told him you were patricians when you first came to visit us."

Antonius scrunched his face. "I don't remember, it was too long ago. I know that my grandparents are patricians. I guess if they are then I must be one too. But why does it matter if I'm a patrician?"

"Because I'm not," Marcus replied bluntly.

Antonius appeared confused. "Because I am and you're not, we can't be friends? That seems kind of silly."

Marcus shrugged his shoulders. "That's what my father said."

Antonius slightly shook his head and said. "Your father doesn't have to know we're friends. I can teach you how to use a gladius and let you ride in my chariot and you can teach me how to shoot your bow."

Marcus lowered his bow and looked at the bright, shiny new chariot with the two large stallions pawing at the ground. It was almost as if they were beckoning to him. He couldn't resist the temptation. Looking around to see if his father was anywhere nearby, he said, "I accept, on one condition. We cannot ride anywhere near my house, and my father must not see us together."

"Agreed," Antonius said, holding out his arm to seal the agreement.

Marcus had never clasped arms with anyone before, so Antonius gripped his arm and said, "There. Now we must keep our word."

Marcus smiled and nodded.

Both boys stepped up into the chariot and Antonius took the reins.

"Hold on tightly or you will find yourself landing on your backside," Antonius warned his new friend.

Marcus threw his bow on the ground then gripped the rails tightly as instructed. With a shout, Antonius snapped the reins, and the chariot lurched forward. A few heartbeats later, they were traveling as fast as the two horses could take them. Frightened at first, Marcus eventually developed confidence in Antonius's ability to control his chariot and began to feel the rapture that only the combination of speed and adrenaline could provide. They rode until the horses became winded then Antonius brought them back to where Marcus' bow lay on the ground.

"Well, how did you like your first chariot ride?" Antonius asked as Marcus stepped off.

"When would you like your first archery lesson?" came the reply.

After that, Marcus decided that becoming friends with the boy who lived on the vineyard was worth his father's ire, should it ever be discovered. From that moment on, he secretly met with Antonius at the vineyard when he had finished his chores. There they would spar with wooden swords and go for chariot rides. Eventually, Antonius even allowed him to drive. But like all secrets, they inevitably become discovered.

One night well after supper, Marcus walked in after spending part of the evening with Antonius at the vineyard.

"Where have you been?" Sergius asked him.

"Uh, practicing with the bow," Marcus replied.

Sergius gave him a questionable look and asked, "At your usual spot?"

"Yes," Marcus replied, avoiding his father's gaze.

Sergius knew this was a lie because he had gone to Marcus's "usual spot" and discovered his son was not there. Following a hunch, he walked down the hill toward the vineyard until he heard two young excited voices challenging each other behind the vineyard stable. Peering around the corner of the stable, he saw Marcus and Antonius sparring with wooden swords. He could have said something then but he decided to confront Marcus later and see if he would tell the truth about where he went. Hurrying back up the hill, Sergius returned to his dwelling before Marcus came home.

Continuing with his interrogation, Sergius asked, "And how did you do with your bow?"

"I'm able to hit the target farther back now," Marcus said with a pleased smile.

Sergius gave him a blank stare and said, "As far back as the Licinius's vineyard?"

The blood rushed to Marcus's face, as he realized his secret was exposed. Being at the rebellious age of seventeen, he boldly proclaimed, "I don't understand why you hate the Licinius family. They have done nothing to us except try to be our friends."

Sergius nodded. "Yes, they may pretend to be our friends, but later they will want to extend their property. Then they will call on their real Praetorian friends and steal our land from us like they did with my father."

"What are you saying? They do not want our land! You are talking crazy," Marcus said, challenging his father.

Enraged by his son's defiance, Sergius shouted, "Do not raise your voice to me! I am your father!" He then swung a backhand at Marcus's face. Before it could inflict the intended punishment, however, Marcus grabbed it. Gritting his teeth, he said, "No, Father, you will not strike me anymore. I will do my chores, but when I've finished, I will do as I wish," loosening the firm grip on his father's hand.

Sergius curled his lip, but he didn't follow up with any further aggression. He had just been made aware that his son was now stronger than he was.

Walking out the door, Marcus went to the hill overlooking the vineyard and sat under an old Willow tree. Looking down at the vineyard house, he wished he lived there, and Galerius was *his* father.

****

The next day, as Marcus toiled in the field, he wiped the sweat from his brow and stood up to stretch some of the stiffness out of his back. Sergius worked in silence at the opposite end. They needed to plant rows of carrots, cucumbers, onions, squash, and tomatoes. Part of their crop would feed them for the year, and the rest would be sold in town to pay for necessities. They also had a large number of chickens, ducks, and pigs for meat. For the most part, they were self-sufficient.

"Make sure you're planting carrots in that row," Sergius yelled.

Marcus nodded.

As the sun disappeared behind the distant rolling hills, they finished for the day then silently walked to the house. Their evening meal was quiet and somber as usual.

Later, as a cream-colored moon rose in the sky and crickets chirped their nightly lullabies, Marcus left the house and went up on the hill. He sat down on the grassy knoll under his Willow tree and watched Lampyridae[11] a short distance away as they danced around like sparks from a fire. Hearing footsteps behind him, he turned to see his mother approaching.

"Oh, it is you," he said, thankful it was not his father.

"I thought I would see what you were up to. Mind if I sit down and keep you company?" she asked.

"I don't mind," he said, picking up a discarded twig from the tree and tossing it.

Looking up into the indigo sky, she said, "It's a beautiful night, isn't it?"

"I suppose," Marcus replied. His tone of voice betrayed his true feelings.

"What troubles you, son. Do you want to talk about it?" she suggested.

Marcus hesitated a moment then asked, "Why is Father so angry all the time? He barely talks to me and won't even speak to the Licinius's. Why does he hate them so? They have done nothing to him."

Camilla put her head down and knew the time had come to tell her son the real reason behind her husband's seemingly irrational anger. "Marcus, there is something you must know about your father. When he was a boy, his family lived in Rhegium and his father had a small shop that sold fishing supplies. His father knew a lot about catching fish, but it took quite a while to get established. Eventually, they began to do well and his family lived in a flat that was in the back. One day, a patrician from Rome came into the shop and asked your grandfather if he would sell it to him. The man was looking to expand his holdings in Rhegium at a good profit. Your grandfather told him he was not interested in selling, but the man kept insisting. Finally, your

---

11-Winged beetles commonly called "fireflies"

grandfather asked the patrician to leave and not return. This infuriated the man. He told your grandfather he would have the shop one way or the other.

A few weeks later he did return, but this time he had two Praetorians with him. They informed your grandfather that they were seizing the shop because he had failed to pay all of his taxes. Your grandfather knew it was a lie because he had always paid his taxes. When he told the Praetorians that he was not leaving, one of the Praetorians took hold of him. Your grandfather pulled away then the other Praetorian drew his sword and killed him. Your grandfather died in front of Sergius, and shortly afterward the patrician forced your father's family out of their home. It was winter at the time, so your grandmother needed to find shelter for them. An old fisherman, who came to their shop often for his supplies, offered to put them up temporarily in his small cottage. But with four children, there was little room, so your grandmother had to sleep out in a small shed near the cottage. With only a blanket to keep warm, the cold and dampness became too much for her. She eventually became ill and died. Being the oldest, your father had to care for his brother and two sisters.

A few years later, the old fisherman died. Since he had no relatives, Sergius and his brother and sisters continued to live in the cottage and inherited the fisherman's small boat. Fortunately, your father learned about fishing from your grandfather, so he was able to catch enough fish to feed them and trade for seeds to plant a garden and grow vegetables.

One day a man came by and offered to trade a small farm nearby for the cottage and the fisherman's boat. Your father had grown to love working in the garden more so than fishing, so he decided to take the man's offer. He moved here and has been here ever since. That is why you shouldn't judge him too harshly, my son. He lost his father and mother because of some evil men's actions."

Marcus shook his head. "But that doesn't mean the Licinius's are evil. Why can't father give them a chance?"

Camilla stroked his tousled hair. "Some things stay with you and never leave, my son. The hatred your father has carried for the men who killed his father will always be there. I'm not saying it is right, but he is afraid to trust anyone who is a patrician or a Praetorian now. I think he fears that what happened to his father might happen to him someday."

"You ask me not to judge him too harshly, yet he judges them harshly," Marcus argued.

Camilla put her hand on her son's shoulder. "Yes, but you are better than your father, Marcus. Sergius has been wounded too deeply to change his way of thinking, so you must learn from his mistakes and not make the same ones. It is good that you judge the Licinius's by their actions now and not by what class they belong to or by who they were in the past. Someday, perhaps, he will see that the Licinius's are good people."

"Then you think they are good people?"Marcus asked.

"Yes, I do," came her quick reply. "Come now; we must get back to the house. It's getting late."

Marcus looked down at the vineyard and said, "You go back. I think I'll stay here awhile."

"Don't stay too long or I will worry," she told him.

"I won't," Marcus promised. After she left, his thoughts turned to his father and he wondered how much longer he take his father's contempt.

****

While Marcus looked up at the moon from his hilly vantage point, Antonius lay on his bed, looking at the same crescent-shaped moon from his window. His deliberation, however, was not of his father but of joining the army. He was of age to serve in Rome's military, and had been thinking of talking Marcus into going with him and signing up. If he did well as a soldier, he would surely be asked to join the Praetorian Guard like his father. The admiration and respect would certainly follow. There was no respect or admiration for stomping grapes. He wanted people to recognize him for something more than helping to make wine. It wasn't that he hated working on the vineyard; he didn't mind it, but he wanted to get out and see the rest of the world and make a name for himself. The only way he could accomplish that would be to join the army. He would talk to his parents about it when they went to Rome for Saturnalia[12] at the end of the year. They would be in good spirits then and more likely to grant his request.

In another room, Octavia put down the scroll on philosophy she was reading and rubbed her eyes. She thought of the day when they first arrived in Aletium. She was a little apprehensive about their new home and learned from a shopkeeper that most of the locals living in the area were tenant farmers. They were not very receptive to new people moving in, especially patricians from Rome, as evidenced by Sergius's reaction. Usually, the only patricians they saw on a regular basis were the wealthy landowners who only appeared occasionally to check on their holdings and take what they wanted. Camilla was Octavia's atypical savior.

12-A festival celebrated in honor of the deity Saturn, held December 17-23

Even though Octavia was well educated and Camilla had no formal education, Octavia found her refreshingly honest, sincere and humble–qualities she found lacking in most of her patrician friends back in Rome.

She admired Camilla for her devotion to her children and the patience she had for her husband, even though he could obviously be difficult at times. But then Galerius had his moments as well. Octavia also discovered being friends with Camilla was relatively easy, as Camilla had many of the same qualities that she possessed. Had it not been for Camilla's secret defiance of her husband's edict to avoid association with Octavia and her family, Octavia would probably have been friendless in the small community.

As the late hour weighed down her eyelids, she stretched and decided to retire for the night. She felt content, as she walked over to Galerius, who was sitting across from her in the atrium, reading a scroll on a different kind of wine he was thinking of making.

"Will you be up late again, Galerius?"

"Just awhile longer. I want to finish reading this scroll," he replied.

"Well, don't stay up too late," she counseled, kissing his cheek.

He smiled and said, "I won't."

As she departed, he watched her until she was out of sight. He felt fortunate to have such a beautiful and patient woman for a wife.

****

A few hours later, Galerius tossed and turned in his bed. The same dream that plagued him repeatedly unfolded once again. He stood out in a field surrounded by a thick mist. Dressed for battle, he held a gladius in one hand and shield in the other.

Suddenly, phantom warriors stepped out of the haze, each bearing fatal wounds Galerius had given them in battle. They surrounded him, then stared with their white, lifeless eyes into his. After a moment, they began to chant. "Death to the slayer! Death to the slayer!" The chant became louder and louder until they screamed it. Then suddenly, they became silent. Raising their weapons, they screeched an unearthly cry and charged him.

Galerius raised his gladius and shield in defense. But a cutting of grapes had replaced his gladius, and his shield became a dinner plate. He looked up at the macabre apparitions rushing toward him and braced for their assault. Just before they struck their deadly blows, he cried out and awoke.

Catapulting up in his bed, he frantically looked around the room. There were no foes, no mist, only the darkened shapes of his bedroom furniture.

Octavia, awakened by his cry, placed her hand on his shoulder. "Is it the dream again?"

"Yes," he replied, rubbing his forehead and laying back down.

Octavia massaged his chest with her hand to calm him and whispered, "Do not be troubled my husband; it is just a dream. Go back to sleep."

Galerius thought it ironic that a man who had feared no one on the battlefield was now afraid to fall asleep in his own bed.

****

CHAPTER III-THE PREFECT

Just off the western coast of Italia and a day's sail from Rome, lay the island of Capreae. It had become the preferred home of the Roman emperor Tiberius Caesar. Surrounded by water and a few cohorts of Praetorians, he felt relatively secure. Although several villas had been built on the island, his favorite was the Villa Jovis. High on a hill overlooking the Bay of Naples, it gave him a sense of detachment from the responsibility that royal appointment had forced upon him. He never really embraced the idea of ruling a profusion of people and his self-imposed exile to the island supported that feeling.

Besides having Germanic bodyguards and Praetorian guards for security, Tiberius also had philosophers, poets, grammarians and scholars on the island to keep his mental faculties sharp. He remained single after the death of his second wife, Julia the Elder, seeing no reason to remarry. He was forced by Augustus, the emperor at the time, to divorce his first wife, Vipsania—whom he adored, to marry Julia—whom he despised. The marriage to Julia was an extremely unhappy one for him. Adding to his unhappiness, his only son, Drusus, died at the age of thirty-six by what the physicians believed was caused by alcohol poisoning from overindulgence. The diagnosis of Drusus's death seemed logical to many as they surreptitiously referred to him as the "royal winebibber."

It is from the Villa Jovis that Tiberius ruled Rome, passing his decisions onto his Praetorian Prefect—Lucius Sejanus, who commanded his Praetorian Guard. Developing a close relationship with Sejanus, Tiberius referred to him as "The partner in my toils."

****

Inside the massive Praetorian Guard fortress called the Castra Praetoria, Sejanus sat behind a large wooden table and stared at a petition that required his immediate attention. Lately, everything seemed to require his immediate attention. The long hours and lack of sleep from his demanding schedule made his eyelids heavy as he doggedly fought the incessant attacks of fatigue determined to defeat him. For the Praetorian Prefect, it was just another day of important decisions that had to be made.

A Tuscan by birth, Sejanus had rugged features and was in good shape for a man in his mid-forties. Customary for the day, he wore a white toga and a pair of caligae[13]. Sitting back in his chair, he looked briefly around the room, which was neither elegantly furnished nor Spartan-like. Several com-

---

13-Classic Roman military sandals or hob-nailed boots

mendations and a few weapon displays decorated the walls. Simple wooden chairs lined the wall across from his table and two comfortable fabric chairs flanked either side of it. His helmet and segmented armor rested on a stand off in the corner.

He had been the Praetorian Prefect almost sixteen years now—all of them under Tiberius, so he knew the emperor well. Many also knew Sejanus, but no one knew who he really was. Considered a trusted confidant and advisor by Tiberius, he even convinced the aloof emperor to build the immense fortress for the Guard. It stood adjacent the northeastern city wall and was erected so that Sejanus could "facilitate operations in the city" better. Prior to that, the emperors of Rome were quite reluctant to allow any large military force inside or near the city walls for fear some disgruntled commander might start a coup, kill the emperor and take the throne. Allowing over 5,000 well-trained Praetorians to have immediate access to the city was an affirmation of the trust Tiberius had placed in his Praetorian Prefect. Sejanus was the second most powerful man in Rome, but he wasn't satisfied. He wanted to become emperor and had been taking steps to assure his success.

The senate feared him and he dealt with those who stood in his way. One of them was Agrippina, the widow of Rome's most beloved general—Germanicus. Nephew and adoptive son of Tiberius, Germanicus was well known for his victories in Germania and Asia. When Tiberius assigned him to put down a rebellion by Roman soldiers, rather than pit Roman against Roman, Germanicus ended the mutiny by reasoning with the rebellious soldiers. In appreciation, they implored him to become emperor and pledged their support. Germanicus, however, refused to even consider it.

When Tiberius learned that his army in Germania had petitioned Germanicus to be their emperor, he gave Germanicus a new command in Asia. While in Asia, a feud arose between Germanicus and the Roman governor of Syria—Calpurnius Piso. A short while later, Germanicus developed a sudden illness and died. Piso was accused of poisoning him. A great outcry arose when the citizens of Rome learned that their beloved Germanicus may have been poisoned. Tiberius had no choice but to have Piso arrested and transported to Rome for trial. The trial never took place, however, as Piso was found dead in his cell before the proceedings began. Many believed he too was poisoned.

After many honors and eulogies, Germanicus was buried. All of Rome wept for him, with the exception of Tiberius. Agrippina suspected that he had ordered her husband's death but without proof, all she could do was support those senators who secretly opposed him. Overtly, however, she made Tiberius aware that either one of her eldest sons, Nero or Drusus, would be an excellent successor to the throne. Since Germanicus was a hero to many people in Rome, Agrippina was confident she had their support.

Although Sejanus would have preferred being chosen by the emperor to succeed him with approval from the senate, he knew it was highly unlikely. He was an Equestrian and emperors were chosen from the senatorial class. Successors related by blood would always be the first choice. Nero and Drusus were eligible, therefore, he must eliminate them somehow.

First he needed to convince Tiberius that Agrippina and her sons were a danger to him. His chance came one evening when Tiberius invited many notables to a dinner party he hosted at the palace. Agrippina, her sons, a few senators and Sejanus were among those who attended.

The guests marveled at the beautifully decorated tables adorned with flowers, assorted delicacies and fruit from around the empire while musicians played in the background. Tiberius liked to make an entrance, so people mingled while they waited for his appearance.

As Sejanus surveyed the crowd, he saw Agrippina. He also saw a senator, who was one of his spies. Walking up to him, he whispered, "Follow me, Secundus."

The senator nodded.

Going to a remote section of the palace, Sejanus turned to the portly gentleman with a bulldog face and bad complexion. "I have a task for you," he whispered.

The senator smiled, knowing he would be well rewarded. "What would you like me to do, Prefect?" he asked.

Sejanus passed along his instructions, then returned to the party.

Senator Secundus waited a moment so it wouldn't appear that they had been together. When he was sure enough time had passed, he returned to the party and sought out Agrippina.

Walking up to her, he asked, "Lady Germanicus, may I have a word with you in private?"

Agrippina gave him a curious look and replied, "What is it, Senator?"

Secundus drew near to her and whispered, "What I have to say is for your ears only, Milady."

"Very well. We can go out on the balcony," Agrippina suggested.

As they walked out, Secundus remarked, "May I say you look very lovely this evening, Lady Germanicus."

She smiled and said, "Thank you, Senator. Now, what is this mysterious message you have for me?"

Looking around to make sure they were alone, Secundus said, "I just happened to overhear a rather intriguing conversation I thought you should know about."

She gave him a curious glance and asked, "What did you hear?"

He drew near to her and said, "One of Tiberius's scholars was saying to another that Tiberius went into a tirade about you the other day after you left his presence."

Her eyebrows went up. "Really? When was this?"

"He didn't say, but he also mentioned that Tiberius said he was tired of your incessant badgering about your eldest sons and how either of them would make a fine emperor some day. What distressed me the most was when he said Tiberius told him that perhaps it was time to silence you once and for all so that he could have some peace and quiet. I fear for your life, Milady."

Agrippina gave him a dubious look and said, "I doubt the emperor would go that far, senator. But, perhaps I have been a little too overbearing on the matter. I will let it rest for awhile."

She was about to leave when Secundus took ahold of her arm and said, "Poison has silenced many a person who has fallen into disfavor with the emperor, you know." He then hurried off.

Agrippina stood there for a moment and thought about what Secundus had said. Her first thought was to dismiss it as an idle concern. But the apprehension in his voice disturbed her. If Tiberius was indeed behind the poisoning of her husband, did he feel it was time to get rid of her too? Did the senator know more than he revealed?

Sejanus walked up to Tiberius and said, "I heard the senate convicted Claudia Pulchra of plotting to poison you, Your Majesty."

"Yes," Tiberius confirmed, "that and performing incantations."

"Wasn't she Agrippina's friend?" Sejanus asked.

"Yes, she was," Tiberius stated reflectively.

Sejanus narrowed his eyes slightly and said, "That must be why Agrippina was upset."

Tiberius' curiosity was now aroused. "What did she say?" he asked.

Sejanus gazed upward and replied, "The other day she mentioned that Claudia's sole crime was being her friend. It almost sounded like she accused you of indirectly punishing her by having Claudia arrested."

Tiberius shook his head slightly. "I know she was upset over the trial, but I had little to do with that. The delator[14] Domitius Afer presented enough condemning evidence to convict the woman. I think Agrippina is overly suspicious of everyone's intentions."

"Still, I'm surprised she even came this evening," Sejanus said, hoping to make her appear even more rebellious.

Tiberius gave him a curious look and asked, "Would you refuse a dinner invitation from your emperor, Prefect?"

Sejanus smiled and said, "Only a fool would do that, Highness."

When the servants served the food, Tiberius insisted that Agrippina sit next to him. Remembering what Secundus said, she stared at what was on her plate for a moment and hesitated.

"Is the food not to your liking?" Tiberius asked her.

"She looked at Tiberius then back at her plate. "I'm sorry, your highness, but I'm not feeling well. Please excuse me."

She stood up and left abruptly.

Sejanus, who sat on the other side of Tiberius, leaned toward him and said, "I spoke with Agrippina earlier and observed no indication she was ill. Perhaps she refused to eat as a protest for her friend's incarceration."

"Whatever her intentions, her behavior was rude," Tiberius muttered.

"Sometimes rude behavior can be dangerous," Sejanus suggested.

Tiberius nodded.

****

Later, when Tiberius took up residence on Capreae, Agrippina and her sons felt emboldened in speaking out against him. He was too far away to hear her words, but Sejanus's spies were listening.

Fortunately for Agrippina, Tiberius's estranged mother-Livia Augusta, sympathized with her plight and took Agrippina under her protective wing, so to speak. Sejanus knew Livia hated him. Consequently, he dared not move against Agrippina because of her. But Livia Augusta was getting old. When she died at 86 a few weeks later, Sejanus saw his chance. With Tiberius's approval, Sejanus arrested Agrippina and Nero-her eldest son and had them tried in the senate for disloyalty to the emperor. The verdict was predictable as no senator wanted the ire of both Tiberius and Sejanus. Agrippina was banished to the island of Pandataria and imprisoned there. Nero was sent to the island of Pontia. Shortly afterward, Sejanus imprisoned Agrippina's other son, Drusus. Sejanus had conveniently removed three more obstacles

---

14-Chief accuser

to his quest for the throne. The only other possible successors were Germanicus's brother Claudius and Agrippina's other teenage son, Gaius. But Claudius had a speech impediment and was hardly considered by many in the senatorial class to be leadership material. Nero and Drusus's younger brother, Gaius, nicknamed Caligula[15] by his father's troops, was still approaching adolescence. Sejanus dismissed them both as inconsequential and felt that the time was drawing near to make his move. As he pondered the situation, his aide, Thaddeus, knocked on the door.

"Yes, what is it?" he called out.

"Senator Secundus is here to see you, Prefect," Thaddeus replied.

Sejanus rubbed his forehead. "Very well, send him in."

The portly senator appeared.

"Thank you for seeing me, Prefect," Secundus croaked with his gruff voice as he took a seat.

"What do you have for me, Satrius?" Sejanus asked.

Secundus smiled a wry smile and said, "It seems that your name was mentioned again today in the senate."

"What was the context this time? No, let me guess… overstepping my authority," Sejanus stated sardonically.

Secundus chuckled. "It's always about you overstepping your authority, Prefect."

Sejanus raised one eyebrow then said, "Who was it this time?"

Secundus took in a breath and said, "I'm sure it will be no surprise to you, but Senator Fabius Quintillus gave an oratory on how dangerous you are becoming to the Senate."

Sejanus gave him a bored stare and said, "Really? What did the illustrious senator have to say?"

"He was concerned about why you arrested other senators who have spoken out against you and were never given a trial to plead their innocence and simply disappeared," Secundus rattled off.

Sejanus smiled. "If it were up to Quintillus he'd make the Praetorian Guard disappear. What was the senate's reaction to his words?"

Secundus lifted his head slightly and said, "Those loyal to you tried to refute what he was saying and convince the rest that the senators who disappeared weren't arrested but feared they could be, and simply left Rome."

"What was his response?" Sejanus asked, stifling a yawn.

"He called them your lackeys and cowards, accusing them of being bought

---

15-Caligula meant "Little Boots." The soldiers under Germanicus gave his son, Gaius, the nickname because Agrippina would dress him in a little soldier's uniform, complete with small hob-nailed boots.

and paid for to think the way you would have them think," Secundus replied.

Sejanus sat back in his chair. "I thought by now the senate would know I am not a man to be trifled with."

Secundus put his hand to his chin and said, "Apparently, a few still wish to do so, Prefect."

With a deadly earnest look, Sejanus said, "I can't have scurrilous talk like that continue. It might embolden others to speak out against me and their complaints might reach the emperor's ears."

"Then I suggest you deal with Quintillus at your earliest convenience," Secundus suggested.

Sejanus gave him a piercing stare and said, "Are you telling me how to handle my problems, Senator?"

By Sejanus's tone, Secundus realized he had inadvertently given offense. He had to clarify the misunderstood remark so as not to fall into disfavor with his benefactor.

"Oh, no, Prefect. It was just a-a suggestion," he stammered.

Sejanus studied him for a moment then said, "Anything else, senator?"

"That is all I have to report for now," Secundus said, nervously tapping his fingers on the chair.

Sejanus got up and walked over to a large chest in the corner of the room and unlocked it with a key that hung around his neck. He took out a handful of gold coins and handed them to Secundus. "That should be enough to reward you for your information."

With a greedy smile, Secundus put the coins into his purse. "As always, it is a pleasure to assist you, Prefect." He then grinned and waddled out.

Sejanus sat back in his chair and narrowed his eyes. He would have to do something about Senator Quintillus.

"Thaddeus!" he shouted.

"Yes, Prefect?" his aide replied, entering his office.

"Have Varius and Castor report to me."

Thaddeus saluted and left.

An hour later, two Praetorians in their late twenties, marched in perfect step down a familiar hallway. They had taken this route many times before and would take it many times again. Their well-toned bodies manifested their prime physical conditioning. They were Sejanus's speculatores[16] who would occasionally be called on to do what he referred to as "delicate matters." Both were dangerous men with a look about them that said, "Do not

---

16-*Bodyguards, couriers, law enforcers and sometimes, executioners*

trifle with us." Their very presence was intimidating. They had spent many hours in the wings of the senate and attended numerous parties where notables were present. They knew every senator and public figure by sight.

After turning down a few corridors, they came to the large black wooden door that bore a metal nameplate with the inscription, "Prefect Lucius Aelius Sejanus." Approaching the two sentries holding pilums[17] who flanked the door, Julius came face to face with one. He gave the sentry an intimidating smile, like a bully would to his next victim, and muttered, "The Prefect is expecting us."

The sentry nodded and motioned them in.

Sejanus's aide stood up and said, "Ah, Varius and Castor. I'll let the Prefect know you're here." He walked over and knocked on the door to Sejanus's office.

"Yes?" Sejanus called out.

"Varius and Castor are here, Prefect," Thaddeus informed him.

"Send them in," Sejanus replied.

Thaddeus opened the door, and the two entered.

After removing their helmets, they saluted and stood at attention.

Glancing up, Sejanus said, "Stand easy."

Relaxing their stance, they awaited their instructions.

Sejanus sat back in his chair and said, "I have another delicate matter for you to handle. Senator Fabius Quintillus has been accusing me falsely in the senate. I want him arrested and taken to the prison." Sejanus then smiled. "Of course, if he tries to escape, you'll have to stop him. Unfortunately, I'll be forced to seize his holdings. You two won't let him escape, now will you?"

The two men looked at each other knowing exactly what Sejanus meant. They answered in unison, "No, Prefect."

"I didn't think so," Sejanus said, raising his eyebrows.

"Go to the records office and get Fabius Quintillus' address then report back to me in the morning once you've resolved the matter. That is all; you are dismissed."

The two speculatores saluted and left to carry out their orders.
****

A short while later, in an affluent sector of Rome, Senator Quintillus was reading in his tablinum[18] when he heard a knock on his entry door. A servant answered, then walked back to where the senator was reclining on a couch.

"Excuse me, Master, but there are two Praetorians here who wish to see

____

17-Javelins used by the military
18-Study

you," the servant said.

"Two Praetorians?" Quintillus asked, appearing baffled. "What do they want?"

"They didn't say," the servant replied.

Quintillus furrowed his brow. "Why would Praetorians want to see me?" he thought. After a brief pause, he said, "Very well, send them in."

The servant returned with Julius and Felix. "The Praetorians, Master."

After waving him away, Quintillus put down the scroll he was reading and sat up. With a stern countenance, he asked, "What is this all about?"

In a cold monotone, Julius replied, "Fabius Quintillus, by order of Prefect Lucius Sejanus, we are to place you under arrest."

Quintillus reared his head back slightly and furrowed his brow. "On what charge?" he said raising his voice slightly.

"You'll have to ask the Prefect. All we know is he ordered us to make the arrest," Julius replied in one breath.

"This is ludicrous!" Quintillus bellowed. "I deserve to know what I'm being charged with!"

"You'll find out at your trial," Julius stated with a cold stare. Under his breath he muttered, "If there is one."

Quintillus jumped to his feet and pointed his finger at the two Praetorians. Raising his voice, he said, "This is all a ploy by Sejanus to destroy me because I...." he stopped in mid-sentence.

"Because you what, Senator?" Julius asked.

Quintillus tightened his jaw then said, "Never mind. I will go with you since I have no choice, but I demand an audience with the Prefect to learn why I'm being arrested."

Felix grabbed his arm and said, "We'll let him know. Now come along."

Accompanying the senator to the front door, Felix opened it and Julius pushed him out. The senator gave him a condescending look and growled, "There is no need to get rough."

"If you drag your feet I'll push you again," Julius warned.

As Quintillus walked down the road between his two guards, he felt his blood begin to boil. It was obvious to him now that he had been too bold in his accusatory remarks against Sejanus and now his only hope for redemption was that the other senators would protest his arrest. But then he remembered the other senators who spoke out against Sejanus had all disappeared. He would likely be another who would never be seen or heard of again. Turning to Julius and Felix, he curled his lip and said, "You Praetorians may think you are the great protectors of Caesar, but you're nothing more than the Prefect's hired assassins."

To his surprise, Julius said, "You're right, Senator. We are the Prefect's hired assassins. But... even assassins have a price."

"What do you mean?"

Julius looked at his companion then said, "Pay us 200 gold pieces and we'll say we couldn't find you."

Quintillus studied Julius for a moment then replied, "I don't have any money on me."

"Go back to your villa and get it," Julius ordered. "We'll wait for you here. If you don't return quickly, we will come looking for you. You don't want that."

Quintillus narrowed his eyes. "You would let me go?"

"We'll tell the Prefect you left the country. Of course, it would be wise for you to actually leave," Julius replied.

The senator stood there for a moment wondering if the same offer had been given to the other senators who disappeared. It was either dying for nothing or fleeing with what he could take with him. His choice was easy. He would have his servants take what they could pack and carry then catch the next ship leaving for anywhere that sounded good. He could make a new life for himself in Greece he thought. Undoubtedly, Sejanus would take his villa in Rome, but it was better than taking his life.

"Very well, I will go and get the gold," he said with an exasperated sigh.

He turned and began walking back to his villa when Julius yelled, "We don't have all night. Run, rabbit!"

Quintillus picked up his gait but only managed a few steps when he felt something strike him in his back. It hit with such force that it drove him to his knees. Then came the pain. He began to feel nauseous and dizzy then suddenly his vision went black. He fell forward, striking the cobblestones with his face.

Felix walked over to Quintillus's body and pulled his dagger from the dead senator's back.

"Nice throw; you're getting better," Julius commented, as he joined his cold-blooded companion.

Felix smiled and replied, "I've been practicing."
****

Early the next morning, they reported back to Sejanus.

"How did the arrest with Quintillus go?" Sejanus asked, already knowing what the answer would be.

Julius smiled and said, "Unfortunately, the senator *did* try to escape while we were escorting him to prison."

"That is unfortunate," Sejanus remarked, slightly shaking his head. He pulled open a drawer from his desk and took out two small purses filled with gold coins. Tossing them to his two henchmen, he said, "Here is a reward for attending to the matter so expeditiously. Go enjoy yourselves. I'll call on you when you're needed again."

They saluted and left.

Sejanus sat back in his chair. A satisfield smile slowly formed on his face. He could add the senator's holdings to the others he had already acquired.

For the past few months, he had been ensuring the loyalty of his officers by dispensing special gifts of land and money to them, seized from those in the senate who spoke out against him. He knew he could buy their loyalty for the most part, but there were still some idealistic officers in his ranks who might side with the emperor once he began his coup. Sejanus had not been the brilliant general on the battlefield like Tiberius was in his prime and had no significant military accomplishments that would garner the men's respect. He had even inherited his position as Prefect from his father. He needed a hero on his side—someone Praetorians would rally behind. The name of an old friend suddenly came to him in an epiphany.

"Galerius," he said out loud.

****

CHAPTER IV-THE INVITATION

Two young warriors challenged each other under a dusky mauve sky.

"Prepare to die, barbarian," one warrior snarled, pointing a sword at his similarly armed foe.

"You are the barbarian, Roman pig!" shouted his fair-haired opponent. Dropping his guard, Marcus asked, "Why is it that I always have to be the barbarian and you get to be the Roman soldier?"

"Because I have the helmet," Antonius replied, smiling and pointing to his father's helmet that fit loosely around his head.

"Then I shall lop off your head and the helmet will be mine," Marcus declared. He swung his sword toward Antonius's head, who ducked. Marcus then quickly gasped as he felt the blunt tip of Antonius's wooden gladius poke his abdomen.

Reeling back a few steps, Marcus asked, "Where did you learn that move?"

"My father showed that to me," Antonius replied, with a cock sure grin. "Don't tell him I said that. I don't want him to think I've actually been paying attention."

"Gods forbid!" Marcus exclaimed.

Dropping his guard, Antonius said, "Marcus, I've been thinking about joining the army. Why don't you join with me? You are skilled with a bow and I am skilled with a gladius…"

"A wooden gladius," Marcus reminded him, pointing at his sword.

"Just the same, we know how to defend ourselves and I don't want to wind up on this vineyard for the rest of my life. I want to see what the rest of the world looks like," Antonius said, looking past Marcus.

"I've thought about leaving the farm," Marcus said, gazing up the hill. "My father hates me and I dread every day around him, but it might put a hardship on the family if I do."

"You don't think your brothers could take over your chores for you?" Antonius asked, cradling his wooden sword.

Marcus shrugged. "I guess both probably could."

Antonius lowered his sword to his side and asked, "Then what's stopping you?"

Marcus quickly whacked him on the arm with his sword and took a defensive stance. "Certainly not you, Roman," he said mockingly.

Antonius rubbed his arm and smiled. "Oh, you will pay for that one." As he circled his chuckling opponent, Marcus suddenly put up his hand and said,

"Wait! Riders are coming and it looks like they're heading for your house."

Antonius snorted and said, "Nice try, but I'm not turning my head so you can strike me again."

The sound of horses' hooves, however, convinced him Marcus was telling the truth. Cautiously, he turned and saw the three riders approaching. "They look like Roman soldiers. I wonder why they are coming here?"

"Maybe they're coming to conscript us into the army," Marcus suggested.

Antonius shrugged slightly and said, "Maybe we won't need to join. Let's go to the house and see what they want."

"Lead the way, Tribune," Marcus said, as the two warriors scampered toward the vineyard house.

A short distance away, three armor-clad riders arrived at the large stone and stucco house and dismounted.

Inside, Galerius sat in a chair examining a grapevine clipping that rested on a paunch he had developed, while Octavia sat across from him on a couch in the atrium[19] examining one of his tunics that had a rip in it. She set the garment down and looked at him. "Galerius, if you don't stop gaining weight, the cost of new tunics for you will break us."

"If you hadn't become such a good cook, Octavia, I wouldn't gain the weight," he countered.

"Where would you be if you didn't have a wife to blame?" she asked.

"Probably still in the Praetorian Guard," he replied. "Back in those days, I could still see my feet when I looked down."

"Oh, Father," Augustina exhorted, walking in from the kitchen, "with all that bulky armor, I find that hard to believe."

"Well I could see them when I took the armor off." Grabbing his stomach, he said, "This won't come off."

"I don't think my cooking is the problem, I think it is your willpower, my husband," Octavia remarked.

"I have lots of willpower," Galerius retorted. "I just can't seem to find it when you set a plate in front of me."

"Perhaps you need a smaller plate," Octavia suggested, peering out of the corner of her eye.

"A smaller plate would do no good, Mother. He would just get more servings," Augustina said with a teasing smile.

Galerius gave them a spurious scowl and said, "Ganging up on me again, eh? Where is Antonius when I need…"

19-Formal room where the owners received guests

Before Galerius could finish, a loud knock on the door startled them.

Augustina dashed across the room. "I'll see who is there!"

Opening the door, she gasped. Standing before her was a large man wearing a red-crested helmet and segmented armor. Inscribed on the front of his cuirass[20] were impressions of the moon, stars and a scorpion signifying he was a member of Rome's elite Praetorian Guard.

A head taller than Augustina, he looked down and gave her a courteous smile. "Hello, young lady."

"Father, there is a soldier here," she said, taking a step back.

Galerius stood up and smiled. "He is no ordinary soldier, Augustina; he is a Praetorian."

Sejanus smiled and said, "Galerius, your daughter has grown into a beautiful budding flower. If I were a younger man, I would be tempted to court her."

Augustina blushed and backed away.

Galerius feigned indignation. "And knowing you like I do, I would never allow it!" His frown turned to a smile as he walked over and grasped Lucius's arm. "Lucius, good friend, please come in. Here I go years without talking about the Guard and when I do, you show up. It must be fate."

Sejanus took off his helmet and said, "Octavia," acknowledging her with a nod.

Octavia politely smiled.

He then turned to his two speculatores standing by their horses and yelled, "You two remain outside. I shouldn't be too long."

Julius and Felix nodded.

Galerius noticed the two men as he closed the door and asked, "Is this a social visit, Lucius, or did you come to arrest me?"

Sejanus chuckled. "Only a fool would try to arrest the best swordsman Rome has ever known. No, Galerius, I came to ask a favor."

With a puzzled look, Galerius asked, "You came all the way from Rome to ask a favor? It must be serious."

"It is," Sejanus replied.

Octavia felt her stomach tighten.

****

As Sejanus' two bodyguards outside conversed, they saw two armed men running toward them. Quickly drawing their swords, they took defensive stances. When Antonius and Marcus came closer, Julius could tell they were no threat. "Stand down, Felix; the swords they carry are only wooden toys."

20-An armored breastplate and backplate

"Toys that could leave a bruise on you," Marcus replied, referring to himself, but Julius took the remark as being aimed toward him.

"Boy, you are speaking to Praetorians," he gruffly stated. "The swords we carry are real and we would cleave you in two before you even raised yours. The next time you address a member of the Praetorian Guard, you had better show some respect."

Marcus turned a bright crimson. "No, I meant..."

Antonius removed his helmet and came to his friend's defense. "We apologize, Praetorian. We meant no disrespect. Why are you here?"

"Our Prefect has business with the man who lives here. Who are you and where did you get that helmet?" Julius asked as he and Felix sheathed their swords.

"I am Antonius Licinius, son of Galerius Licinius; I live here with my family. The helmet belongs to my father. He was a Praetorian Tribune. He isn't in any trouble, is he?"

"Go inside and discern for yourself," Julius replied haughtily.

As Antonius and Marcus walked toward the house, Felix turned to his companion and said, "Galerius Licinius? Isn't he the legendary swordsman?"

"Yes. They called him Galerius Magnus[21]," Julius replied.

On the way to Aletium, the speculatores asked Sejanus where they were going. His only reply was, "to see a friend."

Antonius opened the door and walked in with Marcus behind.

"Ah, here is Antonius now and his friend, Marcus," Galerius declared. "Come in, boys. We are honored to have the Praetorian Guard Prefect himself pay us a visit."

Sejanus extended his hand and clasped arms with Antonius. "I am Lucius Sejanus. You must be Galerius's son; you have your father's look about you."

Antonius smiled.

Marcus clasped arms with Sejanus and said, "I am Marcus Flavius."

Sejanus looked them over and said, "How old are you two?"

"Eighteen," Antonius replied.

"Seventeen," Marcus replied.

Sejanus reminisced in his mind and said, "Ah, if I could only go back to that time."

"Sit down, boys," Galerius said, pointing to stools nearby. "Lucius was just about to tell me the purpose of his visit."

Antonius and Marcus sat down then all focused on the man sitting on the

____

21 *"The Great"*

44

couch across from them. Sejanus leaned forward and interlocked his fingers, revealing a large gold ring that glinted in the lamplight. A black obsidian with a raised golden scorpion on top completed the setting.

Sejanus furrowed his brow and said, "Galerius, I am here to ask for your help. The emperor has given me more responsibilities than I can handle and I have no one in my ranks with the leadership skills that you possessed. I need you now, good friend. Rome needs you now. I am asking you to consider returning to the Praetorian Guard."

Antonius and Marcus turned to Galerius with wide eyes and open mouths. Octavia, however, looked at him with apprehension.

Galerius rocked back slightly in his chair. "Well, I must say I am flattered, Lucius. But I really have no desire to return to the Guard."

"Galerius, I wouldn't ask this of you if it wasn't serious," Sejanus coninut-ed. "There are men in Rome who seek to destroy not only me but also the Guard itself. Many influential members of the senate have been trying to persuade the emperor to do away with us. That would leave the princeps[22] vulnerable as well as myself. I know you and Tiberius had your differences when you served under him, but without the Guard, Rome would be plunged into chaos. I need someone who can stand with me on this, someone I can count on to watch my back. You are the only person I trust."

Galerius looked at Octavia and saw the trepidation in her eyes. Turning back to Sejanus, he replied, "I'm sorry, Lucius, but I'm afraid I must decline your offer. I truly wish I could help, but I have a vineyard to run. My family needs me here."

Sensing an opportunity, Antonius asked, "What about me, Father? I'm old enough to join and you've trained me how to use a gladius and pilum like a soldier. I could become a Praetorian."

Galerius smirked. "Son, it's not that easy to get into the Guard. They pick from the strongest and bravest men in the army who accept orders without question and have proven themselves in battle. It is a select brotherhood."

"Then what if I joined the army now and proved myself worthy like you did?" Antonius pressed.

Now Sejanus sensed an opportunity. "You look like you're in fairly good shape, young man. It just so happens we're recruiting strong lads into the Guard now to replace the ones who have retired. Each year on the first of June we begin a training camp for those we select. Of course, the training isn't easy and the term of service is for sixteen years. Normally, military

22-Literally means "first citizen," referring to the emperor

experience is required, but since Galerius has been training you... I could overlook the military experience requirement."

Marcus perked up. "What about me?"

Sejanus looked him over. "Have you ever used a gladius before?"

"Antonius and I spar practically every day. He has taught me what his father taught him," Marcus replied anxiously.

"He is also an exceptional archer," Antonius added.

Lucius rubbed his chin. "A Sagittarius, eh? Well, you would still have to prove yourselves in training, but if you want to sign up I can arrange it."

Octavia, who kept silent during the exchange, could contain herself no longer. "Galerius, I thought we had agreed that Antonius would take over the vineyard someday. That day is drawing near."

"What?" Antonius exclaimed. "You discuss my future as if I have no say!"

Octavia looked at him with pleading eyes and said, "But my son, you are too young."

"Father went into the army when he was my age," Antonius countered.

Not wanting to have his friend witness a family argument, Galerius said, "Perhaps it would be better to talk about this another time." He followed his comment up with a look, implying there would be no further discussion.

Octavia pressed her lips together tightly then turned to Sejanus and asked, "Have you and your men had supper, Lucius?"

Sejanus gazed up in thought then said, "Truth be told, we haven't eaten since this morning, Octavia."

"Then I shall fix you something to eat," Octavia declared.

Sejanus put up his hands and said, "Please don't go to any trouble."

Octavia shook her head slightly and said, "No trouble at all. You can call your men in when it is ready."

Sejanus gave her a surrendered look and said, "Thank you, Octavia, you are most kind."

"Come, Augustina, I will need your help," she said as she started toward the kitchen.

Sejanus turned to Galerius with a furrowed brow and asked, "Octavia is going to prepare the food? You don't have a cook?"

Galerius smiled. "Do not be worried, Lucius. Octavia has become quite a good cook since we've been here."

"Oh, I have no doubt she is, I am just surprised she doesn't have someone to prepare your food and serve you," Sejanus stated, scratching his head.

Galerius smiled and said, "It was her choice not to have servants."

Sejanus reacted with an upward nod.

Awestruck by the large man in armor, Marcus asked, "Did you fight in any great battles, sir?"

Sejanus smiled. "Nothing compared to what Galerius fought in."

Antonius gave his father a pleading look and said, "Tell Marcus about the battle you were in at Teutoburg Forest."

Galerius shook his head. "That is a painful memory, son."

"What happened there?" Marcus asked, opening his eyes wide.

Sejanus's curiosity was also aroused. "Yes, what happened at Teutoburg, Galerius? I heard our troops walked into an ambush and lost many men."

Galerius took in a deep breath then said, "All right, I'll tell you about Teutoburg. Many years ago, Emperor Augustus ordered the invasion of Illyria, Moesia, Pannonia and Germania. My cousin Albinus and I were under the command of Publius Quinctilius Varius at the time, serving in the seventeenth legion. Arminius, a trusted advisor of Varius, reported a local rebellion in Germania so Augustus sent three legions there to put it down. My legion was one of them. We left our outpost and marched until we reached the forest at Teutoburg. There had been a terrible storm the evening before, so the terrain was quite muddy and difficult to travel. Our forces were strung out for miles with no advanced reconnaissance, which proved to be a fatal mistake. After traveling some distance through the forest, it began to rain. Not water, but arrows. The barbarians had men in the trees and on our flanks. We quickly formed testudos[23] but the arrows claimed many of us before we could set up our defenses properly. Then they attacked from all sides.

The battle raged on until late in the evening when it started to rain water this time instead of arrows. That caused a lull in the fighting. As we waited for another assault, we heard their war drums. They didn't attack, they just kept pounding on those drums. It finally stopped raining then a thick mist spread through the forest. Varius asked for volunteers to slip through the enemy lines and bring back reinforcements. Albinus and I were two of the four who volunteered. We went into the forest and the other two entered the bog in the opposite direction. As we started out, we could barely see our hands in front of our faces, due to the thick mist and moonless night. Fortunately, the enemy couldn't see that well either. Somehow, Albinus and I managed to slip past them and entered a clearing just as dawn broke. We thought we

---

23-*Forming a shield wall around the sides and top of a formation*

were in the clear when two arrows sailed over our heads. 'Run!' I yelled to Albinus, as more arrows came dangerously close. I was in the lead then I heard him cry out. I turned just as he fell with an arrow in his back. I ran over and helped him to his knees, but he told me his legs would not work. His last words were, 'Save yourself and tell my family I died bravely.' Then he drew his gladius and fell on it just as another arrow struck him." Galerius paused. "After that, I kept running until the arrows stopped. That was my worst day as a soldier."

"What happened after that?" Marcus asked.

"I traveled for a few days until I reached a Roman outpost. I tried to obtain reinforcements to go back, but after describing the situation to the Tribune in charge, he refused to send help. He had only a cohort[24] under his command and was afraid they would be slaughtered. Later, I learned he was stripped of his rank and banished by Augustus. That was certainly better than what happened to Varius and the rest. When daylight appeared the day after Albinus and I left, the barbarians attacked. One Centurion, Eggius, made a final charge at the enemy and died bravely, while another Centurion, Ceionus, surrendered with his men. When Varius saw that all was lost, he and a few others fell upon their swords. Those who surrendered paid a heavy price for their cowardice, though. The Illyrians cooked them alive in large pots so their bones could be used for their heathen religious ceremonies. After hearing that, I made up my mind I would never be taken prisoner and fight to the death or die on my gladius. The heathens released one soldier to tell us that more Romans would die the same way if we didn't leave their country."

Lucius nodded and said, "That was a dark time for Rome."

"Yes, a dark time," Galerius agreed. "We lost a lot of good men."

"They also lost three legion eagles[25], Antonius remarked. Putting his hand on his father's arm, he said, "Tell Marcus what the barbarians looked like."

Galerius's eyes narrowed. "In all the battles I fought and all the foes I came up against, I never saw an enemy like the barbarians. Every part of their body that wasn't covered was stained black. The only things you could see were their eyes. Although we were better equipped and better trained, they rendered our tactics and strategy useless. Arminius turned out to be a traitor and executed a brilliant battle plan against us."

"What was your cousin like?" Marcus asked.

Galerius smiled. "A lot like you and Antonius. We even joined the army together." He turned and looked out the window. "I miss him," he said, as his

24-A military unit consisting of 480 men
25-A Roman military standard topped with a golden eagle

thoughts remained two decades in the past in a far away Germanian forest.

The room suddenly became quiet. There were no more questions, as all seemed to sense the solemnity of the moment. It remained that way until Octavia shouted from the kitchen, "The food is ready! Lucius, you can call in your men."

Sejanus stood up and went over to the entry door. Opening it he shouted, "Varius! Castor! Come inside and have something to eat."

Felix shouted back, "You have but to command me, Prefect." After entering, they took off their helmets and placed them on a rack near the door where Sejanus had hung his helmet.

Marcus leaned over to Antonius and whispered, "I like that. 'You have but to command me.'"

"These are my two bodyguards, Praetorians Julius Varius and Felix Castor," Sejanus said, introducing them.

Octavia nodded and said, "Everything is ready. Come into the dining room if you will."

After directing where each person was to sit, she went back into the kitchen and returned with Augustina, carrying large trays of bread, sausages and vegetables. While they placed them on the table, Galerius took out an amphora of his best wine from a cabinet nearby before taking his seat.

Seeing that places were only set for him and his bodyguards, Sejanus said, "I would feel better if everyone had something to eat with us."

"Oh, Lucius, we already had our supper and couldn't eat another bite," Octavia replied

"I could!" Antonius blurted out.

"I could as well," Marcus added.

Galerius gave them a stern look, which caused Antonius to amend his comment.

"I guess I'm full after all." Antonius declared, elbowing Marcus, who nodded in agreement.

After Augustina dished out the food, the two bodyguards began devouring their portions while Sejanus took his time. Sitting across from the two hungry speculatores, Augustina looked back and forth at each one, admiring their rippling muscles. When they would glance up at her, she would give them her best smile.

"Where are your homes?" Octavia asked Julius, attempting to direct the two speculatore's attention away from her pretty young daughter.

Felix, who had just filled his mouth, looked at Julius.

Julius swallowed and replied, "I come from a town in the Umbrian province called Reate, and he comes from Volsinii."

Sejanus added, "These two were both masters with the gladius and pilum in their respective training classes, so I made them my speculatores."

"What's a speculatore?" Augustina asked.

Julius gave her a sinister smile and replied, "We protect the Prefect and do whatever he tells us to do."

Augustina nodded.

"Have you two been in the Guard long?" Galerius asked.

With a half-full mouth, Julius replied, "I've been in ten, Felix has been in nine."

Turning to Sejanus, Galerius said, "Lucius, why don't you tell the boys a little about the Praetorian Guard."

For the next half hour, Lucius described their function while his speculatores filled their plates again. When the trays were empty, Octavia brought in another tray of apple pastries.

"These look wonderful!" Sejanus declared. "Galerius let me borrow Octavia for awhile."

"Oh, no. If I did, you would never return her," Galerius replied, pulling her close.

A short while later, the pastry plate contained only crumbs.

Lucius wiped his mouth and said, "Octavia, that was a most wonderful feast. I hope you will allow me to return and visit again."

"You are welcome any time," Octavia politely replied.

Sejanus smiled at her, but his mind was still on convincing Galerius to return to the Guard. He knew his only chance of changing his mind, however, was to get him away from Octavia. He swirled the last dregs of wine in his mug and gazed into it, formulating a plan. Finally, he spoke. "Come, Galerius. Before I leave, let's take a walk and you can show me this wonderful vineyard of yours."

"Certainly," Galerius replied.

Octavia noticed the invitation extended only to her husband and reacted with a furrowed brow.

"Can Marcus and I come?" Antonius asked.

"Why don't you let your father and I spend some time by ourselves," Sejanus replied with a commanding look.

Antonius nodded as the two speculatores stood up.

Sejanus shook his head, so they both sat back down and focused their attention on Augustina.

As the two old friends walked out into the cool evening air, Sejanus spoke first. "Galerius, there is one thing that still vexes me. You were a Tribune in the Guard with a magnificent villa in Rome, servants to care for all your needs and a senator's daughter for a wife. You had position, power, wealth, and status. Now I don't mean to give offense, but why would you forsake all of that for a laborious life such as this?"

After a brief hesitation, Galerius replied. "When we served under Augustus, the Guard was different then. Do you remember what he used to drill into us all the time?"

Sejanus smiled. "Ah, yes... morality, discipline, justice and courage. Who could forget that? But you seemed so happy being a Praetorian. I guess it is hard for me to understand how a man who seemed so satisfied with the Guard could turn around and leave it."

Galerius shifted his gaze northward in the direction of Rome. "It is true there was a time when I enjoyed the respect, rewards and privileges I received as a Praetorian. But when Tiberius allowed our enemies to come into Rome..."

"You mean the Germanic bodyguards," Sejanus stated.

Galerius slowly nodded. "Yes. Even though their camp was outside the city, I couldn't bring myself to work with them after their kind killed my cousin and friends at Teutoburg. I just couldn't do it."

"I understand," Sejanus said, patting his shoulder. "Do you ever regret your decision to leave the Guard?"

Galerius smiled. "I know this simple way of living may seem crude to you when compared to Rome, Lucius, but we are happy here."

Sejanus stopped and gave Galerius a piercing glance. "Are you sure this is what Octavia wants, Galerius? Doesn't she miss all the excitement and splendor of Rome?"

Galerius's look turned pensive. "I was worried that she might. But she could tell I was unhappy after the Germanics came. When she asked what was wrong, I told her I wanted to leave Rome. I was afraid she wouldn't go with me. But she said, 'Quando tu Gaius, ego Gaia,[26] repeating her wedding vow. If you think it is best for us to leave, we will leave."

Sejanus's brow furrowed. "I would think the daughter of a senator, who was used to being pampered and catered to all her life, would never agree to

---

26-*Phrase uttered by the bride to the groom during the marriage ceremony; it means "Where you go, I will follow."*

having her lifestyle altered so radically."

Galerius raised his eyebrows and said, "Yes, it surprised me as well. But I learned something about Octavia that day. She chose my happiness over her own comfort."

"Well, Galerius, I still think you should be enjoying the good life that Rome and the Guard have to offer. And speaking of such, I will pay you twice what you made before you left, give you a fine villa and make you my second in command if you return."

Galerius flashed a quick smile then took a deep breath. "That is a most generous offer, Lucius, but I really can't accept. My family and I are happy here."

Realizing he wasn't going to change Galerius' mind, Sejanus nodded. "I'm glad for you, Galerius." After a brief hesitation, he asked, "What about your son? How would you feel if he became a Praetorian?"

Galerius sighed deeply. "If that is his desire, I will support him. But if he doesn't measure up, put him in the army. Don't feel obligated to make him a Praetorian because he is my son."

Sejanus nodded. "If he isn't ready then a few years in the army will season him up."

Galerius clasped Sejanus' arm and said, "Thank you, Lucius."

As they walked back to the house, Galerius asked, "Is the emperor still living on Capreae?"

"Yes," Sejanus replied. "He hasn't been in Rome for sometime now."

Galerius nodded slightly. "I can only imagine the pressure you must be under, trying to keep both the Guard and Rome in line."

Sejanus took in a breath and let it out. "I will admit, it has been difficult and becoming more so as time passes. It isn't like the old days when we knew who our enemies were on the battlefield. Now, they could be wearing a senator's toga or a Roman soldier's uniform. One must be careful with whom he trusts."

Galerius nodded. "Times have changed."

Sejanus placed his hand on Galerius' shoulder and said, "Well... if you should change your mind, the offer will always be there, my friend."

Galerius smiled. "Thank you, Lucius. I wish you well with your fight to keep the Guard strong."

Sejanus lifted up his hands then let them fall and said, "It would have been a guaranteed victory with you at my side, Galerius. But I understand that a man has to do what is best for himself... and his family, of course."

Seeing no sense in tarrying any longer, Lucius looked up in the dark sky and said, "It is getting late. I had better be on my way back to Rome."

"Why don't you spend the night with us," Galerius offered. "We have plenty of room and riding in the dark can be dangerous."

"That is generous of you, Galerius, but I don't want to impose on your kindness any more than I already have. Besides, I have pressing matters awaiting me and we had a good rest before we came here."

"I understand," Galerius nodded.

"The next time you are in the city, come to my office and bring an amphora of your magnificent wine," Lucius suggested as they walked back to the house.

Galerius stuck out his chest and said, "I'll do better than that. I'll bring you a whole barrel."

Sejanus slapped him on the back as he opened the door and said, "I will hold you to it, good friend." Giving his speculatores a stern glance, he said, "Grab your helmets, men. We start back for Rome tonight."

"But the hour is late!" Octavia exclaimed. "At least stay with us until morning, Lucius."

Sejanus smiled politely. "Thank you, Octavia. Your husband already tried to convince me, but I really must be going. So much to do."

"Well, if you must," Octavia conceded. She then put up her hand and said, "I can't let you leave empty-handed, though, wait here."

Returning with a full wineskin a moment later, she said, "I'm sure your journey back will make you thirsty. He is a little wine to remedy that." She handed it to the bodyguards.

Sejanus smiled. "Galerius, this woman is truly a goddess; guard her well."

"I never let her out of my sight," Galerius quipped as he put his arm around Octavia's waist.

Sejanus turned to Antonius and Marcus. "If you two are serious about coming to the training camp, fetch me some writing materials and wax."

A moment later, Antonius handed him parchment, a stylus and some ink. Sejanus wrote out the invitation on a nearby table then rolled it up and sealed it with some melted wax Octavia provided. He pressed his ring on the wax and said, "There. This should get you into the Castra Praetoria."

Antonius and Marcus grinned like hyenas.

Walking back outside with his speculatores, Sejanus gave Antonius and Marcus a stern look and said, "Now you two stay in shape. The training won't be that easy so be prepared to work hard."

"We will," Antonius assured him.

Galerius grasped Sejanus's arm and said, "Thanks for coming, Lucius.

I'm sorry your trip was for naught."

Lucius smiled. "Nonsense. A trip is never for naught when you can visit with old friends." He then mounted his horse and said, "Next time you're in Rome you must pay me a visit."

"I have tried, but you're never around," Galerius replied.

Sejanus gave him an apologetic look and replied, "The demands of my position, I'm afraid. Take care, Galerius."

"Keep an eye on those senators," Galerius shouted as they left.

****

Sejanus galloped down the road with his two speculatores close behind. "Your friend appeared to be a likable fellow, Prefect, but I find it hard to imagine him being the legend so many have talked about," Julius stated.

Without turning, Sejanus replied, "Don't let his present appearance fool you. In his prime, he could kill twenty men without breaking a sweat. I have never seen anyone handle a gladius as skillfully as that man did… you included. Men who fought alongside him in different campaigns said he personally killed over 100 men in one battle."

The two speculatores glanced at each other with raised eyebrows.

Sejanus was disappointed that he couldn't convince Galerius to return to Rome, but having his son in the Guard could be the next best thing. Only time would tell.

CHAPTER V-LEAVING HOME

Marcus said his goodbyes, making sure he gave Augustina a special smile, then mounted his horse and headed for home.

After closing the front door, Antonius turned to his father.

"What did you and the Prefect talk about during your walk?" he asked.

"The price of grapes and the weather," came Galerius's facetious reply.

Antonius frowned. "No, I'm serious. Did he try to change your mind about returning to the Guard?"

"Yes, but I told him I would rather deal with difficult children than difficult soldiers," Galerius jocularly exclaimed.

"Oh, Father!" Augustina blurted, as Antonius rolled his eyes.

Octavia shook her head. "Children, it's late, so off to bed with you. We can address the matter further in the morning." Which meant Octavia wanted to verify for herself that Galerius had indeed turned Lucius down.

Antonius and Augustina whined as she kissed both of them on their cheeks. After watching their children go to their respective rooms, Galerius and Octavia retired to their own cubiculum[27].

Beginning her evening ritual, Octavia washed her face from a basin and anointed herself with scented oils. She then changed into her sleeping tunica and began to brush her shoulder-length reddish-brown hair. Galerius removed his tunic, washed his hands, face and upper body then looked at Octavia. He couldn't help but admire her beauty. She was in her early forties, an age where life's priorities cause most women's figures to retain weight rather than lose it. But Octavia was a light eater and kept busy maintaining the house and assisting in the vineyard. This regimen enabled her to maintain an attractive shape that could still turn a man's head.

Feeling his eyes on her, Octavia asked, "You and Lucius were gone for awhile. I know he tried to convince you to return to Rome. What did you tell him, Galerius?"

He sat down on their bed and replied, "I told him my place was here with you and the children."

Octavia stopped brushing her hair, walked over and sat down next to him.

"You really aren't going to allow Antonius to join the Guard, are you, Galerius? That is sixteen years of his life!"

Galerius sighed. "If it is his wish, I will support him. Besides, he could be

27-Bedroom

conscripted anytime now into the army. It would be better for him to serve in the Guard than an army unit."

"But what about the vineyard?" she said raising her voice. "We need him here!"

Galerius replied calmly, "We can always hire someone to help, Octavia."

"But if you were unhappy with the Guard, don't you think he would be as well?" she asked.

"My situation was different," Galerius explained, "and besides, Antonius is not a boy anymore. He is old enough to make his own decisions."

He then crawled into bed and pulled a light cover over him. Usually, when he did that, it signified the end of the discussion. But Octavia wasn't ready to end it.

"I think this is happening too fast," she argued, slipping into bed next to him. "They only have less than a month. That is not enough time to consider all the consequences."

"Let's not worry about it now. I'm tired and I wish to caress my wife before I sleep," Galerius replied, turning to the lovely but dismayed woman at his side.

Octavia folded her arms. "Your wife is not in a caressing mood."

Galerius heaved a heavy sigh and rolled over.

****

The next morning, Antonius sauntered into the dining room and saw his father and sister at the table eating porridge.

"Gruel?" he asked.

"Yes," Galerius answered, "and it's cold."

"Where is mother?" Antonius asked.

Augustina answered him. "Outside somewhere. You'll have to serve yourself."

Antonius looked at Augustina who raised her eyebrows. It was clear his mother wasn't happy about the invitation he received from Sejanus, but she would get over it he thought. At least he hoped she would.

After forcing the cold porridge down, Antonius, Augustina, and Galerius went out into the vineyard as usual to begin their work.

"Antonius!" Octavia called out to him. "Come talk with me for a moment."

Antonius walked over. "What is it, Mother?"

She took in a breath then said, "I know you have this idea that you want to serve Rome like your father, but you need to understand the consequences of what a soldier has to face."

"Mother, I know..." he said, putting up one hand.

Leaning her head in the direction of Galerius, she said, "You've seen the scars on your father's body and how he limps on his left leg, haven't you?"

"Yes," came Antonius' curt reply.

"He also has headaches and awakens in the middle of the night, crying out from a nightmare that continually plagues him. That is what serving Rome has done for your father," she explained.

Antonius looked at his father then back at his mother. "I have never heard him complain about his service to Rome."

Octavia shook her head. "That is not in your father's nature. He chose to become a soldier and was willing to accept whatever the consequences were going to be."

"And I am also willing to accept whatever the consequences are!" Antonius snapped back.

"But you can see what your father has to endure," Octavia pleaded. "He had no example to learn from like you have and could not see that serving Rome would leave him a broken man."

Instantly, Octavia regretted her choice of words.

Antonius felt the blood rush to his face. "I don't see Father as a broken man; I see him as a great man who helped Rome become great. I have a chance to do that as well. If it causes me some pain afterward, then so be it! I am willing to make that sacrifice!" He turned and stormed away, heading toward the lake just up the hill from the vineyard.

Octavia put her hand to her mouth, wishing she could take back what was said. She then closed her eyes and muttered, "Vesta[28], why did you let me say that?"

Augustina witnessed the exchange and started to go after him.

Octavia saw her and shook her head. "No, my child; let him be," she admonished her daughter.

Augustina nodded then returned to her work.

Galerius also noticed his son leave in a huff. He walked up to Octavia and asked, "What was all that about?"

Hanging her head, she began to cry. "I'm afraid I have said something horrible to your son that I now regret."

Galerius put his arm around her. "Tell me what you said to our son that was so horrible."

Looking at him through teary eyes, she related the conversation.

---

28 Roman goddess of hearth and home.

"I'm sorry, my husband. I really don't think of you as a broken man; I just didn't know what else to say to make Antonius change his mind."

Galerius softly caressed her back. "I know. I'll speak with him."

The lake not only provided irrigation for the Flavius farm and Licinius vineyard, it was also a place of solace for Antonius, especially when he wanted to be alone. After a short walk, he arrived at the lake's edge and sat down. He began to throw pebbles into the bluish-gray water as a frog croaked somewhere along the bank. Any other time, he would have looked for it, but he was not in the mood for chasing frogs. He stood up and tossed a pebble as far as he could throw it. The small stone hit the water with a "plunk!"

"Nice throw. But I'll bet I can throw my stone farther."

He turned and saw his father approach, limping slightly. "Father, are you in a lot of pain?" he asked.

"What do you mean?" Galerius asked.

Antonius looked out on the glistening lake and said, "Mother told me you are in constant pain from all the battles you fought and that you don't sleep well at night."

Galerius sat down on the bank and said, "Sit down, son." After Antonius sat down beside him, he continued. "It is true that I experience some discomfort from the wounds I received, and occasionally I have bad dreams. That is the price I must pay for being a soldier. I know I have told you many stories about the battles I've fought and lands Rome has conquered. I'm sure they sounded glorious to you. But being a soldier of Rome is not all excitement, glory and honor. Most soldiers are wounded, some lose limbs, and some die. Some you may be close to." Galerius hesitated, thinking of his cousin. "If you're lucky, you survive, but every survivor must pay a price. It might be physical pain or it might be the pain of things your mind will not let you forget. It might be both. But that is the reality all soldiers have to face. If you feel it isn't a road you want to travel down, then you should be content with what you have here on the vineyard."

"But being a Praetorian is different than being a soldier, isn't it?"

"Not necessarily. There have been times when the emperor has sent entire Praetorian units into battle. A Praetorian is also a soldier and can be called upon to fight for Rome at any time, if needed."

"Do you ever regret the things you did when you were a soldier?" Antonius asked.

Galerius gazed in the distance and replied, "Everyone has regrets."

"Do you regret the men you killed?" Antonius asked.

Galerius snorted and said, "Not the ones who were trying to kill me."

"Did you have to kill anyone who wasn't trying to kill you?" Antonius asked, looking into his father's eyes.

Galerius looked out over the lake and a pained expression came upon his face. He heaved a heavy sigh and said, "I have been in battles where I was ordered to slay women and children who were armed along with their men. I admit, I had to kill them or be killed. I didn't like it, and it took me a long time to get over it, but I did what I had to do. Some men in my unit slew unarmed women and children. I couldn't do it. After I became a Praetorian I had to arrest a few who were executed for plots against the throne, but the emperor's executioners had that distasteful job. If I had been ordered by the emperor to kill someone for no good reason, I don't know if I could have done it. Fortunately, the situation never arose. It is one thing to take a life to protect your own or someone you're guarding. That is your duty. To kill without sense or reason is murder. In our society, killing in the line of duty or self defense is justified. One who murders another must be punished. That is called justice."

Antonius nodded. "Do you think I should become a Praetorian, Father?"

"I think you should do whatever your heart tells you to do. You are the one who has to live your life. But whatever you choose, be prepared to accept the consequences and think it over carefully before you decide," Galerius suggested.

"You are beginning to sound like Mother," Antonius said with a crooked grin.

Galerius narrowed his eyes and said, "Sounding like her is not so bad. Looking like her is another matter."

Antonius stifled a chuckle. "Sixteen years is a long time. How will you manage the vineyard without me?"

"Actually, I was thinking of hiring another permanent hand anyway with the seasonal workers we get for harvest," Galerius replied. "If you leave, I will just have the new hire take over your responsibilities."

Antonius picked up a good-sized pebble and stood up. "What is the bet if my stone goes farther than yours?"

Galerius pursed his lips then said, "I'll do your chores tomorrow."

Antonius smiled. "Prepare to lose, Tribune."

****

April seemed to crawl. As each day passed, it became harder and harder for Antonius to concentrate on his work. Finally, the day before he was to leave for the Praetorian training camp arrived.

Worried about the reaction he would receive from his father, Marcus had procrastinated telling his family about leaving. Now he could wait no longer. After everyone had sat down for a late supper that evening, he blurted out, "Antonius and I received an invitation."

"An invitation to what?" Camilla asked.

Marcus looked over at his father then back to his mother. "To attend the Praetorian training camp in Rome."

Camilla gasped.

Slowly looking up at Marcus, Sergius glared at him. "What did you say?"

"I'm going to the Praetorian training camp," Marcus replied.

Sergius clenched his teeth and snarled, "That Licinius boy talked you into this, didn't he?"

With flinty eyes, Marcus replied, "No, I talked myself into it. Why should I stay here when you hate me?" Without waiting for a response, he stood up and left the table before Sergius could react.

"Come back here!" Sergius shouted.

Marcus ignored him and lunged out the door. He would go where he was appreciated.

On the other side of the hill, Octavia strolled through the vineyard. Her thoughts were on her son and she was afraid she would never see him again. Hearing footsteps, she turned to see Augustina approach.

"Are you all right, Mother?"

Octavia smiled and said, "Yes, just a little worried."

"About Antonius becoming a Praetorian?"

Octavia nodded. "You will understand when you have children of your own."

With a resolute countenance, Augustina stated, "When I do, I'm going to make sure they are all girls."

Octavia gave her a sideward glance. "That will be up to the gods and not you, my child."

They walked in silence for a moment then Augustina asked, "Mother, at what age can I marry?"

Octavia tittered. "Your father and I will let you know."

At that moment, Galerius came up behind them. "We will let her know what?"

"When she can marry and leave us," Octavia replied, turning around.

Galerius's face brightened. "Leave us? She can get married tomorrow!"

"Oh, Father, you're hopeless," Augustina giggled.

"Where is Antonius?" Octavia asked.

"I think he and Marcus are sparring behind the stable," Galerius replied.

Octavia shook her head. "Every time I turn around, he and Marcus are fighting."

"Sparring," Galerius corrected her. "They need to get all the practice in that they can before training camp.."

"I'll go and see who's winning," Augustina said, hurrying away.

As she approached the stable, she could hear the "Clack! Clack! Clack!" of their wooden swords. Going around it, she came upon the two Titans, trying their hardest to best each other.

"Defeat him, Marcus!" she shouted with her hands on her hips.

The combatants stopped just long enough for Marcus to smirk.

Taking advantage of his inattention, Antonius whacked him on the arm with his rudis[29].

"Ow!" Marcus yelled, rubbing where Antonius swatted him.

Antonius chuckled and said, "I owed you that."

Augustina furrowed her brow and yelled, "That was cheating! You hit him when he wasn't looking!"

Shrugging his shoulders, Antonius said, "When your mind is not in the battle, you will feel the sting of your enemy's sword. Father taught me that."

Not wanting to admit the blow hurt as much as it did, Marcus said, "It felt more like a bee sting."

"You are such a scoundrel, Antonius," Augustina chided her brother.

Just then, Galerius and Octavia walked over.

"You two think you're ready to go up against seasoned army veterans?" Galerius asked.

"We're ready," Antonius replied confidently.

An unsure nod was all Marcus could offer.

"Marcus, what did your parents say when you told them you were leaving tomorrow?" Galerius asked.

Marcus looked down and replied, "They weren't very happy about it."

Galerius nodded. He could only guess how Marcus' father reacted and chose not to press him any further.

"Come, Augustina, let's return to the house; it's getting late," Octavia said.

Augustina gave Marcus a smile as she departed with her mother.

29-Wooden gladius

Marcus sighed and said, "I suppose I had better go home and get ready for the trip to Rome." Then his face went ashen. "Wait! I can't go."

"What's the matter?" Antonius asked.

"We only have one horse. I can't take it to Rome, my family needs it for plowing the fields. Perhaps it would be better if I didn't go." Marcus lamented, hanging his head.

"No," Antonius said, thinking quickly. "You don't need a horse. We'll take the chariot! Mercury and Mars can pull it. Is that all right Father?"

"I don't see a problem with that," Galerius replied.

Hope replaced the disappointment in Marcus's face. "You are sure that is all right? I don't know; perhaps I *should* stay home."

Antonius gave his friend a stern look and decisively said, "We're both going, Marcus."

"You can leave the horses and chariot at our villa in Rome when you two arrive," Galerius instructed. "Just let Ignatius know I'll pick them up the next time I'm in the city."

Marcus gave them both a relieved smile and mounted his horse. "Tomorrow, then."

"Tomorrow," Antonius confirmed, as his friend rode away, giving out a whoop halfway up the hill.

After watching Marcus ride out of sight, Galerius turned to his son and said, "Sixteen years. Won't you miss your racing friends in town?"

Antonius furrowed his brow. "How did you know I was racing?"

Galerius smugly grinned. "I know a lot of things you don't think I know. I just hope you're not betting money on the outcomes."

Antonius smiled. "I only bet what I can afford to lose… but I never lose."

"Well, just remember—there is always someone better who will be happy to take your money," Galerius warned.

Antonius nodded.

"Are you sure joining the Guard is what you want, son?" Galerius asked.

Antonius looked him squarely in the eyes. "It's what I want, father."

Marcus rode to the top of the hill and stopped. He didn't feel like going back to his house and facing his father again. Dismounting, he gave his horse a slap on its hindquarters and sent it to the stable. He sat down on the knoll and felt excited the day had finally arrived for him to leave, but sad that he would probably not see his family for a long time.

The sound of a familiar voice made him turn around.

"I thought I would find you here when the horse returned," his mother said as she approached. "I put him in his stall."

"Thanks, mother," Marcus said.

Sitting down beside him, she brushed the hair out of his eyes and said, "Marcus, there is something I must ask you, and I want you to be honest with me. Do you want to become a Praetorian because Antonius wants to?"

Marcus gave her a defensive look and replied, "No... no! I am of age to be conscripted into the army anyway and would have to go if called. I would rather go as a Praetorian than as a regular soldier. I have an opportunity here to be something better and I think I should take it."

Camilla nodded. "When do you leave?"

Marcus hesitated, then turned to her and said, "Tomorrow."

She felt her throat tighten as she asked, "How long will you be gone?"

Marcus grimaced slightly. "Sixteen years."

"Sixteen years!" Camilla cried. "Oh, Marcus, that is half your life!"

"It will go by fast," he tried to assure her. "When I return, I'll have enough money saved to build us a better house and maybe even a better barn. We can't do that if I remain on the farm."

As a tear rolled down her cheek, Camilla took him by the shoulders and said, "If that is what you want then be the best Praetorian you can be." She embraced him as another tear followed the track of the first.

After a brief tender moment, she released him. "Come. It is late. We should get back to the house. I would feel better if you walked me back."

Marcus nodded and asked, "Is Father still awake?"

"He went to the tavern in town. I doubt he will return until much later," she replied, relieved that there wouldn't be another confrontation between them that night.

The moonless sky was now the color of raven's feathers as they walked along. Marcus wondered if he was doing the right thing by joining the Guard and leaving his family. Then he thought about his father and knew he had to leave.

****

At that moment, Galerius walked through the vineyard and gazed up into the same dark sky. He wondered if he was doing the right thing by allowing Antonius to join the Guard and recalled his last day as a Praetorian. He was going off duty, when Sejanus came up to him.

"Galerius, did you hear?"

"Hear what?" Galerius asked.

Sejanus hesitated, then said, "Tiberius has brought Germanics to Rome."

Galerius replied nonchalantly. "A lot of Germanics are brought to Rome as slaves."

"No, not as slaves, as bodyguards for his family," Sejanus replied.

Galerius's look was as if Sejanus had stabbed him in the heart.

"Are you serious?" he blurted.

Sejanus nodded. "I am. Go speak with Tiberius and he will tell you."

"I shall!" Galerius said, leaving in a huff.

After entering Tiberius's chamber and giving his customary "Hail, Caesar," Galerius began in a civil tone. His tone, however, escalated as the conversation progressed. "Germanic bodyguards, Your Majesty? You remember these are like the barbarians that killed our men in Teutoburg, boiled our surviving officers alive and captured our eagle standards!"

Tiberius narrowed his eyes. "I am well aware of that, Tribune. That is why I recruited them to be my bodyguards. It took a great deal of courage to stand up to our legions when we went against them. Besides, they are reliable and I don't have to worry about their loyalty. They don't care who is emperor as long as they are well paid and enjoy the luxuries Rome has to offer."

"But they are enemies of Rome!" Galerius cried.

Tiberius narrowed his eyes at Galerius's outburst and said, "They are not our enemies anymore, Tribune. They have sworn their allegiance to Rome. Get used to the fact you'll be working with them and put aside any ill feelings you have that stem from the past. Now, I wish to rest, so leave me."

Galerius wondered if Tiberius had brought the Germanics in to insult him, being one of the lone survivors of the Teutoburg debacle, or if he actually had more trust in their abilities over his Praetorians. One thing was for certain-any further argument would be pointless. With clenched teeth, he saluted, turned sharply then quickly marched out of the palace.

The next day, he handed Sejanus his resignation. Two days later, he left to look over a vineyard he heard was for sale in Aletium. He said no more about his feelings; elaborating to others would only put him and his family in danger. Tiberius had many informants and sometimes even minor complaints could be interpreted as treason. He wasn't about to take that chance. Octavia had given him her blessing, so he decided to get as far away from Rome as possible. Aletium would be perfect.

Galerius shook his head as he finished recollecting the past. He had walked through the entire vineyard and the hour was quite late. Opening the door to his house, he quietly tiptoed to his son's bedroom. Looking in, he noticed Antonius lying on his side, facing the window. He was about to call to him and have one last father to son talk, but it was late, and he knew Antonius had a long journey ahead of him. He walked farther down the hall and looked in on Augustina. As he watched her sleeping peacefully, he was impressed that she was turning into a lovely young woman like her mother. Entering his bedroom, he quietly removed his tunic and slipped into bed trying not to awaken Octavia. His efforts proved unsuccessful, however. She stirred and put her hand on his arm acknowledging his presence. A sigh escaped her lips. He smiled and kissed her shoulder. She had forgiven him for allowing their son to follow his dream. She knew any attempts to make Antonius stay on the vineyard would only cause him unhappiness. Above all, she wanted her children and her husband to be happy.

On the other side of the hill, Sergius returned from the tavern and fell out of the wagon. He lay there for a moment with his face in the dust and cursed. Finally picking himself up, he weaved over to the water pump and trough. Pumping the handle, he splashed a handful of water onto his face, rubbed the dirt off then shook his head. Upon entering the house, he staggered into his bedroom.

Camilla lay there, afraid to say anything and pretended to be asleep.

Taking off his tunic, he climbed into bed and stared up at the timbers in the ceiling. It didn't take long for the alcohol he had consumed to dull his anger and take him to a place where rebellious sons didn't matter.

****

The next morning, Antonius gazed out his window as a blazing golden sphere peeked from behind the distant citrine-colored hills. He managed little sleep, due to the excitement of realizing his dream was about to come true sooner than he expected. Hearing a cock crow from the Flavius farm, he turned and jumped out of bed to get dressed. Galerius standing at his doorway made him flinch slightly.

"Father! How long have you been up?" he asked.

"I'm afraid I didn't get much sleep last night," Galerius replied.

"I wasn't able to sleep much either. Too excited, I suppose," Antonius stated, taking in a deep breath.

"Before you go, I want to show you something in the stable. Get dressed and come with me," Galerius said, in a tone sounding more like an order than a request.

Antonius threw a tunic over his head and followed his father out of the house. As they approached the far end of the stable, Galerius grabbed a broom leaning against one of the stalls and tossed it to his son. Pointing to an area on the floor covered with hay, he said simply, "Sweep."

"Are we going to clean the stable before I leave?" Antonius asked, baffled by his father's actions.

Galerius smiled but said nothing. After a few swipes of the broom, Antonius cleared the hay and dirt away from a small trap door set into the ground.

"What is that?" Antonius asked.

"You'll find out." Galerius walked over, opened the small door and pulled out a wooden chest a half cubit wide, a cubit long and a half cubit deep.

"What is in there?" Antonius asked.

"You might call it your future," Galerius replied. Opening the chest, he removed a red satin bag and pulled the drawstring on the end. Sliding a richly crafted pugio[30] out, he displayed it proudly in both hands. The pommel was made of pure gold with several large black tourmalines as the grip. Each side of the blade had an eagle's head at the base. Its wings formed the handguard, and black obsidians had been inset for the eyes. The white sheath had gold trim with a black scorpion in a gold circle embossed on the side.

Antonius gasped. "That is magnificent! Where did you get it?"

"Emperor Augustus Caesar gave this to me just before he died," Galerius answered, beaming with pride. "He wanted to thank me for my loyalty and service to him. It means a lot to me, Antonius. Someday it will be yours."

"You should display it in our home," Antonius suggested.

"Your mother asked me to keep it hidden when we first moved here. As valuable as it is, she didn't feel safe with it being in the house and felt something bad might happen if we kept it there. You know how your mother is with her superstitions."

Antonius nodded

"There is also a great deal of money in the chest as well." Galerius turned it so Antonius could see the gold, silver and brass coins that filled half of the interior. "Should anything happen to us while you're gone, I want you to know where it is."

"Nothing is going to happen to you, Father. Why, just the mention of your name and people cower in fear," Antonius remarked dramatically.

"I'm afraid not even your mother fears me now," Galerius chuckled, as he returned the dagger and money back to their hiding place.

"Well, I suppose I should get the chariot and horses ready for the trip," Antonius said, walking over to Mercury and Mars.

"I'll help you," Galerius offered.

30-Dagger

After they had attached the horses to the chariot, Galerius pressed a purse of coins into his son's hand. "Here, you'll need this until you are paid. Don't spend it all in one day."

"Thank you, Father, I won't." Tying the purse to his belt, he patted it and smiled.

"Let's return to the house and have your mother fix you a hearty meal of moldy bread and pig entrails before you leave," Galerius said, as Antonius laughed out loud.

As they walked back to the house, Marcus scampered down the hill with a small bundle of belongings slung over his shoulder.

"You're early," Antonius shouted. "We haven't even had our morning meal yet."

Marcus grinned. "I'd say I'm right on time then. What are we having?"

Antonius gave his father a wink and replied, "Pig entrails and moldy bread."

Marcus returned a doubting look.

Galerius chuckled and put his arms around both boys. "Antonius is pulling your leg, Marcus. But if you're ever in the field and you're hungry enough, you'll eat it."

"Is that what you ate when you were a Praetorian?" Marcus asked.

"More times than I care to mention," Galerius replied, trying to keep a straight face.

Antonius shook his head and said, "Set your belongings here by the door, Marcus. You can put them in the chariot after we eat."

Marcus threw down his bag, then three hungry men went inside.

Treated to a grand meal that Octavia and Augustina prepared, they recalled monumental grape fights; accidental dunkings in the wine vats; fishing in the lake; sleeping under the summer stars; and defeating barbaric foes with wooden swords. After emptying their plates and clearing the table, everyone walked out of the house to say their goodbyes.

Octavia handed Antonius a bag of food she had prepared for the trip and a wineskin filled with mulsum. She then took him by the shoulders and said, "Do your best, my son. Above all, treat others with kindness and respect. The gods will favor you if you do."

"Yes, Mother," Antonius replied. He embraced her, followed by a kiss on the cheek. She smiled and quickly wiped her tears away.

He then turned to his father.

Galerius cleared his throat. "Do not give your trust easily; men must earn it first. Speak only when you have something to say and select your words carefully with much thought beforehand. You can't take back words you regret once they have been spoken."

Antonius nodded and remembered the saying his father told him during one of their sparring sessions. Galerius had been pressing him to defend himself better and had put several bruises on his arms. Antonius finally reached his boiling point and shouted through clenched teeth, "I hate you!"

Galerius stood there for a moment. Then he lowered his sword and said, "Once a sword has made its cut, it is too late to withdraw it." He then walked away leaving Antonius feeling instantly sorry.

Antonius later apologized, and Galerius explained what he meant. Antonius never forgot it.

"Do you have your key to our villa in Rome?" Galerius asked him.

Antonius nodded.

"Don't lose it. Ignatius and Lucia might not be there when you arrive." Galerius suddenly put up his hand. "Wait! I almost forgot. I have something for the both of you."

Hurrying into the house, he returned with a gladius in its sheath and a bow with a quiver of arrows. He handed the gladius to Antonius. "Here, this is the last gladius I used in the Guard. It is a little worn from use, but it's still sharp."

"Father, I am honored, but I can't take your gladius. What if you should need it?"

"I still have my spatha. Besides, you need protection as you travel. There are many dangers out there, so be observant."

"I will," Antonius said, then embraced him.

Patting his son heartily on the back, Galerius added, "Pay close attention to your trainers and do all they ask of you. It might save your life someday."

"I will, Father," Antonius assured him again.

Giving his son one last look, Galerius walked over to Marcus. "Marcus, I hope you don't mind me giving you this. I know your father needs his bow for hunting, and I saw this in Aletium and thought you might like it. Please accept it as a gift of friendship from our family."

Marcus's jaw dropped, as he took the expertly carved bow from Galerius along with the quiver containing a dozen arrows. "This is for me? I... don't know what to say." Fighting back the lump in his throat, Marcus simply said, "Thank you."

Galerius tapped him firmly on the shoulder. Imparting one last word of advice to them, he said, "Since you aren't soldiers yet, you are forbidden to enter a town carrying weapons so keep them in the chariot and don't take them out unless you're in danger. When you get to our villa in Rome, you can leave them there. We'll see you in a few months when you've completed your training."

They both nodded.

Turning to Augustina, Marcus smiled.

"Don't let Antonius hit you when you aren't looking," she said, embracing him with a smile.

Marcus looked over at Antonius and replied, "Don't worry, I won't."

Octavia was the last to embrace him. Then, holding him at arms length, she said, "Marcus, you and Antonius take care of each other."

"We will," Marcus assured her.

Antonius looked at his father, mother and sister one last time. Then he and Marcus climbed aboard the chariot and waved goodbye. Snapping the reins vigorously, Antonius shouted, "Run like the wind, Mercury and Mars!"

The two stallions responded, bolting down the path to the main road.

As Octavia watched them rumble away, she wiped the tears from her eyes and asked, "Do you think the boys will be all right, Galerius?"

"They are not boys anymore, Octavia, they are men," Galerius replied.

****

After going quite a distance, Antonius noticed the horses began to wheeze slightly. "We had better slow the pace, Mercury and Mars are getting winded," he said.

Marcus nodded. "How long will it take before we arrive in Rome?"

"If we travel from sun up to sun down, it will take a good seven days. Our first stop will be Tarrentum. We should reach it this evening."

Marcus looked at the sword tied to the bundle on Antonius's belongings, then back at the bow and arrows tied to his bundle. He felt slightly ashamed that he received a going-away present from Antonius's father and not his own. At least his mother gave him a knife and sheath she had traded for vegetables in Aletium, telling him not to mention it to his father.

"What did your parents say when you left?" Antonius asked.

Marcus looked down and said, "My mother just cried."

"And your father?" Antonius asked in a quieter voice.

Marcus hesitated. "My father told me not to return."

Antonius looked at his friend and said, "That must have been hard to hear."

Marcus shrugged. "It's not like I didn't expect it."

"What are you going to do when your sixteen years are up?" Antonius asked.

Marcus shrugged. "I don't know. Find work somewhere I guess."

Antonius' eyes brightened. "You can always work on our vineyard. My father will hire you."

"But will you return to the vineyard when your time is up or stay in the Guard like your father did?" Marcus asked.

Antonius turned and looked down the road. "I don't know. I'll have to see how I feel. I don't think I'll miss the vineyard, but I will miss my family."

Marcus thought a moment, then said, "I don't think I will miss the farm either, but I will miss the talks my mother and I had. I might even miss my brothers and sisters. What about you? Will you miss Augustina?"

Antonius shook his head. "My sister has always been my little shadow. Now I'm finally free of her it might seem strange not to have her around. I'll probably miss her."

Marcus stretched and asked, "How much farther to Tarrentum?"

Antonius chuckled. "The morning has not yet ended and you ask how much farther? When the sky grows dark we will be close. Until then, have a grape." Antonius threw the purple projectile, hitting Marcus in the head.

"Ow! Remember what your sister said about hitting me when I'm not looking," Marcus reminded him.

"I never listen to my sister," Antonius said with a grin.

As midday drew near, Antonius noticed Marcus flexing his legs. "Let's pull off the road and have something to eat... I'm hungry," Antonius suggested.

"Good idea. My legs are getting a bit stiff," Marcus remarked.

"You know, you don't have to stand when I'm driving the horses. I plan on sitting when you are the charioteer," Antonius remarked.

"I will take your advice," Marcus replied as they came to a stop. "Will we be camping out for the night?"

"No, actually we'll be staying at an inn tonight," Antonius replied in a boastful manner.

Marcus's eyes grew wide. "But I only have a few coins my mother gave me. I can't afford an inn."

Antonius waved his hand. "My father trades wine with the owner for lodging. I'm sure he'll let us stay without having to pay."

"Without having to pay is good," Marcus said, feeling relieved.

That evening, they entered their first town and came to the inn, just slightly off the main road. The spacious, well-built structure surrounded by olive trees overlooked the gulf, providing a breathtaking view of the sea up and down the coast.

As they stepped off the chariot and grabbed their things, Marcus looked around in amazement. Even though the sky cast its darkened shroud over the landscape, the full moon revealed a well cared for property with beautiful gardens, fountains and pools bathed in torchlight.

"I didn't know such beauty existed," Marcus exclaimed.

"If you think this is impressive, wait until you get inside," Antonius remarked with a nudge.

Stepping inside, Marcus noticed tables and chairs that flanked the entry and a polished wooden counter with a marble top stood at the far end. Tapestries, small statues and brightly colored vases containing vivid floral arrangements rounded out the decor. He sighed in wonder as he gazed about the room. Eventually, his gaze fell on a stout, middle-aged man standing behind the counter discussing some last minute details to a servant. As the man turned, his eyes lit up. "Young Antonius! Isn't it a bit late for a wine run?"

"Hello, Crassus," Antonius replied. " I'm not here for a wine delivery. My friend and I are on our way to Rome. Marcus, this is Crassus Varinius. He is the owner of the inn."

Marcus bowed. "Your inn is magnificent, sir."

"Thank you, young man. I am fairly pleased with it," Crassus responded. Giving them a mischievous grin, he said, "Going to Rome, eh? Are we looking to sow a few wild oats with a meretrix[31] or two?"

Antonius smiled. "Oh, no. Marcus and I have an invitation to join the Praetorian Guard."

Crassus reared back and said, "Well, good for you, Antonius! I thought it would only be a matter of time before you followed in your father's footsteps. How is your family? Are they well?"

"They are well, Crassus, and yours?"

The innkeeper sighed and shook his head. "Always demanding, always demanding. Now, since the day is done, I assume you both need a room?"

Antonius pulled at his collar nervously. "I know we are not on an official wine run, but is there by chance a room available that Marcus and I could stay in for the evening? My father can pay you for it when he comes to deliver your next wine purchase."

Crassus smiled. "I'll just see that he gives me an extra barrel when he's here. Miko!" he barked, turning to his servant. "Show these young lions'

---

31 Prostitute

upstairs to room number three and tend to their needs."

The large man nodded. Picking up their bundles in each hand, he carried them up a flight of marble stairs while they followed. Proceeding down a hallway lit by oil lamps, they came to a door marked "III." Miko set their bundles down, unlocked it and placed the bundles just inside. He then lit the oil lamps on the tables in their room and walked over to the balcony. Opening the drapes, which allowed the moonlight to illuminate the room partially through the honeycomb windows, he asked, "Will there be anything else, masters?"

"Yes. We could use a bath after our ride," Antonius replied.

"I'm afraid our baths are closed, but you can still soak yourselves in the main pool."

Antonius nodded. "That would be fine."

"I'll bring you some towels," Miko said then quickly departed.

Gazing about the room, Marcus noticed ornately carved wooden tables and cushioned beds with satin spreads and numerous colorful pillows. A larger wooden vanity table with an oil lamp sat opposite the beds with an intricately sculpted bronze-framed mirror on the wall above it. Two smaller tables with oil lamps sat next to each bed. Used to bare necessities all his life, he was overwhelmed. He had never been exposed to such luxury before and felt as though he was in a magnificent dream. He walked over and lay down on one of the large, olive green cushioned beds. Putting his arms behind his head, he gazed up at the ceiling. "Yes, becoming a Praetorian was a good idea," he muttered.

Just then, a loud knock on the door startled them. Antonius walked over and opened it.

Miko stood there with towels in one hand. "Would you like me to escort you to the pool?" he asked.

"I know where it is," Antonius replied.

"Very well," Miko said as he handed the towels to them and left.

Located under a covered extension at one end of the inn facing the bay, was a large circular marble pool. Around the interior's sides, painted charioteers drove their horses and chariots in a never-ending circle. A fountain rose up from the middle where three large marble dolphins spewed water as they sat atop their sculpted marble splash. Columns every few paces around the pool held up the tented roof allowing access to the gardens surrounding it. Since the hour was late, the pool was unoccupied. Antonius and Marcus arrived, removed their tunics and undergarments then eased in.

"Oooh, this feels good," Marcus exclaimed.

Antonius looked at his friend and smiled. "I could probably stay here the rest of the night."

Marcus leaned back against the side and smiled.

"Just think, Marcus. In another eight days we will be training to be Praetorians."

Marcus flexed his arm muscles. "Once they see my gladiator-like body they will probably make me a Tribune."

Antonius laughed. "My sister has larger muscles than you."

"Oh she does, does she?" Marcus retorted, splashing him. After a brief water fight, they sat back against the side and closed their eyes.

In the darkness, a hand slowly reached out, inching toward Antonius. Just as it was about to touch him, another hand pulled it back. Afraid of being discovered, the observers moved farther back into the darkness making a slight noise.

Marcus turned around and said, "What was that?"

Antonius looked around and replied, "I don't see anything. Getting a little jumpy, gladiator?"

Marcus shrugged and slid back down in the water.

After a good soaking, they wrapped towels around themselves and returned to their room while their mysterious watchers gathered to discuss their observations.

Slipping on a tunic, Marcus walked out on the patio and looked at the moon's reflection on the bay. It's creamy light shimmered on the water as circling seabirds screeched their sad sounding lullabies and the sea's dull roar ebbed and flowed with each pounding wave. He listened to one of nature's symphonies, and it mesmerized him for a moment. Gazing up at the constellations, he remembered hearing his mother say that the lights in the sky were good people who died and were allowed to shine over the earth. Bad people who died had no light. He believed her as a young boy, but now he wasn't so sure. "Antonius… do you believe there is an afterlife?"

Antonius, who was laying in his bed, replied, "My father and I don't believe in it, but my mother does. She says that after we die we go to one of three places. Elysium if we are brave and virtuous, the plain of Asphodel if we are average and live our lives with no real accomplishments or Tartarus where the evil will go and suffer."

Marcus cocked his head and said, "Who determines where we go?"

Antonius shook his head. "I think our actions do, but we had better make the most of our time here before we die. Afterwards is only uncertainty."

"Perhaps, but I would like to think there is something more beyond this life where we can be with those we love," Marcus stated.

"You're not planning on dying on me, are you, Marcus?"

"If I do, I hope I don't wind up in Tartarus," Marcus replied with a smile, as he walked back inside and closed the door.

"Actually, it would probably be better if you did. Then you could keep my sister company," Antonius chuckled.

With a twinkle in his eye, Marcus teased, "I would rather be there with her than you in Elysium."

"Ah... traitor!" Antonius yelled, springing from his bed and wrestling Marcus to the floor.

They playfully grappled for a while until eventually both became winded from the exertion and called a truce. Extinguishing the lamps, they lay down on their beds. Antonius rolled over on his back and stared up at the ceiling. He wondered how hard the training would be while Marcus wondered if they would make it through.

CHAPTER VI-ROME

Sunlight stealthily crept into their room the next morning diluting the dark shadows while the commanding yellow orb arose into a brilliant orange sky. Finches chirped noisily outside causing Marcus to stir as he fought for one more moment of sleep. Antonius, deep in rapturous repose, was oblivious to their cries. A loud knock, however, opened his eyes and, being closer to the door, he rolled out of bed and opened it.

Miko stood there smiling. "Young travelers. Your morning meal has been prepared. My Master thought you would want to be on your way early so you will be served before the other guests. I hope you're hungry."

"Hungry?" Marcus shouted, rolling over and rubbing his eyes. "I could even eat pig entrails and moldy bread."

Miko scrunched his face.

Antonius chuckled and said, "We'll be down as soon as we are dressed."

"Very well, I shall tell my Master," Miko said, then turned and left.

Antonius closed the door and smacked his lips. "We had better enjoy good food while we can. It may be the last we receive for some time."

Marcus scrunched his face. "Is Praetorian food really that bad?"

"We'll find out," Antonius replied with a yawn. "Now get dressed."

"You have but to command me," Marcus replied, saluting his friend.

After dressing, they hurried downstairs.

Miko was waiting for them at the bottom. He bowed and motioned for them to enter a door to the right of the entrance. Both boys cheerfully obeyed. Once inside the large room, they came to a sudden stop when they saw several girls of various ages sitting around an enormous table. Somewhat embarrassed because of their neglect in grooming themselves before they left their room, both quickly tried to groom their hair as best they could.

"We weren't aware there would be a..." Antonius stammered.

"A roomful of girls?" Crassus said, sitting at the head of the table. "These are my daughters, young lions. That is Drusilla, Silvia, Tullia, and Viviana. Daughters, this is Antonius, the son of our wine supplier, and his friend Marcus."

The girls giggled and smiled. Antonius and Marcus smiled back.

Marcus leaned over to Antonius and whispered, "You didn't tell me Crassus had daughters."

"I never knew that until now," Antonius whispered back.

Crassus motioned for them to take their seats. "Come, sit down. I know how large the appetites of young lions can be, so eat all your stomachs can hold. This may be your last good meal before you become Praetorians."

Marcus flashed a concerned look at Antonius, who just smiled. They found two open seats, strategically located between two of the oldest and prettiest girls, then sat down as the girls giggled again.

Marcus leaned over to Antonius and muttered, "Where's the food?"

Crassus held up one finger then clapped his hands.

Immediately a servant appeared, carrying a large tray with grapes, plums, strawberries, quinces, apricots and melons. Another servant followed carrying a tray filled with pastries and breads and behind him a third servant brought a tray filled with cooked meats and sausages. The boys' eyes opened wide as the servants placed the feast before them. After arranging all the food on the rectangular wooden table, the servants left. Satisfied with the variety, Crassus exclaimed, "You may eat!" He then looked at his daughters and said, "Take your portions quickly, my daughters, before the young lions devour it all."

The girls smiled and began dishing out their food. Marcus went to reach for something as Antonius cleared his throat and shook his head. His mother had chastised him often for serving himself before the women took their portions in his house. Marcus looked a little puzzled, but followed Antonius's lead and waited until the girls had taken what they wanted.

Crassus smiled. "Oh, we have well-mannered young lions with us. Your mothers have taught you well. I just hope my daughters leave you enough to fill your stomachs," he chuckled, watching his daughters pile generous portions of food on their plates.

After the girls had served themselves, Antonius and Marcus filled their plates and began to enjoy the feast. Between bites, the girls hurled questions at them like pilums.

"Have you ever been to Rome? Where do you live? How strong are you?"

"Please excuse them," Crassus apologized. "They spend most of their time in Rome being tutored. We have them on an occasional weekend and I'm afraid they are taking their boredom out on you, having little to do here. But, I promised I would introduce them and I have, so no more questions now, girls. Let them enjoy their meal."

A few sporadic groans rose up, but the girls knew better than to try their father's patience. They ate in silence, but gave the two handsome young men at their table alluring looks spawned by hyperactive hormones.

After everyone had finished eating, Crassus addressed his daughters. "Girls, you may be excused now so these aspiring young Praetorians can be on their way."

More groans but the girls stood up and began to leave. One of the oldest leaned over to Marcus before she departed and whispered, "The next time you bathe, make sure you are alone, gladiator." She gave him a sultry smile and left. Marcus appeared puzzled for a moment then blushed as he realized the noise he heard in the bathing area the night before must have been from Crassus' daughters.

After the girls had left, Crassus threw up his hands. "I'm afraid the gods have not smiled on me by giving me sons, so I hope you don't mind the barrage of questions from my daughters. Now I know you are anxious to be on your way and I have other guests to feed so I will let you go. Make sure you say goodbye before you leave."

Antonius and Marcus nodded then went back upstairs to collect their things. A short while later, they returned to the reception area where Miko and Crassus were waiting for them.

"Your horses have been rubbed down and fed so they are ready to travel," Miko informed them.

Antonius bowed slightly and said, "Thank you, Miko, and thank you, Crassus for everything."

The innkeeper smiled. "You are most welcome. You and your friend have a safe journey now, Antonius."

Nodding farewell, Antonius and Marcus climbed back into the chariot and rumbled down the paved path leading out to the main road.

By dusk, they entered the town of Blera and decided to travel a little farther until their stomachs began to growl. Finding a spot just off the road in a wooded area, they thought it would be a good place to set up camp and have their supper. After gathering some wood, they built a fire and ate some of the food Octavia gave them. When they had their fill, they laid down on their blankets and talked about the glorious battles they would fight and the tales people would tell about their heroic exploits. As the night grew late, the warmth of the fire made their eyelids feel like stones were attached. Antonius poked at the fire with his gladius until both were fast asleep as if they were the gods Hypnos and Thanatos[32].

As Antonius slept, he dreamed he was in the Circus racing his chariot. He yelled at his horses to run faster but to his surprise, one turned and growled.

32-In Greek mythology, Hypnos was the personage of sleep; Thanatos was his twin brother, death.

The scene seemed to melt away as he realized he was waking up. Blinking a few times, he saw two yellow eyes reflected in the moon staring back at him a short distance away. He heard the growl again. Focusing a little better, he saw the shape of a large wolf approaching. Now Mercury and Mars began to whinny, attempting to pull away from the chariot while kicking at two other wolves snapping at their legs.

"Marcus!" he yelled, grabbing his gladius just as the animal lunged. Instead of landing on its prey, however, the alpha male landed on the sharp point of Antonius's blade. Falling to the ground with a yelp it died quickly. Another wolf followed after the first and was on Antonius before he could react. As he rolled on the ground with the large animal, Marcus sat up as more menacing growls rumbled from nearby hungry mouths. Two other wolves approached him. He looked over to the chariot where his bow was and then back at the wolves. It was almost as if they were daring him to try for it. Taking a deep breath, he jumped to his feet and dashed to the chariot just as they ran toward him. Reaching his bow, he quickly nocked an arrow and let it fly. One wolf fell. Before he could ready his bow again, however, the other wolf lunged.

The struggles for life and death took only a moment, as one predator finally met the fury of Antonius's gladius while the other felt the sting of Marcus's knife.

Pushing the dead animals off them, they jumped up, ready to take on any more. But there was only one other wolf, and he wasn't prepared to meet the same fate as the rest of the pack. He let out a howl from his safe vantage point and scampered off to look for easier prey.

"Are you hurt?" Antonius shouted to Marcus.

"Just a few scratches. How about you?"

"The same. Do you think more will attack?"

"They might if we don't get the fire going again," Marcus replied.

Antonius looked at the ashes of their campfire.

Marcus rubbed his forehead. "I should have known better. We let the fire go out. I've been hunting with my father too many times to make this kind of mistake. He was always strict about making sure the fire burned all night long. Now I know why. Let's start the fire again."

After getting the fire started again, they sat back on a nearby log with gladius and bow in hand.

"We have enough wood to last until morning. We should take turns stocking the fire through the night from now on," Marcus suggested.

Antonius nodded. "I'll stay up until daybreak. You get some rest."

"I don't know if I can get back to sleep after that," Marcus said, feeling wide awake. "We had better drag the carcasses away from the camp before they attract even bigger predators."

Quickly disposing of them in the woods, they returned to the safety of their fire. Marcus leaned against the log with his bow in his lap and closed his eyes, while Antonius stood nearby with gladius in hand. The darkness lasted but a few more hours.

As the sun's rays filtered through the tall trees, Marcus opened his eyes.

"Get any sleep?" Antonius asked as he poked at the fire with his gladius.

"Not much," Marcus replied. "I kept thinking the fire would go out again and more wolves would return."

Antonius nodded. "Let's break camp and make our way to the next town before they do."

After packing up, they left the woods and returned to the road.

****

The next few days went by routinely: traveling until dark, setting up camp then continuing on the next morning.

As they began the last day of their journey, Marcus asked, "You said we would stay at your family's villa tonight?"

"Yes, we'll spend the night there and report to the Castra Praetoria in the morning."

"What are your caretakers like?" Marcus asked.

Antonius smiled then turned to Marcus with a straight face. "Our caretakers happen to be patricians who are very strict about protocol."

"Protocol? What's protocol?" Marcus asked.

"It's the required way of doing something," Antonius replied. "For example: when a plebeian, such as yourself, wishes to speak with a patrician, they must bow and ask for permission to speak."

"I should do that?" Marcus asked.

"Yes," Antonius replied with a stern look. "That is how things are done in Rome. If you do not follow protocol, they would probably be offended and might not even allow you to stay the night."

Marcus lifted his head and said, "Oh, I understand."

"Good." Antonius turned away so that Marcus would not see the impish grin on his face.

Anxious to reach their final destination, they ate as they traveled. Eventually, they came to the towering walls that serpentined around the city like a giant concrete snake.

Marcus's eyes opened wide as he beheld the sight. "This is Rome?"

"This is Rome," Antonius replied.

As they approached the southeastern gate known as Porta Appia, they stood in line as soldiers on either side checked the people entering the city.

When it was their turn to go in, one large, gruff-looking soldier asked, "What is your business in the city?"

"We are here to become Praetorians, Tribune," Marcus replied with an enthusiastic smile.

The guard, twice Marcus's age, replied in a deep voice, "I'm no Tribune, boy, I'm a milite[33]. I work for my keep."

The other guard overheard the remark and laughed. "They'll learn the difference between a milite and a tribune soon enough."

The first soldier nodded in agreement. He looked at the invitation Antonius handed to him and said, "If you're going to be Praetorians, may the gods help us all." He handed the invitation back and said, "Pass on through."

Antonius snapped the reins and they entered the large gates, feeling somewhat reproved but happy to be back in Rome.

"They're laughing now, but we'll be the ones laughing when we become Tribunes," Marcus said, as Antonius rolled his eyes.

After proceeding a short distance, they turned onto a road and eventually came to a large, one-story main structure with a stable in back. Antonius pointed and said, "There. That is our villa."

Different varieties of trees and plants made up the landscape around the villa, which also included a small fountain surrounded by a rock and flower garden. A four foot stone wall emcompassed the property with a gate at the front, large enough for a carriage to pass through..

Marcus's eyes went wide as he asked, "Your family owns this?"

Antonius replied matter-of-factly, "Oh yes, we stay here when we come to Rome for holidays and visits. My mother and father still have friends here."

"What about you? Do you have friends here as well?" Marcus asked.

"No, I was too young to make friends when we left. Besides, I really only have one friend now." He punched Marcus in the arm.

"Ow!" Marcus yelped. "You need to treat your friends better."

Antonius chuckled as they pulled up in front of the main entry.

After hopping off the chariot, they removed their belongings and walked up to the front door. Antonius took the key from his purse and unlocked it

---

33-Common footsoldier

80

then sauntered in with Marcus behind him.

"Ignatius!" he shouted.

A balding man in his mid-forties appeared. "Antonius? What an unexpected surprise. What brings you here?"

"My friend and I received an invitation to the Praetorian camp. We'll stay the night and leave for the Castra Praetoria in the morning."

"Your parents aren't with you?" Ignatius asked.

"No, just my friend and I," Antonius replied.

Ignatius held out his hands and said, "Here, let me take your things."

Taking both bundles from Antonius and Marcus, he was about to call his wife, Lucia, when she came into the vestibulum[34], large, robust and smiling. "Antonius!" she said, embracing him. Turning to Marcus, she said, "And who is this handsome young man?"

Antonius gave Marcus a nod.

Following his friend's advice, Marcus bowed and said, "Permission to speak."

Both Ignatius and Lucia looked at him strangely.

"We are not royalty," Ignatius exclaimed. "You don't need to bow or ask permission to speak to us."

Marcus gave him a confused look and said, "But, Antonius said that..."

Antonius's laughter interrupted him before he could finish his sentence.

"I think Antonius has played a trick on you," Lucia stated, shaking her head. "I thought you had outgrown that by now, Antonius."

"No, I'm afraid I haven't, Lucia," Antonius said, still chuckling.

Realizing he was the victim of a ruse, Marcus said, "Antonius told me that since you are patricians and I'm a plebeian, I would have to ask permission every time I wanted to speak to you."

"You can speak to us as you would your own parents. Don't believe everything that Antonius tells you," Ignatius said.

"I'm beginning to realize that," Marcus replied, lightly punching Antonius on his arm.

"What is your name, young man?" Ignatius asked.

"I am Marcus."

Ignatius bowed slightly. "I am Ignatius and this is my wife, Lucia."

"It is nice to meet you," Marcus said, as he gave Antonius a reproachful glance.

Motioning for them to follow her, Lucia said, "Well, you two must be

---

34-A small entrance hall into the house

hungry after being on the road all day, so come into the triclinium[35] and I will fix you something to eat."

"I'm hungry," Marcus declared.

"I think we both are," Antonius added, rubbing his stomach.

Lucia quickly prepared some cheese, bread and fruit and set it before the two hungry young men.

"How is your family?" she asked Antonius.

"They are well," Antonius replied between bites.

She then turned to Marcus and said, "And yours, Marcus? Tell me about them."

"I have two sisters and two brothers. We have a farm and sell vegetables in town," Marcus replied with his mouth half full.

"Your parents are still alive, I hope," Ignatius commented.

"Yes, they are still alive," Marcus said, and left it at that.

"Well, we'll let you two eat. Come and get me when you're done eating and I'll clean up," Lucia stated. "Antonius, you know where your room is and Marcus can sleep in Augustina's room."

After Antonius and Marcus finished eating, they bade Ignatius and Lucia a good night and retired to their rooms. Sleep, however, was fleeting for two excited Praetorian hopefuls.

****

The next day, Antonius and Marcus arose early to the smell of baked bread, cooked pork and eggs. They quickly dressed and bade their hosts a good morning then hurriedly devoured their food.

Lucia chuckled at their haste. "Goodness, Antonius. If you and your friend eat any faster, you might accidentally swallow the plates along with your food."

Both smiled.

"So you're going to be Praetorians, eh?" Ignatius asked, as they cleaned the last morsels from their plates.

"Yes... if we pass the training," Marcus replied.

"We'll pass," Antonius stated confidently.

"I imagine your father wasn't too disappointed about your decision, but how did your mother take the news, Antonius?" Lucia asked.

Antonius swallowed his last bite. "She wasn't too excited."

"I don't imagine she was. She always told us you were going to take over the vineyard from your father."

35-Dining room

"That is what they wanted, but it isn't what I wanted," Antonius stated with a rebellious tone.

"How about your parents, Marcus?" Ignatius asked. "How did they feel about you becoming a Praetorian?"

Marcus hesitated then said, "They weren't too happy about it."

"Well, you are both men now and can make your own decisions," Ignatius declared.

Both young men nodded.

After finishing their meal, Antonius stood up. "Thank you, Lucia, for the wonderful meal."

"Yes, thank you," Marcus added.

"You are certainly welcome," she replied.

"How are you getting to the Castra Praetoria?" Ignatius asked.

"My father suggested we leave the horses and chariot here so he could pick them up later. I suppose we can walk."

Ignatius scrunched his face and said, "That's a long walk. I'll take you in the wagon. You can get there faster and get settled quicker."

"I was hoping you'd offer," Antonius grinned.

Ignatius smiled and said, "I have to keep the son of my master happy or he might dismiss us as your caretakers."

Antonius shook his head. "My father would never do that, Ignatius. He thinks too highly of you and Lucia."

Ignatius gave Antonius a determined look and said, "Then I shall just have to keep it that way. While you get your things, I'll hitch up the wagon and pull it around to the front."

"We'll leave our weapons here, since we aren't allowed to be armed until we're Praetorians," Antonius informed him.

"As you wish," Ignatius said, hurrying out the door.

A short while later, the three were on their way. Rolling through roads lined with buildings, houses, shops, and stands with a variety of merchants selling their wares, they finally came to the entrance of the Praetorian fortress.

"Here we are... your new home," Ignatius said, as he brought the wagon to a stop.

Antonius and Marcus quickly jumped off and grabbed their belongings.

"Thank you for bringing us, Ignatius," Antonius said.

"You are most welcome, Antonius. You two take care of yourselves."

"We will," Antonius assured him, as Ignatius waved and rumbled off.

Marcus turned and looked up at the massive fortress and was awestruck for a moment. The stone wall stood nearly five meters high like an impassable obstacle, daring him to approach.

"Am I sure this is what I really want?" he thought.

Antonius made up his mind for him. "Come, gladiator. It's time to become Praetorians."

Marcus nodded and took the dare.

A large arch stretched from one side of the gate to the other. Surprisingly, it gave the entrance a more decorative rather than ominous look. Four large Praetorian sentries, holding pilums and shields, stood guard.

As Antonius and Marcus approached them, one sentry put up his hand. "You there, state your business!"

"We were invited to the Praetorian training camp," Antonius replied, hoping he didn't sound too anxious.

"Do you have your invitation?" the sentry asked.

Antonius fished in his pocket and handed it over.

After reading the invitation, the sentry handed it back then stood away from the entrance allowing Antonius and Marcus to enter. "Take them to the Prefect," he ordered one of the sentries inside.

The sentry nodded. "Come with me."

Entering an open courtyard with building complexes on both sides, they approached several chariots.

"We'll ride from here," the sentry informed them. "The Prefect's office is at the other end of the Castra. The chariots only hold two, so you will have to ride together. Have you driven a chariot before?"

Antonius smiled. "Once or twice."

"Good. Take the one on the end and follow me." The sentry then untied the horses to his chariot and stepped onto it. After seeing that Antonius and Marcus were ready, he nodded and snapped the reins.

"Lets give these new trainees a taste of Praetorian dust," he thought. Bringing his horses to a full gallop, he turned his head expecting to see Antonius and Marcus choking from the dust kicked up from his wheels. Instead, he saw them riding alongside with Antonius grinning like a merchant who had sold all his wares. The Praetorian smiled back.

As they proceeded down the main thoroughfare called the Via Praetoria, Marcus felt as though they were in a city within a city. The interior of the fortress was much bigger than he had imagined. After passing a few sprawling complexes, their escort came to a stop in front of a large building at the end and said, "This is where the Prefect's office is." He stepped down from his chariot and secured it to a post then said, "Follow me."

Antonius and Marcus secured their chariot then followed him inside the building.

Arriving at the entrance to Sejanus's office, the Praetorian pointed to a table and said, "If you have any weapons, leave them here while you visit with the Prefect. Anyone who isn't a Praetorian cannot take weapons into his office. Protocol."

"Of course, protocol," Marcus said, smiling at Antonius.

"We have no weapons," Antonius assured him.

The escort went through their belongings to make sure, then escorted them past the two sentries into the aide's office. "Two new trainees, Licinius and Flavius. They were instructed to report to the Prefect."

The aide walked over to Sejanus's door and knocked.

"Yes?" a voice called out from the inside.

"Two recruits are here to see you, Prefect. Licinius and Flavius."

"Send them in," Sejanus replied.

Antonius and Marcus walked into the office, gave the Praetorian salute Antonius' father had taught them, and stood before him at attention.

Sejanus smiled at their eagerness in decorum. "Looks like you two took me up on my offer. I trust your journey from Aletium went well."

"We did have a little trouble with some wolves that attacked us near Blera while we camped, but we were able to kill four of them," Antonius replied, nonchalantly.

Sejanus leaned back in his chair, intrigued. "Wolves in the woods near Blera? Really? And you were not injured?"

"No, sir, nothing serious, just a few scratches," Antonius replied.

Sejanus smiled. "Good. Well, train hard and you'll be Praetorians before you know it. My aide will give you your oath of allegiance before taking you to your barracks. You will begin tomorrow. I've taken a big chance on allowing you both to take the training , so don't let me down."

"We won't, sir," Antonius promised.

"Do either of you have any questions?" Sejanus asked.

"No, sir!" they both replied in unison.

Sejanus turned his head and shouted, "Thaddeus!" His aide appeared from the adjoining room. "Give these two new recruits the oath of allegiance then take them to the trainees' barracks."

Thaddeus gave a slight bow and said, "Yes, Prefect."

Turning his attention back to Antonius and Marcus, Sejanus said, "And

Tribune Falconius will be your commanding officer. He will see to it that you are well-trained. That is all; dismissed."

The boys saluted then followed Thaddeus into the next room.

Reaching into a desk drawer, the aide pulled out two printed sheets of parchment.

"These are your enlistment agreements. Each term of service will be for sixteen years, and your starting pay is 240 denari every four months, in January, May, and Septembris. It is a long time to your next pay allotment so spend it wisely. We will provide your meals, uniforms, main weapons, and living accommodations during your training but anything beyond that will come out of your purses. After your term of active service has expired, you will serve in the reserves for four years, earning a sum of money for retirement. The amount will depend on your rank when you leave, if you decide to leave, that is. Do both of you understand your commitments?"

Antonius and Marcus nodded.

"Place your right fist over your heart. This will also be a salute that you are to give every senior officer or member of the royal family whenever you approach them or you are dismissed from their presence. As you repeat the oath, leave your fist over your heart. Repeat after me... I, state your names, swear that I will protect and defend the emperor and any other members of royalty or any officials, whether public or senatorial I may be assigned to guard, and will fight to the death if necessary wherever and whenever I am called on to protect and defend them. I will obey all commands given to me by senior officers and will act upon all threats toward Rome or its provinces when ordered to."

After repeating the oath, they saluted and signed their agreements.

"You are now officially soldiers of the empire," Thaddeus said taking their enlistment agreements. "What army units were you in?" he asked.

"Uh, we haven't been in the army," Antonius replied.

Thaddeus gave them a blank stare for a moment, then said, Well, since both of you weren't in the army, you'll need to be branded."

"Branded?" Marcus asked.

"Yes. Every soldier must be branded with the letters 'SPQR' and the date of their enlistment on their arm. It identifies them as a soldier of Rome. It also helps us keep track of deserters."

"When will we receive it?" Antonius asked.

"After you are issued your training uniforms and given your barracks assignment. Now, follow me."

After walking down the main thoroughfare, they entered a large building. Two attendants stood behind a long counter. Thaddeus approached and pointed to Antonius and Marcus. "I have two new trainees here. They will need their bedding, uniforms, caligae and identification papers."

The attendants nodded. After measuring their foot size, they obtained the needed items for Antonius and Marcus, placing them on the counter. Procuring two pieces of parchment with imperial seals from a drawer, an attendant wrote down their personal information. After obtaining all the details needed, he handed the papers to them and said, "Do not lose those or you will not be allowed back into the Castra if you aren't in uniform."

Both Antonius and Marcus nodded.

"Good. Follow me," Thaddeus said as he walked out of the building.

Proceeding to a building across the way, they entered a long corridor. As they passed many rooms containing other trainees, Thaddeus would glance into each one then continue. Finally, he stopped.

"Each room holds eight men and there are only six in this room, so I will assign you here. Down the hall on your left is the latrine and bathing area. Farther down the hall on the right is the dining hall where you will have your meals. Your training Centurion will come by each night and order all lamps to be out. If any lamp is lit again after his rounds, you will be subject to punishment. The door to your room is to be left open at all times while your lamp is burning. You may close it at night after the lamp has been extinguished. In the morning, your training instructor will come by and order you out of bed. You will take care of your personal needs, dress in your training uniforms and report to the dining hall. It has two large green wooden doors. The last two who report to the dining hall do not eat. After your meal, you will report to the training field outside. Your training begins tomorrow. Until then, you can familiarize yourselves with the area and get to know your bunkmates. As of this moment you are restricted to the Castra. Any questions?"

They both shook their heads.

"Good. Find an empty bunk and leave your things then come with me to the stables."

Both nodded and walked into the room, feeling self-conscious as the other trainees looked them over. Finding two empty bunks, they put their issues and personal items down and quickly walked out.

A short while later they returned to the barracks branded and tattooed and sat down on their bunks..

Waving his arm to cool off the branding, Antonius said, "I don't know which is worse—the getting branded or the ointment they put on afterwards.

It smells like horse urine."

Overhearing his remark, a muscular trainee walked up and asked, "You two had to be branded?"

"Yes," Antonius replied, "Who are you?"

"I'm the contubernium leader for this group," the muscular one with scars on his neck and jaw replied. "If you didn't transfer from the army then that means you have no military experience. How did you get in?"

"The Prefect is a friend of his father," Marcus replied, as Antonius shot him a disapproving glance.

The muscular trainee half-nodded. Turning to the others, he said, "Let's go see how big this latrine with walls is, you iron heads."

Antonius and Marcus stood up to go with them, but the muscular trainee put up his hand and smirked. "I just meant those of us that were in the Sixth Ferrata. That's a legion, in case you didn't know."

"I know what a legion is," Antonius shot back.

The muscular trainee snorted and left with his companions.

After they left, Marcus scrunched his face and said, "They didn't seem too friendly."

Antonius stared at the wall and said, "I get the feeling they don't think we should be here." Turning his head abruptly toward his friend, he added, "Let's take our own tour of this latrine with walls, Marcus."

With a smile, Marcus replied, "You have but to command me."

After exploring the fortress all morning, an attack of hunger forced them to visit the dining area in the barracks. As they approached, they saw a line stretching down the hallway.

Marcus turned to Antonius and asked, "Why don't they go in?"

An older trainee in front of them turned and said, "The doors are locked. They open at a certain time and close at a certain time."

"Oh," Marcus replied.

After waiting a few more minutes, the doors opened and trainees began to file in. When Antonius and Marcus went in, they noticed a long serving area, lined with various meats, bread, vegetables and fruits.

Marcus's eyes went big as he turned to Antonius and said, "Pig entrails and moldy bread, eh?"

Antonius smiled.

Being used to rations of grain used to make gruel and bread and whatever animal they could kill and roast for meat, this was a veritable feast for those who had come from army units in the field. After getting what they wanted,

Antonius and Marcus sat down at one of the tables and began to eat. Looking around, they noticed their bunkmates nearby whispering to those around them. Soon, everyone at their table was staring at them.

When they finished eating, one of their bunkmates walked over and said, "You know, not everyone here will be good enough to make it through." He stuffed a piece of bread in his mouth and smiled as he walked away.

"What do you think he meant by that?" Marcus asked.

Antonius leaned toward Marcus and said, "Ignore him. Let's go back to the room."

After returning to their room, they went over to their bunks and noticed large chests at the end. Turning to the other trainees, Marcus asked, "Can we use these to put our personal belongings in?"

"No, that's where you take a dump," the muscular one answered.

His comrades broke out in laughter, causing Marcus to blush.

Angered by the intended ridicule, Antonius spoke brazenly. "My friend asked a simple question. You didn't have to make him feel like a fool."

The muscular trainee stood up and walked over until he stood face to face with Antonius. Antonius clenched his fists and tensed his body, ready to react at the first sign of aggression.

The trainee looked Antonius up and down then snarled, "Every man in this room has earned the right to be here except for you two. Maybe you were allowed in because your daddy is the Prefect's friend, but I'll see to it that you'll wish you never came here, starting right…"

"Are we having a disagreement here?" bellowed a voice behind them.

Everyone turned to see a short, stocky, bald man in a Praetorian uniform standing in the doorway. He had a Centurion's helmet nestled in his arm.

"Attention!" the muscular trainee shouted.

Everyone in the room immediately snapped to attention.

"Well, are we?" the Centurion asked again.

"No, Centurion," everyone replied in unison.

"I didn't think so. Save the aggression for your training. You'll need it." He studied everyone for a moment then walked away.

The trainees relaxed, and the tall red-haired trainee whispered to the muscular one, "Don't waste your effort on them, Darius; they'll wash out quick enough."

Darius snorted and went back over to his bunk.

Feeling as though he had gone from one bad situation at home to another, Marcus turned to Antonius and whispered, "Oh, yes, just like I dreamed it would be."

"Let's go outside. I could use some fresh air," Antonius suggested.

Walking past condemning eyes, they left the barracks and approached a large oval track adjacent the building.

"How are we going to become Praetorians if everyone here hates us?" Marcus asked.

"We'll just have to prove that we belong," Antonius replied. "We can't let them discourage us; we have to ignore what they say and just concentrate on doing our best."

Marcus nodded as they walked onto the track.

A small concrete border a few inches high lined the inside and outside of the track, with a large grassy field in the middle. A small group of umbrella pine trees stood majestically at either end.

As they walked around the cinder-filled oval, Antonius said, "This is like the track at the Circus, just a little smaller. It has no spina in the middle as well."

Marcus scrunched his face. "What's a spina?"

"It's an island made of concrete with statues and obelisks in the middle of the track. That's where they count the number of laps that are run. This track just has an open field instead of a spina," Antonius informed him.

Marcus had more questions and Antonius had more answers.

"What are obelisks?"

"Very tall four-sided shafts made of stone that come to a point at the top. They are used for decoration mostly."

"Did you go to many races at the Circus?"

"My father and I would go every time we came to Rome. Sometimes Ignatius would join us and we would watch races all day long. My favorite team is the blue team."

"How many teams are there?"

"Four—the red, blue, white, and green teams."

"How is it you know so much about everything?"

Antonius smiled. "My mother and father taught me quite a bit, but I also ask a lot of questions."

Marcus nodded. "I need to start asking more questions."

After finishing their walk around the track, they decided to go back to their room.

Lying down on their bunks, they listened to the trainees in other rooms talking, laughing, and telling stories until they heard a voice down the hall, shouting, "Lamps out! Lamps out!"

The trainee nearest the door arose, extinguished the lamp and returned to his bunk. A tense silence seemed to fill the air in their room. The night was an uncomfortable one for Antonius and Marcus.

CHAPTER VII-Tiro* Troubles
*A Praetorian recruit

Just before dawn the next morning, Antonius and Marcus awoke to a loud, booming voice. "On your feet, you slimy gutter rats! Do your business then report to the dining hall! Last two go hungry."

Startled by the centurion's booming voice, Antonius and Marcus sprang out of their beds and noticed their bunkmates running out of the room. As they followed them into the hallway, several other trainees jostled them while they headed for the latrine. They relieved themselves then quickly washed their hands and faces from a long wooden trough that contained fresh flowing water.

They were about to return to their room when Marcus released an organic vapor and said, "Wait, Antonius. I have to go."

Antonius scowled and said, "Well, hurry up! We don't want to be the last two."

A short while later, Marcus appeared. "We can go and get dressed now."

The two hurried back to their room, put on their training uniforms, caligae, and helmets then ran down the corridor to the dining hall. Upon entering, they noticed everyone was already seated and eating. A feeling of dread came over them as they remembered the centurion's last words.

He motioned for them to approach his table then said the words they dreaded: "You trainees are the last two according to my count. For that you go hungry. Get down on your hands and feet on either side of the door and do not let your bodies touch the floor until I tell you… NOW!"

Quickly obeying, Antonius looked over at Marcus. "If you hadn't taken so long in the latrine, we wouldn't be doing this."

"Sorry, I couldn't help it," Marcus replied.

"No talking!" the centurion barked.

Both Antonius and Marcus faced forward and watched the other recruits devour their food. Occasionally a trainee would look over and smile at them, thinking the two soft non-military trainees wouldn't last long.

Minutes seemed like hours for Antonius and Marcus. Their muscles burned like fire and their arms began to shake. Just when they were on the verge of collapsing, the Centurion yelled, "Meal time is over! Take your utensils to the washing area then report to the training field!" Looking down at Antonius and Marcus, who had just collapsed on the floor, he said, "I didn't say you could relax! Get back up!"

Antonius and Marcus quickly resumed their torturous positions.

The other trainees filed out, snorting at the two non-military tiros as they passed. Antonius and Marcus kept their gaze to the floor, hoping the bald centurion would end their misery soon. As their muscles strained once again, they felt beads of sweat form on their heads and arms. Finally, the centurion wiped his mouth on the back of his hand, stood up and stretched. After patting his stomach, he said, "Ahh. That is the best meal of the day." Looking over at Antonius and Marcus, whose knees occasionally helped to prop them up, he yelled, "Are you still here? Join the others you dawdling sloths!"

They jumped to their feet and ran out, shaking their sore arms. After they put on their uniforms and reported to the field, the centurion yelled, "Form ranks! Four rows with twenty-five across facing me at arm's length from the man next to you and the row in front of you. You should all be familiar with this so don't dawdle."

The trainees scrambled as the centurion slapped the vitis[36] in his hand. Eventually, they formed the four rows and stood at attention.

"That was pitiful!" the centurion yelled. "I've seen sheep line up faster than that. The next time I tell you to line up, you will do it immediately or I will have you running laps around the mountains! Now remember who is next to you and who is in front or behind you."

The men looked at those around them.

"You will line up exactly the same way each time. Now, for those of you wondering 'Just who is this madman?' I will introduce myself. I am Centurion Taurus, your training instructor. I am an expert with the gladius, spatha, pilum, spear, bow and arrow, ax, dagger and just about any other weapon you can think of. I will be instructing you mostly on advanced techniques with the gladius, since that will be the main weapon you will be using. But I will also teach you how to be proficient with the bow and arrow and the pilum. You will learn to master these three main weapons or one day you will die by the hand of someone who has. On the final day of training you will compete against one another and the trainee who is the most skilled with any of the weapons will receive a plaque, 50 aurei and be called 'Master' for that weapon. If any of you should be the master of all three weapons, you will be awarded the title of 'Grand Master,' have his name put on a plaque and receive 150 aurei. But do not get your hopes too high. We have had only one

---

36-A vine staff similar to a riding crop

Grand Master of all the men who trained here."

"Who was that, Centurion?" a trainee asked.

Taurus puffed out his chest and strutted before them. "Me," he smirked. He then held up a scroll and shouted, "I will call out your name each time you form ranks in the morning. When I do, say 'Here,' step forward, and then step back in line. Do I make myself clear?"

"Yes, Centurion!" the trainees shouted.

"What was that? I didn't hear you!" Taurus shouted.

"YES, CENTURION!" the trainees roared.

Taurus gave one nod and said, "That's better!"

He then began calling out their names. When the roll was completed he said, "There are 100 of you now but by the end of training camp there will only be 80. So take a good look around you. One out of every five will either quit, be asked to leave, or die," he added with a grim smile. "Each week we will train for six days and you will have one day of rest." He gave them a intimidating smile and said, "You will need it. Now, before I begin your instruction, we will do some conditioning. You should already be in good shape, so this shouldn't be too difficult for you. We will start with some exercises to warm up, then a little running and marching. I will demonstrate the movement and you will follow on my count."

Taurus took them through each exercise until they had stretched and warmed up sufficiently. When they had finished, Taurus bellowed, "I will be watching you closely during the exercise period and the trainee that does the movements better than the rest will lead you on the following day. It is a great privilege to be the leader, so strive to do your best. Now, run to the end of the track and back. If I don't think you are running fast enough, you will run again. Now, RUN YOU MISERABLE ILLEGITIMATE SONS OF PROSTITUTING MOTHERS!"

The trainees sprinted down the field, and upon returning learned that they had to run again and again. Along the way, a few donated their meals to the ground. Taurus chuckled as he watched them try to avoid stepping in the vomit as they ran. Since Antonius and Marcus were deprived of eating, they had nothing to regurgitate. When Taurus felt they had given their best efforts, he yelled, "All right, form ranks!"

This time they did it much quicker.

Taurus grinned. "Next time, perhaps, some of you pigs will not eat so much before training, eh? Right face! Forward, march!"

They marched for the rest of the morning. After Taurus had decided they had marched enough, he brought them to a halt. Pointing to a detail of Praetorians returning from the stables nearby, he said, "You see those Praetorians over there? They are Rome's best. They *are* what you will soon *become*... if you survive the training and pay attention to what I say. Do you want to be Rome's best?"

"YES, CENTURION!" the men shouted with what strength they had left.

"That is music to my ears. To the dining hall! The last two go hungry!"

The trainees ran to the door, causing a mass of flailing arms and legs resembling a battle of octopuses trying to get in. This time Marcus and Antonius were able to watch two unlucky ones try to keep their bodies from touching the floor. After obtaining their food, Antonius and Marcus sat down at a table and nodded to the other trainees. The redheaded trainee from their room named Cornelius, sat down across from them.

"How does your father know the Prefect?" he asked Antonius. "Is he a senator or legate?"

"They were Praetorians together. He was a Tribuni Augustaclavii[37]."

"What is his name?" Cornelius asked.

"Galerius Licinius," Antonius replied.

Cornelius was about to take a bite and stopped. "The one they called Galerius the Great?" he asked.

"Yes, that's what they used to call him," Antonius replied, looking at Marcus out of the corner of his eye.

"Galerius the Great," Darius commented snidely as he sat down across from Antonius. "Rumor has it he killed over 100 men in one battle by himself. To me that sounds a bit exaggerated. I've been in battles before and on a good day I've killed 30 or 40, but 100 seems like someone was counting the bodies three times."

"Really, and who vouched for the men you killed?"Antonius asked, challenging Darius' claim.

Darius' face turned red and he was about to reach over the table and start something when Cornelius sitting next to him said, "Darius was the optio in my unit, and I can vouch for those numbers."

"What's an optio?" Marcus asked.

Darius gave him a cold stare. "Second in command."

"Oh," Marcus said.

"Where are you two from?" Cornelius asked.

"Aletium in Calabria," Antonius replied.

37-An equestrian class Tribune serving as a tactial commander

"Antonius's family owns a vineyard, and my family has a farm nearby," Marcus added.

Darius turned to Antonius. "Did your father teach you how to use a gladius or did you just stomp grapes?" The comment drew a few chuckles from some of the trainees at the table.

With a serious expression, Antonius replied, "He has been training me ever since I was small on both the gladius and the pilum. For the past few years, Marcus and I have been sparring and practicing together. Marcus is also quite a good bowman."

With a derisive snicker, Darius said, "It's one thing to shoot at targets. It's another to shoot at a man."

He gave Marcus an unnerving stare until Taurus barked out, "Meal time is over. Put away your eating utensils and report back to the field!"

The rest of the day was spent marching, lifting large rocks as a group and walking a short distance with them then doing squats as a group while holding large logs. Just when everyone was on the verge of collapsing, Taurus yelled, "FORM RANKS!"

One hundred trainees scrambled to get to their assigned positions while Taurus watched with amusement. Once they located their places and stood at attention, Taurus barked, "Well, you trained like women today, but you'll do better tomorrow or you *will* run laps around the mountains. "DISMISSED!"

All the trainees ran toward the door, pushing and shoving, trying anything to keep from being the last two. Fortunately, Antonius and Marcus once again avoided that dishonor.

As they sat down to eat, Darius stared at Antonius for a moment. "Born to a father who was considered by some to be a legend might get you in, but as the Centurion mentioned, you still have to complete the training. I'm betting you'll be two of the twenty who won't."

A hush fell over the table as the rest of the trainees focused on Antonius to see how he would respond.

He wasn't about to let Darius intimidate him. With a steely look, he said, "I have five sesterces that say we will."

"Make it ten," Darius countered, with a self-assured smile.

Antonius put his arm across the table and Darius grasped it hard.

"It is a wager then," Antonius said out loud.

After Taurus had finished his supper, he stood up. "I recommend that you get plenty of rest tonight, eunuchs. You will need every ounce of strength for tomorrow. Now, go bathe yourselves; you smell like piles of horse dung."

Antonius and Marcus arose with the rest of the trainees and turned in their bowls, cups and spoons. Then they slowly shuffled out of the dining hall, mustering up the last ounce of energy they had to even walk.

"Where do we bathe, Centurion?" Marcus asked before he left.

"The bath house is on the east side of the barracks," Taurus replied curtly.

Marcus nodded. Turning to Antonius, he asked, "Do we all bathe together in a pool like at the inn we stopped at?"

"A typical Roman bath house has three pools—a caldarium or hot pool, a frigidarium or cold pool and a tepidarium or warm pool. After you go into all three pools, servants anoint your body with oils then scrape your skin with metal instruments to remove the impurities."

"That sounds painful," Marcus said, shuddering.

Antonius shook his head. "It's not as bad as what we just went through."

When they had finished the bathing ritual, Antonius and Marcus slowly walked back to the barracks with the others.

"How do you feel?" Antonius asked his friend.

"Like I've been skinned," Marcus replied.

They collapsed into their beds, never hearing Taurus come down the hall a short while later, calling, "Lamps out! Lamps out!"

****

As the training progressed, Antonius and Marcus learned that eating light helped them avoid becoming sick from the exertion. They also noticed their bodies were beginning to work out the soreness and stiffness and their muscles were becoming more toned. Although the training was difficult, being shunned by the other trainees was even more difficult. Whenever they asked questions, the other trainees would answer with a shrug or tell them to "Go ask the Centurion."

Fortunately, they had each other for support.

One evening, Taurus was unloosening his caligae when he heard a knock on his door. "Enter!" he shouted.

Darius appeared and closed the door. After a brisk salute, he said, "Centurion, may I have a word with you?"

"What is on your mind, Aurelius?"

"I'll come right to the point. Licinius and Flavius shouldn't be here. They have no military experience and are only here because Licinius's father knows the Prefect. If it came to a life or death struggle, I believe they would freeze and put the rest of us at risk."

Taurus studied him for a moment. "Those two may not be veterans like the rest of you, but they are fast learners and have quick reflexes.”

“But they haven’t been tested in a real fight. I think they would turn and run like cowards,” Darius said, emphasizing the last word.

Taurus looked down his nose at him and said, “Those are strong words.”

“I’m only thinking of the other men,” Darius said in a monotone.

Taurus stared at him for a moment then said, “Every man in the army feels like running away the first time they’re in battle. If trained properly they’ll stand their ground. I’ll watch Licinius and Flavius closely. If I feel they don’t measure up, I’ll send them to an army unit for more training. Anything else?”

“No, Centurion.”

“Very well, dismissed,” Taurus said, pointing to the door.

Darius saluted and abruptly left. He had given the intended message; now he had to do what was needed to make Taurus’s decision easy.

****

Another week passed. One day after training, Antonius and Marcus were in their room listening to the others talk about how many men they killed on the battlefield.

“Darius and I have killed our share in Pannonia,” Cornelius boasted.

Wanting to enter the conversation, Marcus exclaimed, “Wolves attacked us on our way to Rome. We killed some. I don’t know if that counts.”

His bunkmates reacted with condescending smirks.

“How many?” Cornelius asked.

“Four, but we heard at least one other,” Marcus replied.

“What did you kill them with?” Cornelius asked.

“Probably a hoe,” Darius interjected, causing a brief bout of laughter.

Marcus and Antonius, however, remained expressionless. “I had my bow and knife and Antonius had the gladius his father gave him.”

At that moment, Taurus walked in.

“Attention!” Darius shouted.

“As you were,” Taurus ordered. “Are you men talking about women again?”

“No, Centurion,” Darius replied. “We were talking about animals and men.”

Taurus smirked and said, “From what I’ve been told by many women, they’re the same.”

Laughter filled the room, breaking the tension but it quickly returned after Marcus asked, “Centurion, why is it we have to wear a helmet but you never wear one?"

Everyone in the room went silent. Darius and the other veteran soldiers knew that one never questioned a centurion's decisions. They waited for Taurus to come down hard on the naive trainee.

Instead, Taurus smiled and replied, "Because it makes me look like a strutting peacock, that's why."

Marcus expelled a nervous laugh as Taurus turned to the rest. "Be proud you've made it this far, grunts. You only have to endure a few more months of the most grueling, torturous training anyone has ever experienced."

"Yes, only a few months," Cornelius said, rolling his eyes.

"For those who last," Darius added, looking directly at Antonius and Marcus.

"At least we have one day off each week," Marcus said with raised eyebrows.

Cornelius sneered at him. "What can we do? We can't leave the Castra."

"You could watch the chariot races," Taurus suggested. "Some of the Praetorians get together and race each other on your rest day."

Antonius's ears perked up. "Chariot racing, here?"

"Yes," Taurus replied. "It's open to all Praetorians and the races are held on the training field race track."

"Could I race my chariot?" Antonius asked.

Taurus furrowed his brow and said, "You're not officially a Praetorian yet… but I'll ask Tribune Falconius and let you know what he says. Anyone else want to race?"

The rest of the men in the room remained silent.

"Very well, then. Carry on." Taurus turned and strode out.

Antonius thought for a moment. Perhaps chariot racing could be his escape from the unfriendly atmosphere he and Marcus had to deal with since they'd been there. Lightly slapping his friend's arm, he said, "I'm going to have Ignatius bring my chariot here."

"How will you contact him?" Marcus asked. "Didn't they say we aren't allowed to leave the Castra."

Antonius nodded gloomily. He then perked up and said, "The centurion can leave the Castra. Perhaps he would give Ignatius a message for me."

Marcus gave him a dubious look.

****

The next morning the training regimen was the same as usual–running, lifting and marching. The trainees formed ranks and Taurus addressed them.

"Congratulations, sons of cattle, you have all survived the first month. Next month we'll be focusing on more conditioning."

The trainees groaned.

"And, you will also be working with this." He pulled his gladius from its scabbard and held it up. As he brandished the short sword before them, Daris muttered, "It's about time."

He wasn't alone feeling that way. Every trainee looked forward to showing off his prowess with it.

Taurus pointed to a pile of dulled swords and said, "First, we shall warm up with a short run. TO THE TREES AND BACK, YOU SLOTHS!"

After returning from the run, Taurus had them choose a blunt gladius and pair off.

"Just like old times, eh?" Marcus said to Antonius, with a smile.

Getting their attention, Taurus yelled, "You should all know how to use a gladius, so impress me. Let me see what you can do with one. Half speed."

As the trainees began to spar with each other, Tribune Falconius walked up. Seeing him approach, Taurus saluted. "Tribune."

Falconius nodded and they both watched the trainees spar.

After observing awhile, Falconius said, "It appears they at least know how to use a gladius."

"They had better know how to use it," Taurus replied. Pointing to Antonius and Marcus, he said, "Those two over there have had no military experience but they seem to know how to use a gladius quite well. So far they both seem to keep up with the other men."

At that moment, Thaddeus, Sejanus's aide, walked up. "Tribune Falconius, the Prefect would like to see you."

"Very well," Falconius said, leaving the field with him.

A short while later, Thaddeus knocked on Sejanus's door. "Tribune Falconius is here, Prefect."

"Send him in," Sejanus replied.

Falconius entered and stood at attention.

After he finished signing a document, Sejanus looked up. "How do the new trainees look so far, Tribune?"

"I think we have some good prospects. Only time will tell just how good they will be."

"I'm sure, with your supervision, we will have another fine crop of Praetorians," Sejanus remarked with a polite smile.

Falconius returned his smile and said, "I will see to it they do not disappoint you, Prefect."

Sejanus nodded. He then arose from his table, walked over and closed the door to his aide's room. Drawing near to Falconius, he whispered, "The reason I sent for you is to discuss a matter that must be kept confidential between us. There are two trainees I want you to pay particular attention to. One is Antonius Licinius, and the other is his friend, Marcus Flavius. How are they doing with the training?"

"Surprisingly quite well for two who have had no military experience," Falconius replied with a surprised look.

Sejanus nodded "Is the name Galerius Licinius familiar to you?"

"Of course. Centurion Taurus told me the more muscular one is his son."

Sejanus leaned close to Falconius and said, "Galerius is a good friend of mine and I want to make sure his son does well in the training. Your task is to see that he does. Make sure his friend completes it as well. Since they haven't had military experience, they will need tutoring in other areas such as tactics, formations and the like. I'm counting on you to see that they receive it. Of course, you will be rewarded for your effort."

Falconius gave a nod and said, "Don't worry, I will see to it, Prefect."

On the way back to his chair, Sejanus said, "Excellent. Keep me informed of their progress and remember, you are to keep this confidential."

"I understand," Falconius replied. "Of course, I will need to inform Centurion Taurus, since he will be working directly with them."

Sejanus pointed to him and said, "Just make sure this goes no further than the three of us. Tell him I'll make it worth his while as well. That is all."

Falconius saluted and departed. He knew that special consideration could be a blow to the other trainees' morale if discovered, so the extra training would have to be held on the rest day and conducted somewhere private. The recreation area in the Tribune barracks would work, he thought. It had a few large tables and documents about formations, tactics, and battle plans. It was the ideal place and he would be able to assist in their training.

Back on the training field, Taurus walked around observing the men spar for a while and were impressed with what he saw. "All right, everyone, find another sparring partner!" Taurus barked.

Antonius and Marcus gazed about and noticed everyone turned their backs on them and looked for other partners.

"It doesn't look like anyone wants to spar with us," Antonius said.

"I'll spar with you," Darius challenged Antonius with a smirk.

"And I'll be the farmer's sparring partner," Cornelius said.

Strutting in front of Antonius with a smug smile, Darius said, "Show me what your father taught you, vineyard boy."

Antonius gripped his gladius a little tighter as Darius attacked. Cornelius did the same with Marcus. The sparring was supposed to be at half speed, but Darius and Cornelius came on them full bore. To Darius and Cornelius's surprise, Antonius and Marcus held their own until Taurus walked over and shouted, "I said half speed!"

Antonius and Marcus stopped but Darius took advantage of the sudden distraction and struck Antonius hard on his helmet, knocking him to the ground.

Taurus stormed over and bellowed, "Did I not make myself clear, Aurelius? I said half speed!"

"I guess it's hard for me to slow down in the heat of battle," Darius replied, winking at Cornelius.

"Well, we're not in a battle here. Licinius, are you all right?" Taurus asked.

Antonius stood up with a slight wobble and nodded.

"You two find other opponents," Taurus ordered Antonius and Marcus.

"No one wants to spar with us," Marcus replied.

Taurus gritted his teeth then yelled, "Balbus! Scipio! You two spar with Licinius and Flavius."

The two he called, walked over. It was evident on their faces that they were not thrilled with the order.

Darius walked away with a smile while Antonius gave him a grim stare. The sparring resumed, this time at half speed.

Taurus watched them to make sure they obeyed then went on to observe the others.

Walking up behind him, Falconius asked, "How are trainees Licinius and Flavius doing, Centurion?"

Taurus turned and saluted. "They are holding their own, Tribune, especially Licinius. I was just watching him spar with Aurelius. He was doing well enough until I distracted him. It is certainly apparent that someone quite skilled with a gladius has been teaching him."

"Someone has. No doubt you've heard of Galerius Licinius?"

Taurus turned abruptly. "Galerius the Great?"

Falconius nodded. "Yes. That is his son."

Taurus rubbed his chin and said, "He's following in his father's footsteps, eh?"

"It appears so. Come to my room after training this evening, Centurion. I have a matter I wish to discuss with you," Falconius ordered.

Taurus looked surprised and said, "Very well, Tribune."

That evening at the Tribune barracks, Taurus knocked on Falconius's door and heard Falconius say, "Enter!"

"What did you wish to see me about, Tribune?" Taurus asked, as he stepped inside.

"Close the door and have a seat," Falconius replied, pointing to a chair.

Taurus closed the door and sat down on the nearby chair.

Falconius took in a breath through his nose and breathed out. "Licinius and Flavius. How do you feel about them?"

Taurus hesistated a moment then said, "They certainly have skills, but the rest of the trainees resent them because they're not military. I was thinking of transferring them to an army unit to maintain comraderie among the remaining trainees."

Falconius shook his head and said, "That would be a mistake."

Taurus furrowed his brow. "How so, Tribune?"

Falconius leaned toward Taurus and said, "They are favorites of the Prefect. He wants us to tutor them so they will be as knowledgeable as the rest when it comes to tactics, formations and procedures."

Taurus shook his head. "I don't think the other trainees will take that well. They will be hated even more."

Falconius leaned back and folded his arms. "That's why the other trainees can't know about it. You and I will instruct them in the tribune recreation area here in my barracks on their free day."

Taurus snorted and said, "You're asking me to give up my free day as well."

"The Prefect told me he will compensate you for it," Falconius quickly mentioned.

Taurus thought for a moment. It would be unwise to say 'no' to Sejanus and the extra money would be a welcome bonus. Taurus pursed his lips then said, "Those two do seem to be pushing themselves harder than the rest. I admire that. All right, if it is the Prefect's wish, I will do it."

"Excellent!" Falconius exclaimed. "That is all I wanted to discuss."

Taurus stood up, saluted, and was about to leave when he turned back and asked, "Oh, Licinius wanted to know if he would be allowed to race his chariot with the other Praetorians on his rest day. I told him I would ask you."

Falconius rubbed his chin. "I don't see a problem with it as long as it doesn't interfere with our tutoring and his training."

"And if it does?" Taurus asked.

"Try it for a few weeks and see if he can handle everything," Falconius suggested. "If he can't, discontinue it."

"I'll do that," Taurus said as he left.

A short while later, Antonius and Marcus were about to fall asleep when Taurus appeared in the doorway.

"Licinius and Flavius!" he shouted.

Everyone sprang out of their bunks and stood at attention.

"I just need Licinius and Flavius. You two put on your tunics and come with me. The rest of you remain in your room," Taurus ordered.

Antonius and Marcus knew what it meant to be called to Taurus's room. Two other trainees had received the same invitation before and the following day they were sent back to their original army units.

Crestfallen, Antonius and Marcus left the room while their bunkmates smiled and Cornelius uttered, "Good riddance!"

After the long walk to the centurion's barracks, Taurus motioned them into his room and closed the door.

Antonius and Marcus felt as though they had a large rock in their throats as they waited for the dreaded words that would end their Praetorian careers.

Taurus gave them his usual stern look then smiled. "You two are fortunate the Prefect likes you. He has asked me and Tribune Falconius to teach you military tactics and maneuvers so you can know as much as the others."

Both their mouths dropped open.

"We are not being sent to an army unit?" Marcus asked.

"No, but you will have to give up your rest day for tutoring," Taurus informed them.

"We'll give up whatever you want as long as we can continue training as Praetorians," Antonius exclaimed with a smile.

"I like your attitude, Licinius. Now, every rest day you will go to the Tribune barracks. Do you know where that is?"

"Yes," Antonius replied, "it's next to this barracks."

"That is correct. Tribune Falconius and I will meet you there at the first hour and we'll go over formations, tactics, and other procedures that the rest of the men are already familiar with. We'll talk you through a few formations and by the end of your training you will know as much as the others. You can practice your weapons skills on your own time after each training day is finished. Do you think you'll have enough stamina to do it?"

"We'll have it," Antonius assured him. Marcus nodded in agreement.

"Good. Now, some of the trainees will probably think I called you here to reassign you to an army unit. They will begin to wonder, when you show up for training the day after tomorrow. If they should ask, just tell them I threatened to dismiss you if you didn't improve. That should appease their curiosity. Any questions?"

They looked at each other then Antonius asked, "Did you by any chance ask Tribune Falconius if I could race?"

"I did," Taurus replied. "He approved it as long as it doesn't interfere with your tutoring and training. Do you still want to do it?"

"Yes!" Antonius exclaimed. "My chariot is here in Rome; I just need to let the caretaker to my father's villa know to bring it to the Castra. Could you deliver the message for me since I'm restricted?"

Taurus hesitated a moment, then said, "For a denarius."

Antonius nodded. "I can give you directions to the villa."

"One last thing," Taurus said. "Don't think you have it made because the Prefect wants you to pass the training. If I see either of you giving me less than a full effort or if I see you not trying to get along with the other trainees, I will send you to an army unit, no matter what the Prefect wants. Do you understand me?"

"Yes, Centurion," both replied with solemn expressions.

"Now return to your room. Tomorrow is your rest day so I will see you both at first light in the tribune building recreation area."

They saluted and quickly left. Walking back to the barracks, they both looked at each other and exchanged silent smiles.

Returning to their darkened room, they undressed and lay down on their bunks feeling extremely relieved.

"They must be shipping out in the morning," Darius thought, as he noticed they weren't packing. He fell asleep with a smile on his face.

When Darius awoke the next day, Antonius and Marcus were gone.

Waking up the other bunkmates, he said, "It looks like we got rid of those two jackals after all."

"I'm not so sure," Cornelius remarked, looking into their footlockers. "Their things are still here."

At midday, Antonius and Marcus entered the dining hall after finishing their morning tutoring session.

Seeing them sit down at a nearby table, Darius walked over. "Where have you two been?"

Antonius gave him a "none of your business expression," and replied, "Don't worry, we stayed in the Castra."

Darius shot him a doubting look. "What did the Centurion say to you the other night?"

"Go and ask him," Marcus replied with a smile, emulating the same curt response he had heard from Darius and the others so often before.

Darius glared at them then walked back to his table.

CHAPTER VIII-MASTERS

As promised, every evening after their regular training, Antonius and Marcus returned to the practice field and worked on their weapons skills. During their day off, they trained with Taurus and Falconius in the Tribune barracks. Taurus also delivered Antonius's message to Ignatius about bringing his chariot to the Castra.

The training continued, including long marches with weapons and jumping into a ten foot pool with full armor. Trainees had to remove their armor and return to the surface while holding their breath. Fortunately, no one drowned, but Taurus had to resuscitate two trainees. At the end of the second month, ten trainees had been disqualified. Three were due to injuries and the other seven because the physical requirements were too much for them to endure.

Despite the fact that Darius tried everything he could think of to make Antonius and Marcus quit by urinating and defecating in their footlockers, spitting in their food and getting the other trainees to shun them, Antonius and Marcus withstood the humiliations and kept improving.

On the next training day, the remaining trainees assembled outside to begin their usual regimen. After Taurus called the roll, he strutted past the front of the formation and addressed them in his usual degrading way.

"Congratulations on making it this far, you sons of squid. As you probably have noticed, ten are no longer with us. Which of you will be the next to go?" He heard a few grunts from the formation and smiled.

Darius glanced over at Antonius and Marcus with clenched teeth. His efforts to get rid of them had been unsuccessful so far. Their determination to become Praetorians was much stronger than he had anticipated.

The day began with conditioning in the morning and weapons training in the afternoon. The trainees finished the day with wrestling matches. Determining the winner was simple. You won by forcing your opponent to yield.

After choosing Antonius as the first wrestler, Taurus asked for a volunteer to be his opponent.

"I'll wrestle him," Darius said, stepping forward with his usual condescending smirk.

"Very well," Taurus said.

Antonius glared at his chief antagonist. Galerius had taught him how to wrestle proficiently, but he knew Darius was strong. They had both won all their previous matches, so it would be a good contest.

Taurus raised his hand then signaled for the match to begin.

Darius immediately rushed Antonius and they began to grapple. As they struggled against each other, trying to apply a hold that would force their opponent to submit, Antonius slipped on the grass. Darius took advantage and quickly spun around behind, placing him in a chokehold. Seeing no way out, Antonius tapped on his arm and muttered, "I yield." But Darius would not let go. Antonius tapped again, but Darius wouldn't release his grip. Antonius felt himself passing out when Taurus shouted, "That's enough!"

Prying Darius's arm off Antonius's throat, Taurus lightly slapped Antonius's face a few times. "Licinius! Wake up, Licinius!"

Enraged, Marcus started toward Darius. "He was submitting! You should have released him!" Just before he reached Darius, he heard Antonius cough. Looking down at his friend, he said, "Antonius. Are you all right?"

Still dazed, Antonius looked around and said, "Yes, I'm all right."

Taurus looked up at Darius and said, "The next time a man yields, release him immediately. Am I clear, Aurelius?"

Darius shrugged his shoulders and said, "I didn't hear him."

As they had their evening meal, Marcus leaned over to Antonius and whispered, "I thought Darius was going to break your neck."

Through clenched teeth, Antonius replied, "That's the second time he's tried to hurt me. There won't be another."

The next day was their rest day. After finishing a day of tutoring in the Tribune's barracks, they were about to return to their room when Taurus said, "Licinius. Your chariot is at the stables. If you hurry, you can make the races this afternoon."

"Thank you, Centurion!" Antonius exclaimed. Turning to Marcus with a giant grin they hurried out.

Running all the way to the stables, they approached Appius, the head stableman.

"What's the hurry, you two?" Appius asked.

"My Centurion said that my chariot was brought here. It is blue with two light bay stallions as the team," Antonius replied, slightly out of breath. Seeing his chariot sitting just inside the stable, he pointed to it. "That's it. Are my horses here as well?"

"Yes, they are in one of the stalls. Did you want to race with the others this afternoon?"

Antonius nodded exuberantly. "Yes!" he exclaimed.

Appius pointed to his chariot and said, "Then hook up your chariot and don't tarry or we'll race without you. The other Praetorians are hooking theirs up now."

"I will," Antonius replied. "Come, Marcus, you can help me."

"You have but to command me," Marcus replied.

After both quickly hooked Mercury and Mars to the chariot, Antonius went over all the fittings to make sure everything was in place. The other Praetorians had already departed for the track.

"You're lucky I start the races," Appius stated, "now go join the others, I'll be right behind you."

Antonius and Marcus hopped aboard the blue chariot and charged out of the stables with Appius right behind them in his.

When they arrived at the track, they noticed a few Praetorians who had gathered to watch the races.

Marcus patted Antonius on the back and said, "Good luck, Antonius." He then stepped off the chariot and joined the other spectators.

Antonius gave him an anxious nod.

"Your attention, Praetorians!" Appius shouted.

Appius cleared his throat then announced, "We will have two races as usual, but today we have a new entry. Four chariots will be in the first race and four in the second. Our new charioteer will be in the second race. He pointed at Antonius, who tried not to appear nervous. "Now don't kill him his first time on the track," Appius said with a sly smile.

A few of the charioteers chuckled while Antonius swallowed hard, hoping the head stableman was joking.

"Now, listen as I call the names for the first race." Appius then called out four names. "Those who I didn't call will be in the second race."

Antonius looked around and briefly studied the seven other Praetorians as they climbed aboard their chariots. They were older and apparently had already spent a few years in the Guard. One, approximately ten years his senior rode by with the first group of charioteers and gave him a nod. Antonius nodded back. Antonius and the second group then waited for their turn just outside the track.

Appius walked over to the 'start and finish mark' and lined up all the chariots for the first race. When he was satisfied they were even, he bellowed, "You all know the rules. If you see someone thrown from their chariot, slow down and stop if possible to avoid further injuries. Remember, this is for recreation not money so let's be gentlemen."

A few racers looked at each other and smiled, knowing that wagers had indeed been made between them. Nothing like that made in the Circus.

Appius then raised his arm to begin the race while all four charioteers tightly gripped their reins and leaned forward. After a brief hesitation, Appius dropped his arm and the race began. Antonius watched closely as the four chariots circled around the track. All the drivers seemed to be going at a good pace but no one appeared to be trying to force the other racers into a dangerous situation. He assumed the reason was to avoid injuries. He had seen many mishaps while attending the Circus with his father, some of them fatal, so he wasn't surprised at the tactics. On the last lap, the pace quickened and the racers really pushed their horses. Antonius thought to himself, "If the second race is similar to the first, I will start fast and build a good lead then no one will be able to catch me." He felt confident about his plan and watched the victor of the first race cross the finish line amidst the cheers of his supporters.

As he pulled his chariot onto the track with the others, the Praetorian in the chariot next to him leaned over and said, "I wouldn't get too close to the rail if I were you, unless you can afford to replace your wheels."

"The rail?" Antonius asked.

"The concrete border on the inside of the track," the Praetorian replied.

Antonius looked at it and said, Oh, yes."

Just tall enough to break a chariot wheel, the veteran charioteers kept well away from it. Antonius would keep that in mind.

The next four chariots took their positions at the starting line. Once Appius was satisfied they were lined up evenly, he gave the signal and the second race began. Antonius's chariot lurched ahead of the others, causing Marcus to shout, "Yes, Antonius!" and raise his fist in the air.

As Antonius's chariot streaked down the straightaway, he didn't notice anyone in his peripheral vision which encouraged him. Taking the first turn, he looked back to see a few chariots a short distance behind him and snapped the reins to make his horses run faster. On the next turn, he was still in the lead and snapped his reins again, encouraging Mercury and Mars to increase the pace. As he passed by the stable master each time, he knew he was in the lead and felt confident he would win. Finally, one lap remained.

Glancing over at the spectators, he saw Marcus waving and shouting. As he turned back, a chariot passed him. He snapped the reins and shouted to his horses to run faster, but they didn't respond. Another chariot went past him, then another. As his winded horses slowly trotted across the finish line, he realized he had come in last. Reining his horses to a stop, he stepped off his chariot and shook his head in discouragement.

The Praetorian, who passed by him in the stable and nodded before the race, walked over. "You have fast horses, young Praetorian, but you should have paced them better." He smiled and walked away.

"Thanks for the advice," Antonius shouted to him.

The Praetorian turned his head and nodded.

Marcus walked over and said, "At the beginning, I thought you were going to win easily."

Antonius grimaced and said, "I started them too fast. I know better than that. I just wanted to win the other Praetorians' respect."

Marcus smiled and said, "You just wanted to win."

Antonius smirked and said, "I suppose."

Marcus clapped him on the back and said, "Well, it *was* your first race. Think of it this way, you won six laps!"

Antonius looked at his winded horses and said, "I should rub Mercury and Mars down before we return to the room."

"I'll help you," Marcus volunteered.

As they entered the stable, Appius stopped Antonius and asked, "Did you say your name was Licinius?"

"Yes. Antonius Licinius."

"Any relation to Galerius Licinius?"

"He is my father," Antonius replied.

Appius's eyes grew wide. "Your father is Galerius the Great?"

Antonius took in a deep breath and replied with a dead-pan look, "Yes, my father is Galerius the Great."

****

The last week of training finally arrived. After the warm-up calisthenics, Taurus had the trainees assemble in ranks and addressed them with an ominous grin.

Strutting in front of the formation, he slapped his vitis in his hand and declared, "If you think your training has been hard so far, think again. Today, I will introduce you to Hercules' chariot. For you see, a Praetorian is not just a man; he is a thoroughbred. And, like thoroughbreds, you must pull the chariot. Attention! Right face! March!"

Marching over to the track, the trainees noticed four chariots that had been brought out sitting side by side. As they drew nearer, they could see large rocks had been piled up inside each basket[38] with the back enclosed. There were no horses, only a pole and crossbar extending from the rider's compartment resting in the dust. Taurus brought the trainees to a halt and had them stand at ease. "Today you will work together as a team," he declared. "Each row will be a separate team and two from each team will take their turn pulling the chariot around the track then hand it off to the next two in line. The team who crosses the finish line first, after all their teammates have taken a turn, has permission to go into the city for the evening."

The men cheered.

"The losing teams will remain in the Castra," he added.

Each row began to point at the others.

"I will even up the rows so that you all have the same number," Taurus declared. He then had each trainee count off in fours. As he counted them off, Darius and Cornelius made sure they were on the same team. Seeing their tactic, Antonius did the same with Marcus. After all the rows were even, Taurus pointed to each one and said, "This row will pull the red chariot and be the red team. This row the white team; this row the green team; and this row will be the blue team."

When Antonius saw they were assigned the blue team, he whispered to Marcus. "The same colors as the chariots that race in the Circus! We are on the factio veneta[39], my favorite team."

In the blue row, since Marcus and Antonius were the fastest in the footraces during training, they were chosen to be the ones running the last lap for their team. Darius and Cornelius were chosen to run the last lap for their team.

When Taurus had seen that all the teams were ready, he shouted, "First two runners for each team, take your place and begin when I give the signal."

After each team was ready, Taurus drew his gladius and raised it above his head. After pausing slightly, he swung his arm down and shouted, "RUN YOU STEEDS OF HERCULES!"

The first two men in each team grunted and strained, finally moving their respective chariots. As they returned from their lap, the next two took over. After a few laps, all four teams remained fairly close to each other. As each team passed the chariot to their next teammates, they would collapse to the ground, gasping for breath. While each duo awaited their turn, Tribune Falconius and Prefect Sejanus walked over to observe. The race continued with

---

38-*The inside of the chariot where the charioteer stood*
39-*The name of the Blue Team that raced professionally in the Circus Maximus*

the lead changing back and forth until the race was primarily between the blue and red teams. Cornelius and Darius grabbed the pole from their teammates for the last lap. Straining to move the heavy load, they proceeded down the track just as the chariot from the blue team arrived. Antonius and Marcus quickly took over and pulled with all their might to catch up with Darius and Cornelius. They flew down the track, their feet hardly touching the cinders.

Darius looked back to see Antonius and Marcus gaining on them and yelled to Cornelius. "PULL HARDER!"

Antonius and Marcus inched closer and closer to them.

With only a short distance remaining, they were almost even. All the men from each team roared encouragement to their respective teammates.

As both chariots crossed the finish line, Darius and Cornelius leaned slightly breaking the plane before Antonius and Marcus.

"The red team wins!" Taurus shouted, as both teams brought their chariots to a stop and fell to their knees, completely exhausted. The red team cheered, patting Darius on the back while the blue team groaned in defeat. Antonius looked up and noticed Darius's condescending smile as they both gasped for air. He was sure Darius would rub salt in his and Marcus's wounded egos over the race and didn't look forward to what they would say in the barracks.

"I'm sorry, Antonius," Marcus gasped. "I couldn't run any faster."

"It's just a race," Antonius remarked between breaths.

Taurus raised both his arms and shouted, "Now that you have all experienced the chariot, proceed quickly to the archery range. I want the first person in line ready to shoot when I get there."

As the trainees ran to the archery range, Sejanus leaned over to Falconius. "That was a good race. For a moment, I thought Licinius and Flavius were going to have a come-from-behind win."

"So did I," Falconius replied. "If Aurelius and Cornelius hadn't leaned at the last moment, it might have been a tie."

"How are Licinius and Flavius doing?" Sejanus asked.

Falconius pursed his lips then said, "Licinius is likely the best with the gladius and Flavius possibly the best with the bow. But Aurelius is good with all three weapons. It will be interesting to see who wins the Master's titles."

Sejanus nodded. After watching the men spar for awhile, he commended Falconius for his good work then returned to his office.

For the rest of the afternoon, the trainees sharpened their skills on the archery range. When the training was over, Taurus formed them into ranks and shouted, "A word of advice for you men who won the evening's pass."

Darius and his red team members gave him their attention.

With a stern countenance, Taurus said, "Don't fraternize with women older than your mothers, and be back in your rooms before the sun rises. That is all. DISMISSED!"

Cheers intermingled with laughter as everyone dashed for the dining hall. On the way, Antonius tripped and skidded across the grass. Darius had seen to it that his legs became tangled. Marcus helped his friend up, but the delay cost them. They entered the dining hall as the last two and went hungry again.

After the evening meal was over, Antonius and Marcus went back to their room and prepared for the baths. Occupying an area away from the others, they soaked quietly as Darius and the others on the red team laughed and talked about their victory in the chariot race. Antonius and Marcus were the last to leave.

As they walked into their room, Darius sneered and said, "I guess your father never taught you how to run, eh Licinius?"

Antonius wanted badly to smash his taunting face in, but he remembered Taurus's warning. He gave Darius a seething look and remained silent.

Darius, however, continued to gloat. He pretended to show a sympathetic look and said, "My condolences, Licinius. It is a shame you get nothing for second place and have to go hungry besides. That's what happens when you challenge real soldiers."

Cornelius added to the mockery. "The only ones they're good at challenging are little girls."

Darius and the others in the room broke out in laughter.

As Antonius and Marcus sat on their bunks, they gritted their teeth and looked straight ahead.

After Darius and his companions had left for their night on the town, Marcus looked over at Antonius, gritted his teeth, and said, "I'll be glad when this is all over. If I have to deal with Darius much longer..."

Antonius took on a glum countenance and said, "If we are assigned to the same unit after our training, we may just have to."

Marcus shook his head and shuddered at the thought. Then he took a deep breath and said, "Well, at least we won't go hungry." He pulled out two large biscuits and two apples from underneath his pillow.

"Where did you get those?" Antonius asked.

Marcus proudly displayed them and said, "I took these during the midday meal and brought them back to our room before going back to the training field. I thought I might be hungry later on so I hid them. I guess it's a good thing I did. Here!" he said, tossing s biscuit and apple to Antonius.

Antonius caught them then chortled and asked, "Is there anything else under your pillow?"

Marcus replied with a toothy smile.

Later, as Taurus cleaned his armor, he heard a knock on his door. Opening it, he saw Sejanus's aide.

"What is it?" he asked.

"The Prefect wants to speak with you," Thaddeus replied.

Taurus gave him an annoyed look and asked, "Now?"

"Yes, Centurion," the aide replied.

Taurus sighed and said, "Very well." He put down the cloth he was using and followed Thaddeus to Sejanus's office.

When they arrived, Taurus noticed the sentries were gone, which seemed unusual, but the hour *was* late. Thaddeus approached Sejanus's open door and said, "Prefect, Centurion Taurus is here."

Sejanus motioned for Taurus to enter.

Taurus went in and saluted.

Sejanus nodded to his aide. "Thank you, Thaddeus; you may go off duty now. Close the door on your way out."

"As you wish, Prefect." Thaddeus said, closing the door behind him.

"Centurion Taurus," Sejanus began, "I appreciate you and Silvanus taking the extra time to tutor Licinius and Flavius. It appears they will complete the training."

"Yes, they were quick learners and worked hard to become two of my best trainees."

Sejanus beamed. "Good. I have another task for you. It will require an additional sacrifice on your part, but I will reward you well if you accept it."

"I'm at your disposal, Prefect," Taurus replied without hesitation. The extra tutoring had proven to be quite lucrative for him.

Sejanus sat back and folded his arms. "There are Roman governors in Creta and Judaea that have requested more men. Caesar thought it would be good to send some of the new Praetorians there for a little seasoning. I have decided to send twenty to Creta[40] and twenty to Judaea. Licinius and Flavius will be among those assigned to Judaea, but I need someone to keep an eye

---

40-*The largest of the Greek islands*

on them. That is why I'm sending you as well."

Taurus looked at him in disbelief. "Me? What about my position here as the training officer? When I made Grand Master, you promised me I could be the permanent trainer."

Sejanus's glare suddenly made him feel uncomfortable. Speaking slowly and deliberately, Sejanus said, "I know being the head trainer here is a position I'm sure you feel you deserve. No one disputes that. But I have an important future purpose for those two and need you to report their progress to me and insure they will return to Rome intact when they finish their tour. As for giving up your position here, I will compensate you quite handsomely."

Taurus narrowed his eyes. "How handsomely?"

Sejanus opened a large bag on his table and spilled several gold coins across the top. "There are two hundred aurei in the bag. You will receive a bag like this each year they are alive. Of course, this will be in addition to your regular pay."

"I only have to make sure they stay healthy?" Taurus asked.

"In essence, yes," Sejanus replied.

Taurus narrowed his eyes. "What happens if they are maimed or killed and I can't prevent it?"

With a steely glare, Sejanus said, "Then the payments stop. Here is your first one in advance," he added, pushing the bag toward Taurus.

Taurus took it and asked, "Then I can resume my position as training officer when I return?"

"Yes," Sejanus replied expressionless.

The gold coins shining on top of the Prefect's table quickly convinced Taurus that wealth was more important than the desire to maintain his status quo. With a hint of a smile, he added them to the bag and said, "All right, Prefect, I'll do it."

Sejanus then leaned toward Taurus and said, "This is to be kept strictly confidential, Centurion. If word leaks out, Judaea will be your permanent duty station. Do you understand?"

"I understand perfectly," Taurus replied. "Who will be in charge of the men in Creta?"

Sejanus sat back and asked, "Who would you suggest?"

"Aurelius was an optio in the army and did well in the training; he would probably be the best man for the position."

"Good. I'll promote him to Centurion. Any other questions?" Sejanus asked.

"Yes. How long will my assignment in Judaea be?"

"Two years," came the reply.

Taurus tightened his jaw then said, "You wouldn't mind putting my two year commitment and reinstatement back to training officer in writing, would you, Prefect?"

Sejanus smiled. Taurus was no fool.

****

With only a few training days left, nineteen men had dropped out or were disqualified. One more had to go. Falconius ordered Taurus to meet with him before the day began.

"You wanted to see me, Tribune?" Taurus asked, closing the door to Falconius' room.

"Yes, Centurion. We still need to eliminate one more trainee. Who do you recommend?"

Taurus rubbed his chin and said, "I have an idea who to eliminate but I'll see how they do in their training today."

Falconius nodded. "Very well. Let me know at the end of the day. That is all. Dismissed."

Taurus saluted and reported to the training field.

After the trainees had assembled, he addressed them. "This is your last day of training," he shouted. "We still have one more trainee to eliminate so give me your best efforts."

Aurelius hoped it would be Antonius so he could win the bet. But he was afraid that both of them might advance and it turned his stomach.

Taurus continued. "Tomorrow we will have the weapons master competitions so make every move, throw and shot count. We will begin with our usual exercise routine. Licinius! Front and center! You will be the leader today."

Darius clenched his teeth. He should have been the one leading, not Antonius. He had won most of the competitions.

Surprised, mainly because he had never led the group, Antonius smiled and took his place at the front of the formation. He yelled the instructions to each exercise as he had heard others give them and the trainees responded. After Antonius had completed all the warm-up exercises, Taurus shouted, "Now we'll have sparring practice. Half speed, as usual, I don't want anyone cutting off anything important you may need later on."

Chuckles arose from the formation as one trainee said in a muffled voice, "The Castrated Praetoria."

Taurus smiled at the vulgar reference, then continued. "Pick up a gladius from the pile over there, then pair off."

The men drew their weapons and began to spar as Taurus and Falconius observed.

"Have Licinius and Flavius put in extra time on their weapons?" Falconius asked.

"Yes, sir, every evening after training. Licinius is definitely quite proficient with the gladius, thanks to his father's instruction, and Flavius is as good with a bow as anyone I've seen," Taurus replied.

"What about Aurelius?" Falconius asked.

Taurus scrunched his face. "He could be the next Grand Master, but his arrogance bothers me."

Falconius smiled. "I recall an arrogant trainee some years ago who became the Grand Master."

"That wasn't arrogance, Tribune, that was confidence," Taurus replied with a grin.

Falconius smiled.

After the training day was complete, Taurus knew who to eliminate. "Cornelius, come to my room," he ordered, then walked away.

Cornelius gave Darius a worried look. Darius's eyes showed disgust. They both knew what "come to my room," meant.

"It's not over yet," Aurelius called out as Cornelius left.

Entering Taurus's room after slow-walking there, Cornelius came to attention.

"Stand easy," Taurus commanded him.

Cornelius took a more relaxed stance, but Taurus could see the dread in his eyes. Not wanting to prolong the agony, Taurus said, "I'll make this short and to the point. You didn't make it."

Cornelius's eyes went cold and he shook his head. "You are eliminating me over Licinius and Flavius?" he bellowed. "They shouldn't have been here in the first place!"

"I'm sorry you feel that way, Cornelius. You will be invited back next year and given another chance. That is the best I can do."

"When do I have to leave?" Cornelius growled.

"You can remain in the Praetorian barracks until your orders arrive." Taurus paused, then said, "That is all, you're dismissed."

Cornelius snapped to attention, gave a hard salute then stormed out. Returning to his room, he shared the bad news with Darius and the rest of his bunkmates. When he finished, six faces glared at Antonius and Marcus.

"Let's go get some air; it stinks in here," Darius snarled.

****

The next morning before leaving the room for the final competitions, Darius walked over to Cornelius, who lay on his bunk. He had not arisen and dressed with the others or attended the morning meal.

Leaning close, Darius whispered, "Don't worry, Cornelius. I'll find a way to get you back in."

"How do you propose to do that?" Cornelius muttered half-heartedly.

Darius said with flinty eyes, "Accidents happen," then walked away.

After all the trainees had assembled on the field, Taurus shouted, "Now is your chance for glory, scorpions! First, we will have the pilum competition. You will have three throws at the target. The one scoring the highest will receive the title of Master. If there are tie scores, those who tie will throw one more pilum each until I determine who wins. When I dismiss you, report to the weapon tables. Dismissed!"

The trainees ran over to the tables and found pilums stuck in the ground near each one. Bows and arrows lay on top for the archery competition. The trainees lined up, received their instructions and began. After a few rounds, Darius and Antonius were the last two competing. Darius took his throw and placed his pilum near the center of the target. Antonius readied his pilum and just before releasing it, one of Darius's bunkmates pretended to sneeze. The ploy was effective, and Antonius' pilum hit on the outside of the target.

Incensed by the intended distraction, Marcus yelled at the distractor. "That wasn't fair! You deliberately made that noise just as Antonius was making his throw!"

Darius smirked and said, "In battle there will be all kinds of sounds. If you don't ignore them and concentrate on your training, you'll be killed or get your brothers-in-arms killed."

Marcus turned to Taurus with a pleading expression.

Taurus only nodded in agreement with Darius.

"That's all right," Antonius interjected. "We still have the archery and gladius competitions."

The trainees continued with the archery competition and were allowed three arrows each. In the case of a tie, the targets would be moved back ten paces. After the first round, five trainees, including Marcus and Darius tied. For the next round, the targets were moved back another ten paces. After everyone who was left had completed the second round, only Marcus and

Darius remained. For the last try, the targets were moved twenty more paces and Taurus said, "This time there will be one arrow each. Both of you will shoot at the same target. The arrow closest to the center will be the winner."

Darius was the first to shoot. He took careful aim and released his arrow with red fletching. The arrow sailed through the air and hit the target, just on the outside edge of the center ring. He couldn't see exactly where it hit, but could tell it was close to the center. He smiled, feeling confident he had just won the competition. Walking by Marcus, he said, "You are going to lose, farm boy."

Marcus placed his blue-fletched arrow on his bow with trembling hands. He looked over at Antonius, who gave him an encouraging nod. Throwing up a handful of grass to check the wind, Marcus looked up into the sky and said under his breath, "Help me, Jupiter." Raising his bow and arrow with a steady hand, he aligned the target with the distance mark on the lower part of the bow. Taking a deep breath, he drew the arrow back and slowly exhaled. Just before releasing it, Darius's bunkmate sneezed again. The arrow began its ascent. At its apex a slight gust of wind hit the fletching. Dropping rapidly, the arrow struck the target close to Darius'. As the curious trainees ran down to see who was victorious, Darius, Marcus, and Taurus followed at a slower pace. A combined gasp arose from those gathered around the target as the three quickly made their way to see the results.

Clearing the crowd away, Taurus looked at the target and shook his head in amazement. The arrow with the blue fletching was slightly closer to the center of the target than the red-fletched one. "Flavius is the winner!" he shouted.

Marcus looked at the target with wide eyes and an open mouth as Antonius raised his fist and shouted, "Master Marcus!"

"The hands of the gods had something to do with this," one trainee remarked as he noticed how close the difference was.

Darius yanked his arrow out of the target, snapped it in two and threw it on the ground. "Dumb luck is all it was," he growled. Like the discarded arrow, winning the Grand Master title had just been removed from his grasp.

Taurus grinned, however. His record as Grand Master remained intact. "Now, for the final contest. Report to the middle of the field for the gladius competition," he shouted.

As Darius ran over to the designated sparring area with the others, he still couldn't believe that a simple-minded farmer had beaten him in the archery competition with a lucky shot. Although Marcus had ruined his bid for

Grand Master, Darius could still win two out of the three competitions. He only hoped he would have a chance to face Antonius in the gladius contest.

While everyone assembled in the middle of the field, slaves removed the targets and brought out several barrels containing metal greaves and leather arm wraps. A few veteran Praetorian volunteers stood by to judge the winners of each match. Taurus then put the names of the trainees he had previously written down, into a helmet. From it, he would determine who the pairings would be. After calling the trainees to attention, he went over the rules. "Everyone will wear helmets, greaves, and leather sleeves during your matches. The swords you will use were dulled to prevent serious injury. A veteran Praetorian will observe your match and determine the winners. The match is over when there are three strikes in the opponent's vulnerable areas. These areas are the head and abdomen. If you knock your opponent's gladius from his hand, or your opponent cannot continue, the match is over. Are the rules understood?"

All the trainees shouted, "Yes, Centurion!"

Taurus drew the first pairs of combatants from the helmet and called out their names. After the matches had concluded, Darius, Antonius, and Marcus were among those who advanced. Taurus drew the next pairings. After the second round, Darius, Antonius and Marcus were once again victors in their matches. The competition continued until there were five left. Taurus put the last five names into the helmet. They included Antonius, Marcus, Darius, and two others. Antonius and Marcus were the first pairings drawn then two others, with Darius getting a bye.

Before Antonius and Marcus began their match, Marcus whispered, "It would have to be you."

Antonius smiled.

Marcus gave it his all, but Antonius won 3-1.

After the second match had concluded, three were left. Taurus once again drew the pairings. Darius and the other trainee who won the second match were the first two names drawn. Antonius had the bye this time. One Praetorian observer positioned Darius and his opponent for the next match and signaled them to begin. The two circled each other for a moment then Darius attacked. A few minutes into the match, Darius scored twice and felt confident he would come out victorious. His overconfidence led to carelessness, however. As he went in for the final kill, his opponent parried and struck him hard in the abdomen. The score was now 2-1. Darius smarted inside for allowing the other trainee to score a point so convincingly. The Praetorian observer judging the match positioned them to continue. As soon as he gave the signal for them to begin, Darius lunged at his opponent and delivered a barrage of withering blows. The trainee tried to fend them off as best he could, but the ferocity of Darius' attack made him fall backward. As he did, Darius struck him hard across his unprotected neck before he hit the ground. The Praetorian judging the match pointed to Darius and said, "Winner!"

As Darius walked away from his supine opponent, everyone noticed the defeated trainee was not moving. The judge knelt down to check him and saw blood coming from his mouth. He felt for a pulse then looked up at Taurus, shaking his head. "This man is dead."

Taurus hurried over and also checked the fallen man's pulse. When he couldn't find it, he looked up at Darius.

Darius removed his helmet with no look of concern or remorse.

Taurus approached with a cold stare and said, "I hope you were aiming for his helmet and not his throat."

Darius shrugged his shoulders and said only, "Accidents happen."

Taurus peered into Darius's eyes and saw only emptiness. He then turned to Sejanus and Falconius, who had been observing the competitions.

"A few of you take this man to the Castra medici[41]," Sejanus ordered.

As two men carried the dead trainee away, Sejanus addressed the rest. "It is unfortunate that this happened, but there is always a chance for accidents to occur during training. Continue with the competition, Centurion."

Taurus nodded and turned to Antonius. "Licinius! Prepare yourself for the final match. I shall be the judge of this one. Aurelius, I'll give you a moment to collect yourself."

"There is no need for that," Darius replied, as he gave Antonius a smug look. "I'm ready. Besides, this shouldn't take long."

"Very well. Take your positions," Taurus commanded. He raised his hand to make sure both were ready then yelled, "Begin!"

The two sidestepped each other, moving in a circle and looking for an opening. Then suddenly, they came together with such ferocity that no one could doubt their hatred for each other. After thrusting and parrying for a few minutes, they backed off and circled again. This time, Darius tried a different tactic. After a flurry of moves, he managed to swipe the lower front of Antonius's breastplate.

Taurus raised his arm. "One hit for Aurelius!"

The match continued, and soon Antonius managed to block a blow aimed for his neck, striking Darius hard on his helmet. Darius wobbled back but

---

41-Similar to a medical corpsman of today

maintained his guard.

Taurus yelled, "One hit for Licinius!"

The score was 1-1. Antonius smiled. He had repaid Darius in kind for the first encounter they had on the training field.

Angered by the blow, Darius backed off to clear his head. Then he launched into a blistering attack, trying again for Antonius's vulnerable neck. Antonius deflected each attempt, however. Realizing Antonius was on to his tactic, he attacked high several times then quickly thrust his gladius toward Antonius's abdomen. The tip struck armor.

"Another hit for Aurelius! The count is Aurelius-2, Licinius-1!" Taurus shouted.

Darius smiled, confident that the match would soon be over. "You lack the killer's instinct, boy," he scoffed. "That is why you will lose."

Antonius remained quiet as they circled each other again. Darius charged, but Antonius sidestepped, striking him in the abdomen as he went by.

"A hit for Licinius!" Taurus shouted. "The match is even. The next point wins the title."

"Time to put an end to this," Darius snarled. Again he rained a barrage of blows down upon Antonius. But despite his best attempts to end the match, Antonius met each one with an effective counter move.

Seeing that Antonius was only defending himself, Marcus yelled, "Go after him, Antonius!" but Antonius remained in a defensive posture. Then, as Darius's moves slowed with fatigue, Antonius saw his chance. Feinting low, he swung his gladius around hard, striking Darius solidly on his wrist. As Darius's gladius fell to the ground, Antonius pointed his gladius at Darius's face and smiled.

"That is a kill! The match is over!" Taurus shouted.

"No!" Darius growled, "I can still pick up my gladius and fight!"

Taurus shook his head. "I said before the matches began that if you drop your sword, you lose. Licinius is the victor and Master of the Gladius."

The trainees looked at Darius with raised eyebrows as he clenched his teeth and glared at Antonius.

Antonius, however, continued to smile. He felt a special satisfaction in knowing he had beaten Darius in the competition that mattered the most to him. He would also take great pleasure in collecting the bet they had made for completing the training.

Sejanus and Falconius walked over.

"Well done, men," Sejanus congratulated them.

Just before Sejanus and Falconius walked away, Falconius approached Taurus and said, "Centurion. Go ahead and inform Cornelius that due to the tragic accident today, he will be confirmed with the rest."

Taurus saluted and said, "Yes, Tribune."

Turning to the trainees, Falconius shouted, "Congratulations to all those victorious today in the competitions and congratulations for completing your training. Tomorrow you will be official members of the Praetorian Guard!"

"HUHF!" the trainees shouted out.

Falconius then nodded to Taurus, who turned and addressed the trainees. "The confirmation ceremony will be held tomorrow on the tenth hour at the amphitheater here on the field. Family and friends are allowed to attend. A banquet will be held afterward for all. Those who were awarded the title of Master in each weapons competition will receive their individual awards during the ceremony. Stop by the armory either today or early tomorrow and get your permanent uniforms, togas and armor. You will be required to wear your battle uniform for the ceremony. Several attendants will be at the armory to assist you. Once you have done that, the time is yours to do as you wish. You may leave the Castra but make sure you have returned well before the ceremony begins. It has been my privilege to train you. The Guard has a motto that we live and die by. It is simply, 'To the last!' That means you will fight to the last man and to the last drop of blood in defending your emperor and Rome. I have only one final thing to say before I dismiss you." Taurus drew his gladius and lifted it high above his head. "TO THE LAST!" he shouted.

"TO THE LAST!" the trainees echoed, raising their fists in the air.

After sheathing his gladius, Taurus smiled a rare smile and said, "Enjoy your midday meal. This time, no one goes hungry. Dismissed!"

A cheer arose from the men, but they still ran to the door.

In the dining hall, most of the trainees talked about the accident involving Darius, while some speculated where they would serve. After everyone had finished eating, Antonius and Marcus went outside and let out two whooping yells, slapping each other on the shoulders.

"I recognized that move you used on Darius," Marcus said. "You hit the nerve on his wrist like your father taught you. I remember you doing that to me a few times."

"It worked, didn't it? And you… that was an amazing shot you made to beat Aurelius in the archery competition."

"I think the gods had something to do with that," Marcus admitted.

"No, I think it was all the practicing you did," Antonius disagreed.

Marcus smiled. "Your family will be at the ceremony, won't they?"

"They were planning on it. What about your family?" Antonius asked.

Marcus looked down and said, "I wish they could come, but my father would never allow it."

"Well, at least Augustina will come to see you," Antonius said in a teasing manner.

Marcus gave him a smirk then said, "I think I'll wash up then go get my uniforms before the line is too long."

Antonius put one finger in the air and said, "That's a good idea; I'll join you, Bow Master."

Marcus extended his arm and said, "After you, Gladius Master."

CHAPTER IX-Confirmation

The next morning, a Praetorian Tribune in full uniform marched down the corridor leading to the Prefect's office. As he approached Sejanus's door, the two sentries came to attention and saluted.

"I am Tribune Galerius Licinius and I have an appointment to see the Prefect," he said in a firm tone.

The sentries passed him through and Thaddeus addressed him as he walked into the room. "Did I hear you say you had an appointment, Tribune Licinius? I'm not aware of any."

The prefect and I are old friends and he told me to see him whenever I was in Rome," Galerius replied.

Thaddius lifted his chin slightly and said, "Very well. I will announce you." He then walked over to Sejanus' door and knocked.

"Yes?" Sejanus called out.

"A tribune Licinius is here to see you, Prefect," Thaddeus replied.

"Send him in!" Sejanus called out.

Thaddeus opened the door and indicated for Galerius to enter.

Sejanus smiled and stood up. "Galerius, come in, come in." Noticing he was in uniform, he asked, "Have you decided to take me up on my offer and return to the Guard, Galerius?"

Galerius smiled. "No, I just wore this for the ceremony, Lucius."

"Ah," Sejanus responded with an upward nod. "Please have a seat, my friend," he added, pointing to a chair near his work table.

Taking the proffered chair, Galerius said, "I won't take a lot of your time, Lucius; I was just curious to see how Antonius and Marcus did before I go see them. We received the invitation to their confirmation, so I take it they passed the training."

Sejanus grinned. "Yes; they did quite well actually. Their weapons skills easily equaled or surpassed the other trainees who finished. They just needed some extra tutoring in formations, tactics and a few other things. You'll be pleased to know that Antonius won the title of Gladius Master. I don't imagine that is a surprise to you, though."

Galerius smiled and nodded. "And Marcus?"

"He won the Archery Master title."

Galerius nodded. "That is truly good news. I know this may be presumptuous of me, but can you tell me where they will be assigned?"

Sejanus sat forward in his chair and spoke softly. "Galerius, I have a special assignment for them. I'll share it with you but do not tell anyone else."

"You know I can be trusted," Galerius replied.

Sejanus leaned back in his chair. "For their duty assignment, I've decided to send them to Judaea."

"Judaea? Why Judaea?" Galerius asked in a disbelieving voice.

Sejanus took in a breath then said, "I owe a favor to Pontius Pilate, the Roman Prefect assigned there. This will give your son and his friend a chance to guard a high official."

"That is the special assignment?" Galerius asked.

"Oh, no," Sejanus replied shaking his head. Leaning forward again he said in a low voice, "The two speculatores of mine you met at your vineyard have taken care of many personal assignments and served me well, but they're starting to become known as my enforcers by some in the senate. I would like Antonius and Marcus to replace them when their tour in Judaea is finished. That is the special assignment. They will report directly to me and will be stationed here in Rome for the remainder of their enlistment. How would you feel about that?"

Galerius rubbed the back of his neck. He knew Antonius and Marcus would be put in a dangerous position if Sejanus' relationship with Tiberius ever eroded, but he masked his concern. "That is most generous of you, Lucius. But, since they aren't that familiar with Rome or the senatorial class, don't you think veterans who know their way around the city and senate would be a better choice?"

Sejanus waved his hand. "They can learn their way around over time. Remaining anonymous is more important to me. That is why I need men who are not only weapons masters, but unknown to those in Rome who bear watching."

Galerius put his hand to his chin and looked down for a moment.

Sejanus noticed his reticence. "I thought you would be excited about this opportunity for them, Galerius. It would seem you are against it."

"Oh, no, but as you and I both know, Rome can be perilous to those who are unfamiliar with its pitfalls," Galerius remarked.

"Don't worry, my friend. I will make sure they are well briefed on how to avoid Rome's pitfalls and I have no reservations about their loyalty in serving me. Once they spend two years in Judaea guarding Pilate, they will be ready for the assignment, I assure you."

"Well, if you think so, Lucius." Galerius said, as he stood up. "I know how busy you are, so I won't keep you any longer. I appreciate you giving Antonius and Marcus the chance to join the Guard and I'm pleased they did so well. To show you my appreciation, I have brought you a barrel of our finest wine."

Sejanus beamed. "You were always a man of your word, Galerius. If you wouldn't mind not mentioning my plan to them, I would like it to be a total surprise when the time comes."

"You have my promise," Galerius said, as he opened the door. "One more thing... would you allow me a small favor, Lucius?"

"Name it, my friend."

"I would like to personally give my son his gladius and dagger when they are passed out. I let him have my old gladius from the Guard when he left home and would appreciate it if you would allow him to use that as his service weapon. I also have a dagger I would like him to have."

"Certainly," Sejanus agreed. "Do you have them with you?"

"I do," Galerius replied.

"When the time comes for us to distribute their weapons, I'll have Tribune Falconius call you up when it's your son's turn. Would that meet with your approval?"

"It would," Galerius said. "Thank you, Lucius." Galerius then extended his arm.

Clasping it with his, Sejanus said, "I'll see you tonight at the ceremony."

"Yes, tonight," Galerius affirmed, as he walked through the door and closed it behind him.

Making his way down the corridor to his son's room, Galerius' face revealed a troubled spirit. It was common knowledge that Sejanus had been ordering the arrests of senators and Julians for the past few months. News of their disappearances even spread as far south as Rhegium. While many thought the orders came from the reclusive emperor, some thought Sejanus gave the command in order to clear a path to the throne. Galerius knew that Antonius and Marcus could be caught in the middle if a future power struggle occurred between Sejanus and Tiberius. It worried him, as indicated by his previous concern about their special assignment, but he had no control over future events that affected them. Antonius and Marcus were the masters of their own destinies now.

****

After they finished a hearty morning meal, Antonius and Marcus headed back to their room.

"Once we become Praetorians, women will sing our praises and fall at our feet," Marcus facetiously predicted, patting his friend's shoulder.

"Only if you remember to wash yours," Antonius countered with a chuckle. "And what about Augustina? What will she think about a plethora of women falling at your feet?"

"A plethora?" Marcus asked with a puzzled look.

"Yes, plebeian. That means many," Antonius explained.

"Oh, excuse me, patrician," Marcus retorted. "And where did a grape squeezer like you learn such a big word?"

"He learned it from his mother," a booming voice replied from their room as they entered.

"Father!" Antonius called out and hurried over to embrace him.

Giving Marcus a stern look, Galerius said, "Grape squeezer, eh?"

Marcus grinned.

Antonius pointed to his father's uniform and asked, "You're in uniform. Does this mean..."

"No, no, I just thought I would wear it one last time for your confirmation." He patted his breastplate and said, "It is good to know I can still fit into it, even if it is a little tight."

"Where are Mother and Augustina?" Antonius asked.

"They're at the villa. I came to see what your plans were for the day."

"Actually, we are free until the ceremony this evening," Antonius replied.

"Good. We'll go to the villa then; your mother is anxious to see you."

"I don't suppose anyone from my family came?" Marcus asked, still holding onto a thin thread of hope.

"No, I'm sorry, Marcus. Your mother really wanted to attend but she knew you would understand why she couldn't," Galerius informed him.

Marcus hung his head and nodded.

"Father, do you think it would be all right if we wore our uniforms now?" Antonius asked.

Galerius frowned and replied, "It wouldn't be proper since you won't officially become Praetorians until after the ceremony."

Antonius and Marcus both frowned.

"Before we go to the villa, come with me," Galerius ordered. "I have a task for you two."

"What is it?" Antonius asked, giving his father a suspicious look.

"I brought Lucius a barrel of our finest wine and told him I would deliver it. You two can lift it off the wagon and we'll take it to his office."

"Mere child's play," Marcus assured him as they left.

Walking down to the building where Galerius left the wagon, Antonius and Marcus had the barrel of wine on the ground in a matter of seconds. Putting it on a small cart Galerius had brought with him, they wheeled the large barrel inside and set it down next to Sejanus's door.

"You can't leave that here!" one of the sentries exclaimed.

"I already cleared it with the Prefect," Galerius repled, "you can ask him." Putting his arms on Antonius and Marcus' shoulders, the three marched down the hallway leaving bewildered looks on the sentries' faces.

The ex-Praetorian Tribune and two future Praetorians then returned to the wagon and climbed aboard.

"Do you think we could see some of the city?" Marcus asked. "I haven't had a chance to really see much of it."

"Certainly," Galerius replied. "Let's meet with the rest of the family then we can decide where to go."

The answer brought a smile to Marcus' face.

A short while later, they rolled up in front of the Villa Urbana[42]. Before the wagon stopped, Antonius and Marcus leapt out and ran to the door causing Galerius to shake his head at their exuberance.

Bursting through the entrance first, Antonius saw his mother and Augustina sitting on a couch.

"Mother!" he shouted, walking briskly over to her. Octavia stood up and happily embraced him. Her eyes immediately filled with grateful tears. "My son… Marcus… it is so good to see you. We've missed you both."

"Well, at least one of you," Augustina added, as she directed a flirting glance toward Marcus.

Antonius smirked and said, "It is good to see you too, Augustina."

Octavia took Marcus by his shoulders and said, "Your mother sends her love and says she misses you terribly."

Marcus smiled.

Augustina couldn't help but notice his physique. He had put on some weight and his muscles were now well-toned. Putting both hands on his right upper arm, she said, "You look much stronger than when you left. Was the training difficult?"

"It wasn't easy," Marcus replied with a convincing expression. He also couldn't help but notice how she had blossomed in just four months. Her girlish features were becoming a woman's. He liked what he saw.

42-Main living quarters of the villa

Galerius walked in and said, "Marcus suggested we see the city sights. The women can take the carriage and the men will take the wagon. Octavia, you can follow us." Turning to Ignatius and Lucia, he added, "Everyone is invited. Ignatius, why don't you drive the carriage."

"I will be happy to," Ignatius said.

Augustina really wanted to ride with Marcus but she knew her mother wouldn't allow it, so she kept quiet.

Soon, the occupants of both the carriage and wagon rolled out of the villa to see Rome's attractions. They rode by the lavish emperor's palace and mansions owned by the well-to-do on the Palatine hill; the plush Gardens of Lucullus with its luxurious Persian gardening style; the towering aqueducts of Virgo, Marcia and Alsietina; the numerous statues praising gods, goddesses and rulers; the temples located in the Forum Boarium and other impressive architectural wonders.

As the day grew later, the sightseers grew hungry. Octavia suggested they return to the villa and have something to eat. Marcus and Antonius were especially grateful for her suggestion.

After Lucia prepared some pasta with cheese, bread and vegetables, they all sat down to a delightful meal.

Antonius smiled at his mother and Marcus smiled at Augustina, who made sure he sat next to her. Soon, everyone was happily eating while Antonius and Marcus talked about their battles with wolves, the indignities they suffered from their bunkmates, and the welcomed distractions of the Castra chariot races. Of course, they included the fact they were both Masters in the weapons competition. The disclosure drew some "Oohs and ahhs," especially from Augustina.

After relating all they could think of, Antonius asked, "How is the vineyard doing, Father?"

"Quite well," Galerius replied. "The man we hired to take your place seems to be an able-bodied fellow and a quick learner. In fact, he has done so well that he's watching the vineyard for us while we're here."

"I'm sorry I'm not there to help," Antonius said with a pained expression.

"No apology is necessary. We will be fine," Galerius replied.

"Do you know where you will be assigned yet?" Octavia asked.

Antonius shook his head. "No, we'll find out after today's confirmation ceremony."

Galerius wanted to tell everyone what he already knew, but he remembered his promise to Sejanus and remained silent.

After finishing a tasty meal, Antonius and Marcus patted their stomachs and sat back in their chairs.

"We still have plenty of time before the ceremony begins. What shall we do?" Galerius asked.

Almost simultaneously, Antonius and Marcus said, "The Circus."

Placing her hand on Galerius's arm, Octavia said, "Very well, you men go to the races; we women have some shopping to do."

Galerius patted her hand. "Don't be too long, we don't want to cause Antonius and Marcus to be late for their confirmation."

"We won't," Octavia assured him.

"And remember, my dear, there are few opportunities in Aletium to wear the latest fashions," Galerius said with a teasing gaze.

Octavia returned his gaze with an impish smile. "Oh, I wasn't thinking of shopping for me, my husband. I was thinking of finding you some larger tunics while we're here."

Augustina and Lucia tittered slightly.

Smiling at his father, Antonius remarked, "I think Mother just ran you through with her gladius, Father."

Galerius grinned. "Since you've been gone, I'm afraid she has become quite a worthy sparring partner."

Octavia smiled. "Only with words, Antonius."

Shaking his head, Galerius turned to Antonius and Marcus. "Shall we go before I'm run through again?"

"Yes!" came the collective response.

"Come with us, Ignatius," Galerius suggested.

Ignatius' eyes brightened.

Since the Circus was just a short distance away, the four decided to walk. Taking the road from the Forum Boarium that passed by the Circus, Antonius and Marcus acted like giddy schoolboys, while Galerius and Ignatius spoke of what had transpired in Rome. As they neared one of the entrances to the hippodrome framed by a massive arch, they heard the cheering of the crowd inside. Antonius and Marcus picked up the pace as Galerius and Ignatius tried to keep up with them.

"How does anyone build something this big?" Marcus exclaimed.

"On a festival day it can hold 150,000 people and when the emperor is present, they will throw bread out to the spectators," Galerius answered. "I was assigned here many times to control the crowd if they became unruly."

"Do you think the emperor will be here today?" Marcus asked.

"I doubt it," Galerius replied. "He would normally be seated in the private enclosure just across from the finish line, but he hasn't been to Rome for some time now."

Marcus frowned.

"Hurry!" Antonius exclaimed. "We don't want to miss the blue team scoring another victory."

"What makes you think the blue team will be victorious?" Ignatius asked.

"When I am here, they are always victorious," Antonius replied confidently.

"Well, we'll see. Personally, I'm partial to the green team," Galerius retorted. "They have better horses."

"But the blue team has better charioteers," Antonius countered.

Galerius smiled. "Would you care wager with me on a race, Antonius."

Antonius grinned at his father and replied, "The last time I did, I had to carry you on my back from the inside of the Circus all the way to the outside. What kind of wager did you have in mind?"

Galerius rubbed his chin. "The terms are thus. If the green team wins, at the end of the race you must stand up and shout as loud as you can, 'The green team is the best team in Rome. I was a fool to cheer for the blue team!'"

Antonius smiled. "All right, but if the blue team wins, you must do the same."

Galerius thought for a second then grasped Antonius's arm. "Agreed."

Arriving at the entrance, they entered the arena just as an official announced the next race. Finding the section reserved for Praetorians, they started down a row to take their seats when a Praetorian in the row noticed Antonius, Marcus and Ignatius enter. Seeing they were in tunics and not in uniform or Praetorian togas, he gruffly asked, "Are you Praetorians?"

"They are with me," Galerius replied.

"Sorry, Tribune," the Praetorian apologized. "I just wanted to make sure they were in the right section."

"No harm done," Galerius remarked as they sat down on the smooth stone bench.

Marcus' gaze was immediately drawn to the spina in the middle of the track. He pointed to an obelisk that stood 24 meters high and asked, "Is that an obelisk, Antonius?"

"Yes. Do you know anything about it, Father?" Antonius asked.

"Yes. It came from the Egyptian pharaoh Ramses II. Augustus had it brought to Rome."

"What about those statues in the middle?" Marcus asked.

"I know those," Antonius declared. "The one on the left is Victoria, goddess of victory; the one in the middle is Cybele, goddess of fertility; and the one on the right is Messia the goddess of cultivated earth."

"Messia," Marcus stated, as though he had received an epiphany. "I've heard my mother say her name before, hoping she would bless our land so it would be easy to till. What about the woman riding the lion?"

"That is Cybele again," Antonius informed him.

Marcus chuckled. "She must be brave to ride a lion."

Galerius turned to him and smiled. "Riding a stone lion is much easier than riding a real one."

Antonius gave Marcus a look of skepticism and said, "My father would know."

Marcus pointed to three conical pillars at the end of the spina. "What are those three things called?"

"Metae," Antonius replied. "Those pillars let the charioteers know where the turn is."

"Oh. Where do they start from?" Marcus asked.

Antonius pointed and said, "There, on the west side. You can see the starting gates called carceres[43]."

"Oh, yes, I see them," Marcus said, shading his eyes.

"Any other questions, Marcus?" Antonus asked.

Marcus grinned and said, "I told you I needed to ask more questions."

Antonius smirked and looked at his program. "Ah. You may as well get ready to stand and shout for the blue team now," he smugly told his father. "Pontius Epaphroditus is the blue charioteer for this race. He never loses."

"We'll see," Galerius replied.

"I'll cheer for him, too," Marcus volunteered, as Galerius sported a wiley smile.

"Do you want to be included in the wager, Marcus?" Galerius asked.

Marcus shook his head. "Oh, no, I don't know the charioteers well enough to do that. I'll just help Antonius cheer."

"As you wish," Galerius stated with a smug look on his face.

Marcus again pointed to the platform where laps were counted and asked, "Antonius. What are those large oval things that look like wooden eggs?"

"Lap counters. When a lap is completed, an egg is lowered," Antonius replied.

43-*Starting gates*

"Ah," Marcus said, lifting his head slightly.

They watched in anticipation while eight chariots lined up at the starting gate for the next race. Everyone in the stadium stood up and began to chant, "Conquer! Conquer! Conquer!" As the trumpets sounded the "make ready" signal, the charioteers focused on the mappa[44] the starter held in his hand. After determining the charioteers were all ready, the starter dropped the linen, the gates opened, and the race began to the roaring of the crowd. As the chariots hurtled around the track, Antonius and Marcus stood and shouted encouragement for their charioteer while Galerius and Ignatius sat back, watching them with amused grins.

The race was fairly even until the fifth lap when the blue chariot and green chariot pulled away from the field with the red chariot close behind. A white chariot struck the spina on the fourth lap turning too sharply, cracked its wheel and had to leave the race. As the three leading chariots thundered down the straightaway for the sixth lap, the horses for the red chariot began to fade. The green chariot moved up to challenge the blue chariot and its driver, Pontius Epaphroditus. Now one lap remained, and Antonius and Marcus were shouting at the top of their lungs.

Galerius turned to Ignatius. "Antonius should save his shouting for the end of the race."

Ignatius smiled and nodded.

The green and blue chariots were even as they rumbled down the last straightaway. Antonius and Marcus held their breaths as the chariots crossed the finish line. The blue chariot was victorius by half a horse length.

"Hah! Hah!" Antonius shouted raising his fist, as Marcus excitedly pounded him on his shoulder.

He turned to Galerius after regaining his composure and said, "I think you should honor our wager now, Father."

"Are you sure you don't want to make it the best two out of three?" Galerius suggested.

"No Father, honor your wager," Antonius demanded.

Galerius shrugged and stood up. "Very well." He cleared his throat and yelled, "The green team is the best team in Rome. I was a fool to cheer for the blue team!" He then sat back down with a smile. Several Praetorians sitting nearby looked at him oddly.

"No, Father. You were supposed to say it the other way around."

Galerius smiled. "I think not, Antonius. If I recall our words, they were

____

44-*The large handkerchief used to start the race*

thus: I said you must shout those words if the green team won. Then you said if the blue team won I must do the same. Those were the same words, so I honored our wager."

Ignatius chuckled. "That was the wager, Antonius."

Antonius shook his head then turned to Marcus. "You were smart not to bet with my father. He will twist your words."

Galerius gave his son a sly look then said, "Well, we should probably return to the villa before it gets much later."

The four men made their way out of the large hippodrome and headed back to the villa. A short while later the women returned with oils, perfumes, new sandals and larger tunics for Galerius.

****

As the hour drew near for the ceremony to begin, Galerius ushered everyone out of the villa. He then helped the women into the awaiting carriage that Ignatius would drive, and climbed aboard the wagon with Antonius and Marcus, carrying something wrapped in a blanket.

"What's in the blanket?" Antonius asked.

Galerius gave him a "none of your business" look and said, "You'll find out later."

It wasn't long before they arrived at the Castra and found a place for their conveyances. Walking over to the entrance at the southeastern gate, Galerius went up to a sentry and said, "We are here for the confirmation ceremony for our son and his friend."

The sentry saluted and said, "Welcome, Tribune. Families are instructed to wait in the reception hall until the ceremony begins."

Galerius nodded.

"Open the gate!" the sentry shouted.

Antonius and Marcus led the way to the reception hall. There they joined the other family members and friends who had come to support the new Praetorians.

Seeing them enter, Thaddeus, Sejanus's aide, recognized Galerius and quickly walked over. "Welcome, Tribune Licinius. Feel free to mingle with the other guests. The ceremony will begin shortly."

"Thank you," Galerius replied.

"The new Praetorians are to go to their rooms and put on their uniforms and then wait there until they are called for," Thaddeus informed them.

"Very well," Galerius replied, looking at Antonius and Marcus to make sure they heard the instruction.

They nodded and hurried off.

"Where do you think Antonius and Marcus will be assigned?" Octavia asked her husband.

Galerius shrugged his shoulders. "It could be anywhere."

A moment later, Taurus entered the reception hall. "All family and friends of the new Praetorians will follow the aide to the amphitheater where the ceremony will commence shortly."

Back in their room, Antonius and Marcus put on their uniforms. When they were satisfied that every button was hooked and all was in its proper place, they sat on their beds and shared colossal smiles. Darius, Cornelius, and two other trainees who made it through put on theirs as well and occasionally shot a scowl in their direction. A tense silence filled the air until finally, they heard the sound of a familiar voice.

"Praetorians! Line up outside your room and form two rows behind me when I pass!"

"You heard the centurion," Darius said, as the six roommates lined up outside their door.

Falling in line with the others, they headed toward the field as if to begin another training day. Upon arriving at the small amphitheater next to the training field, Taurus ordered them to form a single line and stand at attention facing their now-seated families and friends. He then stepped to the side and took his place next to them.

Falconius, who was seated on the other side of Sejanus, came forward to a small podium and began his presentation. "To family and friends of our trainees, on behalf of our esteemed emperor, Tiberius Caesar and the staff at the Castra Praetoria, I bid you welcome. I am Tribune Thracius Falconius, the training commander here. This year's group has been an extraordinary one. We have had men recommended from legions such as the First Germanica..."

"Huhf!" went the battle cry from its members.

Falconius continued naming the other legions, followed by the customary battle cry.

After the last unit was mentioned, Darius added under his breath, "And a couple of eunuchs with no military experience." Cornelius, standing next to him, suppressed a laugh.

Falconius continued. "The men have worked hard and those who withstood the rigorous training stand before you now, the best-conditioned and best-trained soldiers Rome has to offer."

The audience applauded.

"I have no doubt they will represent Rome well in whatever duty they are assigned and will not hesitate to give their lives if necessary for their emperor and Rome. We are proud of their achievement and you, as family and friends, should be proud as well. We will now have a brief awards ceremony for those who mastered the three main weapons a Praetorian must know well. When I call their names, each trainee will step forward and receive his award from Centurion Taurus, our chief instructor. For mastering the pilum, Praetorian Darius Aurelius." Darius stepped forward bearing a disgruntled look and quickly took his plaque and monetary reward. The crowd politely applauded.

"For mastering the bow, Praetorian Marcus Flavius." Marcus stepped forward. He exhibited a slight smile when he heard Augustina cheering in the audience while everyone else clapped.

"For mastering the gladius, Praetorian Antonius Licinius." Antonius stepped forward and accepted his award with an austere expression. The audience politely applauded again.

"Now we will present each one of our new Praetorians his official gladius and dagger. Bring them in."

Four veteran Praetorians came forward, two carrying large quivers of brightly polished swords and the other two carried wooden crates of daggers. They handed the weapons to Falconius, as he congratulated each graduate and handed them their gladius and dagger, followed by a salute. Each new Praetorian returned the salute after sheathing his weapons. When Falconius reached Antonius, he turned to the crowd. "This Praetorian's gladius and dagger will be presented by his father, a well-known and well-respected Praetorian Tribune, now retired... Galerius "Magnus" Licinius."

The audience rose to their feet and cheered as Galerius stood and made his way to Antonius. Octavia and Augustina looked on in surprise. Galerius approached carrying the dagger and gladius, wrapped in a blanket. Standing before his son, he took them out and said, "Praetorian! This gladius has seen its master through many battles successfully. May it see you through any battles you may have as well. Take care of it and it will take care of you." He then handed it to Antonius.

"Yes, Tribune," Antonius said solemnly, as he sheathed his sword.

Galerius then held up the dagger. It was the dagger that Augustus had given him. "This dagger... well, you know all about it. Guard it well."

"I will," Antonius said, sheathing it and saluting his father smartly. Bursting with pride, Galerius returned the salute and went back to his seat. Octavia smiled at her husband and took his hand as he sat down.

Down the ranks, rancor mounted within Darius as he mumbled, "How touching."

After all the new Praetorians had received their swords and daggers, Falconius returned to the podium.

"Now I'm sure those of you who are family and friends of our new Praetorians are anxious to know where they will be serving, so I won't keep you in suspense any longer. Two provinces are in need of more security so three contuberniums will be stationed in Judaea and two contuberniums will be sent to Creta. The assignments are for two years. Once they have completed them, the men will return to Rome and be assigned to permanent units. The remaining men who graduated will fill in vacancies left by retiring Praetorians in Rome."

Antonius and Marcus exchanged excited looks and hoped they would be two of the forty assigned in Rome.

"The following Praetorians will be serving in Creta. Praetorian Darius Aurelius was promoted to Centurion and will be in charge of that group."

Antonius and Marcus once again exchanged looks. They were worried looks this time. When Falconius finished reading the sixteen names, Antonius and Marcus breathed a sigh of relief that they weren't included. He then announced, "The following will be serving in Judaea. Centurion Taurus will command that group."

When they heard their names read, Marcus gave Antonius a perplexed glance. Antonius nodded. He knew where Judaea was, thanks to his mother's geography lessons. Although it was on the other end of the empire, he would get to see a new land. He was surprised they would be serving so far away and even more surprised when he heard Taurus would be their commander.

Falconius continued. "The ship for Creta and Judaea will leave tomorrow morning and will drop off those serving in Creta then continue on to Judaea with the rest. We will conclude the ceremony with our Praetorian Guard motto then everyone is invited to the banquet held in honor of the new Praetorians."

Taurus stepped to the front then turned left and marched down the row of men until he stood at the middle of the formation. Turning toward them, he raised his gladius in the air and shouted, "To the last!"

The new Praetorians drew their swords in unison and shouted, "To the last!"

"Dismissed!" Taurus shouted.

After breaking formation, Marcus and Antonius quickly walked over to where Antonius's family was standing.

"We're going to Judaea!" Antonius said, beaming.

Galerius smiled. He knew the reputation Judaea had, some calling it the armpit of the empire, but he said nothing. It was his son's moment and he didn't want to spoil it.

Octavia grasped a hand of Antonius and Marcus into hers. Her eyes showed concern. "I wish you could have stayed in Italia, but it is wonderful that you did so well. I'm proud of you both," she said, giving each hand a gentle squeeze.

Antonius and Marcus beamed.

"Congratulations, Praetorians!" Taurus said to Antonius and Marcus.

They turned and noticed he had people with him. "Thank you, Centurion," they replied.

Gesturing to his guests, Taurus said, "Let me introduce you to my sister's family. This is Sidonius Cato, his wife Juliana—my sister, and their two daughters, Julia and Serina."

Galerius extended his hand to Sidonius and said, "It is a pleasure to meet you. This is my wife Octavia, my daughter Augustina, son Antonius, and his friend Marcus Flavius. I am Galerius Licinius."

While everyone was being introduced, Julia and Antonius made eye contact and exchanged smiles. Antonius felt instantly attracted to her.

"You are the famous Tribune they call Galerius the Great, aren't you?" Sidonius asked.

Galerius modestly replied, "That was a long time ago."

"Not that long; it is an honor to meet you," Sidonius said, as Galerius took his arm again.

"We have others to meet so we should probably take our leave," Taurus suggested. As they walked away, Antonius noticed Julia look back at him and smile.

As he tried to remember her name, Marcus grabbed his arm. "Food," was all he said.

Antonius smiled and said, "I'm right behind you."

They headed for one of the large tables heaped with food and drink, far surpassing their fare during training. As Antonius filled up his plate, he noticed Julia on the other side of the banquet table choosing some of the displayed delicacies as well.

"You are wise to serve yourself before all the Praetorians come through.

There might not be anything left," he warned her.

Julia smiled. "You sound as if they don't feed you that well here."

"Pig entrails and moldy bread," Antonius replied, glancing peripherally to catch her reaction.

She laughed lightly, neither haughty nor annoying, but a sound that pleased him.

He then glanced her way and asked, "Your name again was…"

"Julia," she replied. "And yours?"

"Antonius."

"Well, Antonius, will you be stationed in Rome?" she asked.

Antonius shook his head. "Unfortunately, I'm being sent to Judaea."

With a furrowed brow, she said, "Oh, what a pity. My family and I live in Rome and I was hoping we could get to know each other better."

Antonius's heart raced at her apparent interest in him. "Perhaps I can take furloughs and visit you. Where do you live?"

"The Cato villa on the Palatine hill," she replied.

Antonius nodded once and said, "I will remember that."

As she turned to leave, he called out, "Wait! Before you go, if you don't mind me asking, how old are you?"

"Sixteen," she replied with a smile.

"Sixteen," he thought to himself. "She will be married by the time I return." He watched her walk away for a moment then turned to find Marcus behind him, puckering his lips.

"What?" Antonius asked.

"Oh, nothing," Marcus replied. He then made a kissing sound.

Antonius frowned and punched him on the arm.

"Ow!" Marcus reacted. "I'm telling Taurus you're not getting along with me and he'll send you to an army unit."

"Too late," Antonius retorted with a guffaw.

As the remainder of the evening progressed, Antonius occasionally glanced over at Julia, who sat a few tables away. When he caught her gaze she would quickly avert her eyes, making him smile. Eventually the night grew late and families and friends began to leave, saying their goodbyes. As Julia and her family stood up from their table, she looked back at Antonius and smiled.

He gave her a slight wave of his hand, causing her sister to giggle.

Seeing that Octavia looked tired, Galerius said, "The hour is late and we should return to the villa. I'd like to get an early start back to the vineyard."

Realizing it might be a long time before she saw her son again, Octavia hugged him then Marcus. "You two take care of yourselves and watch out for each other," she admonished, through teary eyes.

Both nodded.

Augustina took her turn embracing them, spending a little more time with Marcus. "I will miss you... yes, even you brother."

Galerius cleared his throat and said, "Remember, you two represent not only Rome but your families as well."

"We will remember," Antonius promised.

Galerius grasped their arms and gave both a hearty pat on the back, then all waved goodbye.

As Antonius and Marcus watched them leave, Marcus rubbed his hands together and said, "Well, let's see if there is any food left."

"You're still hungry?" Antonius asked.

Marcus put up both hands and said, "We can't let it go to waste! Tomorrow we could be having pig entrails and moldy bread."

Antonius slapped his friend lightly on the back and said, "Spoken like a true Praetorian."

Joining the rest of their peers around the food table, which now had only scraps of fruit, cheese, meat and bread here and there, they jockeyed for the last morsels.

Sejanus and Falconius congratulated the men one last time then bade all a good evening.

Standing on a nearby chair, Taurus bellowed, "Attention, everyone! When you get up in the morning, I want you to have your morning meal then clean your areas. I will inspect them so they had better be clean. Those leaving for Creta and Judaea will then depart for the ship that will take us to our destinations. The night is getting late, so I suggest you retire. You will need to arise at your usual training time."

Everyone groaned and began to disperse, knowing their late night revelry would make it difficult to arise at the appointed time in the morning.

"Should we put on our uniforms before the morning meal, Centurion?" Aurelius asked.

"No," Taurus replied, shaking his head. "Knowing how some of you pigs eat, you'll have stains all over them. Put them on after you finish cleaning your areas. Any other questions?"

When Taurus could see there weren't any, he jumped down and headed back to the barracks. As he did, Antonius took out his father's dagger and marveled at its beauty. A few of his fellow Praetorians noticed it as they passed by. Darius and his other bunkmates were among them.

"Darius!" Antonius called out.

He turned and glared at Antonius.

"About that bet we made the first day in training. I believe the wager was ten sesterces?"

Darius frowned. Reaching into his purse, he pulled out the agreed wager and tossed it on the ground in front of Antonius. "There. Have your farmer friend pick it up for you; he's used to groveling in the dirt anyway." He turned his back on them and walked away, hoping for a challenge.

Marcus was about to oblige and started after him.

Antonius grabbed his shoulder and said, "Remember Taurus's warning."

Marcus nodded and asked, "What are you going to do about the wager?"

"Leave it there," Antonius replied. "I don't want anything from Aurelius."

After returning to their room, Marcus noticed the bow and quiver of arrows Galerius gave him on his bed along with his knife. Galerius had dropped them off before returning to the villa.

"My bow and knife!" Marcus exclaimed, rushing over to his bunk. Turning to Antonius, he asked, "Do you think Taurus will let me keep them?"

"Ask him tomorrow," Antonius replied. "Right now, I want to sleep and dream of a beautiful young Roman girl."

"I'll bet I know who she is," Marcus teased.

Soon afterward, they were both dreaming of beautiful young girls.

As the moon was at its peak, a solitary figure approached Antonius's bed. Carefully opening the chest next to it, he removed the item he wanted and slipped out of the room. Making sure the hallway was clear, he approached the latrine clutching a prized dagger.

CHAPTER X-PIRATES

"On your feet, scorpions!" Taurus' voice boomed down the hall, disturbing the morning's peace and 80 new Praetorians. "Report to the dining hall and have your morning meal then return to your rooms and make sure they're clean!" he shouted.

Rolling out of their bunks, Antonius and Marcus ran out the door along with their bunkmates and proceeded to the dining hall.

As they sat down to eat, Marcus whispered to Antonius, "I hope we're not put in the same century with Darius once our time in Judaea is up."

Antonius gave him a sideward glance and said, "Even if we are, don't forget, we're still brothers in arms."

Marcus nodded, and they continued eating. After a short while, Taurus bellowed, "Finish your meal and go clean your areas now! When I finish mine I'll come and inspect your rooms."

Marcus nudged Antonius and asked, "Do you think I should ask him about my bow and knife now?"

"Sure," Antonius replied.

Marcus stopped at Taurus' table and said, "Centurion..."

Taurus looked up and asked, "What is it, Flavius?"

"Antonius' father gave me a bow and quiver of arrows and my mother gave me a knife. Can I take them with me to Judaea?"

Taurus didn't take a moment to think about it and replied, "Yes. From now on, you'll be my official bowman when we're in the field."

"Thank you, Centurion," Marcus said with a smile.

Taurus waved him away and said, "Now go clean your area and let me finish my meal."

Marcus hurried out of the dining hall and joined Antonius and his bunkmates as they began to clean their area.

When Darius was satisfied with the results, he said, "That's good enough. Put on your uniforms."

After dressing, Antonius went over to his footlocker and opened it to obtain his father's dagger. "No!" he cried.

"What's wrong?" Marcus asked.

"My dagger is gone!" Antonius cried.

Marcus looked at the contents and asked, "Are you sure you didn't put it somewhere else?"

Antonius's face turned red. Raising his voice, he said, "I put it right on top! I went through everything several times; it's not here!"

With flaring nostrils and narrowed eyes, he turned to his bunkmates. "Which one of you took my father's dagger?"

Each bore a look of innocence.

"Are you accusing us of stealing?" Darius snarled.

"Prove me wrong and let me search your things," Antonius countered.

"You're not touching mine," Cornelius said.

Darius gave Antonius a scathing look. "Be careful who you call a thief, Licinius."

"Why don't you report this to Centurion Taurus and have everyone in the barracks searched?" Marcus suggested.

Antonius glared at each man in the room, feeling certain that one of them was guilty, then walked out into the hallway. He spotted Taurus waiting to inspect, and walked over. "Centurion. Someone stole the dagger my father gave me. I think one of my bunkmates took it."

With a shocked look, Taurus said, "Thieves in our ranks will not be tolerated. Attention!" he shouted. "Everyone remain in your rooms until I tell you to leave!"

Darius walked out and asked, "What is going on, Centurion?"

"You'll find out shortly," Taurus replied, then hurried out of the barracks.

A moment later he appeared with four veteran Praetorians. Two immediately went down to the end of the hall, and the other two stayed with Taurus.

"Praetorians!" Taurus yelled. "Everyone step outside your rooms now and stand along the wall at attention!"

After everyone lined up in the hall, Taurus nodded and the Praetorians he brought with him began their search. As they came out of each room, they also searched the occupants. Each time they exited a room, Antonius hoped to see a sign of discovery, but instead they just went into the next room to continue the search. Finally, they came to Antonius's room. After an intensive search, they came out and searched Darius and the rest. Turning to Taurus, they shook their heads and returned.

Taurus stood silent for a moment then said, "You are probably wondering why this was necessary. Someone stole a valuable dagger belonging to Praetorian Licinius. If you have seen anything that would help us locate it, come forward now."

When no one stepped forward, Taurus said, "Very well. If the thief is among you, I assure you that your career as a Praetorian will be a short one.

Return to your rooms now and make sure they are straightened up before you leave."

As Antonius and Marcus went back to their room, Marcus said, "Antonius, I am truly sorry. I know how much that dagger meant to you. Why don't you take mine? I have my knife and sheath."

Antonius shook his head.

"Please, Antonius. Take it then we'll both have knives. Otherwise, you'll have an empty sheath, and it will look funny."

Reluctantly, Antonius took it and said, "Thanks, Marcus."

Marcus hung his head and said, "I feel bad for you. You had it for such a short time."

Antonius hung his head and said, "I feel bad for my father. It meant so much to him coming from the emperor himself."

"It's bound to turn up. Someone will eventually notice it," Marcus said, trying to cheer him up.

"I hope you're right. I'm not looking forward to telling my father a thief stole his dagger. I couldn't even take care of it for one day. I have shamed his trust," Antonius stated, looking down at his feet.

"When do you plan on telling him?" Marcus asked.

Antonius shook his head slightly and said, "I won't be able to before we leave, so I don't know."

As they entered their room, they noticed their bedding on the floor; their chests rifled, and their belongings strewn about.

"Thanks for making us clean our room twice, Licinius," Darius growled when he saw the mess.

Antonius glared back at him.

After remaking their bunks and picking up their personal things that had been cast about, one of the men in the room mumbled he needed to use the latrine and slipped out. Once there, he checked to make sure no one was around then jumped up and grabbed the wooden beam just above his head. With one hand, he felt for something he had placed on top. After retrieving it, he put it in a cloth bag then stuck it inside his tunic. He smiled thinking he made the right decision to hide it there. Returning to his room, he quickly placed it in his knapsack while everyone else in the room was re-packing their knapsacks.

A short while later, after giving each room a cursory look to make sure they were clean, Taurus shouted, "ATTENTION! Those assigned to Judaea and Creta report outside your rooms! The rest remain here until the Prefect's aide comes and gives you your duty assignments."

Those leaving on the ship, quickly appeared with their gear and stood at attention as Taurus walked down the hallway to inspect them. As they held their positions, one also held his breath, hoping there wouldn't be another search. Satisfied that everyone was ready and accounted for, Taurus returned to where he started. "Follow me in twos!" he shouted.

Two by two, they filed out of the barracks and onto six large open wagons used mainly for supply transport. Antonius and Marcus threw their gear onto one of the wagons and climbed aboard with the others and took their seats on large grain sacks. Taurus climbed on top of another wagon along with Darius and turned to the driver. "To Portus Augusti," he commanded.

As the wagons slowly made their way to the naval port, Marcus turned to Antonius and asked, "Where is Judaea?"

"It lies to the east, across the sea," Antonius replied.

"Will it take long to get there?" Marcus asked.

Antonius looked up and said, "A few weeks I'm guessing."

Marcus felt a twinge of excitement mixed with anxiety. "I've never been in the sea. It will be a new experience."

Antonius looked at Marcus with raised eyebrows and said, "I have a feeling we'll have many new experiences."

After the short ride to their ship, everyone jumped off the wagons. Workers then quickly unloaded the provision sacks and carried them over to a large merchant vessel.

Sejanus had learned that one was bound for Judaea and thought there was no sense in making Praetorians suffer on a long voyage in a trireme's[45] cramped quarters. Sending them to Judaea was bad enough, so he arranged for them to sail to their destinations on the merchant ship. The captain had no objections having the extra protection.

Taurus motioned for everyone to gather around him then pointed to the large vessel. "This is our ship, men. Pick up your things and assemble on deck, quickly now."

After they had assembled, the ship's captain walked over and acknowledged Taurus's salute with a nod then addressed the men.

"Welcome aboard my ship, Praetorians. We will get underway shortly but before we do, let me outline the rules of my ship. The sailors on board are Roman freedmen, not slaves, so treat them as such. You will be responsible for the evening watches on board once we are underway. I have set aside an

---

45-A warship with three rows of oars on each side; the ship usually carried around 200 men including 180 oarsmen

area below for your sleeping quarters next to our cargo. You may also come up on deck for your meals and exercise. We ask that you restrict yourselves to those areas so my men can perform their tasks without distraction or interference. The voyage to Judaea will take four weeks with a good wind. We will be making one stop in Creta. Your main responsibility is the safety of this ship."

"Are you clear on that?" Taurus shouted at the men.

"Yes, sir!" thundered their reply.

Taurus turned to the captain and said, "Anything else?"

"Yes," the captain replied. Turning to a grizzled-looking man in his forties, the captain said, "Didius here will take you below now and show you where you'll be sleeping."

Taurus shouted, "Praetorians, follow this man and take your things below then report back on deck. Dismissed!"

"This way, Prae-tor-i-ans," Didius uttered, pronouncing each syllable slowly as if he were mocking them. Leading them down to the cargo area, he pointed to some makeshift cots that had been set up. Antonius and Marcus looked over the cramped space and had a feeling the voyage would be a long one. Everyone put their kits and knapsacks under the cots they chose to sleep in then hurried back on deck.

After they had assembled, Taurus shouted, "During the voyage, you will exercise on deck each day to maintain your conditioning. Uniforms will be tunics only; battle dress when you stand your watches. Aurelius will post a roster for guard duty just outside the entrance to our quarters below. Check it daily to see when your times are. Any questions?"

"No, Centurion!" the men replied in unison.

"Very well. Dismissed!" Taurus barked.

Antonius and Marcus headed toward the port side of the ship with several other Praetorians. Leaning against the rail, they watched Ostia slowly fade in the distance. They were now official members of Rome's most elite band of soldiers heading for their first assignment. Bursting with pride, Marcus turned to Antonius and said, "Well, Antonius, we made it."

"Yes, we did," Antonius said with an air of uncertainty. For a brief moment, he wondered if they had done the right thing. He quickly dismissed the feeling as a brief bout of homesickness and the fact they wouldn't return to their homeland for two years. They were Praetorians now sailing to a far- off Roman province assigned to protect the Roman governor. Perhaps if they did a good job, they might be assigned to guard the emperor. The thought made

Antonius smile. He was going to see the world he longed to see.

After the midday meal, Antonius and Marcus stopped to inspect the watch list. There were two watches—the first being just after supper til dark and the second from then until dawn. The ship's crew would stand watch during the day. Finding their names, they learned they would be standing guard together on a few of the watches.

"Looks like we get the dark to dawn watch tonight," Antonius said un-enthusiastically.

"At least we're not on that watch the whole voyage." Marcus remarked.

Antonius snorted. "I'm surprised we're not if Aurelius was in charge of assigning the watches. Perhaps Taurus assigns them and Aurelius just posts them."

Just then, they heard Taurus's distinct voice shout, "All Praetorians on deck for conditioning! Tunics only!"

They both quickly removed their armor then reported topside.

The exercise period lasted for an hour, interrupted occasionally by a nauseous participant running over to the side of the ship.

After feeling they had worked hard enough, Taurus dismissed them to settle in before the evening meal.

Being one of those who experienced a touch of seasickness, Marcus wiped his mouth as he headed for the hatch leading below.

"Having trouble adjusting, gladiator," Antonius said, with a chuckle.

"I didn't know the sea was this rough," Marcus said, suppressing a belch.

Antonius looked up in the sky. "I would imagine it gets worse during a storm."

Marcus turned to Taurus, standing nearby, and asked, "Do you think we'll run into any storms, Centurion?"

Taurus looked up in the sky and said, "It's up to Jupiter."

"Jupiter's the god of the sky and thunder isn't he?" Marcus asked.

"He is, if you believe in the gods," Taurus said with a wry smile.

Later, those who could eat, had a supper of smoked fish, carrots, bread and fruit, then returned to their cots to rest. Antonius and Marcus managed a few hours sleep before one of the two assigned for the first watch shook them awake and said, "Your watch. Report to Aurelius at the bow of the ship."

After a few yawns, Antonius and Marcus put on their uniforms then climbed the ladder to go on deck. Spotting Darius on the bow they headed toward him unsteadily as the ship rocked back and forth. When they reached him, he handed each one a long spear and gave them their instructions. "Stay alert and if you see any ships approaching, wake me!" he exclaimed then went below.

Antonius marched to his post with head erect and shoulders back. He felt important for the first time in his life. His training had given him the confidence to accomplish physical feats he never thought possible, besides sharpening his senses. He heard the occasional creaking of the ship's timbers as the waves gently tossed it to and fro, splashing methodically against the hull. He smelled the salty aroma of the sea as it sprayed its porous blanket over the bow of the ship. He could still taste the fish he had for supper as the flavor lingered in his mouth. Continuing around the side of the ship, he met his counterpart and nodded. He did a crisp about-face then headed back toward the bow where he saw Marcus approaching from his side of the ship.

"See any ships on your side?" Marcus asked.

The temptation was too great. Antonius feigned a look of concern. "No, but I think I saw something that appeared to be following us in the water."

"What did you see?" Marcus asked with wide eyes.

"I don't know what it was, but it was large and appeared to have scales and bumps on its back. It could have been a sea serpent. They've been known to follow ships. My father said he was on a ship once when one snatched a man from the deck. They never found him."

Marcus lifted a single eyebrow giving Antonius a doubting look.

"No, I'm serious, Marcus. My father told me he saw it happen."

Marcus suddenly felt goose bumps rise on his arms. "You... think it was following us?"

Antonius furrowed his brow and said, "It appeared to be. Make sure you keep a sharp lookout and don't turn your back on the sea."

Marcus's eyes went at big as brass coins.

Antonius shrugged his shoulders. "Well, we had better continue back around before Darius finds us talking and throws us overboard. We don't want to make it easy for the beast if it *is* out there."

Marcus nodded.

As they turned and walked in opposite directions, one kept chuckling to himself while the other kept a very close eye on the water.

****

The next several days were like the first: eating, exercising, regurgitating, resting and standing watch topside. So far, they were favored with good weather and Creta was only a day away.

As the sun began to disappear in the horizon, Antonius and Marcus put on their uniforms after supper to stand the first evening watch this time. They climbed the ladder until they reached the deck then met Darius at his usual spot at the bow. After handing each one their spears he said, "Stay alert and report any ships you see," then went below.

Both nodded and began their vigil around the opposite sides of the ship.

After his first pass around the ship on his side, Marcus approached the bow and noticed Antonius focusing on something in the distance. "Do you see something?" he asked.

"There is a little speck on the horizon, there," Antonius said, pointing to the east as dusk was just beginning to set in. "It might be a ship."

"Does it look like it is heading for us?" Marcus asked.

"It's hard to tell, but we should probably tell Aurelius," Antonius replied. I'll keep an eye on it, and you inform him."

Marcus hurried away and returned shortly with Darius.

Darius walked up to Antonius and said, "Flavius said you believe you saw a ship."

"Well, it could be a ship," Antonius replied, pointing to the speck.

Darius looked where Antonius pointed and said, "Keep a watch on it and see if it gets bigger and heads for us. I'll go below and notify Taurus that we have spotted a possible ship that could be approaching."

A moment later, he returned with Taurus.

"What do you think?" Darius asked.

Taurus stared at the spec that began to take shape as it drew closer and said, "It's a ship all right, sailing with no visible lights. That means one of two things–plague or pirates. Neither is good. Aurelius go below and inform the captain we have a suspicious ship approaching us."

Darius saluted and went below.

On the other vessel, a greasy man with a large red bandana wrapped around his head came up on deck from below and approached the helmsman. "This had better be good," he barked.

The helmsman replied, "It looks like a Roman merchant ship, Captain–a big one judging from its outline on the horizon. I steered toward it in case you wanted to take its cargo, since we haven't plundered any ships for awhile and we could use the haul," he added with a hopeful smile.

"A merchant ship, eh?" said the captain, as he strained his eyes to see. "They should be laden with all kinds of goods if they haven't unloaded them yet. I'll get the men ready for battle. Make sure no lights are visible on our ship. Hopefully, the merchant ship won't see us approach until it's too late.

We'll have to postpone our little pleasure cruise with the women down below for now. Maybe the merchant ship will have a few trinkets on board we can give them. That should put smiles on their faces."

The man with the red bandana smiled greedily, already counting the treasure he would obtain, as he went below to inform his men their pleasure would have to wait. What he did *not* count on was forty new Praetorians—young, well trained and eager to prove it, on board the merchant ship.

Darius returned on deck and told Taurus that he informed the captain. Taurus took another look and could make out that the approaching ship was still running dark.

A moment later the merchant captain joined them and asked, "What do you see, Centurion?"

"A ship heading for us with no lights. Looks like a liburnian[46]. Cretan pirates often use that tactic to avoid being spotted at night. If they drop their sails and pull alongside, they will attempt to board us. They'll kill those who resist and take whatever plunder they can, then sink us. When I was stationed here before, I knew of a merchant vessel that met that fate."

The captain's face showed concern.

Taurus turned to Darius and said, "Centurion, go below and prepare the men for battle just in case it is a pirate ship."

"What if the ship just passes us by?" Marcus asked.

"Then it will be a good drill for us," Taurus responded.

"Bucklers[47] for shields?" Darius asked.

"Yes, and bring me my ax," Taurus replied. "Go below now and get the men ready."

Darius quickly left.

The captain followed him and said, "I'll get my men ready as well."

Taurus nodded.

"How many men do you think are on that ship, Centurion?" Marcus asked.

Without hesitation, Taurus replied, "A liburnian can hold 100 men. If it's a pirate ship, it will most likely be half that many."

"You think it *is* a pirate ship?" Antonius asked.

"Yes. It appears to be steering directly toward us instead of just drifting if it were plague," Taurus replied.

They watched the approaching vessel for a few more minutes until Darius

---

46-A small galley ship used for raiding with two rows of oars
47-A small, round battle shield used for close combat

returned with the captain and the rest of the Praetorians.

Handing the double-edged battle ax and shield to Taurus, he said, "Your ax and buckler, Centurion."

The captain put his hand on Taurus's shoulder and said, "Centurion, my men are ready and will stay below until we know the intentions of the other ship."

"I'll have my Praetorians remain out of sight until we determine if those on the other ship mean to board us and which side they plan on boarding," Taurus stated. "Once they commit, I'll spread my men along that side of the ship. As soon as they come on board, we'll engage them."

The captain nodded. "My men will remain below, armed and ready if you need reinforcements. I'll go below now and inform them of the plan." The captain was about to leave when he turned back. "We are fortunate to have you Praetorians on board. If the other ship is a pirate ship, we'll have a little surprise for them."

Taurus's smile quickly turned serious. Turning to his men, he said, "Line up along the side of the ship and sit down with your backs to the rail. Take out your swords and keep your eyes on me. I'll give the signal to attack. No one does anything until then."

Every man nodded and took their positions as the approaching ship headed straight for them and dropped its sails. No doubt remained in Taurus's mind now; it was a pirate ship. Antonius and Marcus glanced nervously at each other as the pirate ship slowly came alongside. A few seconds later, grappling hooks sailed over. Landing with numerous "thumps" they scraped across the deck as the pirates quickly pulled them toward the side of the merchant ship. In some cases, Praetorians had to dodge the hooks to avoid being pinned against it. As the ships drew together, Antonius and Marcus could hear muffled voices on the other vessel. A moment later, a wave of pirates dashed across the gangplanks they placed between the two ships.

"NOW!" Taurus yelled.

His men jumped to their feet and fiercely attacked.

Surprised by the onslaught of well-trained defenders, the pirates quickly learned they had chosen the wrong ship to plunder.

Antonius's first adversary was a large, swarthy man missing his front teeth. Holding a curved sword, he snarled and swung his sword at Antonius. It caromed harmlessly off the buckler. Antonius crouched low and lunged with his gladius just underneath the pirate's rib cage.

"Uhh!" the pirate grunted, giving a look of surprise and pain as he fell to his knees and slumped to the deck. Yanking his gladius from the body, Antonius had no time to react to his first kill. Another pirate quickly sprang at him swinging his sword wildly.

Nearby, Marcus had his hands full. Fighting defensively against his ferocious opponent, he quickly realized he would be the one lying on the deck if he didn't end it. Remembering a move Antonius taught him, he quickly went on the offensive and struck the pirate on his wrist, severing his sword hand. The pirate's weapon clattered onto the deck, his hand still clutching the handle. Letting out a blood-curdling scream, the pirate grabbed his wounded arm. Marcus's gladius ended his misery, striking him between his neck and shoulder.

The battle raged on. Antonius quickly killed two more pirates and engaged another when one rushed him from behind. Seeing the man about to strike Antonius, Taurus hurled his ax. Tumbling end over end, the ax made a "woo woo woo" sound as it flew through the air. One edge penetrated deep into the pirate's back. He screamed in agony then dropped to the deck. Antonius turned just in time to see him fall then noticed Taurus draw his gladius and give him a nod. He acknowledged with a wave and looked for another opponent.

Suddenly, Antonius heard Marcus shout his name and noticed two pirates attacking him at the same time. Before he could assist, another pirate engaged him. Darius, who had just finished with an opponent, also saw Marcus in trouble. He smiled and turned to find another adversary.

The two pirates slashed furiously at Marcus, who tried his best to fend off their blows. Steadily, they backed him up to the side of the ship. They would either kill him or force him into the sea. Antonius finally dispatched his opponent, but not before Marcus was cut deeply on his arm by one of his attackers. Fortunately for him, his buckler and armor stopped most of the pirates' blows. Rushing over, Antonius engaged one of the attackers. A moment later, both pirates lay dead at their feet.

"Thank you," Marcus said, holding his lacerated arm and trying to keep the loss of blood to a minimum.

The battle was over and all but one pirate lay dead on the deck. The last survivor was the pirate captain in the red bandana. Realizing it was futile to continue, he threw down his sword and knelt at Darius's feet. Placing his hands on his thighs in submission, he surrendered in Greek.

Darius sneered and beheaded him with one quick swipe of his gladius.

Although the fighting had been ferocious, Antonius was shocked at Darius' callousness. Scrunching his face, he said, "You didn't have to do that.

He was surrendering."

Darius's clenched his teeth and snarled, "Don't ever dispute the actions of a superior officer!"

Antonius looked on in disgust, as Darius wiped the blood off his gladius.

Taurus glanced around and noticed three of his men had obviously been killed. The rest had significant to minor wounds, including Marcus. He nodded and said, "Well done, men. Aurelius, assign some men to take our dead below and see that the wounded are tended to. Tell the captain the fighting is over. I'll take a detachment of men and board the pirate ship to see if any more are left."

Darius nodded then escorted Marcus and the other wounded Praetorians below as ordered.

Taurus and the remaining Praetorians carefully made their way onto the pirate ship. Antonius started down below when Taurus said, "Wait! You could wind up with a spear in your chest. Someone bring me a lantern!" A Praetorian quickly produced one from the merchant ship and handed it to him. Cautiously lowering it into the darkened hold below, Taurus waited for a response. When there was none, he stuck his head into the opening and looked around. At the stern of the ship, he saw several silhouettes huddled together.

Taurus shouted in Greek, "Drop your weapons and come out; we will give you quarter."

"Like you did our men?" a feminine voice replied.

"You are women?" he shouted.

"Yes," came the reply.

"Are there any men with you?" he asked.

"No," the woman assured him.

Taurus slowly stepped down the ladder until the lantern shed enough light to reveal that the figures were indeed women, all scantily dressed and quivering. One woman with dark red hair stood brazenly in front of the group, holding a sword. The rest, armed mostly with daggers, bunched up behind her.

"We will not harm you as long as you put down your weapons," Taurus assured them.

"I know what you Romans do," the redheaded woman with blazing eyes replied. "You will make slaves of us all."

Pointing his gladius at her, Taurus replied, "Your men would have done worse to us. Is it not better to live and serve as slaves, than resist and die as plunderers and murderers?”

The woman remained silent.

Taurus was fierce in battle against hardened soldiers and pirates, but slaughtering civilian women was another matter. He would give them a way out and let them decided whether to live or die. Directing his remarks to the red-haired woman, he said, “I take no pleasure in killing women but if you refuse to surrender, we’ll burn you with your ship. The choice is yours.”

The woman looked around at her frightened companions. Without another word she dropped her sword on the floor and said, “We surrender.”

The rest dropped their weapons.

Motioning for the men on the ladder behind him to come down, Taurus said, “Pick up their weapons then search for any others they might be hiding then search the ship. When we have all who are on board, find some shackles to chain them together. There should be some on this ship.”

A brief search of the ship did reveal shackles the pirates used to secure their captured prisoners. The women sneered as two Praetorians chained them together. Leading them on deck, Taurus motioned for them to walk across the gangplank to the merchant ship. They began to cross with the redheaded woman in front. Looking up, she saw a sailor throw the pirate captain’s head overboard. “Roman swine!” she screamed. “May your enemies roast you alive!” Then she jumped off the gangplank between the two ships. The women chained to her were forced to follow one by one. Antonius tried to grab them, but the weight of so many bodies in chains were too much. Screaming and crying, the doomed women sank into the Tartarean sea. Taurus and his men watched in shock as the unforgiving waves claimed their last victim.

“Why did she do that?” Antonius asked, shocked by the redheaded woman’s last act of defiance.

Taurus shook his head. “I don’t know. Women have always been a mystery to me I’m afraid.”

“At least we don’t have to worry about them now,” Darius remarked. “The whores probably would have slit our throats if given the chance.”

Turning toward Darius, Antonius mumbled in a low voice, “They may have been whores, but they were somebody’s daughter or sister.”

Darius gave him a cold glance. “They were still our enemies, Licinius. Feeling sorry for them will only get you and others with you killed.”

Intervening, Taurus said, “All our enemies are dead now.” Turning to the rest of his men, he said, “Search the pirate ship, from top to bottom. Take anything of value for yourselves before we torch it."

Praetorians shouted their approval then hurried below to see what treasures they could find. After a thorough search, they returned to the merchant ship with jewelry and a few other trinkets of gold and silver they found.

A few sailors set the pirate ship adrift, then lit torches and threw them onto the deck. The liburnian quickly became a blazing inferno. Before long, the hungry sea swallowed the flaming vessel, leaving only a few remnants of burning debris on its surface.

As the Praetorians gathered around their fallen comrades below to say goodbye to their friends, some of them watched, feeling fortunate they were not the ones lying there.

Taurus allowed them a moment to express their feelings, then said, "Licinius, continue with your watch. Brucius, you take Flavius's place. We will be docking in Creta soon. Hopefully, the people there will be a little more hospitable."

Antonius went back on deck and was about to resume his sentry duty when Taurus approached and gave him a smile and solitary nod.

Antonius nodded back. He felt more confident after surviving his first battle, but the unexpected action of the pirate women jumping to their deaths somehow took away all the glory he had imagined. As he walked across the deck, he noticed the numerous crimson bloodstains and was thankful they weren't his. Returning to the bow, he met up with Brucius and they began to talk about the battle. Hearing someone approaching, they turned with their spears ready to meet the threat.

Marcus smiled and put up his hands. "Don't worry, I'm not a pirate."

Antonius furrowed his brow. "You should be below having your wound tended to."

"I just needed a bandage. Thanks, Brucius. I'll finish the watch," Marcus replied.

"Are you sure, Flavius? You were wounded."

"It isn't bad; I can take over."

Brucius shrugged his shoulders. "Well, if you insist." He then handed Marcus his spear and went below.

"That was a nasty cut," Antonius said, looking at the blood seeping through the bandage on Marcus's arm. "I thought you would stay below."

"It's just a scratch." Marcus replied, not wanting Antonius to know how painful it was. He paused for a moment then looked out to sea. "Antonius."

"Yes?"

"We killed those men," Marcus said, as the realization of what had just occurred fully hit him.

"We had to, Marcus. It was like the wolves in Blera. Kill or be killed."

"But these were men." Marcus shook his head. "I didn't even have time to think about it. It happened so fast."

Antonius placed his hand on his friend's good shoulder and said, "I'm just glad you weren't seriously injured or killed."

Marcus grinned. "So am I."

Realizing they had better get on with their duty, they turned and walked their assigned posts. Marcus proceeded to the middle of the ship and vomited over the side.

****

Gray skies and thick rumbling clouds appeared the following day, hiding the sun. After the morning meal, the surviving Praetorians assembled on deck to honor their fallen comrades.

"Praetorians, remove your helmets and let us pay one last tribute to those who are no longer with us," Taurus ordered.

After everyone had bared their heads, Taurus looked up in the sky. "Mars, God of War, if you can hear me, we return three of your warriors to you. May they go to Elysium with the other valiant ones. We now release their bodies to the sea and hope their families will remember them well."

A detail of sailors slid the covered, weighted bodies over the side as somber Praetorians watched their brothers sink into their watery graves.

The ship arrived at the port of Gortyn later that day. After picking up provisions and dropping off Darius and his detachment, it departed the next day without incident

As Darius watched the merchant vessel fade out of sight, he couldn't help but remember a painful memory that had tortured him for many years. The incident with the liburnian was not Darius's first time dealing with pirates.

When he was a young boy of nine, he was on another ship with his parents. His father was a Tribune assigned to the Roman Prefect in Egyptus and was sailing there to assume his duties with a century of men.

Late one night, a pirate ship approached, similarly to the ship that approached the merchant vessel. Because it was another new moon and cloud cover hid the stars, the sentries didn't spot the vessel until it was upon them. Darius and his family were below at the time and heard a commotion on deck. His father recognized it as the sound of battle and drew his gladius. He turned to his wife and child with a concerned look and said, "Keep the door locked until I return." He put his ear to the door for a moment then opened it and ran out. He never returned.

Darius remembered huddling in the corner with his mother as they heard ferocious shouts and painful screams coming from above. Then all went quiet. Trembling as she held her son tight, his mother stared wide-eyed at the door. Hearing several footsteps approaching, she told him to hide under the bed and pushed him as far back as he could go. A moment later, the door came crashing open. His mother uttered a yelp and shrank back in the corner. All Darius could see were four pairs of dirty feet rushing into the room. He heard a snicker then saw the tip of a curved sword one of the men lowered. Blood was slowly dripping down the blade. Darius felt his heart beating faster than it ever had before. He watched in horror as the dirty men forced his mother to the floor then took her, one after the other. He still remembered her terrifying screams.

When the last man finished, he callously plunged his dagger into her heart.

Darius looked into his mother's eyes as precious life flowed out of her body. They were pleading eyes, but they would plead no more. Darius lay there, unable to move. It was as though a large slab of stone pressed down on his body, forcing the blood to his head.

After the dirty men left, a whimper escaped his mouth. He kept looking at his mother's face, unable to take his eyes off her. Waiting until he could hear no more voices, he slowly crawled from under the bed. Kneeling by his mother, he put his hand on her cheek and began to cry. Then he heard a crackling sound and a faint odor of smoke wafted into the room. He stood up and hurried to the door. Peeking out, he noticed smoke billowing from above. He ran over to the wooden steps and sprinted up, barely feeling each one as he went. Once on deck, he saw the pirate ship pulling away. Fire was everywhere and dead bodies littered the deck of the ship. His father was one of them. As the flames threatened to engulf him, he ran to the side and jumped into the burning sea.

Seeing a ship on fire in the distance, a Roman trireme that happened to be in the area, headed toward it. By the time it reached the sinking vessel, the pirate ship had vanished into the black night. The trireme picked up only one survivor, a young boy with burns on his neck and jaw.

CHAPTER XI-CAESAREA

The next several days passed without incident, but bad weather threw the merchant ship slightly off course. On the last day of the voyage, the sun appeared as though it was rising from the depths of the sea. Every man on board was happy to see it, after a brief storm tossed them about like a cat playing with a dead mouse. The cry of "Land, ho!" was especially a welcome relief to those whose stomachs were unsettled. Gathering near the bow to catch a glimpse of their final destination, Praetorians and sailors stood side by side, glad that their journey was almost over.

"There! There is Judaea!" Taurus exclaimed, pointing at the land coming into view.

As the ship drew nearer, they could see several large towers looming in the distance with numerous masts jutting out between them. Gliding into the harbor, it pulled up to the large pier and moored.

"All right, scorpions!" Taurus yelled. "Get your things and assemble on the dock!"

After retrieving their knapsacks and kits, they disembarked then formed ranks. A bearded man, dressed in a tunic toga robe tied with a gold sash in the middle and a gold band around his head, immediately approached them. "You are the Praetorians sent from Rome?" he asked.

Taurus looked at him suspiciously and replied, "Yes. Who are you?"

"I am Demosthenes, a humble servant of his Excellency Pontius Pilate. I will escort you to the palace if you will allow. It is just down this road."

Taurus gave him an upward nod then said, "Very well." He then turned to his men and shouted, "Form two ranks!" When they had lined up, he said to Demosthenes, "Lead the way."

Demosthenes bowed then turned and proceeded down the coastal road to the palace with Taurus and his men close behind.

Pilate's palace stretched from well inland out to the edge of a small peninsula that extended into the sea. High walls surrounded the enclosure with walkways where Pilate had posted guards on the parapets to be on the alert for any approaching danger. Guards were also posted at the only gate.

Demosthenes waved to the guards at the gated entrance who opened the gates, then he led Taurus and his men through the courtyard and inside the palace proper. Walking down a few hallways, he came to two large double doors flanked by guards and stopped. "Wait here while I announce you to his Excellency."

Taurus nodded.

One of the guards then opened a door and allowed Demosthenes to enter.

A moment later he appeared and said, "His Excellency will see your centurion now in the judgment chamber."

Taurus turned to his men and said, "Wait here." He then entered the chamber with Demosthenes.

Striding up to Pilate, he saluted and said, "Lucius Sejanus sends his best wishes, Governor, along with three contuberniums of Praetorians."

"Ah, Sejanus kept his promise," Pilate exclaimed with a smile. "What is your name, Praetorian?"

"Centurion Taurus, Governor," Taurus replied.

"Centurion Taurus, my servant will familiarize you with the palace while I attend to other matters. I will meet with you later and go over your duties. You may take your leave now." Pilate said, waving him away.

Taurus slightly bowed and said, "I will await your summons, Governor."

Demosthenes stepped forward and said, "Come, Centurion. I will show you where you and your men will be quartered."

After leaving the judgment chamber, Taurus and his men passed through a few corridors then entered a spacious hall containing nearly 500 bunks lined up in rows of ten.

Turning to Taurus, he said, "We usually accommodate visiting soldiers from Syria or the Antonia fortress here. This will be your barracks. As the one in charge, you can have your own room just down the corridor. I assume you would prefer that?"

"Yes, I would," Taurus replied. He turned to his men and said, "You men choose a bunk close to the entrance; I'll return shortly."

Demosthenes motioned for Taurus to follow him, while Antonius, Marcus and their comrades looked around at their new quarters.

Proceeding down the hall a short distance, Demosthenes stopped and opened the door to a small room. "You can leave your things here, Centurion, while I'll take you to meet Prefect Liberius. He is the Palace Prefect and will be your commanding officer."

After Taurus had dropped off his knapsack and kit, they walked farther down the hall until they came to a large wooden door with a nameplate that said, "Palace Prefect."

Demosthenes knocked.

"Yes? What is it?" a voice bellowed from behind the door.

Demosthenes replied, "The Praetorians have arrived, and their Centurion is here to see you as you instructed, Prefect."

"Send him in," came the reply.

Taurus entered the room and stood at attention. A stocky man in his mid-forties sat behind a dark wooden table with papers strewn about and a helmet on one corner.

"Centurion Taurus of his majesty's Praetorians reporting for duty," Taurus declared, saluting smartly.

Liberius looked up and said, "Stand at ease, Centurion."

"Thank you, Prefect," Taurus replied, taking a more relaxed stance.

"I was told you would be arriving earlier this week. What caused your delay?" Liberius asked, seeming slightly annoyed.

"A little bad weather, but we also ran into some pirates near Creta," Taurus replied stoically.

"Pirates?" Liberius stated, narrowing his eyes slightly. "Yes, I've heard stories about pirates that operate around Creta. You must have defeated them since you are here."

"The sea rats made the mistake of attacking a ship with Praetorians on board," Taurus stated with a slight smile.

"Well, down to business," Liberius said gruffly. "Since you have been assigned directly to the governor as his bodyguards, I will be your commanding officer. Your orders will come from me, the governor, or his wife and no one else. Pilate often travels to Jerusalem but he prefers being here in Caesarea to avoid the religious zealotry there. You will provide the escort for him as well as any security needed whenever he or his wife goes to Jerusalem. Occasionally he takes trips into Caesarea for recreation. He attends plays at the amphitheater and chariot races at the hippodrome located next to the palace, so be prepared for that as well."

"One of my men raced his chariot at the Castra and did quite well," Taurus stated.

"Just make sure he pays attention to the governor and not the races," Liberius warned him.

"I'll make sure he does, Prefect. How have the people here reacted to Roman rule?" Taurus asked.

Liberius sat back in his chair and said, "The Jews, for the most part, have accepted their lot as a conquered people. Occasionally, however, suicidal zealots will try their hand at fame and martyrdom by attempting to kill Romans, so keep your men on their toes. You brought twenty-four men with you, correct?"

"Twenty-two," Taurus replied. "I lost two assigned here to the pirates."

Liberius snorted and said, "I'll have to adjust your posts." He made a notation on a scroll, then said, "You will be responsible for your men's training, fitness and discipline. If any of your men get out of line, I expect that you'll have them scourged. I have little tolerance for disobedience."

Taurus nodded. "I will see that my men behave themselves."

Liberius gave Taurus a quick glance and replied, "No doubt you will. I will expect a copy of your duty roster every day, so I know where you've posted your men. How you rotate their watches is up to you, but it is imperative that the governor has protection at all times. You will assign two men as the governor's personal bodyguards to remain close by him wherever he is, two men outside the doors of the judgment chamber, and two men outside the door to the governor's living quarters at all times. Here is a diagram of this palace and another diagram of the palace in Jerusalem," Liberius said, handing two documents to Taurus. "Familiarize yourself with both of them so they're committed to memory. Any questions?"

"When should I begin assigning my men to their posts?" Taurus asked.

"I'll give you a day to become familiar with the palace before you have to post your men. Any other questions?"

"No, Prefect."

"In that case, welcome to the land of leprosy and camel dung," Liberius quipped.

Taurus saluted and left the room. Returning to Demosthenes, he said, "I would like to brief my men now so take me back to where they are housed."

Demosthenes nodded and led the way.

Before Taurus entered the barracks, Demosthenes said, "I have some information for your men if you would allow me to share it with them."

Taurus nodded. Entering the barracks, he shouted, "Attention, Praetorians! The Greek here has some information to pass on to you."

After giving Taurus a disparaging glance for not referring to him by name, Demosthenes began. "Again I am Demosthenes," he said, accentuating his name, "and it would do well for you to remember it and familiarize yourselves with your surroundings. As soon as you are ready, I will take you on a tour of the palace." He then turned to Taurus.

Seeing that his men had already claimed their bunks and put their equipment underneath, Taurus said, "They're ready."

Demosthenes gave Taurus a nod then said, "This way, then if you will,

Praetorians."

As they walked through the palace, Antonius and Marcus were impressed with what they saw. The late king, Herod the Great, had spared little expense in providing himself with the luxuries that Roman governors and their supporting staffs now enjoyed. The palace was similar to a huge Greco-Roman mansion with a private bathing pool, tropical courtyards, and numerous plushly decorated staterooms. The conscript barracks adjoining the Praetorian barracks housed 3,000 men. They were mostly conscripts from Syria and Samaria, with a few Roman Centurions in charge. After the tour concluded, Demosthenes led Taurus and his men back to their barracks.

"The time is yours, Centurion, until the governor calls for you," Demosthenes stated. "There is one other thing I should mention," he added.

"What is that?" Taurus asked.

"A banquet will be held in the palace gardens tomorrow. Many Jewish officials and members of the Jewish hierarchy will be attending. You and your men will need to provide close security for the governor and his wife," Demosthenes related, waiting for a possible outburst because of the late notice.

Taurus squinted and asked, "When will the festivities take place?"

"On the sixth hour," Demosthenes replied.

"That doesn't give us much time to prepare," Taurus said with a scowl.

"I'm sorry, Centurion, but you were expected a few days sooner, and the invitations have long been sent. Will you be able to provide the governor's security or should I tell him his conscripts will have to do it?"

Taurus didn't want Pilate to think Praetorians couldn't adapt at a moment's notice. "I'll provide it," he replied with a stoic look.

"If you will come with me, I'll show you where the gardens are," Demosthenes stated.

"Lead the way," Taurus commanded.

The next morning Taurus strode into the Praetorian barracks and shouted, "On your feet, scorpions!"

Twenty-two men scrambled out of their bunks and stood at attention.

Taurus took a deep breath then announced, "The governor is holding a banquet in the palace gardens on the sixth hour. Our job is to provide his security. I will come and get you in the fifth hour and assign your posts, so finish your morning meal then remain in the barracks until I return. The dress will be battle uniforms with scutums and pilums. The banquet is your first official assignment here in the palace, so make me proud. Any questions?"

"No, Centurion!" came the response.

"Good." Taurus turned sharply and departed.

After finishing their meal, the Praetorians anxiously prepared for their first official detail. Antonius and Marcus were busy cleaning their equipment when one of their comrades walked over to them.

With a serious expression, he said, "Licinius and Flavius, I have something to say to you."

"What is it?" Antonius asked, expecting a criticism.

The Praetorian looked down then back up. "In training, Aurelius told us that you two were dangerous and would cost some of us our lives if we ever went into battle. After seeing how you fought against the pirates, I think Aurelius was wrong. The rest of the men here feel the same. I just wanted you to know that." Without waiting for a response, he quickly turned and walked away.

Antonius and Marcus looked at each other and smiled.

On exactly the fifth hour, the barracks door flew open. Before anyone had a chance to yell attention, Taurus shouted, "Make sure your uniforms are in order and report to the gardens immediately! Licinius and Flavius, you will be the governor's personal bodyguards. Watch for any threats but don't interfere with the governor's movement—swords and daggers only for you two, pilums and shields for the rest. Any questions?"

When no one responded, Taurus shouted, "Well, don't stand there like piles of horse dung, line up!"

A short while later, twenty-two Praetorians dressed in their impressive black-leather-trimmed armor stood at their posts. Their uniforms, shields, and pilums, along with glaring expressions, made their very presence appear intimidating.

Soon, local dignitaries began to arrive. Pilate, dressed in his most brilliant white toga with freshly pomaded hair, stood near the entry to the gardens. He held a small golden scepter in his hand to impress upon everyone that he was most assuredly in charge. After his guests had exchanged insincere greetings with him, they entered until eventually the line dwindled down to one small man dressed in a gray robe. He approached and bowed then reached inside his robe, pulling out a large dagger still in its sheath.

Antonius and Marcus immediately drew their swords and jumped in front of Pilate, ready to pounce upon the man when Demosthenes shouted, "No, no, he means no harm! This is a gift meant for his Excellency. I was told he would present it to him."

They quickly sheathed their swords and returned to their places on either side of Pilate, while the man's eyes returned to their normal size. He said a few words and handed the dagger to Pilate, who removed it from its sheath made of leather. The curved dagger had various semi-precious stones on the iron pommel and handguard, and a carved handle made out of ebony wood.

Pilate nodded his pretended approval but inside he despised it. He would have been impressed with precious gems and gold, but he was dealing with belligerent pious people who hated Romans. The unimpressive bestowal was probably meant to insult him.

The man presenting the dagger quickly bowed again then hurried off.

Pilate leaned over to Demosthenes and said, "Perhaps next time, it would be good to inform the bodyguards that someone will be presenting these types of offerings."

Demosthenes blushed and said, "Yes, Excellency. I do apologize."

After all the guests had arrived, they drank and ate their fill then listened to Pilate's new plans for Romanizing Judaea. When he had concluded his speech, they thanked him for the dinner then left with the notion that Romanizing their country would come with a cost. That meant higher taxes.

****

That night, Antonius and Marcus decided to visit the city to see how palatable Judaean wine was. They left the palace and followed the main road into Caesarea just as dusk began to fall. After walking a short distance, they noticed four Roman army soldiers ahead at the side of the road. A man lay on the ground at their feet. One soldier kicked him, shouting, "Get up, Jew dog! Get up!"

As the man tried to rise, another soldier pushed him back down with his foot. "I didn't say you could get up; he did." The other soldiers laughed as Antonius and Marcus approached.

"Is there trouble here?" Antonius asked.

Looking at Marcus and Antonius with contempt, the largest one said, "Take your leave, Praetorians. This matter does not concern you."

It was then that Antonius noticed they were all Centurions.

To his surprise, Marcus boldly stated, "Do you think it is fair that four armed soldiers should beat one unarmed old man?"

Antonius leaned over to him and whispered, "Marcus, they are Centurions. You don't question them, remember?"

The largest Centurion snarled and said, "You dare challenge a superior officer, boy? Perhaps I should teach you a lesson." He followed the remark by drawing his gladius.

Antonius and Marcus instinctively started to reach for their swords, when a voice down the path shouted, "Have you men lost your senses? Is one Jew's life worth a Roman's? Sheathe your swords and stand down!"

Antonius and Marcus turned to see Taurus' familiar face.

"Who are you?" the large Centurion asked.

"Centurion Taurus of the Praetorian detail assigned to guard the governor. Are you men from the palace?"

"We are Centurions over the auxiliaries," the large one replied belligerently.

Taurus nodded slightly. "If the governor learned you were trying to pick a fight with his Praetorians, he'd probably have you flogged. I would look for action elsewhere if I were you. Perhaps of the female kind."

The four Centurions looked at each other and smiled. One said, "He's right, Florian. Why waste our time on this old Jew when we could better spend our time with his daughter?" They all laughed and headed down the road, but the large Centurion looked back. "You little boys were lucky your centurion came, or we would have shown you how *real* soldiers fight."

"Pay him no heed," Taurus said as the four proceeded farther down the road. "He is an ignorant swine and will probably live a short life with that mouth of his."

Antonius and Marcus nodded and helped the old man up.

"Thank you," the man said, brushing off the dust. "I thought they were going to kill me."

"You speak Latin," Taurus stated, surprised at the man's literacy.

"Yes, I have studied Greek, Latin, Hebrew and Aramaic," the old man replied.

"Ah, a learned Jew. Who are you and where do you live, old man?"

"I am Jacob Itsak, and I live not far from here just down the road."

"I suggest you make haste then. You shouldn't be out past dark anyway," Taurus warned him.

"I was on my way home when those men accosted me," the old man explained.

Taurus lifted his head slightly and said, "A word of advice; next time you see Roman soldiers approach, give them a wide berth."

The old man put out his hands and said, "They came up from behind. I didn't even notice them until they were upon me. I am lucky you men came. I have seen others beaten to death by Roman soldiers."

"We are Roman soldiers too, you know," Taurus said.

"Yes, but you are different. I could tell when you helped me. You care about others. Those men did not." Pointing down a connecting road, Jacob said, "I live down this road in the dwelling with the white door. Thank you again for helping me. If I can ever be of assistance, you have but to ask."

"How could you help us?" Taurus asked. "And why would you want to? We are Romans, and you are a Jew."

Jacob smiled. "In God's eyes, we are all brothers."

"You believe in the gods?" Marcus asked.

"I believe in one God," Jacob replied.

Marcus' eyes grew bigger. "Do you believe in an afterlife?"

"Yes," the old man admitted. "If you would like to know more about my beliefs, I would be happy to share them with you."

"Perhaps another time," Taurus interrupted, as he gave Marcus an impatient look. "Now, we have wine to drink and women to please."

"As you wish," the old man said as Taurus hurried his charges away.

While the three continued down the road, Marcus asked, "Do you believe in an afterlife, Centurion?"

Taurus raised one eyebrow and said, "I believe in this life. Why do you ask, Flavius?"

"Oh... I am just curious," Marcus replied.

Taurus' response was quick. "Well, be more curious about your swordsmanship. Remember, you nearly lost your arm in our battle with the pirates."

Marcus nodded and rubbed his bandaged arm.

"What was that one big soldier's name?" Taurus asked.

"Florian," Antonius replied.

Taurus nodded. "I used to have a horse named Florian. It was a mare."

Antonius and Marcus laughed so hard they nearly fell over. Regaining their composure, they wiped the tears from their eyes and continued into the city with Taurus shaking his head.

After traveling a short distance, they came to a sizable structure called, "The Dancing Goat Tavern.," complete with a picture of a dancing goat.

"This looks as good a place as any," Taurus declared, opening the door. As the three walked inside, they noticed it appeared to be a popular gathering place for soldiers assigned to the palace as several were there. After they found an empty table, a heavyset middle-aged woman came over to take their order.

"What will you three have?" she asked bluntly.

Before Antonius and Marcus could say anything, Taurus replied, "Your finest wine for the three of us."

Antonius and Marcus looked at him with wide eyes.

"Do you want a large or small amphora?" the lady asked.

"A large amphora," Taurus replied, "and none of that watered down swill."

"It will cost six bronze," she said with a bored look.

"It does not matter. Bring the wine, woman." Seeing that his companions appeared concerned, he said, "Don't worry, you plebians, I'll pay for it."

His companions both exhaled in relief.

Gazing about the crowded room, they noticed the four Roman Centurions from the road.

"It looks like our friends are here," Antonius remarked.

"Ignore them," Taurus said. "We came to drink and enjoy ourselves."

However, Marcus and Antonius couldn't help but notice that all the other soldiers in the room were glaring at them.

"Why does everyone keep staring at us?" Marcus asked.

Leaning forward, Taurus put his elbows on the table and clasped his hands. "When you wear the uniform of a Praetorian, you'll find that regular soldiers either envy us or feel our duty is too easy. No matter where we go, the reaction is the same. Get used to it."

Suddenly the big centurion stood up from his table and walked over.

He curled his lip and said, "You Praetorians think you are like the gods, don't you? You can go where you want and do what you want. Well here, we don't step aside for men who think they are better than us. A Praetorian bleeds just like any other man. This is our tavern; you Praetorians are not welcome here."

Taurus gave the large centurion a puzzled expression. "You and your friends own this tavern?"

The large soldier stood there with a blank look for a moment, then said, "Perhaps you should stick to drinking with the governor, shiny head." He turned and smiled at his companions, who chuckled.

Taurus smiled and said, "Perhaps you should stick to picking on old men who can't fight back, you putrid pile of pig dung."

The large centurion's face twisted into a scowl. Drawing his gladius, he snarled, "You dog of a..."

His words went unfinished. Taurus instantly drew his dagger and thrust it deep into the large man's abdomen. The stunned man looked down at his stomach then back up at Taurus before crumpling to the floor. All the other soldiers in the tavern quickly stood up and grabbed the hilts of their swords, including Antonius and Marcus.

Taurus, however, remained seated. Reaching down, he yanked his dagger from the dead soldier and wiped the blood off on the dead man's tunic. He then stood up and loudly proclaimed, "I am Centurion Taurus of His Majesty's Praetorian Guard. I am a master with the gladius, dagger, pilum, bow, and axe. My companions are just as skilled, or we wouldn't be Praetorians. We didn't come here looking for trouble; we simply wanted to drink and enjoy the rest of the evening. But if you would rather have us spill your blood than our wine, we will happily accommodate you."

"WHACK!" went the dagger as he plunged it firmly into the solid oak table top. It sounded like someone chopping wood, and everyone in the room flinched slightly. Taurus then drew his gladius. Marcus and Antonius drew theirs as well.

"Now, who wishes to be the next to die?" Taurus asked, calmly looking around the room.

The challenged soldiers glanced at each other to see who would take him up on his offer. Then, one by one, they released the grip on their swords, sat down and returned to nursing their drinks.

Taurus, Antonius, and Marcus sheathed their swords and sat back down as well. The dead soldier's three companions cautiously came over. After glaring at Taurus, they dragged their dead companion outside.

"That will be eight bronze," their server said, plunking the large jar of wine down. "Six for the wine and two for the mess."

Taurus paid her without argument and removed his dagger from the tabletop. After re-sheathing it, he poured the wine.

"We're sorry for the trouble," Marcus said to the woman, as she wiped the blood from the floor.

She looked up with a tired face and replied, "I would rather have you killing each other than killing us."

Taurus raised his mug and said, "To Rome!"

Antonius and Marcus raised their mugs and echoed his toast. Then they drank the wine that cost eight sesterces and one life.

Later, as they left the tavern, Marcus turned to Taurus. "When all those soldiers stood up, I thought we were in trouble."

Taurus snorted. "Most soldiers usually don't want to fight a Praetorian. The large fellow was an exception. I told you his mouth would be his end."

****

The next day, an auxiliary centurion appeared at Liberius's office. He was one of the centurions at the tavern and was there to file a complaint. Liberius sent for Taurus.

"You wanted to see me, Prefect?" Taurus asked, after saluting.

"Yes," Liberius replied. "This centurion says three Praetorians murdered his companion last night. What do you know of this?"

"He was one of them!" the centurion exclaimed, pointing an accusatory finger at Taurus.

Taurus gave him a dismissive look. "To set the record straight, I was the only Praetorian who killed the man in question. He approached our table and said we were not welcome and told us to leave. He drew his sword, so I drew my dagger and defended myself. Praetorians Licinius and Flavius were with me and can testify as to what happened."

"Well I saw you stab my companion without provocation," the auxiliary centurion snapped.

"I thought you said all three of us killed him," Taurus replied calmly.

"Yes, all three of you, I meant," the centurion quickly added.

Taurus smiled. "It appears that one of us is lying. Why don't you and I go outside and settle this with our swords, Centurion?"

Liberius put his hand up. "I don't think that will be necessary." Turning to the complainant, he said, "Centurion, if the dead man had stayed at his table, none of this would have happened. Inform your men to get along with our Praetorians. We have enough people here who want to kill us without turning on each other."

The centurion sneered at Taurus. "If you will talk to your men, Centurion, I will talk to mine."

Taurus nodded.

Liberius stood up and said, "Thank you for informing me of this incident, Centurion. I'll make sure the word gets passed."

The auxiliary centurion saluted and walked out of the room.

Liberius gave Taurus an irritated glance. "Write up a report and have it on my desk today."

"As you wish, Prefect," Taurus replied.

As he saluted and turned to leave, Liberius said, "Tell me, Centurion. Did this man really deserve to die?"

Taurus stopped and turned around. "I had no choice. If I hadn't killed him, he would have killed me. Besides, the man was a pig."

Liberius waved him off then muttered, "Most soldiers are," as he dug his finger in his nose.

CHAPTER XII-RACING AND RELIGION

The racing season in Judaea had started and Antonius was pleased to learn Praetorians would also be guarding Pilate at the local chariot races. Since it was customary for the Roman governor to hand out the awards at each race, Pilate had an obligation to attend.

After arriving at the Caesarean hippodrome and escorting Pilate and Procula to their seats, Antonius and Marcus took up their posts along with the other Praetorians.

As the chariots entered the track, Procula turned to Pilate and asked, "Who do you think will win today, Pontius?"

"Does it really matter?" Pilate replied sardonically. "I wish a few of our Roman charioteers were here. They'd show these pagans a thing or two."

Liberius, who sat on the other side of Pilate, said, "I understand that one of your Praetorians raced back in Rome."

"Really?" Pilate perked up. "Which one?"

Turning to Taurus, who stood next to him, Liberius asked, "Which one of your men raced his chariot in Rome, Centurion?"

"Praetorian Licinius, Prefect. Just races in the Castra," Taurus replied.

"Which one is he?" Pilate asked.

"Praetorian Licinius!" Taurus shouted.

Turning around from just below where Pilate sat, Antonius replied, "Yes, Centurion?"

Taurus turned to Pilate and said, "He's our charioteer, Governor."

Pilate leaned forward and asked, "You raced chariots in Rome?"

"Uh, yes, Governor, but I only raced at a local track near my home and the Castra Praetoria."

"Were you any good?" Pilate asked.

"I won my fair share of races, but I only raced bigae[48] not quadrigae[49]," Antonius replied.

Pilate rubbed his chin then turned to Liberius. "I think it would be good for us to have a charioteer representing Rome in these races. Perhaps I should purchase a chariot of my own and have the young Praetorian here drive it for me. What do you think, Procula?"

"An excellent idea, Pontius. I would have someone to cheer for."

48-*Chariots with two horse teams*
49-*Chariots with four horse teams*

"Then it is settled." Turning to Demosthenes, Pilate said, "After the race, put out the word that I am looking to purchase four of the fastest and strongest horses then find me a good chariot builder. I want to proceed with this as quickly as possible while we still have a racing season left."

"It shall be done, Excellency," Demosthenes replied.

Taurus immediately motioned for Antonius to turn back around.

Before the beginning of the race, the announcer introduced Pilate to the audience. Their reaction was a small amount of applause. Then he introduced the charioteers. As he named each one, the charioteer's fans roared their support, easily exceeding the response shown to Pilate. They hailed from Syria, Samaria, Phoenicia, Greece, Judaea and one from Cypress, owned by a merchant in Caesarea. His charioteer's name was Sargon. A merciless and intimidating man, Sargon had already caused the deaths of a few charioteers who seriously challenged him. His ruthless reputation branded him as one to avoid during the race. As set by the rules, the chariots lined up with the winner of the previous race beginning on the inside lane. Since Sargon always won, he always started on the inside.

After the preliminary announcements concluded, the chariots took their positions. When all were lined up and ready, the starter dropped the mappa and six chariots charged down the track as the crowd cheered.

Pilate watched more intently now while they sped around the oval track, kicking up dust and cinders high in the air. As predicted, the other charioteers held back to avoid confronting Sargon. He remained in the lead throughout the rest of the race until the Greek driver in the red chariot saw an opening on the inside. Bravely, he made his charge. But Sargon had intentionally left the opening for him. When the red chariot came along side, Sargon swerved hard, forcing it into the spina. The Greek tried to rein in his horses, but he reacted too late. His inside wheels disintegrated from contact with the concrete sides of the spina and the red chariot tumbled over and over, throwing the driver onto the track. Gasps arose from the stands, as horses' hooves and chariot wheels pounded his body unmercifully.

Procula covered her eyes and Demosthenes grimaced at seeing one of his countrymen trampled to death. Antonius swallowed hard.

That evening while he reclined on his bunk, he thought about the Greek charioteer. These were not friendly races he'd been accustomed to, and he wouldn't be racing a two-horse team with friends or other Praetorians. He would be racing a four-horse team against charioteers who most likely would want to kill him. Representing all of Rome even made him more nervous.

As he thought about Pilate's offer to be his charioteer, Marcus thought about Jacob's offer to share his views about the afterlife. He couldn't dismiss the idea and decided to see what the old man had to say about it.

The next morning, he put on a tunic and told Antonius he was going for a walk in the city since he and Antonius didn't have a post to stand until the evening.

"Wait and I'll go with you," Antonius offered.

Marcus put up his hand and said, "Actually, I would rather go by myself."

Antonius furrowed his brow. "Are you sure? Remember, Taurus said we shouldn't leave the palace alone."

"I'll be all right. I won't wear my uniform or weapons, so no one will know I'm a Roman soldier."

"Be careful," Antonius warned.

"I will; I'll be back before we stand our posts," Marcus assured him.

"At least tell me where you're going so I'll know where to look if you haven't returned before then."

"Marcus tightened his lips then said, "I'm going to see the old man who was beaten by those centurions. I just want to ask him a few questions."

Before Antonius could say another word, Marcus hurried out of the barracks. A short while later, he walked down the road that led to Jacob's house. After finding the white door, he knocked. Receiving no response, he turned to leave as Jacob approached him from the road. "Did you wish to see me?" he asked.

"Yes," Marcus replied. "You said you would share your beliefs with me."

Not recognizing him at first, Jacob said, "I'm sorry, but you are unfamiliar to me. When did we speak?"

"I was one of the Praetorians you spoke to after the four Roman soldiers assaulted you the other night," Marcus replied.

Jacob smiled and nodded. "Yes! I remember. You look different without your helmet and uniform. Come in."

Opening the door to his small two-room dwelling, Jacob said, "I'm afraid I live quite simply compared to what you are probably used to. Would you like some water?"

"No, thank you; I'm not thirsty," Marcus replied as he walked in. He noticed a few blankets and a pillow lying on a simple, wooden-framed bed, a small stool, and a table with an oil lamp. A tall cabinet stood in the corner across the room. Jacob's furnishings were not that dissimilar to his. As he looked for a place to sit, Jacob pulled up a stool. "Sit here. I can sit on the bed. What is your name, young Roman?"

"Marcus Flavius. Yours was Jacob, as I recall."

"You have a good memory. Now, what would you like to know, Praetorian Marcus Flavius?"

Gazing solemnly into the old man's eyes, Marcus asked, "You said you believed in an afterlife. What exactly do you believe?"

Jacob smiled. "If you really want to know about the afterlife, there is one who can explain it far better than I can. His name is Jesus and he lives in Nazareth. I was told he will be preaching in Beth-haggan today. Would you like to go and hear him speak?"

"I suppose. Would it take long to get there?" Marcus asked.

"If we ride, maybe a half day there and back. I have a friend who has camels. I'm sure we could borrow them."

Marcus hesitated. "I don't know. I've been told the people here hate Romans. What if they find out I am one?"

Jacob cocked his head and said, "How would they know unless you tell them?"

Marcus knew it was risky, but something inside told him to go.

"Very well, talk to your friend who owns the camels, but I have to be back before dark," Marcus stated.

After obtaining their means of transportation and riding until shortly past midday, they reached Nazareth. As they entered the town, they noticed a crowd had congregated around a man wearing a simple white robe. They seemed to be listening intently to what he had to say.

Jacob pointed and said, "Oh good, he hasn't left yet. The man who speaks is Jesus."

They dismounted their camels, walked over, and listened. Jesus spoke for awhile longer until he told the crowd he had to go and excused himself. He then started to leave with a small group of men as the crowd dispersed. Jacob ran up to him and bowed. "Pardon us, Master, but my companion wishes to know about the afterlife. Couldst thou but spare a moment?" Drawing nearer to Jesus, he whispered, "He is a Roman and does not speak our language."

Jesus turned and smiled at Marcus. "What dost thou wish to know?"

"Is it real?" Marcus asked.

"As real as I am," Jesus replied.

"What is it like?" Marcus asked.

Jesus smiled kindly and said, "Those who live righteously will be in paradise. Those who sin and do not repent will be cast into purgatory."

"What do you mean if they do not repent of their sins?" Marcus asked.

"They must ask God for forgiveness and forsake the sin," Jesus replied.

"What is paradise and purgatory?" Marcus asked.

"Follow me and I will teach thee," Jesus replied.

Marcus shook his head slightly and said, "I can't."

Jesus put his hand on Marcus's shoulder and stood there for what seemed like eternity gazing into his eyes. They were kind eyes and Marcus felt a warmth flow into him.

Finally, Jesus spoke. "My time here is short young Roman and I have much yet to do," he said softly. "Yea, the time runs short for both of us. Make good use of the time that is allotted thee and remember this: All who take the sword shall perish by it. There are others who will perish for speaking the truth. Someday, we both will make a great sacrifice. Prepare thyself for that day as I have."

He turned and departed leaving Marcus wondering.

Marcus turned to Jacob and asked, "What did he mean, 'We both will make a great sacrifice?'"

Jacob shrugged and said, "Sometimes he speaks in ways that are hard for those not close to the spirit to understand."

Marcus lifted his head slightly and said, "I probably should get back to the palace."

Heading back to their camels, Marcus said to Jacob, "Tell me more about this paradise and purgatory."

As they traveled back to Caesarea, Marcus asked many questions about Jacob's beliefs and felt comfortable with the answers he received. Upon entering the barracks just before dusk, Antonius gave him a slight lambasting. "You cut that pretty close. I was just about to get ready for our duty."

"Sorry," Marcus apologized, "it took longer than I thought it would."

Well, did the Jewish old man answer all your questions?" Antonius asked as they hurried and put on their uniforms.

Marcus smiled and replied, "Enough for now."

****

A few weeks later, Taurus marched into the barracks. "Licinius! Report to the stables."

Antonius gave him a wary look. "This isn't a cleaning detail, is it?"

Taurus frowned. "Pilate wants to personally show you his new chariot and horses."

"Should I put on my uniform?" Antonius asked.

Taurus shook his head. "No, just your tunic will be fine."

"Do you think he'll want me to take the chariot out today?" Antonius asked with hopeful eyes.

Taurus raised his eyebrows and replied, "Possibly. Now hurry and don't keep the governor waiting."

Antonius jumped up and ran to the stables. Upon arrival, he saw Pilate stroking the neck of a milky white stallion. Three identical running mates stood in their respective stalls next to him.

Antonius stopped and snapped a salute. "Praetorian Licinius reporting as ordered, Governor."

Pilate smiled then pointed to the horses. "Meet my new adopted children, Praetorian."

Antonius nodded slightly and said, "They are magnificent, Governor."

Pilate rested his hands on their stall. "I think they'll beat any team in Judaea if you learn how to control them. I have named them Mars, Jupiter, Mercury and Pluto."

Antonius smiled. "I named my two horses back home Mercury and Mars."

"Ah, it is an omen!" Pilate exclaimed.

"Have you seen them run yet, Governor?" Antonius asked.

"Of course. The owner brought them here from Cappadocia and demonstrated their abilities against another team before I purchased them. They have been trained to race and the owner felt they were ready. I hope he is right, since I spent a small fortune on them. Jupiter seems to be the most spirited. If you can make him perform to his best, the others should follow his lead. Come, I will show you the chariot."

Pilate led Antonius over to an area next to the stall. A stableman hurried and removed the covering, revealing the small racing chariot. The body and wheels were painted gold with silver spokes and hubs. On each side was a wooden circle showing an eagle standing on a block that said "SPQR."

"The chariot is magnificent, Governor," Antonius said, looking at it with equal eagerness and delight.

"The builder used willow and cypress, so it is light." Pilate then looked Antonius over. "How much do you weigh, 240 libras? 250?"

"The last time I weighed at the Castra Praetoria I was 245, Governor."

"Let's get you down to 235. It would be better if you were at 230, but you would have to starve yourself and you'll need stamina to control the horses and win the race."

"As you wish," Antonius replied.

Turning to the trainer, a man by the name of Galbo, Pilate commanded him to hook up the horses to the chariot. "We'll test it on the track and see if the gold I paid for everything was worth it."

Galbo immediately had two stablemen bridle the horses then fit them into their chest harnesses. Under the watchful eye of Pilate, they backed them into the chariot and fed the reins through their eye fittings, connecting the harness straps to their respective brass clasps on the yoke. When they finished, they nodded to Pilate.

"Now, let us proceed to the track. I am anxious to see how you handle them, Praetorian Licinius. Take Galbo, my trainer, in your chariot and I will ride with Prefect Liberius in another."

"As you wish, Governor," Antonius replied.

After stepping onto the chariot and waiting for Galbo to join him, Antonius gave the reins a sharp snap. The jolt he received from his team both surprised and pleased him.

Entering the hippodrome located just outside the palace wall, both chariots pulled onto the track and stopped. Pilate stepped down from his chariot and turned to Antonius. Looking up at his new charioteer, Pilate said, "One last word of advice. Do not be timid with them or you will lose control. You are their master, so let them know you are and they will respond the way you want them to. Take them out slow for the first lap and let them stretch their legs, then give them their heads on the second and let's see how you do. I will watch from here. Remember, you are handling four now, not two."

Antonius nodded, then gave the reins another snap and started around the oval track. He could tell the horses wanted to go faster but he kept them reined in to a trot. After the first lap, he gave them their heads, yelling, "Run, Jupiter, Mars, Mercury, Pluto!" The horses responded immediately and flew down the track as though their tails were on fire. Keeping his team tight on the inside, Antonius completed the lap and thundered past Pilate and Galbo.

The trainer turned to Pilate and smiled. "I think you have yourself a charioteer, Governor!"

****

Three weeks went by quickly. The evening before the race, a solitary figure sneaked into the royal stables and went directly to Pilate's chariot. With some effort, the man worked the linchpin out of the axel holding the wheel and replaced it with a defective one that was nearly sawed through. The saboteur sneaked back out undetected.

The next day, throngs of people came to the hippodrome for the race.

They heard that Pilate had entered a chariot and were anxious to see how good the Roman charioteer was and if he would meet his fate on the track. Rumors spread that the other charioteers made bets to see who would cause his demise.

After entering the hippodrome, Pilate went to the stables to give Antonius some last words of encouragement. As he approached, Antonius stood at attention and saluted.

"How do you feel, young Praetorian?"

"Anxious to race, Governor."

"Eagerness is good. Now remember, driving a chariot is like painting a picture. If you control the brushes well, you will paint a masterpiece. Your horses are the brushes and you are the artist. Is my meaning clear?"

"Yes, Governor. I will heed your advice."

Pilate gave Antonius a solitary nod then walked over and patted each of his stallions on the neck. "Run well, my children, and there will be a reward in your buckets tonight."

Turning to Galbo, Pilate asked, "Any words of advice for our young charioteer?"

Galbo nodded. "One thing you should keep in mind at all times, Praetorian. The other charioteers will show you no mercy, so do not let your attention stray or you will wind up under their wheels. Here is a curved knife called a falx. I will attach the knife in its sheath to your chest. Should your horses become separated from the chariot and you are pulled from it, use the knife to cut the reins, but make sure you don't free yourself in front of another chariot."

Antonius gave a serious half nod and said, "I'll remember that."

Taurus, who escorted Pilate to the stables, said, "Represent Rome well, Praetorian," then followed the governor out.

Pilate had barely taken his usual seat when a middle-aged man approached coming down the stairs.

Taurus stopped him and said, "You can't enter this area."

The man put up his hands and said, "I am only a humble merchant who wishes to wager on the race with his Excellency. I have no weapons. You can search me if you want," the middle-aged man with a salt and pepper beard replied.

Turning to Pilate, Taurus said, "Governor, this merchant wishes to wager with you on the race. Should I let him pass? He carries no weapons."

Pilate gave the man a curious look then asked, "Who are you, merchant?"

The man smiled. "My name is Abaddon, Excellency. I heard you have a chariot in the race and I would like to wager that my chariot will be victorious over yours."

Pilate glanced at him with narrowed eyes and asked, "A wager, eh? Which chariot is yours?"

The merchant smiled. "The black one with the black stallions, Excellency."

Pilate laughed. "Your charioteer is a brute! No wonder you want to wager on him. He has the inside position and never loses."

Pilate rubbed his chin then said, "All right, I will make you a wager. I'll bet one hundred silver pieces on my chariot to beat yours."

"Are you sure you would not like to wager one hundred gold pieces?" the merchant suggested, wringing his hands.

Pilate smiled. "This is only his first race. Perhaps next time."

"Very well. The bet is one hundred silver pieces," Abaddon said, his tone hinting of disappointment. He returned to where his servant stood and said, "The Roman governor must not be too sure of his driver. Place wagers with everyone you can who bets on the Roman. Give good odds to encourage them. Pilate just might need another charioteer after this race."

The servant quickly departed. At the same time, Pilate instructed Demosthenes to go around and boast that Antonius had won many races at the Circus in Rome. Then he was to anonymously bet on the merchant's chariot, with one taker just in case the young Praetorian charioteer fared badly.

In the stables, Antonius finished putting on his xystis[50] and watched closely as Galbo attached his knife then checked the harnesses and chariot fittings, making sure everything was secure. When he completed his inspection, he stepped back. "They are ready to run, Praetorian."

A race attendant, holding several colored scarves, approached Antonius and looked at his chariot. "Since your chariot is mostly gold, I will give you the golden scarves, Praetorian. Tie them around your upper arms." He handed them to Antonius and departed to disseminate the other scarves to the rest of the charioteers.

Antonius tied his on then nervously stepped onto the chariot. Taking a deep breath, he thought, "This is my chance for glory. I must not fail."

Seconds later, trumpets sounded. Eight chariots then proceeded onto the track, hailing from Phoenicia, Phrygia, Galatia, Cappadocia, Syria, Cypress, Judaea and Rome. After taking a slow warm-up lap, they entered the starting gate and took their positions. Since Antonius was the newest entry,

---

50-A long garment charioteers wore, fastened at the waist with a simple belt

he was assigned the outside position. The announcer made his usual pre-race announcements as Antonius nervously awaited the start.

From his ominous-looking black chariot and horses, Sargon gave him a defiant sneer. Antonius glanced at him then turned back to the front and focused on the starter's arm as he raised the mappa. The crowd went silent as they also watched the starter's arm. The horses interrupted the silence with their snorting and whinnying, as they pleaded with the charioteers to let them run. When it seemed like the race would never begin, the linen floated like a feather from the starters hand. Charioteers shouted for their steeds to run and the crowd roared their delight as thirty-two horses leapt forward with flaring nostrils and pounding hooves.

As expected, Sargon took the lead and made the first turn slightly ahead of the silver chariot and blue chariot. Antonius slowly passed one chariot after the turn and gained on the next two, running side by side down the straightaway. After taking the second turn, he overtook them slightly. By the end of the first lap, Antonius was already in fifth place. As he made the next turn, one of the chariots he passed caught up and turned into his chariot, trying to force him back outside. He recovered and continued down the straightaway. On the following turn, Antonius maneuvered in front of the same chariot. The driver over-corrected and the momentum tipped his chariot over. Breaking free from the team, it tumbled over and over, finally hitting the outside wall. The driver lay motionless on the track as the crowd gasped. Several men waited for the other chariots to pass then ran out to retrieve him. The lapkeeper tipped another metal falcon down from its rod perch, ending the second lap. Antonius passed the next chariot on the straightaway and was in fourth place as he went into the turn. He gained a little more ground, bringing his horses even with the front of the blue chariot as they charged down the straightaway. On the turn, the driver of the blue chariot tried to steer into Antonius's chariot, causing the wheels of the two chariots to rub together. Antonius recovered again, snapped the reins and sped down the straightaway. For the next two laps, the black chariot remained in first, with the silver chariot in second and the blue chariot in third, holding Antonius to fourth place.

As the sixth lap began, Antonius managed to pass the blue chariot on the straightaway. After the next turn, he started to gain on the silver chariot. Remembering his lesson at the Castra about pacing his horses, he waited for the last lap before giving them their heads. At the turn, he was neck and neck with the silver chariot. As they rumbled down the track before coming to the next turn, Antonius snapped the reins hard and shouted, "Now, Jupiter!" The silver charioteer steered into Antonius to force him further outside, but Antonius held his ground and on the next turn passed him. The crowd was shouting wildly as Antonius began to gain ground on the black chariot. As he drew near, Sargon turned to him and shouted a curse in his native tongue. He then steered sharply to the outside, causing his chariot to strike one of Antonius's wheels. The defective pin finally snapped and the wheel disintegrated causing the chariot to hit the spinae and break loose from the team. As the reins had been secured tightly around Antonius's arm, his team continued to pull him along the track with the other chariots following closely behind. A vicious crowd screamed for his blood, chanting, "Kill the Roman! Kill the Roman!"

Procula and Pilate both gasped when they saw Antonius's chariot break apart and their Praetorian about to be trampled to death.

Sargon looked back, confident in his victory but wanting to witness the destruction of the brash young Roman. As he approached the final turn, Antonius remembered what the stableman had told him about using his falx to cut the reins. But he was being pulled in front of five other chariots. If he cut the reins, he would surely be crushed. As he approached the turn, he decided what he must do. Removing the falx from its sheath, he readied it to cut the reins as he bounced along the track. When his team went into the final turn, he slashed at the leather straps wound tightly around his arm and freed himself, letting the momentum of the turn roll him to the outside of the track. The other chariots flew by, missing him by only inches. He hit the stonewall surrounding the track hard and felt himself losing consciousness. When he came to, he looked up and saw Taurus standing over him.

"Licinius! Licinius, can you hear me?" Taurus shouted.

All Antonius heard were the loud cheers of the crowd, ringing in his ears. "Am I alive?" he muttered.

"Yes, you're alive," Taurus replied. "Can you stand?"

"I think so," Antonius replied as he stood up, wobbling a little.

Taurus grabbed him by the arm and said, "You were lucky you rolled out of the way. A chariot almost took off your head. Are you all right?"

"Yes, just a little dizzy," Antonius replied, putting his hand to his head.

Taurus walked him over to the side of the track as Pilate, Procula and Liberius made their way down, accompanied by their Praetorian escort.

"Thank the gods you are alive," Pilate exclaimed. "For a moment, I thought you would be crushed to death. When you cut the reins and rolled out of the way on the last turn, there was so much dust I couldn't tell if you were trampled or not. But you don't appear to be badly injured."

Antonius looked himself over and said, "Just a few scratches. The chariot is ruined I'm afraid. I'm sorry, Governor. I will win next time; I assure you."

Just then, Demosthenes came up to Pilate and whispered to him, "Excellency, the merchant wishes to know when you will pay him the agreed upon wager."

"Have him come to the palace after the race and pay him," Pilate whispered back to him.

Demosthenes bowed and left.

"Well, let's go and give the victors their due," Pilate said, drearily.

Liberius and a Praetorian escort accompanied Pilate and Procula to the winner's circle where the awards were presented. On the way, Demosthenes came up to Pilate and whispered, "You won ten silver pieces from the wagers, Excellency."

Pilate snorted.

After handing out the usual awards and uttering a few insincere words of congratulations, Pilate turned to Liberius and bellowed, "Take me back to the palace!"

As Procula waited in their carriage, she said, "It was too bad about our charioteer's showing, but I like him, Pontius. I think he will win next time. He seems to have... gravitas."

Pilate sat down beside her and remarked, "Yes. I have a feeling he will be quite an asset for me in the long run."

"For us," Procula interjected.

"Yes, my dear, I meant for us," Pilate corrected himself.

****

The next day, Taurus watched Antonius and Marcus spar during their free time. Walking over to them, he said, "Licinius, come with me. I want to try something new with you."

"What about me?" Marcus asked.

"You're my archer. Practice with your bow," Taurus shouted back.

After finding a secluded spot on the palace grounds, Taurus turned to Antonius and said, "This is good. Now, I know you can handle a sword with your strong hand; let's see how you are with your weak hand."

"What?" Antonius asked.

"Put your sword in your other hand," Taurus ordered.

Antonius switched hands.

"Now," Taurus began, tipping his head up slightly. "Suppose you are fighting an enemy. He cuts you on the arm or hand that holds your sword and you cannot use it any longer."

"Then I am a dead man," Antonius replied.

"Not if you can fight with your other hand. A worthy enemy will try to disarm you if he can't kill you outright. Knowing how to fight with both hands might save your life someday. Even the best get cut. When you have foes coming at you from all different directions, it is almost inevitable. If you are badly wounded on your normal fighting arm, you can still continue to fight if you know how to use your weak hand. Are you up for it?"

Antonius smiled. "I'm up for it," he said, accepting the challenge.

Taurus took a stance across from him and said, "Now, just apply what you've learned with your strong hand and do the same with the other. Let's walk through a few basic moves."

Antonius gave him a nod and said, "I'll try."

Taurus gave him a deadly serious look and said, "Those who only try, die Licinius. If you believe you *can* do something, you will do it!"

Antonius nodded.

They squared off and began to spar. At first, they ran through the basic movements slowly. After an hour, they became a little more fluid. After two hours, Taurus picked up the pace.

Stopping for a moment to catch their breath, Taurus said, "You have a gift, Licinius. Your reflexes are the fastest I've ever seen." He rubbed his chin and said, "Let's see how fast they are."

With a puzzled look, Antonius followed him over to where Marcus was shooting at a target attached to a vertical hay bale.

Nodding to Antonius, Taurus said, "Go down and stand by the target. Flavius, when he's in place, I want you to put an arrow in the center of the hay bale."

"I don't understand," Antonius said.

Taurus smiled. "Before the arrow hits the target, I want you to grab it. Do you think you can do it?"

Antonius was about to say, "I'll try," but remembered Taurus's admonition. Instead he showed a determined look and said, "I'll do it."

He ran down to the hay bale and shook his arms to loosen them up. He then went into a slight crouch and gave a nod he was ready. Calling out to Marcus, he said, "Remember, you're shooting at the target and not me!"

Marcus grinned then drew the arrow back and lined up his bow with the target. When he was sure his aim was true, he let the arrow fly. Antonius's eyes narrowed as he concentrated on the flight of the arrow. The arrow seemed to glide to the target in slow motion as he followed its flight. At the last second, he reached out. Looking down in his hand, he saw the arrow in his grasp. The tip was an inch from the target.

Marcus's jaw dropped.

Taurus smiled. "This exercise will also help you to be proficient when you have a weapon in both hands, like your gladius and dagger. That can help when you're facing two attackers."

"I'll remember that," Antonius assured him.

****

For the next few months, Antonius practiced with Taurus in secret until he was proficient with either hand. At the end of one session, Taurus said, "I think you have the hang of it now, but continue practicing with both hands."

"Thank you, Centurion," Antonius exclaimed. "There is one thing that puzzles me, though. Why have you singled me out for this training?"

Taurus glanced at his gladius. "Everyone needs a protégé he can pass his secrets down to. I won't live forever and the others don't have your skill. But, of course, I didn't say that." He smiled and walked away.

The next day, Taurus gathered the off-duty Praetorians for their usual gladius training. Giving Marcus a glance, he said, "Today we'll work on fighting two men at a time."

Marcus remembered the two pirates who attacked him at the same time on the ship and wished he had that training before then.

"Here are some basics about fighting two men at a time when you're alone," Taurus began. "Whenever two adversaries engage you, first watch your opponents as they approach. If they have been trained well, one will try to engage you from the front, while the other one will try to get behind you. What is the next thing you should do?"

"Make sure no one can get behind you," Antonius replied.

"That is correct. And how do you make sure no one can get behind you?"

"Make sure there is a wall or tree behind you," Marcus added.

"Very good. Now, well-trained soldiers will still try to flank you, which is why you must eliminate one as quickly as possible. It is best to pick the weaker or less skilled adversary and attack him first before they attack you at the same time."

"How can you tell which one is weaker cr less skilled?" Marcus asked.

"Watch them. Study their faces. If one looks more confident, he probably is the better of the two. Look for nervousness. Is one trembling? Do you see fear in his eyes? Is one perspiring more than the other? These are signs to watch for. They will tell you which one to attack first."

All the Praetorians nodded.

"What if they both just rush you and you don't have time to tell which one is the weakest?" Marcus asked. "That happened to me when the pirates attacked us."

"Then do your best and hope someone comes to assist you."

Marcus nodded and looked at Antonius.

"What if you are in the open, and there is nothing you can use to protect your back?" Antonius asked.

"Wait for them to split up, then quickly go on the attack against the weaker man and try to put him between you and your other opponent. Now, you two come at me and I will demonstrate for the rest. Remember, your swords aren't training swords and they're sharp so a tap on the armor will do."

Antonius and Marcus smiled at each other and began to circle him. Since they were in the open, Taurus waited for them to get far enough apart then sprang at Marcus, keeping to the side away from Antonius. Quickly registering a kill on Marcus, Taurus turned to Antonius and defeated him after a longer exchange.

Slightly out of breath, Taurus stated, "Timing is critical when you're in the open. If you attack one man too soon when the other is close, you will be fighting both of them at the same time. Sometimes that happens anyway and you'll have to use both your gladius and dagger to defend yourself as best you can. Again you must determine who the weaker opponent is and try to get rid of him as quickly as you can. Licinius! Let's see if you learned anything. Albertus and Erasmus, attack him."

The two began to circle Antonius, as he waited for them to distance themselves from each other. When the distance was sufficient, he immediately attacked Erasmus. After registering a kill on Erasmus and thwarting Albertus's assault, he turned on Albertus and defeated him.

"Like that?" Antonius asked, giving his opponents a look of consolation.

"Yes. Exactly like that," Taurus replied. "Flavius! You're up. Crispus, Golthius, you be the attackers."

Two more Praetorians came forward and began to circle Marcus, who studied them for a moment. Turning to Taurus, he said, "What happens when you have to fight two men who both look confident?"

Taurus smiled. "Then use your bow and don't let them get close."

Laughter filled the courtyard.

Marcus took his turn, but the outcome was less successful for him, as one Praetorian put up enough resistance to allow the other to register a kill. Marcus nodded after he felt the sword hit his armor and said, "Next time I'll use my bow on you two."

More laughter rang out until Taurus curtailed it with a gruff announcement. "We'll continue with this exercise every day until it becomes second nature to all of you. Now form into groups of three and practice it."

For the rest of the training period, two fought against one until everyone felt fairly confident in being able to handle multiple attackers. The training session would prove to be invaluable later on.

CHAPTER XIII-THE NAZARENE

In Rome, Julia had not lacked for suitors, thanks to her parents. However, no one interested her enough for a serious relationship and she told her parents she wouldn't marry if she didn't love the man they chose. So far, she didn't. She couldn't get the handsome young Praetorian she met at the promotion ceremony off her mind. As she sat in her bedroom, wishing he had been stationed in Rome, an idea came to her. It was a daring idea, too outrageous to propose, but Julia decided to propose it anyway.

That evening, as her family gathered around the table for their supper, Julia said, "You know, my birthday is coming soon and I thought of a wonderful gift you could give me, Father."

"What is that?" Sidonius asked.

"I would like to see a little more of the world outside of Rome. I thought it might be interesting to visit Uncle Taurus in Judaea."

"Judaea?" her mother exclaimed. "That country is on the other side of civilization! I'm afraid your father doesn't have the time on his hands to waste on that type of trip to a backwards country, Julia."

"I know he is busy, but Serina could go with me."

Serina shook her head. "Oh, no! Don't include me in your plans. I get seasick when we sail on the coast."

Sidonius shook his head and said, "Traveling across the sea by yourself is out of the question, Julia."

Not about to give up on her outrageous proposal, Julia said, "Then have Domitia accompany me."

"Two women in a far off country... I still don't like it," Sidonius shook his head.

"Then send Vergilius as well. Uncle Taurus would see that nothing happens to us and I'm sure he would be thrilled to have a member of his family visit him. He must be terribly lonely, being so far away."

"If I know your uncle, I would be quite surprised if he was lonely," Sidonius said, raising his eyebrows.

Juliana gave him a disapproving look.

"Perhaps her reason for going is to see that Praetorian she met at the confirmation banquet," Serina suggested.

Julia gave her sister a scowl. Now she had to play down her interest in the dashing young Praetorian who showed an interest in her.

"I met many Praetorians that night," she countered, hoping that her tone deflected suspicion.

"Wasn't he the handsome one who waved to you when we left?" Serina asked with a teasing smile.

Ignoring her, Julia said, "I want to see how other people live... their culture, their attractions... just something different from Rome."

Sidonius wasn't moved. "I still don't like the idea," he said with a stone face.

Julia turned to her mother with pleading eyes.

Clasping her hands together, Juliana said, "You know, when I was a young girl, I went on a trip to Greece once. This was before I met your father."

"I didn't know you visited Greece," Julia said, as Sidonius gave her his full attention.

"Yes, I traveled with my mother and your uncle. We went by ship one glorious summer. We had heard so much about the Greek culture that we wanted to see it for ourselves. I shall never forget the many wondrous sights we saw. So, you see, my dear, I do understand your desire to see the world. I'm just surprised that you would choose Judaea over Egypt or Greece."

"But Mother, Uncle Taurus is in Judaea. He could show me the sights and protect me while I'm there."

"From what I've heard there are not many sights to see in Judaea other than camels and sand," Sidonius commented.

Juliana saw through her feigned reasons and could have sided with her husband but she thought it would be good for her daughter to experience other cultures like she had. And, perhaps a brief fling with this Praetorian she seemed enamored with would encourage her to marry a suitable young man when she returned home. Her brother would certainly see that she was well chaperoned at all times. Turning to Sidonius, she said, "I think we should allow her to go on this trip, as long as Domitia and Vergilius go with her."

But Sidonius would not give in. "The Jews in Judaea are not as passive as the ones in Rome from what I've heard. It could be dangerous. And besides, if we let Domitia and Vergilius go with her, who will do the work that is needed in the villa?"

"We can hire someone to do the cooking and cleaning. It would only be temporary," Juliana replied, which made Sidonius heave a heavy sigh. He could see, however, that his wife was not going to side with him and he would wind up being the ogre that forbade his daughter to spread her wings. Taking a deep breath, he said, "Very well. If she wants to go that badly she can. But only if Domitia and Vergilius accompany her."

"Oh, thank you, Father!" Julia exclaimed, jumping up from her place and hugging him tightly. "All will be well; you will see." She gave her mother an appreciative hug as well, along with a soft "Thank you."

After dinner, Julia heard a knock on her bedroom door.

"Julia, it is Serina. May I come in?"

Still upset at her sister's attempt to sabotage her trip, she replied, "I don't know if I should let you in or not."

Serina opened the door and stood halfway in. "I'm sorry, Julia. I suppose I was just jealous that you were going to a far off land and I would be stuck at home by myself."

"You could have gone with me," Julia reminded her.

Serina gave her a sarcastic look and said, "You know how sick I get on the sea. I probably would have died before we reached land."

Julia smirked and said, "Yes, I remember."

Sitting down on Julia's bed, tears welled up in Serina's eyes. "At least you have someone who is interested in you."

Julia put her arm around her little sister and said, "You have me, Serina. You will always have me. Besides, you'll have suitors when you're older."

"I know, but you are prettier than I am," Serina pouted.

Julia furrowed her brow and said, "You shouldn't talk like that, Serina. You are pretty, but you're still very young. It won't be long before young men will show interest in you."

"You think they will?" Serina asked in a soft, high-pitched voice.

"Yes, I do," Julia replied. Standing up, she pointed to the door and said, "Now go and let me brush my hair so men don't think I am your ugly older sister."

Serina smiled and gave Julia a hug. "You are the best sister anyone could have. Forgive me for what I said at dinner?"

"Of course I forgive you, now go," Julia said, feigning anger.

Standing up, Serina gave Julia one last hug, wiped her eyes and departed.

Alone again, Julia sat down and began to brush her hair. "Will you be the one, Antonius?" she wondered.

The next day, her mother began making arrangements for Julia's trip. She sent Vergilius to the shipping office to obtain a schedule of ships bound for Judaea and when they returned. She would also have to inform her brother so he could arrange lodging. She decided to have Sidonius send him a dispatch as soon as the shipping lanes opened and schedule Julia's trip two months afterwards to allow him time to receive it. Julia and her two servants would leave for Judaea the end of June.

****

On April first, Pontius Pilate was in Jerusalem for the Jewish celebration of Passover. He sat in the judgment hall with Antonius and Marcus flanking him as his guards and had been ruling on matters of law requiring the death penalty. He had already condemned a man named Bar-Abbas for murder.

"What is next on the docket?" he asked Demosthenes.

"Excellency, the Sanhedrin have brought another criminal for you to judge. His name is Jesus of Nazareth."

Marcus, who had been looking straight ahead as trained, now glanced at Demosthenes.

"What has this man done?" Pilate asked.

"They claim he has been preaching sedition against Rome," Demosthenes replied.

"Very well. Bring him in," Pilate barked.

Demosthenes opened the entry doors and said to the waiting assemblage, "The governor will see you now."

Two large men pushed a shackled man in. Wearing torn and bloody clothes from being beaten by henchmen of his accusers, Jesus appeared exhausted but had a gentle look in his eyes. Members of the Sanhedrin followed closely behind.

"Why have you brought this man before me?" Pilate formally asked.

Joseph Caiaphas, the chief priest, stepped forward and pointed back at the prisoner. "He is a malefactor and should be judged by thee."

Pilate raised one eyebrow. "Then judge him according to your law."

Caiaphas shook his head. "He claimeth to be our king but Caesar is ruler over us. By your law he preaches sedition."

Pilate looked at the shackled man. "Do you claim to be the King of the Jews?"

Jesus raised his head and answered sarcastically, saying, "Did thou learn this of thyself or did others tell it to thee?"

Pilate replied, "Am I a Jew? Your own countrymen have delivered you unto me and accused you of claiming to be their king. What do you say?"

Jesus replied in a tired voice. "My kingdom is not of this world. If it were of this world, then would my servants fight to deliver me from the hands of those who seek my destruction. Dost thou see any here to rescue me?"

"Are you a king then?" Pilate asked again.

Jesus looked at Pilate with piercing eyes and said, "Thou sayest that I am a king. To this end was I born, and for this purpose came I into the world, that I should bear witness unto the truth. All who are on the side of truth will listen to my voice."[51]

Pilate guffawed and said, "Indeed, what is truth?" He then turned to the priests. "I find no fault in this man other than being delusional."

But Caiaphas's jaw was set. "But he preaches sedition! He should be condemned to die!"

"He may be mad, but I find no evidence of sedition against Rome here. Clearly, you want him crucified because of religious offenses not political ones. He is in Herod's jurisdiction so let Herod condemn him."

A murmuring arose from the Sanhedrin, but they knew better than to argue with Pilate. Roman consent had allowed them to continue their religious leadership over the people and Roman consent could be removed. Caiaphas turned and stormed out of the chamber, saying only to his entourage, "Bring him!" They roughly led Jesus out.

Herod, however, was not as big of a fool as Pilate had hoped. He remanded Jesus back to him later that day.

Demosthenes approached Pilate and said, "Excellency, the Sanhedrin delegation has returned with the Nazarene."

"What? I told them to take him before Herod Antipas!" Pilate growled.

"They did, Excellency. Herod sent them back to you for a ruling," Demosthenes stated timidly.

"I suppose I will not be rid of them until we conclude this matter," Pilate muttered. "Send them in."

"As you wish," Demosthenes replied with a bow.

Pilate scowled as he watched them enter. The man they wanted crucified would have to be popular with the people if he was speaking out against Rome. His execution could lead to civil unrest. Then an idea came to him on how to solve the whole issue. It was customary on Passover to release a prisoner of the people's choosing. He turned to Antonius and Marcus. "Sentries, escort the accused to the balcony where the people can see him."

Antonius and Marcus took Jesus by the arms and led him out. As they did, Jesus turned to Marcus and gave him a sad smile.

Pilate followed them out and observed the crowd that had gathered in the esplanade. In a loud voice, he cried, "People of Judaea! It is the custom of your Passover to have a prisoner released. Therefore, I give you a choice.

51-John 18: 30-38 King James Bible

I can release the man named Bar-Abbas who has committed foul crimes against you, even murder, or I can release this man Jesus whose only crime is claiming to be your king. What say you?"

Since the Sanhedrin had made sure most of the crowd there thought Jesus was a blasphemer, the result was inevitable. "Crucify him!" they yelled.

Pilate cursed silently. He still felt uncertain about crucifying this man. Again he faced Jesus and asked, "If you are not of this world, from whence do you come?"

His question was met with silence.

"Speak up, man," Pilate exclaimed. "Don't you know I have the power to crucify or release you?"

Jesus quietly replied, "Thou couldst have no power over me except it were given to thee from above. Therefore, those who deliver me unto thee have the greater sin."

Caiaphas could see that Pilate was stalling. Coming forward, he asked to speak with him privately. Taking him aside, Pilate asked, "What do you have to say to me, Priest?"

Caiaphas chose his words carefully. "Excellency. The matter before thee is most serious to us. Give us this man's life and we will take full responsibility for the consequences. If you free him, word might reach Caesar that you refused to punish a man who preached sedition against Rome. I'm sure Caesar would not view that well." Putting the final touch to his threat, he narrowed his eyes and said, "Crucify the Nazarene."

Dripping with sarcasm, Pilate asked, "Shall I crucify your king?"

Caiaphas replied smugly, "I have no king but Caesar."

Pilate glared at him then turned to Demosthenes. "Bring me a basin." Looking down at the crowd, who continued to chant, "Crucify! Crucify!" he wished he could crucify the lot of them.

A moment later, Demosthenes appeared with the basin of water. Washing his hands in full view of the crowd, Pilate shouted, "I am innocent of this man's blood! However, if it will appease you..." he turned to Liberius and said, "Take the prisoner out, scourge[52] him then crucify him."

The crowd cheered as Pilate dried his hands.

"What would you have inscribed on the cross's plaque, Governor?" Liberius asked.

Pilate looked at the condemned man. "Put, 'This is the King of the Jews' in Latin, Greek, and Hebrew, so that all may know who he claimed to be."

Liberius saluted then ordered two Praetorians at the entry door to take

---

52-Whip

the prisoner out. "Find a Centurion for the auxiliaries and tell him to assign a quaternio[53] to carry out this man's sentence."

Marcus desperately wanted to ask Jesus what he meant by the sacrifices he foretold that both of them would have to make, but he could not abandon his post. He was afraid the meaning was going to die with the man.

After stripping Jesus down to his undergarment to add to the humiliation, a soldier tied him to the whipping post used for public floggings. Taking a few steps back, he readied the flagrum[54]. The crowd went silent as they waited for the piercing "Crack!" from the whip. Animosity was evident in the eyes of most who had gathered while sorrow and compassion showed in the eyes of a few.

During the verberatio[55], Jesus winced in agony as each of the thirty-nine lashes from the whip tore into his flesh. After the brutal beating, Jesus slumped to his knees in shock when they untied him from the whipping post. A man from the crowd threw a crown of thorns on the ground before him, saying, "He claimeth to be king; let him wear a crown!"

A soldier picked it up and placed it upon Jesus's head, pressing it down to make sure the thorns drew blood. Two soldiers then laid the stipes[56] across his lacerated back for him to carry. They marched him through the city and up the hill to Golgotha then drove large spikes through his flesh as they nailed him on the cross. Hours later, when his body finally succumbed to the pain and agony, he released his last breath. The skies immediately grew dark and a great storm commenced. No one had ever witnessed a greater storm in all the land.

In the palace, replacements relieved Antonius and Marcus from their posts. As they walked down the palace hall on their way back to the barracks, they heard the deafening lightning and thunder outside.

"What do you think is happening?" Antonius asked.

Marcus gave him a worried look and said, "I don't know. It's almost as if the gods are angry."

Antonius gave him a doubtful look and facetiously said, "Maybe the gods are angry because this fellow whom Pilate crucified spoke out against Caesar and Rome."

Marcus shook his head. "I was told he only spoke out against the religious leaders. That is why they feared him and wanted him dead."

53-*Death squad consisting of four men who scourged then crucified the prisoner*
54-*A whip consisting of three tendrils, usually having metal or bone fragments on the ends*
55-*The severest form of scourging that sometimes resulted in death*
56-*The main wooden post used for crucifixion*

"Do you think his death will cause the people to revolt?" Antonius asked.

Marcus thought for a moment. "No, I don't think so. He told the people to love even their enemies. Many thought of him as their Savior."

"Love your enemies," Antonius stated with a snicker. "How can you love someone who is trying to kill you?"

"From what I was told by the old man we met, love will save the world," Marcus remarked.

Antonius guffawed. "You can choose love if you want to, but I choose a sharp gladius and a well-balanced pilum as my saviors."

Marcus wasn't sure that love would save the world, but he wasn't convinced that weapons of war would save it either.

****

For the next three hours, there was a great upheaval in the earth and the midday sky turned so black that people were afraid to even move. Then the rain came down in torrents.

When the strange occurences had abated somewhat, Demosthenes approached Pilate once again. "Excellency, the Sanhedrin are here again and ask for an audience."

Pilate closed his eyes and shook his head. "What do the pious priests want now?"

"They said they must speak with you on a matter of grave importance."

Pilate exhaled a long breath and said, "Very well, send them in."

As the high priests entered the judgment chamber, Caiaphas stepped forward and said, "Your Excellency, the man Jesus thou didst crucify..."

Pilate put up his hand. "You mean the man *you* had crucified."

"As you wish, Excellency, but we have a predicament now."

"Oh? What is your predicament, Priest?" Pilate snarled.

"This man's followers claim he will be resurrected in three days. They say his disappearance will prove he is the Son of God. We are afraid they will remove his body from the sepulcher then say he was resurrected. We humbly ask thee to have your soldiers guard the tomb, so the criminal's disciples cannot remove his body."

Pilate looked at him in amazement. "Don't you have guards of your own to manage the task?

"Yes, Excellency, but if the man's followers see Roman soldiers guarding the tomb, they are much less likely to try and remove the body or cause a disturbance."

Pilate sighed. "All right, I will send a few auxiliaries."

Caiaphas shook his head. "That might cause more trouble. Auxiliaries do not get along favorably with our people."

Pilate sat back in his tribunal and frowned. "What do you want me to do, send my Praetorians?"

Caiaphas thought for a moment. "Your Praetorians are Rome's best, are they not?"

"Yes, but they are meant to protect me, not the tomb of some religious derelict," Pilate growled.

Caiaphas rubbed his chin and said, "But if thou couldst spare just two, Excellency, none would dare challenge them."

Pilate's patience was growing thin. "How long do you need my Praetorians for this guard detail of yours?" he asked sarcastically.

"For the next three days?" Caiaphas replied.

Pilate glared at Caiaphas for a moment, then finally said, "Very well. I shall arrange it. Now leave me, Priest."

Caiaphas bowed then ushered his companions out with a satisfied smile.

Pilate beckoned for Taurus to come forward.

"Yes, Governor?" Taurus stated.

"Assign two Praetorians to guard this Jewish sepulcher for the next three days. We shall return to Caesarea after that, if this cursed weather ever clears up," he snarled.

Taurus responded with a salute.

For the next two days, Praetorians watched the tomb where Jesus had been placed. For those two days, nothing happened and the rain never ceased. On the third day, Taurus walked into the barracks and bellowed, "Licinius! Flavius!"

"Attention!" Antonius shouted, springing to his feet with the others.

Taurus smiled and pointed to him. "You and Flavius will relieve the guards at the tomb this evening. No one is to enter it. Your watch will end at first light then you can return to the barracks. Do you understand your instructions?"

"Yes, Centurion," both acknowledged with a salute.

After Taurus left, Antonius looked over at Marcus and said, "Great. We get to stand in the rain all night."

That evening, as they relieved the other Praetorians at the tomb, they noticed three women sitting across from it, wailing and lifting their arms up in the air to mourn the loss of their Master.

"Who are those women?" Antonius asked one of the Praetorians.

The Praetorian replied with a smirk. "The Nazarene's followers. They have been here every day since the man was entombed. They cause no trouble, they just sit under their canopy and weep. It appears they have no sense to go in out of the rain," he stated, mocking them.

With a wry expression, Marcus said, "At least they have a covering."

The Praetorian nodded and said, "The watch is yours. Try not to catch your death of cold."

After taking their places on either side of the massive round stone in front of the tomb where Jesus was laid, Antonius and Marcus pulled their wet cloaks tighter around them.

Looking over at the three distraught women, Marcus wished there was some way he could comfort them, but he was a Roman soldier. His comrades had just crucified their master. They would desire no solace from him.

Sometime later that night, the rain suddenly stopped. Feeling thirsty, Antonius turned to Marcus and asked, "Did you bring a water flask?"

"No, but I could use a drink right now?" Marcus replied.

Antonius chuckled. "Water has poured on us all night, yet we have none to drink." He looked over at the three women and beckoned to them.

Hesitating at first, one finally came out of the canopy and approached.

"Water," Antonius said to her. "Can you bring us some?"

The woman looked at him strangely.

"She doesn't understand you, Antonius," Marcus said.

Antonius repeated the request in Greek and the woman nodded. Going back to her shelter, she returned with a small flask.

"Thank you," Antonius said, taking it from her.

He took a long drink then handed it to Marcus, who also drank his fill then handed it back to her. Touching her hand, he said, "Thank you."

At first the woman appeared as though she didn't understand. Then she gave him a kind nod. Returning to the others, she said something to them, then they took down their canopy and left.

Antonius chuckled and said, "I will never understand Jewish women. They sit out in the rain then return to their dwellings when it stops."

Marcus nodded then looked up at the stars breaking through the thinning clouds. He noticed that one star seemed to stand out above the others.

"Look, Antonius. Do you see that star in the sky?"

Antonius looked up. "Where? Oh… yes. The bright one."

They gazed at it for a few seconds, becoming almost entranced.

"Does it seem to be growing brighter?" Marcus asked.

"Yes… and bigger."

"What do you... think is causing it?" Marcus asked, unable to take his eyes off of it.

"I don't know, but it's beginning to hurt my eyes," Antonius replied.

Marcus squinted and said, "Mine as well."

They were trained to be fearless in every situation, but something about the phenomena in the sky greatly unnerved them. Finally, the pain became too unbearable for them to keep watching. Both had to turn away. When they turned back, their vision was clouded in darkness.

"I can't see!" Marcus shouted, throwing down his pilum and shield then rubbing his eyes with both hands.

"My eyes are useless as well," Antonius cried, as a long deafening roar of thunder sounded around them.

As they stood there, afraid to move for what seemed to be eternity, dawn broke.

"I... I can see again!" Antonius cried, as his vision finally began to clear.

"I can see again as well," Marcus declared, looking around. The first thing he noticed was that the large stone had been rolled away from the tomb's entrance. "Someone moved the stone!" he said pointing.

Antonius grabbed Marcus's arm and shouted, "The body!"

Rushing inside the sepulcher, all they saw were the cloths used to wrap the body lying on the burial slab.

Antonius put his hand to his chin. "The man's followers must have taken his body during the thunder when we could not see or hear."

Trying to make sense of it, Marcus asked, "You think that star caused our blindness?"

Antonius shook his head. "I don't know. This is very strange." He went back out to look for footprints going into the tomb or leaving it. The only ones he found were theirs and one other leaving the tomb. After looking around and seeing nothing that would indicate that someone took the body, he shook his head. "I suppose there is no reason to stay here now. It is dawn and our watch is over. We had better tell Centurion Taurus what happened."

"Do you think he'll even believe us?" Marcus asked.

Antonius gave him a questionable look and said, "If you were Taurus, would you believe us?"

Marcus swallowed hard. What had happened was almost too hard for him to believe and he experienced it.

Returning to the barracks, they gave their report, including the women, the star and the empty tomb. Taurus stared at them for a moment then shook his head. "Come with me. You can tell your story to Pilate."

Pilate was just having his morning meal with Procula in the royal dining hall when Demosthenes approached.

"Excellency, the Sanhedrin priests are here again."

"What do they want now?" Pilate asked gruffly.

"They are concerned about the disappearance of the man Jesus's body, the one guarded by your Praetorians."

"His body disappeared?" Pilate barked. He shook his head and thought, "These Jewish badgers will be the death of me yet." "Tell them to meet me in my judgment chamber," he instructed his aide.

Demosthenes bowed and left as Pilate swept his plate of food on the floor.

After Pilate sat on his tribunal, he nodded to Demosthenes who opened the doors to the judgment chamber. "Pilate will see you now," he declared.

Several of the priests, led by a bristling Caiaphas entered. "Governor of Judaea, thy men hath failed us," he angrily stated.

"What do you mean my men have failed you?" Pilate barked.

"Yea, thy Praetorians who guarded the Nazarene last evening did not prevent the man's followers from taking his body," Caiaphas declared with a scowl.

Pilate leaned toward the priest with narrowed eyes and said through clenched teeth, "Are you saying that my men did not do their duty?"

With an accusatory look, Caiaphas said, "They were either bribed or fell asleep. Either way, they were negligent. Now we must deal with his followers who hath claimed he did rise from the dead. They say it was a sign he truly was the Son of God. The men thou didst send to guard the tomb last night must be punished!"

Pilate looked down with a sigh and rubbed his forehead, wishing he had sufficient cause to punish the Sanhedrin. Looking up, he said, "I sent my Praetorians to guard the sepulcher as a favor to you. If you wanted to assure that this man's body was not taken, you should have placed your own men there as well. I will speak with the Praetorians who were posted at the tomb last night and we shall see what they have to say. Liberius!" Pilate shouted.

"Yes, Governor?" Liberius, who stood near the entry door, quickly approached.

"Have Centurion Taurus report to me with the men who were supposed to guard the Jewish sepulcher last night."

"It shall be done." Liberius turned to leave just as Taurus approached.

"Ah, Centurion Taurus. I was just coming to summon you. The governor wishes to question you and the two Praetorians assigned to guard the Jewish preacher's sepulcher."

"That is why I came," Taurus replied. "I have the two with me now."

Pilate leaned forward in his tribunal. "Centurion, are these the two assigned to guard the tomb last evening?"

"Yes, Governor. Praetorians Licinius and Flavius were on duty at the tomb last night."

Pilate gave out an exasperated sigh. It would have to be one of his two favorites. Displaying a gruff facade for the benefit of the Sanhedrin, he growled, "You men have caused me some distress with the Jewish leaders here. They accused you of falling asleep at your posts or being bribed and allowing the dead man's body to be removed. Well, which was it?"

Antonius looked at Taurus, who nodded for him to speak.

"Governor, we swear we did not fall asleep at our post; nor were we bribed," Antonius said as convincingly as he could.

The Sanhedrinists murmured among themselves.

"Then what happened to the dead man's body?" Pilate asked, looking at Marcus.

"We... don't know, Governor. A bright light from the sky blinded us while we stood our watch and when we could see again, the body had disappeared," Marcus replied.

Antonius lowered his head, knowing how unbelievable Marcus's explanation sounded.

"And you heard nothing?" Pilate asked, raising his voice slightly.

"The thunder was so deafening we couldn't hear anything, Governor," Marcus stated with pleading eyes.

Pilate gave Marcus a hard stare then turned to Antonius and asked, "What about you, Praetorian Licinius? Can you confirm what your companion just told me?"

Antonius took a deep breath and replied, "Yes, Governor."

Pilate sat back in his chair. "Do you expect me to believe this story?"

Antonius hung his head and said, "We find it hard to believe ourselves, Governor, but I swear it is the truth."

Pilate gave them a piercing look and was about to have them scourged when Taurus spoke up. "Governor, if I may say something."

Pilate raised his hand indicating for Taurus to proceed.

"Before they experienced this blind condition, one of the women gave them water to drink. She might have put a potion in the water that caused them to be blinded temporarily. I have heard that some potions can do that."

Pilate looked at Antonius and Marcus, as beads of sweat rolled down their temples. After a moment, he finally said, "I suppose that is possible. While they were incapacitated, someone could have removed the body during the din of the storm." He paused and rubbed his chin. "You men are lucky to have a Centurion who will speak up for you. Negligence while performing your duty is punishable by scourging. But since your Centurion's explanation makes sense to me... I will forgo that. I'm sure your Centurion will find other means of holding you accountable for the incident. That is my judgment. Leave me now."

"Yes, Governor," Taurus said, as all three saluted and marched away.

The priests gritted their teeth, but there was nothing more they could do. They asked to be dismissed and left in a huff.

As the three Praetorians walked down the hallway, Antonius turned to Taurus. "Thank you for speaking up on our behalf, Centurion."

Taurus gave him a slight nod. "You won't go unscathed. I just hope you two were truthful and you didn't fall asleep or were bribed."

"We told the truth!" Marcus exclaimed. "Not once did we fall asleep and no one gave us money to allow Jesus's body to be removed. I swear it!"

Taurus gave him a searching look, but could detect no signs of deceit. Before walking away, Taurus said, "Next time, take a water flask with you."

****

Pilate and his escort of conscripts and Praetorians rode out of Jerusalem that day, amidst talk that the crucified man named Jesus had either risen from the dead or his body was stolen by his followers to make it appear that way. Pilate could care less. As far as he was concerned, another delusional Jewish zealot had been eliminated.

CHAPTER XIV-JULIA GOES TO JUDAEA

The night before Julia's ship was to depart, Juliana went to her daughter's room and watched her flitting around like a butterfly trying to decide which clothes and items to take. "Still packing?" she asked.

"Yes," Julia replied, looking as though it was going to take her all night. "I can't decide what to wear in case I meet the Roman governor."

"Let's see what you have so far," Juliana said, as she sat down on the bed and looked at the clothes her daughter had laid out. "I think what you've chosen will be appropriate." She approved of her daughter's choices, mainly because she had purchased them for Julia. Smiling at Julia's obvious excitement, she said, "Are you worried about how you'll look for the governor or the Praetorian?"

Julia rolled her eyes. "The governor, of course," she replied.

Juliana knew her daughter's true reason for wanting to look her best, however. It was time for her to dispense some motherly advice. "Julia, I know you're not going to Judaea merely to be with your uncle. Now is an exciting time in any young girl's life when she feels anxious to experience the thrill of romance. If you have an opportunity to spend some time with this young Praetorian you fancy, just be cautious. I trust you will always be properly chaperoned, but remember, he is a soldier. Soldiers are only interested in a moment's passion, not commitment. Don't put yourself in a position to be alone with him or you may regret it."

"I doubt that will happen; Domitia always accompanies me wherever I go. Besides, Uncle Taurus is his centurion. What could go wrong?" Julia dared a half grin at her mother.

"Well, just remember who you are. Your actions affect your family as well as yourself." Juliana admonished.

Julia embraced her mother tightly. "I will. Please do not worry."

"That is a mother's responsibility," Juliana replied with a smile. "Now, do you have enough money?"

"Yes. Father gave me what he said was a sufficient amount to cover meals, lodging and expenses."

Handing a small purse full of gold and silver coins to her daughter, Juliana said, "Knowing your father, he probably gave you enough for one day. This should last for the whole trip."

Julia embraced her mother again. "Thank you, Mother."

Early the next morning, they departed for the ship. After sharing long embraces at the dock, Julia and her chaperones boarded the ship and waved goodbye. As Juliana watched their ship disappear over the horizon, she said a tear-laden silent prayer to Neptune for her daughter's safety.

After putting their things away below in the ship, Julia and her servants went on deck to see the scenery. Standing at the rail, they observed swimmers, boat people and fishermen as the merchant ship passed by the coastal ports and towns. They even waved to a few. Julia wondered what their lives were like and felt fortunate to be who she was. She had a loving family, loyal servants and lived in a grand villa. Life was good.

Later, their ship passed through the Strait of Messina, rounded the point and headed for the open sea. Julia's excitement to see Antonius began to mount. Would her trip turn out to be a boring sightseeing excursion with her uncle or would she have a chance to spend some time with Antonius and really get to know him?

Almost a month after leaving the port of Ostia, the ship pulled into the Caesarean harbor late that morning. A familiar Praetorian centurion in full uniform stood on the dock, waiting for the ship to moor.

"Uncle Taurus!" Julia cried, running down the gangplank into his arms.

Kissing her warmly on the cheek, he said, "Ah, my favorite niece."

She gave him a playful smile and said, "I thought Serina was your favorite niece."

"But she isn't here," he replied with a grin.

"Oh, Uncle, you are hopeless."

"You've been listening to your father again, eh? I see you made it here safely. No pirates?"

"No pirates," she confirmed. "It appears you received Father's dispatch about us coming."

"Yes. You must have had good weather, your ship arrived on schedule."

"We did, although poor Domitia is not used to sailing and spent most of her time at the rail of the ship."

Taurus laughed, as Domitia blushed slightly.

"Come, I have a carriage waiting. Where is your baggage?" he asked.

"Vergilius is bringing them off the ship for us." Julia pointed to her manservant as he labored down the gangplank carrying their bags.

After placing them at her feet, Vergilius looked up and said, "Master Cicero. It is good to see you."

"Yes, you as well, Vergilius. But let's forget about calling me Cicero and just call me, 'Master Taurus.'"

"As you wish, Master Taurus."

Julia smiled and turned to her uncle. "Have you been waiting long?"

"No, I was in the palace and saw your ship sailing in. I arrived just before you pulled into port."

"The palace must be close by," Julia stated.

"Yes, just down the road from the port," he confirmed.

"Were you able to secure lodging for us?" she asked.

Taurus grinned and said, "I did better than that. I received permission from the governor to have you stay at the palace."

Julia's eyes lit up. "At the palace? That's wonderful, uncle!"

"Yes," Taurus remarked, as if it wasn't that difficult. "The palace has several staterooms that are used for occasional dignitaries and visitors, but they're rarely used. When I told him my niece from Rome was coming for a visit, he insisted you stay in one of them."

"My parents gave me enough money for lodging, so I won't have to spend it by staying in the palace. Thank you uncle, and I will convey my thanks to the governor when I see him." Julia stated.

"I'm sure your parents would prefer the palace over some inn filled with unsavory characters," Taurus added.

"Like you, Uncle?" Julia teased.

Taurus gave her a pretended stern look, as they walked to the waiting carriage.

"How long will you be staying?" Taurus asked.

"One month," she replied.

"You have already arranged passage back to Rome?"

"Yes, Mother took care of that."

"How is Juliana?" Taurus asked about his sister.

"She is well," Julia replied.

"And Sidonius?"

"Over-protective as usual," Julia said, rolling her eyes.

"That is what fathers are for," Taurus replied with a grin. He then pointed to a carriage nearby and said, "I have a carriage for you over there. As soon as Vergilius loads your bags onto it, I'll drive you to the palace. Domitia and Vergilius can ride on top with me."

"Would it be all right if I rode on top with you? Vergilius and Domitia can sit inside."

Taurus frowned. "It's... irregular, but as long as you don't mind."

Julia squeezed his arm and smiled. "I don't mind."

"Very well." Taurus looked at Vergilius and Domitia, who both raised their eyebrows, suprised they would be the ones riding inside the carriage.

After Vergilius loaded their bags and everyone was seated, Taurus snapped the reins and the carriage rolled down the road. Turning to Julia, he said, "Juliana tells me you haven't married yet. You know you are getting up in age. If you wait much longer, you will have to settle for an old senator with a large girth and wads of ear hair."

Julia laughed. "I have had suitors, Uncle; I just haven't been impressed with the right one yet. How is it you never married?"

"Alas, I vowed only to marry a Vestal Virgin. To my sorrow, none of them would have me," Taurus replied, pretending to be heartbroken.

Julia shook her head.

"Ah, here we are," he said, as they pulled up in front of the main gate.

"That was quick," Julia said.

"I told you the palace was close," Taurus stated, giving her a side glance.

The sentries waved to Taurus and opened the gate. The carriage rolled into a large inner courtyard containing several fountains and well-sculpted shrubs and flowers.

"Oh, this looks wonderful!" Julia exclaimed wide-eyed as she glanced about the grounds.

"The inside is even more impressive," Taurus boasted.

"I can't wait," she exclaimed, as he brought the carriage to a stop.

Helping her down, he said, "You must be tired from your journey. I'll take you right to your room and check on you later when you've had time to rest."

"Thank you, Uncle. We are a bit fatigued," Julia said as Vergilius and Domitia stepped out of the carriage.

Taurus then escorted niece and servants into the palace. "Now, Julia, you must tell me. What madness made you decide to visit Judaea? I'm sure there are many other places you could have traveled to, which are certainly more interesting than this unforsaken land."

"Because *you* are here, Uncle. Also, I wanted to get away from Rome for awhile. I thought since you were in Judaea you could show me the sights."

"I'm afraid there aren't many outside Caesarea and Jerusalem. Neither city matches the splendor of Rome, but a few places may be of interest to you. I don't have much time to myself, but what little I have..."

"If you are too busy, perhaps one of your Praetorians could be my escort. Actually, there was one at the confirmation I was hoping to see again."

"And what *is* this young Praetorian's name?" Taurus asked, through narrowed eyes.

"Antonius," she replied.

"Antonius Licinius?"

"Do you have any other men named Antonius?" she asked.

"No, just one," Taurus replied.

"That's the one then. What do you think of him?" she asked.

Taurus raised his eyebrows and replied, "He's one of my best." He then frowned and said, "But I don't know if I would trust him with you."

"You wouldn't have to take time from your busy schedule if you allowed him to show us around," Julia said, batting her eyes at him.

"Why, you minx! You didn't come here to see your old uncle; you came here to see Licinius, didn't you?"

Julia gave him an innocent look. "Not at all!" Putting her arm through his, she said, "You know you have always been my favorite uncle."

"I am your favorite uncle because I am your *only* uncle," Taurus commented.

"On mother's side," she corrected him, drawing a smirk.

Stopping in front of a large oak door, he said, "Here is where you'll be staying."

After unlocking and opening it, he held out his arm for them to enter.

Julia and her servants walked into the spacious, well-furnished atrium and gazed about.

"Oh! The room is beautiful! Thank you, Uncle, and it would be nice if you could arrange for Antonius to escort us while we're here," Julia suggested again, giving Taurus a hug to butter him up.

He gave her a look out of the corner of his eye letting her know he was aware of her true intentions. He then started to leave, but abruptly turned back. "Oh yes... I almost forgot. The governor has invited you to dine with him and the governess in the royal dining hall this evening."

Julia's eyes widened. "Oh! When should I be ready?"

"Don't worry, his Greek servant will knock on your door later this evening. Rest for now; you'll have plenty of time before he comes for you. If you need anything, my room is down the long end of the passageway on the right." Taurus smiled as he walked out.

"Thank you, Uncle," she said as he left.

Domitia closed the door and remarked, "Dining with the governor, Mistress. What an honor."

Julia put her hand to her breast and said, "Yes, I've never dined with dignitaries by myself. My parents have always accompanied me. I hope I don't embarrass them."

Domitia gave her a supportive look and said, "Oh, you won't, Mistress."

Noting a pause in their conversation, Vergilius asked, "Where would you like me to put the bags, Mistress Julia?"

Julia did a brief walk through, winding up in a large bedroom and said, "You can put mine in here. Domitia can take the room next to mine, and you can stay in the room across from us, Vergilius."

"As you wish," he responded.

Julia walked back out into the atrium and looked at the woven tapestries hanging on the walls and several ornately carved tables with oil lamps positioned conveniently about the room. A large couch with several cushioned pillows sat in the middle.

After Vergilius had set her bags down and returned to the atrium, Julia went back into her bedroom. She felt the large bed and was pleased with its firmness. A small table and lamp sat beside it and a large dresser stood on the other side. Her room accessed the courtyard, allowing her a magnificent view through the windows set into the doors. Vases and flowers adorned every corner and a smaller adjoining room contained a marble washbasin and toilet.

"Domitia, would you please arrange my things," she asked.

Domitia responded with a single nod. "As you wish, Mistress Julia."

After Domitia had finished, Julia said, "I think I will take uncle's advice and rest for awhile. Why don't you and Vergilius rest as well; the voyage was a long one."

"Thank you, Mistress," Domitia replied.

A few hours later, Taurus marched up to the governor's living quarters where Antonius and Marcus were standing guard outside the door.

"Everything all right here?" Taurus asked.

"Yes, Centurion!" they both answered.

"Some important visitors have just arrived from Rome. You two will be their bodyguard detail tomorrow. I want you to meet with them in the morning and plan their activities. You will be their escorts for the entire day."

"Who are they?" Antonius asked.

"You'll find out when you get to their stateroom," Taurus replied with a stone face.

Puzzled at why Taurus wouldn't tell them who it was, they looked at each other with furrowed brows.

Taurus continued with further instructions. "Make sure your uniforms are spotless and come to my room after everyone is assigned their posts and I'll show you to their stateroom. Swords and daggers, no shields."

"Yes, Centurion," they both exclaimed.

After Taurus left, Marcus asked, "Who do you think it is, Antonius?"

"Probably some fat senator and his wife on holiday," came the reply.

"Why would they come here?" Marcus asked, with a scrunched face.

Antonius chuckled. "Perhaps it's a senator and his mistress and he wants to get far enough away from Rome so his wife doesn't find out."

Marcus lifted his head slightly.

****

Later that evening, Demosthenes knocked on Julia's door.

Domitia answered.

He bowed and said, "The governor desires the company of your mistress to dine with him now."

Julia entered the room. "Where will my servants be having their supper?"

"In the kitchen," Demosthenes replied. "We can drop them off on our way to the royal dining hall."

Not surprised at the arrangement, Julia replied, "Very well." She then looked at Domitia, who read her mind. "I will get Vergilius, Mistress."

After leaving the room, they walked down the large hallway then entered an intersecting corridor. Demosthenes led them down part ways until they reached an open door. The smells of cooked meat filled the hall making Julia hungry. He pointed inside and said to Julia, "Here is the kitchen. There is a table in the back where your servants can eat. I'll let the cook know who they are." Vergilius and Domitia nodded and went in. After instructing the cooks to feed Julia's servants, Demosthenes and Julia then proceeded down the hall. Entering a wider corridor, they continued until they came to two massive polished oak doors.

Turning to Julia, he asked, "Your name please, Miss?"

"Julia, daughter of Sidonius Cato of Rome," she replied formally, as taught by her mother. Although she felt a little anxiety knowing she would be the focus of attention, she was excited to dine with a Roman governor in a Judaean palace. It was something she could use as a topic of converation with her family and friends when she went back to Rome.

Demosthenes opened the doors and led her into a large sitting room, lined with elegantly carved and upholstered wooden chairs. He pointed to one and said, "You may sit here, Miss until I announce you," taking her hand briefly as she sat down. "The governor and his wife will join us shortly. When they enter, please stand and address the governor as 'Your Excellency' and his wife as 'Governess' or 'Lady Claudia.'"

Julia nodded. While she waited, she felt that she was transitioning from a girl to a woman at last.

A moment later, doors on the other end of the sitting room opened and her host and hostess appeared.

Demosthenes stood erect and announced, "Julia, daughter of Sidonius Cato of Rome, I present his Excellency Pontius Pilate, the Prefect of Judaea and his wife, Lady Claudia."

Julia did her best curtsy. "I am so honored to meet you, Your Excellency, and you, Lady Claudia."

Procula took her by the hand and said, "Oh, formalities are so mundane. Please call me Procula, Julia."

Julia bowed and said, "As you wish."

Pilate smiled and beckoned to her. "Follow us into the dining hall, young lady. Our food preparer has created a wonderful meal and I am anxious to hear the news from Rome."

Julia smiled and followed them into a large room containing a massive table that could seat as many as fifty people at once. Looking around, she caught her breath. The room's opulence easily rivaled those she had seen in Rome. Noticing there were four places set, she wondered who else would be joining them. Demosthenes bowed and withdrew as a man entered the dining room. Dressed in a soldier's uniform, he briskly walked over to the table.

"Ah, Prefect Liberius," Pilate exclaimed. "I see you received my message. Miss Julia, this is Prefect Martinus Liberius; he is in charge of our garrison here at the palace. I've asked him to dine with us this evening; I hope you don't mind. Prefect Liberius, this is Julia, daughter of Sidonius Cato of Rome, here on holiday."

Liberius bowed and said, "Miss Julia."

Procula pointed to a place on the side of the table and said, "Julia, why don't you sit there and Prefect Liberius, you can sit across from her."

Pilate and his wife sat at opposite ends of the table.

After everyone had taken their seats, Pilate smiled and turned to Julia. "Tell me, young lady; what news from Rome have you brought us?"

"Pontius!" Procula exclaimed, giving her husband a disapproving glance. Turning to Julia, she said, "Forgive my husband's eagerness, Julia. Please tell us how your trip was from Rome and a little about your family."

Pilate frowned.

Julia raised her eyebrows slightly and said, "The trip was interesting. The captain allowed us to dine with him and every evening we were serenaded by one of the sailors who played a lyre and sang to us."

"That does sound interesting. How was the weather?" Procula asked.

"We had good weather the whole journey."

Procula leaned forward and said, "Tell us about your family, My Dear."

Pilate squirmed with impatience.

"My father is a judge and hears many important matters of law at the basilica in Rome. We live a short distance from the palace on a comfortable villa with two servants. My mother and sister make up the rest of my family and we also have a villa on the coast near Ostia."

"A family of status; that is good," Pilate interjected. "Now, what can you tell us of Rome?"

Procula threw up her hands and shook her head.

"Well... the emperor still resides on Capreae," Julia began.

"Yes," Pilate impatiently stated, "I read that from a dispatch I received not too long ago. Is Prefect Sejanus still controlling Rome?"

"Some say he is becoming too controlling," Julia replied with raised eyebrows. She immediately regretted her remark.

Pilate leaned forward. "Really? Who said that?"

Julia blushed. For a moment she had forgotten how dangerous it was to say the wrong thing in front of the wrong people. Thinking quickly, she replied, "I'm sorry, Your Excellency. It is not my place to say such things. One evening at supper, my father mentioned in passing he heard that from an acquaintance. I'm sure the report was probably just gossip."

Pilate nodded slightly. "Sometimes gossip turns out to be true." He stared at her for an uncomfortable moment. His gaze finally shifted as a server entered, setting a bowl of soup before him. "Ah, this looks appetizing. Please, begin eating."

Julia took her spoon and dipped it in the steaming bowl. Sipping a small amount, she noticed a generous mixture of vegetables and small pasta bits in a rich beef broth.

"This is wonderful," she remarked.

"Yes," Procula stated, "the man who prepares our food here at the palace has a true gift for taking local ingredients and adding a touch of Italia to them."

"Please forgive me for interrupting your meal," Liberius stated, "but how long will you be staying in Judaea, Miss Julia?"

"One month," she replied, "I'm looking forward to seeing the country."

Pilate chortled and said, "Not much to see in this desolate sun-baked wasteland, but Procula can probably tell you what sights are worth seeing. Has anyone been assigned to escort you around while you are here?"

"My uncle has arranged for two Praetorians to accompany us wherever we go."

Pilate wiped his mouth, and said, "If our Praetorians are going to be your escorts, you should be quite well protected. They have become most familiar with those areas that are safe for Roman citizens."

"Is there a danger to Roman citizens here?" Julia asked.

"There are a few disgruntled zealots who would like nothing better than to bring harm to a Roman. You just have to be careful where you go," Pilate replied.

"My Dear," Procula interjected, "I fear you are frightening our guest. She'll be looking over her shoulder wherever she goes now."

Pilate put up his hands and shook his head slightly. "I apologize if I caused you any consternation, young lady. I'm sure you will be quite safe with our Praetorians at your side."

The rest of the evening's discussions centered on the weather, Judaea, and Rome. When it concluded, Julia thanked the governor and governess for their hospitality then Demosthenes escorted her and her servants back to their stateroom.

After changing into a sleeping tunic, Julia slipped between the covers and thought about Antonius. She hoped her uncle would let him escort them around Judaea. Somehow, she had to figure a way they could be alone so she could talk privately with him and see if he was worth pursuing. She only had a month, then they would be separated a great distance for who knows how long. Was this a good idea to come here hoping for a romantic moment with a young man she had only seen once? Time would tell.

****

The next morning, Antonius and Marcus put on their uniforms and reported to Taurus's room. He looked them over then said, "All right, you look presentable. Follow me."

As they strode down the corridor, Taurus gave them their instructions. "You will escort our visitor and her servants wherever they wish to go. Make sure no harm comes to them. I don't even want to hear they received a rash from the sun. You can start with a tour of the city."

"How long will they be staying?" Antonius asked.

"One month. You'll be their escorts for two days then I'll rotate two others to replace you until everyone in the barracks has a chance to escort them."

Antonius and Marcus looked at each other and smiled. At least that meant easy duty for two days.

"All right, follow me," Taurus commanded.

Upon arrival at Julia's stateroom, Taurus knocked on the door. Domitia opened it and bade them enter.

Walking in, Antonius and Marcus noticed a girl sitting on the couch, slightly in the shadows. As she stood up, Antonius's mouth dropped open.

"Julia! You're the visitor?" he asked.

"You remembered my name," she replied, impressed that he recalled it. "I thought since my uncle was in Judaea, I would come visit him."

"Ah, yes, where every young Roman girl dreams of going," Taurus remarked with an upward glance.

Marcus stifled a laugh.

Taurus gave him a serious look. "Since I feel that my niece would be more comfortable among people her own age, I want you to see that she has an enjoyable stay. Take her to the more interesting sights in Caesarea, and the Dancing Goat is not one of them."

Marcus smiled then nodded. Antonius turned to Julia and said, "Yes, Centurion; I, uh... we will make sure that she enjoys herself."

"I thought I could count on you," Taurus said with half closed eyes. He then turned to Julia. "My dear, Licinius and Flavius here will be your escorts for the next two days then I'll rotate the other men in my command to guard you. You will always have two Praetorians with you wherever you go."

Although Julia felt disappointed she would only have Antonius for two days, she politely smiled. "Whatever you feel is necessary, Uncle."

Taurus turned back to Antonius and Marcus and said, "Remember, my niece is precious to me. See that nothing happens to her. Am I clear?"

"Yes, Centurion!" both exclaimed.

"Good! If I hear any complaints from her, I'll have your entrails for my morning meal!"

Domitia's head reared back and her brow furrowed.

Taurus noticed her shocked expression and said, "Don't look so surprised, Domitia. Entrails don't taste as bad as they sound especially when roasted."

"I'm sure there won't be any complaints, Uncle," Julia said as she gazed into Antonius's hazel brown eyes.

"Just make sure you return to the palace before sundown. Danger most often chooses the night," Taurus instructed.

Putting his hand to his helmet, Antonius said, "I just remembered, Centurion. The first race of the season is in three weeks. I've been taking the chariot and horses out every morning to prepare for it."

Taurus narrowed his eyes. "Ah, yes, the chariot races, I forgot about them. The Governor would have my head if you miss your training. I'll assign two of the other men to escort my niece."

Julia looked as though he had stabbed her in the heart. "Oh, Uncle! Can't you let Antonius escort us at least today? Surely the Governor won't mind if he misses one day of chariot practice. Please, Uncle."

Taurus took in a deep breath then said, "I'll tell him I forgot about chariot practice and assigned Licinius to be your escort for the day. I would suggest you leave before he finds out Licinius didn't show up at the track."

Antonius gave him a worried look and said, "You won't get into trouble, will you, Centurion?"

Taurus took in a breath then said, "I think the governor won't mind you taking one day off to escort my niece."

Antonius nodded.

Taurus walked over and gave Julia a hug and said, "Enjoy your day and if these two reprobates displease you in any way, let me know about it."

Julia smirked and replied, "I don't think that will be a problem, Uncle."

Taurus turned to leave and gave Antonius and Marcus a snake-eyed look.

"What do you have planned for us today?" Julia asked Antonius, after her uncle left.

Opening the door, Antonius replied, "We'll take you to the Inn of the Gilded Horse for your morning meal. They have the best food in Caesarea and the prices are reasonable. After that, we'll see some of the sights the city has to offer."

Julia nodded her approval. "Since my uncle has been kind enough to arrange for our lodging, we will pay for all our meals."

"As you wish," Antonius replied, breathing a sigh of relief internally.

After boarding the carriage that Taurus had arranged for Julia's transportation, Antonius, Marcus, Domitia, and Julia proceeded into Caesarea while Vergilius chose to stay behind and straighten up the room.

"Anything interesting happening in Rome?" Antonius asked, as he and

Marcus sat across from Julia and Domitia in the carriage.

"Your Prefect has been busy. He charged a few senators with maestas and they just disappeared," Julia replied.

Antonius' eyebrows went up. "Really? They left Rome?"

"No one knows," Julia added, "I just heard my father mention it. There is a lot of fear in the senate right now. I hope you don't have relatives who are senators."

"My grandfather was a senator but he and my grandmother passed away," Antonius stated.

"Your father is a Tribune in the Praetorian Guard, isn't he Antonius?" Julia asked.

"He was, but he's retired now and owns a vineyard in Calabria near the town of Aletium. He is actually a good friend of the Prefect and served with him under Augustus and Tiberius for a while. The Prefect even came to our home and asked my father to come back into the Guard. That's how Marcus and I came to join."

"You are fortunate to have a father who was a Praetorian," she remarked.

"Also fortunate that he was a good friend to the Prefect," Antonius added.

Wanting to include Marcus in the conversation, Julia asked, "How do you like being a Praetorian, Marcus?"

Scrunching his face, he replied, "It's different from what I thought it would be."

"What about you, Antonius? How do you like it?" she asked.

He took a deep breath and said, "I thought there would be more action, more recognition and more opportunity for advancement. Unfortunately, most of what we do is routine."

Julia raised her eyebrows. "Routine?"

"Train… stand our posts… guard the governor… nothing too exciting," Antonius replied in a monotone.

"Isn't driving the governor's chariot exciting?" Julia asked.

Antonius snorted. "It would have been, if my chariot hadn't crashed in the first race. I have a new chariot now and, as I mentioned, the racing season will start in three weeks. Will you still be here to see me race?"

"I will," she replied, as her eyes sparkled with anticipation.

"Perfect!" he exclaimed. "You can come and cheer for me then."

Julia smiled and said, "I look forward to it! I have gone to a few chariot races in Rome with my parents, but I never had anyone in particular to cheer for."

"Now you do," Antonius exclaimed. "I'll need all the support I can get. The people here in Judaea would love to see me lose, or worse."

"What do you mean, 'or worse?'" Julia asked.

"You haven't been here long enough to realize that the people of this land despise Romans. They would like nothing better than to see me crushed beneath someone else's chariot wheels."

Domitia's and Julia's eyebrows raised.

"I don't suppose you could choose something else to occupy your spare time?" Julia suggested.

Antonius shook his head slightly. "I'm afraid it's too late. Pilate already expects me to race, and to win. Besides, I don't think he would take it well if I told him I was going to quit. I've let him down once already; I have to redeem myself now. It will be easier to do that if you cheer for me."

She smiled. "Then I shall cheer for you."

"What have you been doing in your spare time, Marcus? she asked.

Marcus mused for a moment then said, "I have been learning about the Jews' religious beliefs."

"That sounds interesting," she remarked, pretending to show interest.

Marcus looked at Antonius and said, "It can be."

"In what way?" Julia pressed.

"They believe in one main god. Some even believe that a Jewish preacher was the son of this one god."

"There are stories of gods coming to earth," Julia said.

"This one was crucified," Antonius added.

"Oh," Julia said quietly.

After arriving at the inn and having a pleasant meal, Antonius and Marcus escorted their charges around the city and showed them some of the few major sights. They included the Temple of Divine Augustus, the Pharos, the statues of Augustus, Roma and the impressive Tiberiéum. They spent the rest of the day shopping and strolling down "safe" avenues. Their first day of sightseeing concluded with a stop back at the inn for supper, since Julia and Domitia had so enjoyed their morning meal there.

As the sun began to set into the sea, Antonius suggested that they should return to the palace. After boarding the carriage, they took the road that ran along the coast, past the main harbor. While they traveled the bumpy road, Julia had an idea. She waited until they were back at their room then turned to her servant. "Domitia, you can go inside. I wish to speak with my escorts alone for a moment."

Domitia gave her a suspicious glance and asked, "You won't go any-where, will you, Mistress?"

"No, Domitia. A few words with them then I will come right in."

Domitia nodded and slowly went inside, giving Marcus and Antonius a squinty-eyed look until Julia closed the door.

Julia gave Marcus an apologetic smile and said, "Actually, I just have words for Antonius. Would you mind, Marcus?"

Marcus grinned at Antonius and said, "I'll see you back at the barracks, Reprobate." He then hurried away.

Turning to Julia, Antonius said, "I was hoping we might have a chance to be alone so we could talk."

Julia smiled and whispered, "I wouldn't say we are completely alone; I'm sure Domitia probably has her ear to the door as we speak." She pulled Antonius away from it and came up close to his ear.

"I would love to go for a walk down by the sea tonight, just the two of us. Can we meet later, after my servants have fallen asleep? Nod yes or no."

Antonius nodded "yes."

"Good. Wait until it is quite late then I will meet you in the courtyard just outside my room."

Antonius nodded again.

Speaking louder, Julia said, "Thank you for escorting us. We had a wonderful time. Good night."

"Good night," Antonius replied, as Julia opened the door and went in, giving him a captivating smile before closing it.

Back at the barracks, he sat down on his bunk and took off his helmet.

"Well? What did you talk about after I left?" Marcus asked, practically bursting with curiosity.

"She wants me to go for a walk with her along the seashore later tonight."

Marcus raised his eyebrows and said, "You're not planning on taking advantage of her, are you, Antonius?"

Antonius gazed at nothing in particular and replied, "It's up to her."

"Just remember, she is the Centurion's niece," Marcus warned him.

Antonius nodded. "Don't worry, I won't let it get out of hand. I don't want Taurus having my entrails for his morning meal."

Marcus chuckled then quickly fell asleep.

****

Later, as Marcus and the rest of the men in the barracks slept, Antonius was wide awake as he thought about his upcoming seaside stroll with Julia.

He could tell she was someone special: confident, intelligent, kind and assertive, but not overbearing. He could wait no longer. He arose from his bunk and tiptoed past sleeping Praetorians until he came to a door that led out into the courtyard. Silently, he opened and closed it then looked up at the full moon suspended high in the sky. The night was clear and the garden crickets chirped their monotone melodies, keeping time with the beating of his heart. Suddenly, he became aware of Julia's presence. Turning quickly, he noticed her standing only a few feet away in sandals and a plain but modest tunic that fell to her mid-calf, secured by a sash. Although it wasn't fancy, she looked beautiful in it. She wore her hair up during the day, but now she had it down and the smooth, light brown tresses flowed past the middle of her back. As she came nearer, the fragrance of myrrh surrounded him. He could feel his body temperature begin to rise.

"I hope you haven't been waiting long," she said. "I had to make sure Domitia and Vergilius were asleep before I left. When they began snoring, I felt it was safe to leave." She tittered.

He smiled then muttered, "You look... radiant."

"This?" she replied, pulling on her tunic. "I had to wear my sleeping tunica in case Domitia or Vergilius awoke and caught me returning. Then I could say that I needed a sip of water."

"It sounds like you thought of everything," Antonius said with a smile.

She gave him a coy look and stated. "I try to look ahead, but sometimes the unexpected happens which can alter plans."

"So... you can predict the future?" he asked, taking her hand and leading her toward the palace gate.

"No, but it doesn't hurt to try and predict what the future may hold."

He stared into her emerald eyes and said, "And what do you think your future holds?"

"Near or far?" she asked.

"Both," he answered.

Julia put her hand to her chin. "Hmmm. In the near future, I will enjoy the company of a handsome young Praetorian while we walk along the seaside and watch the waves wash onto the shore. As for the distant future... I'm afraid it is still a bit hazy."

"You think I'm handsome?" he asked.

She pretended to ponder then said, "A little above average I would say," looking him up and down.

Antonius laughed. "Since you have shared your feelings for me, I will share mine with you. I think you are above average, as well."

She playfully slapped his arm and said, "You are a tease, Antonius. No doubt a trait learned from your father. How does your mother put up with the two of you?"

"She only has one to put up with one now," he replied.

As they approached the main gate, Antonius said to one of the interior guards, "We are going for a walk down by the sea."

The sentry opened the gate and smiled as they left.

Walking down to the nearby shoreline they strolled along the beach, silently gazing out at the moonlit sea. Deciding to take off her sandals, Julia pressed her toes into the cool, soothing sand and felt its gentle caress with each step. A light breeze kissed their faces as it came off the sea, carrying a slight aroma of the saltwater. The night was perfect and Julia acknowledged it. "It is a beautiful evening, isn't it, Antonius?"

"Yes, it is beautiful," he replied. "On our free time, Marcus and I come here and gaze out into the sea, trying to imagine what our families are doing back home."

"Do you miss them?" she asked, turning to him.

"Yes, especially my mother and her pastries," he grinned.

Julia smiled. "How long will you be stationed in Judaea?"

"Two years," Antonius grunted.

"Oh!" she said with a frown. "Do you think they will transfer you to Rome when your time here is up?"

"I hope they do, but I'll just have to wait and see." He pointed to a smooth patch of sand and said, "Why don't we sit down?"

Julia smiled and they sat down, both pulling their knees to their bodies with their arms.

As they gazed out into the sea, a pod of dolphins swam by, leaping and diving as they playfully followed each other.

"I think dolphins are magnificent fish," Julia observed.

"They're mammals," Antonius corrected her.

"How do you know that?" she asked, tilting her head to the side.

"My mother has drawings of them done by a Greek man called Aristotle. He classified them as mammals. We're mammals too, so we're related."

Julia laughed. "They are beautiful to watch, but I hope I don't look like them."

"You may not look like them, but I would say you are beautiful to watch as well," Antonius complimented her.

Julia gazed into his eyes and said, "Antonius, you are a flatterer."

"I speak only the truth," he declared, raising his chin.

She brushed her hand over the tiny particles of weathered rock at her side and smiled contentedly as the waves splashed noisily on the shore. "The sound of the waves is so soothing, isn't it?" she asked.

"Yes. I always feel more relaxed when I come here," he replied, gazing into Julia's eyes.

She returned his gaze and drew closer to him. Their lips met in a first kiss that was exactly as each had imagined it would be.

"I have been wanting to do that ever since I first saw you," Antonius said. They kissed again and again.

Remembering her mother's words, Julia pulled away and said, "We probably should return to the palace."

"Is something wrong?" he asked.

She looked around and said, "I feel like someone is watching us."

Antonius also looked around but saw no one. "If you feel uncomfortable, I'll take you back."

"We probably should go. If Domitia discovers I'm not there, she'll go straight to uncle."

Looking up, he noticed the skyline was becoming brighter. "We had better run before the sun comes up."

Hurrying back to the palace, he dropped her off in the courtyard.

"I'll see you later," she said, slightly out of breath.

He smiled and gave her one last kiss. Returning to the barracks, he lay down on his bunk. He was pleased with his first opportunity to be alone with her. She was not like the other girls he had come to know casually in Judaea. They were only interested in getting money from the soldiers for "favors" and drinking their wine. As he closed his eyes to obtain the small amount of sleep left to him, a figure passed by the door to the barracks. He paused just long enough to verify that Antonius was in his bunk.

"On your feet, you sons of camels!" Taurus bellowed, just before the sun peered onto the Judaean landscape. "We escort the governor to Jerusalem today. Eat a hearty meal or you'll go hungry before we arrive in Antipatris."

Antonius opened his eyes and sighed as the others in the barracks sprang out of their bunks. Chariot training would have been easier than marching all the way to Jerusalem.

"We're going to Jerusalem today?" Marcus asked, rubbing his eyes. "I thought that was next week."

"No, it is today," Taurus replied in a sarcastic tone. "Now get cleaned up.

You smell like..."

"Piles of horse dung!" a chorus of Praetorians finished his sentence.

Taurus smiled and strode out.

Antonius groaned as he sat up.

Marcus chuckled at his friend's bloodshot eyes and tousled hair. "I think someone stayed up too late last night."

Antonius smiled and replied, "It was worth it."

A few hours later, Pilate and his entourage were on their way to Jerusalem. Procula invited Julia to accompany them in their carriage which she happily accepted. Their first stop would be the town of Lydda for a short rest then they would proceed to Jerusalem from there.

As the Praetorian escort marched alongside Pilate's carriage, Antonius wondered what conversations Julia was having with the governor and his wife. As he speculated, Taurus came up and gave him a sharp rap on the arm with his vitis, causing Antonius to flinch.

"Licinius! If I were you, I'd forget about any more late-night encounters with my niece. Now pick up your shield, you're dragging it on the ground!" He gave Antonius a stern look then marched off to the front of the column.

Antonius looked at Marcus. "How did he know about that?"

Marcus shrugged his shoulders.

Antonius grumbled, "My shield is as high as everyone else's."

They reached Jerusalem late that night and entered Herod's other palace, that was Pilate's residence when he was in Jerusalem. It had two main buildings containing baths, banquet halls and accommodations for hundreds of guests. The grounds included gardens, porticoes, groves, canals and ponds fitted with bronze fountains. Recognized for its three ornately designed towers, the palace interior was decorated richly with alabaster, marble, silver and gold. The palace was an obvious example of the Jewish king's extravagance.

After making sure Pilate was secure in the praetorium[57], Taurus assigned his Praetorians their posts. Antonius and Marcus stood the late night to dawn watch over the governor's quarters.

"I think we're being punished for your stroll on the beach with Julia," Marcus remarked.

Antonius furrowed his brow and said, "I can't figure out how he found out about it."

"I didn't tell him," Marcus declared.

Antonius recalled his and Julia's rendezvous by the sea and remembered

---

57-The part of the palace where Roman governors resided

her mentioning she felt like someone was watching them. It must have been Taurus. As he fought to stay awake the rest of the night, he wished Taurus and Julia had not been related.

After being relieved the next morning, Antonius went to the Praetorian barracks in the Agrippeum[58] and collapsed on his bunk. The wooden cot was harder than the one he had in Caesarea, but he didn't care.

Looking over at Marcus in his bunk, he said, "I think you're right. I'm being punished because Julia likes me."

"Just think of what he would do if she hated you," Marcus grinned.

****

Later that morning, Taurus met Julia for a tour of the city. Domitia and Vergilius asked permission to stay behind in her room, which Julia granted. The first stop on Taurus's tour was the temple enclave. Walking through the Hulda Gates, just below the Royal Portico where the Sanhedrin met, they climbed up two flights of stairs past the moneychangers and merchants. Upon reaching the top, they entered the Court of Gentiles. Julia was awe struck by the towering walls and columns in the massive courtyard. Hundreds of people wandered about or stood in small groups conversing or praying. Animal pens lined the walls containing unblemished animals suitable for sacrifice.

"This is much larger than I expected," Julia remarked. Lifting her head slightly, she sniffed the air and asked, "What is that strange aroma?"

"That is the smell of animals being sacrificed along with incense, saffron and frankincense to sweeten the odor," Taurus replied.

"Are there usually this many people?" she asked.

"When they celebrate their festivals, the courtyards are packed with even more people who come from all over the land. The soldiers from Caesarea and the Antonia Fortress are required to control the crowds. If you think the smell is bad now, you should have been here a few months earlier during Passover. They sacrificed animals in the hundreds. The odor of their blood hung in the air like a foul mist," Taurus explained.

"I'm glad I missed it," Julia said as she raised her arm to smell the myrrh-fragranced handkerchief tucked in her bracelet. After browsing around for a while, Julia walked toward a walled-off enclosure in the center of the temple complex where two large temple guards stood.

"You can't go in there," Taurus said, gently grabbing her arm.

"Oh, why is that?" she asked.

____

58-The wing in the Praetorium where the Praetorians were housed

"Some areas are forbidden to Romans," he replied. "There are some other interesting sights in the city. I'll show them to you."

"As you wish, Uncle," she said with a puzzled look on her face.

As they left the temple enclave, Julia asked, "Why are some areas forbidden to us? This is a Roman province. Shouldn't we be allowed to go anywhere we want to?"

Taurus smiled. "That has always puzzled me as well. I asked the governor's Greek aide about that. He said the Jewish people are strict about certain places they consider sacred. Only a chosen few are allowed in those areas. It seems quite mysterious to me, but the Greek said that once a Roman detachment tried to enter what they considered their holiest room. The people rose up in arms and it almost caused a widespread revolt. They set temple guards at its entrance with orders to kill anyone who tries to enter without authorization. The emperor has agreed to allow the Jews their privacy in that one location to worship their gods as they wish."

Julia nodded and said, "I was told they only worship one god."

Taurus said only, "Hmm."

After a breathlessly tiring day of touring the city, Taurus returned Julia to her assigned room in the palace.

A day later, Pilate concluded his business with the city officials and they returned to Caesarea.

****

For the next two weeks, Julia and her servants went to the Sea of Galilee and several of the towns nearby such as Tiberias, Capernaum, Sepphoris and Nazareth escorted by various Praetorians. At the end of the third week of Julia's holiday, she, Domitia, Vergilius, and Taurus returned to the palace after a day spent touring the coast by trireme.

Stopping outside her room, Julia said to her servants, "Go inside. I wish to speak with my uncle."

Domitia and Vergilius entered and closed the door.

Julia looked into Taurus's eyes and said, "Uncle. My time here is almost up. I would really like to see Antonius and Marcus one more time before we leave. Can't you allow them to be our escorts at least one more time?"

His first inclination was to say, "Absolutely not!" But as he looked into her pleading eyes, he couldn't deny her request. He retained the title of her favorite uncle and said, "I suppose I can allow that. I'll assign them on your last day."

Embracing him warmly, she said softly, "Thank you, Uncle. That would

222

mean a lot to me.”

"I'll agree to that as long as you promise to conduct yourself like a lady and don't do anything you'll regret later on."

Julia looked down then back up at him and said simply, "I promise."

As he walked away, she thought, "You are definitely my mother's brother."

CHAPTER XV-THE VICTOR

It was the day before the race and as the city slept, the saboteur once again went to Pilate's chariot in the royal stables. This time he put the faulty pins in both wheels. As he sneaked away he felt confident the Roman charioteer would surely not escape death this time.

The next morning, Antonius awoke early, only managing a few hours sleep. As he thought about the upcoming race, his heart felt as though he was already bolting down the track. He wanted to impress the governor as well as Julia, but he knew that every charioteer would be out for his blood. He would have to be at his very best.

After the morning meal, he and the rest of the Praetorians readied themselves for the hippodrome detail. A short while later, Taurus walked in and barked, "The governor is ready to leave for the hippodrome! Line up for inspection!"

Everyone snapped to attention.

After inspection, they marched to their positions alongside the governor's litter, manned by eight large servants who would carry the governor and his wife. Once Pilate and Procula took their places inside, the company proceeded to the hippodrome led by Liberius and Taurus. Julia, Demosthenes and a few servants followed the litter. After arriving, Pilate gave Antonius some words of encouragement. "You know who you have to beat, but don't let your guard down on the others. Be fearless on the track and I'll see you in the winner's circle this time."

"I won't let you down, governor," Antonius promised with a determined look.

Pilate then proceeded to his place in the stadium followed by his entourage and Praetorian escort. He had barely taken his seat when Abaddon the merchant approached.

Recognizing the avaricious merchant, Pilate instructed Taurus to "Let him pass."

"Excellency, good health to you," Abaddon said, bowing and fawning. "I heard you have a new chariot. Would you care to wager on the race again?"

Pilate rubbed his chin. "Yes. But this time, the wager is one hundred pieces of gold for my golden chariot. I have confidence my chariot will win today and we brought a good luck charm with us." He gestured to Julia. "This time your charioteer will eat my charioteer's dust, merchant."

Abaddon beamed. "Only if your driver's skills are as great as your confidence, Excellency. Five hundred pieces of gold it is. I will be back after the race to collect it," he said, with a confident cackle, then returned to his seat.

Pilate glared at him as he walked away. "Insolent dog. If my chariot doesn't win today, the scoundrel's sarcasm will only get worse."

"I wouldn't worry, Pontius," Procula said, patting his arm. "I have a feeling your Praetorian will be victorius today."

Before the chariots entered the arena, the master of ceremonies announced each region they represented as usual. When he announced "Rome," the jeering of the crowd quickly drowned out the few cheers.

"Crush the Roman, Sargon!"

"Send him back to Rome in a Judaean urn!"

Procula leaned close to her husband. "The crowd appears to be particularly vicious today, Pontius. I hope your charioteer is cautious."

"If he is too cautious, he will lose the race. It would be better for him if he is aggressive," Pilate stated concernedly.

"Perhaps cautiously aggressive," Julia suggested, trying to ease the tension.

"Yes, well said, young lady," Pilate stated.

As Antonius took off his uniform and changed into his xystis, he noticed the other drivers looking in his direction. He wondered how much they had wagered with each other as to who would bring about his demise this time. Tightening his belt, he checked his falx to make sure it was secure. As he donned his leather helmet, Sargon approached.

"You wish to try your luck on the track once more, eh, Roman?" the hirsute man asked. Then lowering his voice, he said, "If you challenge me again, I will personally crush your bones beneath my chariot and feed your bowels to the dogs." He then gave Antonius an intimidating smile and strutted away.

Antonius was now more determined than ever to win. Walking over to his chariot, he noticed his horses bobbing their heads and pawing the ground. They were indeed anxious to run.

Inspecting the chariot, Galbo pulled the pins in the wheels and checked them this time since one had failed in the last race. "Master Licinius, come look at this!" he shouted.

Antonius walked over and saw the two half-sawed through pins and asked. "Are those from the chariot?"

Galbo clenched his teeth and said, "Yes. Someone has sabotaged the chariot. Fortunately we have extras but I'll have to run to the palace stable to get them."

"Well, hurry," Antonius urged.

Galbo nodded and hurried out.

Just then, the trumpets sounded for the chariots to proceed to the track.

Antonius watched anxiously for Galbo to return as the other charioteers left the stable. Finally, he returned and said, "Sorry, it took me awhile to get them."

"Hurry!" Antonius implored him. "The other charioteers are already on the track!"

Galbo hurried to replace the pins and wheels with the help of another stableman and, after a few minutes, the chariot was ready.

Antonius then leapt onto the chariot then Galbo secured the reins to his arm.

Meanwhile, Pilate saw all the other charioteers enter the track and take their usual preliminary lap. All except for Antonius. Standing up, he shouted, "Where is my chariot?" His concern grew as all the other chariots lined up and waited for the signal to begin the race.

Just as the starter was about to drop the mappa, Antonius's chariot bolted toward the starting gates. Looking up at the starter's hand holding the handkerchief, he muttered, "Don't drop it."

Seeing his charioteer racing toward the starting gates, Pilate pointed and exclaimed, "There he is!"

Antonius was still a few lengths away from the others when the starter dropped the mappa. Seven chariots lurched forward to the roar of the crowd with Antonius bringing up the rear. Making the first turn slightly ahead of the two closest chariots, Sargon pressed his horses to build a bigger lead. On the next straightaway, Antonius's chariot accelerated down the track, moving up on the green chariot and coming neck and neck with the silver chariot on the outside. As they made the next turn, the green chariot turned into the silver chariot to force it into Antonius's chariot. Its wheels ground against those of the silver chariot, causing it to swing into Antonius's path. Antonius saw it and sped past the impending obstacle as the first lap ended. Up in the stands, Abaddon smiled, counting the one hundred gold pieces in his mind.

For the next three laps Antonius passed one chariot after another even when they tried to force him into the wall or spina. He knew he had to push his horses harder than he had before and hoped they would have enough stamina to finish the race. At the beginning of the fifth lap, he began to gain on the two chariots ahead of him running neck and neck. Roaring down the straightaway to end the fifth lap, he passed them both on the outside before they could block him. He was now in third place. Going into the next turn, he cut sharply to the inside. The two other chariots slowed to avoid colliding, then jostled for position right behind him. But as they did, their wheels became entangled and, as the charioteers leaned to free their chariots, both chariots' wheels disintegrated, dumping the men out of their chariots. Both chariots crashed into the opposite walls and the charioteers teams continued to pull them into the paths of the approaching chariots. The other charioteers swerved to miss them without success as the two drivers disappeared under pounding hooves and grinding wheels. Procula and Julia both gasped, along with the rest of the crowd.

A bloodthirsty spectator mentioned to his friend, "Perhaps the Roman will be next, eh?"

Track attendants stopped the horses of the two damaged chariots and quickly led them off the track, while others went out to retrieve what was left of the chariots and mangled bodies of their drivers. Antonius still had one more chariot to pass before he could challenge Sargon. At the next turn, Antonius was a full length behind him when the lap keeper removed another wooden egg to end the sixth lap. It was time to push his horses more than he had before. "Now, Jupiter!" Antonius shouted, as his chariot thundered down the straightaway, passing the second place chariot. One lap remained.

At the next turn, he was a length behind Sargon. Now the merchant was nervous. Antonius's chariot inched forward until he came alongside the unchallengeable black chariot.

As they went into the last turn, Sargon pulled hard to the right to force Antonius into the outside wall like before. But Antonius had anticipated his move and pulled hard on the reins to almost stop his horses. As the black chariot cut in front of him, Antonius swerved to the left, taking the inside position. Sargon desperately tried to swerve back, but he cut too sharply. His chariot tipped over and tumbled several times freeing his team. With the reins still wrapped tightly around Sargon's wrist, the torque pulled his left arm from its socket. Bleeding profusely, the unbeatable charioteer lay exposed on the track while the remaining chariots pummeled him over and over. The crowd suddenly went silent.

Focused completely on winning the race, Antonius crossed the finish line unaware that his chief nemesis was dead.

Abaddon stared in disbelief. Not only did he lose his champion charioteer, he also lost a great deal of money. Besides the governor, he had confidently bet with several others who felt the young Roman would win that day, at generous odds.

Antonius slowed his chariot and looked back, expecting to see the fuming expression on Sargon's face. Instead he saw the last few chariots come across the line. The crowd was still in shock, but here and there, a few who had bet on the victorious Roman began to cheer. Antonius turned his chariot around and slowly drove back to where Sargon fell. He watched in silence, as the attendants carried the blood-soaked body of his chief antagonist off the track. Then he noticed Sargon's left arm on the track in a pool of blood.

Moments later Abaddon walked up to Pilate and said, "Here is the agreed upon wager."

"Give it to my aide," Pilate instructed, pointing to Demosthenes. Then he said, "Perhaps the next race we can wager five hundred gold pieces."

With a scowl, Abaddon made a quick bow then silently walked away. His attempts to sabotage Pilate's chariot had proven unsuccessful and his greed would cost him his business.

Pilate turned to Procula and Julia with a smile that could not be contained. "Come, we must congratulate the victor!" He jumped to his feet then hurried down the stone stairs that led to the track with Procula and Julia following close behind.

"Magnificent! Simply magnificent," he declared, as Antonius brought the chariot to a stop.

"Thank you, Governor," Antonius replied. He looked at Julia and smiled.

She took a deep relieved breath and returned his smile.

Sensing an attraction between them, Procula said, "Perhaps your champion could take our young lady for a victory lap, Pontius. Would you like that, my dear?"

Julia looked up at Antonius and replied, hesitantly, "If he promises not to go too fast."

"I promise to only go as fast as the lady wishes," he assured her.

Then holding out his hand he assisted her onto the chariot and said, "You should probably hold onto me."

She placed her hands on his waist as he snapped the reins. The chariot lurched forward giving her an unexpected jolt and causing her to wrap her arms around his waist.

He reacted with a smile and brought his winded team to an easy trot. "Is this slow enough for you?" he asked.

"This will do," she replied, hardly believing she was riding in a racing chariot on a hippodrome track as hundreds of spectators watched them.

Procula took Pilate's arm as they proceeded to where he would hand out the awards and said, "I think they like each other, Pontius."

Pilate gave an upward nod and said, "Maybe we should try and convince her to stay. He seems to perform better with the young lady present."

As Antonius and Julia finished their jaunt around the track, she said, "It is a shame a few charioteers were hurt today."

Antonius looked up at the thinning crowd. "That is why some people come—to see the blood. Some of the charioteers even hope for it."

Julia looked down and noticed a large bloodstain still visible in the hardened track. Looking up at him, she said, "You won't intentionally try to hurt others when you race, will you, Antonius?"

Antonius thought for a moment. "I like to go fast, but not at the expense of someone else's life. I prefer a good, clean race with no one getting hurt." He then looked at Julia and said, "You have my promise I will not intentionally try to hurt anyone when I race."

Looking down, she remarked, "I suppose at every race, there will always be the possibility that will happen."

"Yes," Antonius agreed, "there will always be that possibility."

Finishing his victory lap, Antonius dropped off the chariot to Galbo, waiting near the stables.

"Excellent race, Praetorian," Galbo congratulated him.

Antonius nodded then escorted Julia to the area for the awards presentation. The ceremony was brief, but this time Pilate crowned *his* champion. Placing the wreath on Antonius's head, he leaned close and whispered, "I'm glad you won. I don't think I could have taken any more sarcasm from that merchant swine who owned the black chariot." After handing out the scrolls for second and third place, Pilate declared the contest over and the remainder of the crowd dispersed.

"This calls for a celebration," Pilate shouted. "Let us now celebrate our victory! We shall eat and drink ourselves into oblivion!"

The Praetorians all cheered.

After Antonius cleaned up and changed back into his uniform, they returned to the palace for an evening of revelry. Servants quickly set up the banquet hall and prepared extra delicacies for the festivities.

Julia sat at Pilate's dining table, to the left of Procula at one end with Antonius sitting accross from her. At Pilate's end, Liberius sat to his right while Taurus sat to his left. The other Praetorians occupied the rest of the table on both sides.

Procula turned to Julia and asked, "Have you enjoyed your stay with us so far, my dear?"

"Oh, yes, it has been delightful," Julia replied. "My uncle's Praetorians have shown me so many interesting places and people. It was so kind of you to let them escort me."

Procula touched Julia's arm and said, "I'm glad you were able to come, my dear. It was nice to have another Roman woman to talk to."

Julia smiled at the thought that Procula thought of her as a woman and not a young girl.

Pilate, irritated that the wine had not yet been brought out, bellowed, "Must we be kept waiting until the Feast of Tabernacles? Where is the wine?"

Two servants hurried over to their table with two large amphoras and quickly began to pour.

"Finally, something to wash down the dust of the track," Pilate exclaimed.

When he saw that the servants had filled all the cups, Pilate stood up and said, "I would like to propose a toast!"

Everyone arose from the table.

Holding his cup in the air, he said, "To my magnificent horses... the Praetorian who took them to victory... and the glory of Rome!"

"The glory of Rome!" everyone shouted.

Then came the food. Different kinds of meats, fish, cheese, olives, and a variety of fruits and vegetables.

After consuming enough food with enough wine, Pilate stood up once again and called down to Antonius. "I hope you have enjoyed what victory tastes like, Praetorian Licinius. Keep winning and I will reward you both in palate and purse. Come now and receive your well-earned reward."

Antonius left his place and walked up to Pilate's side.

"Demosthenes!" Pilate shouted, "bring me the winnings from the race!"

Not long afterwards, the Greek assistant carried out a small chest.

"Put out your hands, Praetorian!" Pilate ordered.

Antonius obeyed, then Pilate opened the chest and counted out fifty gold coins, putting them into Antonius's two cupped hands.

"Your first reward," Pilate declared. "Keep winning and there will be more."

"Thank you, Governor, this is most generous," Antonius replied, looking shocked at the unexpected gift.

Pilate lifted his head slightly and said, "You certainly deserved it. Now, it's growing late and I'm sure you all have duties to perform, so Centurion

Taurus, you can dismiss your men."

"Yes, Governor," Taurus said, rising to his feet. "Praetorians! Dismissed!"

Antonius filed out with the others, but before he left, he noticed a certain young lady smiling at him.

****

On Julia's final day in Judaea, Antonius and Marcus appeared at her stateroom as Taurus had promised.

"How would you like to spend your last day?" Antonius asked.

"I want to go somewhere along the seashore and just relax," Julia replied. "Why don't you and Marcus wear tunics instead of your uniforms so you can relax as well."

Antonius shook his head. "We're not supposed to relax on a guard detail. We're responsible for your safety. I don't think your uncle would like that."

"Then bring your swords," Julia suggested. She then muttered, "He can't dislike it if he doesn't know about it."

Marcus shook his head. "Your uncle finds out about everything."

Julia looked daringly at Antonius and asked, "You're not afraid of my uncle, are you, Antonius."

"I am," Marcus answered.

Antonius, however, took her dare and said, "We'll change and come back."

Hustling his unsure friend back to the barracks, Antonius quickly began to take off his armor and helmet.

"Are you sure you want to do this?" Marcus asked.

Antonius scrunched his face and said, "Don't be a mouse. We'll still be protecting her."

"If the centurion finds out, we'll be the ones who will need protecting," Marcus retorted, as he took off his helmet.

Returning to Julia's room after changing, Marcus gazed up at the ceiling and shook his head as Antonius knocked on the door.

Domitia opened it and gestured for them to enter.

"Much better," Julia said, looking them over. "Come, I want to have fun on my last day. Vergilius, bring the blankets, you're coming too," she ordered.

After finding a secluded spot on the shore, Vergilius laid out blankets for Julia, himself and Domitia, while Antonius and Marcus stood behind them in a semi-relaxed stance.

Julia didn't think her feelings for someone she barely knew would run this deep. In the short time she had known Antonius, she felt a strong attraction and desperately wanted to know if he thought of her as just a casual fling or if his feelings toward her were serious. Turning, she said, "Antonius, would you go for a walk with me?"

Domitia immediately rose to her feet, intending to accompany them.

"Remain here, Domitia," Julia said firmly. "We won't go far."

Domitia sat back down, but gave Antonius her squinty-eyed look.

As Julia and Antonius strolled down the shoreline feeling the surf wash up around their feet, Antonius asked, "Have you enjoyed your stay here, Julia?"

"It's given me a chance to know someone a little better," she replied with a coy smile.

He returned her smile and said, "Me as well."

Mustering up what courage she had, Julia asked, "What do you think of me, Antonius?"

He pondered her question for a moment. With conviction he replied, "I think of you as a precious gem."

"Oh, I like that," she said. "How precious?"

He waved his hand. "Far more precious than gold or silver could buy. What do you think of me?"

With a brief hesitation, she said, "I would compare you to a mighty stallion, like those that pull your chariot."

Antonius smiled.

"Are you brave enough to meet me in the courtyard one last time tonight before I leave?" she pleaded.

Antonius thought of Taurus's warning and quickly decided to ignore it. "I'm brave enough," he replied with a smile.

Julia grasped his hand and gave it a gentle squeeze. Then, realizing Domitia would probably be watching, she quickly released it.

Looking back, she noticed they had gone quite a distance down the sandy and rocky shoreline.

"We should probably return before Domitia comes after us," she suggested.

Antonius smiled and nodded.

After Julia had her fill of sun and surf, they left the shore and went into the city where she did some shopping before returning to the palace.

****

That evening, Demosthenes knocked on Julia's door and invited her to dine as usual with Pilate and Procula for supper. After the meal, Pilate tried to convince her to stay.

"You know, Procula would love having another Roman woman of means besides servants to converse with in the palace. Why don't you stay?"

Julia thought for a moment, then said, "I am flattered that you ask, Your Excellency, but I don't feel I'm ready to be on my own just yet."

"Are you sure you won't reconsider, young lady? You're welcome to stay here as long as you like," Pilate said, trying to change her mind.

"Your offer is most kind, but I can't," Julia replied.

"You should at least stay for the next chariot race," Pilate beseeched. "My driver seems to do better when you cheer for him."

"It is tempting, your Excellency, but I really must return to Rome. My parents would worry if I did not arrive when promised."

Procula smiled and nodded. "I am pleased that you think of your parents, my dear. Many young people today think only of themselves. It is refreshing to hear you say that."

"Respecting their wishes is how I show my parents that I love them," Julia replied.

"Well, I hope your stay has been an enjoyable one," Pilate said, realizing he couldn't change her mind.

"Oh, it has been wonderful! You and the governess have been so kind to allow me to stay in the palaces. I shall never forget the hospitality you have shown me," Julia declared.

"When does your ship sail, my dear?" Procula asked.

"In the morning on the second hour," she replied.

Procula turned to her husband and said, "Pontius, we should let Julia return to her room. She probably has to prepare for her journey home."

"Certainly," Pilate replied. "But before you go, young lady, we would like to give you a gift." Pilate clapped his hands and Demosthenes immediately appeared with a box wrapped in silk, tied with a golden ribbon. Pilate nodded toward Julia and Demosthenes walked over and presented it to her.

"You are too kind," she said, taking the box. "Should I open it here?"

"Of course," Pilate replied. "It is merely a memento Procula picked out that we thought you would like."

Julia opened the box and felt her breath taken away as her eyes beheld a stunning gold necklace, trimmed with a few precious gems.

"This is the most beautiful thing I have ever seen!" she exclaimed.

"A beautiful necklace for a beautiful girl," Procula remarked. "We hope your journey back to Rome is a safe one."

"Thank you for your wonderful gift, it is truly breathtaking."

Pilate stood up and said, "You may go now and prepare for your departure. If ever you decide to return to Judaea, you are most welcome to stay with us again."

"My deepest thanks. You have both been most generous. I will remember this trip always," Julia declared, feeling her eyes becoming misty.

Pilate and Procula smiled as Julia bowed her head and departed.

Later that evening, Taurus dropped by her stateroom.

Opening the door, Vergilius stood aside. "Mistress Julia, your uncle."

Taurus walked in and said, "Julia, I apologize for not being able to spend more time with you. I hope your stay was a pleasant one?"

Julia's eyes brightened. "Oh, yes, Uncle. I had a truly wonderful time."

He smiled one of his rare smiles. "Good. I will come by early and escort you to your ship tomorrow."

Looking like a school girl trying to use her charms, she asked, "Would you permit Antonius and Marcus to come see me off as well? I would like to thank them for being my guides."

Taurus gave her a look that said, "I know what you're trying to do." He then sighed and said, "Yes, I'll bring them with me. I can also bring the rest of the Praetorians to see you off since they all were your escorts."

"Oh... well, you can thank them for me if you wish, but I would really just like to say goodbye to Antonius and Marcus," she said, looking up under her eyebrows.

Taurus gave her a slight smile and said, "If that is your wish I will grant it. I'll come for you at the first hour. That should give you enough time to arrive and get settled on the ship."

Julia nodded. "And I want you to know I am leaving Judaea with a clear conscience, Uncle."

He gave an upward nod and left the room, feeling relieved that Julia's stay was free from making any moral mistakes she would have to pay for later. His sister would be pleased.

Julia and her servants packed for the return trip home then retired for the night as the hour grew late. When Julia was certain her servants were asleep, she slipped out of bed for her last meeting with Antonius. Entering the courtyard, she saw him waiting for her. She hurried over and fell into his arms, kissing him warmly. Afterward, Antonius reached into his tunic pocket and produced a small box.

"Something to remember me by while we're apart," he said, holding it out to her.

Julia's mouth opened in surprise. With trembling hands, she removed the top and beheld a silver dolphin pin with a small green emerald for its eye.

"Oh, Antonius. This is beautiful!" she declared.

"The dolphin's eye is an emerald. Remember when you asked what I thought of you and I said... "

"A precious gem," she said, finishing Antonius' sentence.

She looked at his gift once more as tears welled up in her eyes. "I will wear this always. When I do, I will think of you and the most wonderful time of my life." They embraced and kissed again. She then put up her finger and said, "Wait here. I have a gift for you as well." Running back to her room, she silently slipped inside. A moment later, she returned and handed Antonius a miniature white horse carved from ivory.

Impressed with the detail and workmanship, he exclaimed, "This is magnificent! Where did you get it?"

"I couldn't resist. I saw it in one of the shops in Jerusalem and had to buy it for my favorite charioteer. It is to remind you of your promise."

"I will think of you each time I look at it." He then took her in his arms and gave her one last memorable kiss.

Pulling away, she smiled through misty eyes. "I have to leave now while I can still think clearly."

"Must you go? Stay a little longer," he pleaded.

Julia gazed at him longingly then slowly backed away. "I cannot trust myself with you if I do. I love you, Antonius." She quickly turned and ran back to her room.

"I love you, too," he whispered. Looking down at the small carving in his hand, he smiled. He wished they had more time, but the time they shared was enough for him to know—she was the one he wanted to marry.

The next day, Taurus, Julia and her servants boarded a palace carriage that would take them to the dock. Antonius and Marcus escorted them on horseback. Upon arriving, Vergilius took their baggage on board the ship as Julia embraced her uncle and decorously shook hands with Antonius and Marcus.

As she and Domitia walked up the gangplank, her eyes brimmed with tears. Waving farewell, she called out to her three favorite Praetorians, "Take care of yourselves!" she shouted.

The three Praetorians waved as the ship pulled out of port. After it had disappeared over the horizon, Taurus yelled, "Don't just stand there, you two hyenas! Get back to the palace! You have posts to stand!"

On their way back to the palace, Marcus leaned over and asked Antonius,

"What's a hyena?"

****

Julia and her servants stood on deck as their ship pulled into Ostia a few weeks later. "Look! Mother and Sister are here!" she cried, seeing Juliana and Serina standing on the dock.

With tears in her eyes, Julia ran down the gangplank and embraced them as though they had been apart for years. "Mother, Serina... I missed you so much!"

"We missed you too, Julia," her mother replied, her own tears brimming. "It is good to have you back safe."

"Have you been waiting long?" Julia asked.

"All day," Serina replied with a bored sigh. Noticing a sharp look from her mother, she added, "But the wait was worth it to see that you returned home safely."

"Did you have a wonderful time?" Juliana asked.

"Yes! Judaea is certainly not as developed as our country, but there are many similarities in the major cities. I even stayed in two palaces and dined with the governor," Julia stated proudly.

"You dined with the governor?" Juliana asked, raising her eyebrows.

"In two palaces?" her sister asked.

"Yes. Uncle Taurus arranged it so I could stay at Herod's palace in Caesarea. Then we went to Jerusalem and saw the Jewish temple there and stayed at Herod's other palace. It was even more magnificent than the palace in Caesarea!"

"Did you get to see your Praetorian much?" Serina asked.

Julia looked at her mother's concerned face. "Yes. I was able to see Antonius. In fact, he and his friend were our guides for a few days. They conducted themselves like perfect gentlemen, didn't they, Domitia?"

Domitia hesitantly nodded, causing Juliana to smile.

Vergilius walked up to them with bags in hand and asked Juliana, "Where is the carriage, Lady Cato?"

"Just off the dock on the left," Juliana replied, pointing to where the carriage sat.

Vergilius nodded then went and secured the luggage.

"You must tell us everything," Juliana insisted as they all walked over then boarded the carriage.

"Yes! What else did you do?" Serina asked, as everiyone was seated and the carriage pulled away from the dock.

"Many things. I even went to a chariot race Antonius was in," Julia replied.

"A chariot race? Did he win?" Serina asked.

"Yes!" Julia exclaimed. Then she scrunched her face and said, "but three charioteers were killed."

"Oh, my," her mother exclaimed.

"But Antonius really won?" Serina pressed.

"He did. It was his first victory, and the governor thought he won because I was there. He called me Antonius's good luck charm."

Juliana smiled. "I'm glad the trip was wonderful for you dear, but it is good to have you back home."

Julia sighed then said, "Yes, although seeing new sights was enjoyable, I did miss you."

"Did you bring anything back from Judaea?" Serina asked innocently.

"Yes," Julia replied with an exuberant smile. "I have gifts for all–a necklace for mother given to me by the governor himself, a pair of Phoenician sandals for Father, and some Syrian bracelets I purchased in Caesarea for you, Serina."

Serina squealed in delight.

"You brought back nothing for yourself?" Juliana asked.

"I have a very special pin Antonius gave me," Julia replied with a contented smile.

CHAPTER XVI-Death and Desire

A few months later, Pilate went to Jerusalem to see how its new aqueduct was functioning that the Roman engineers had built. He had negotiated with officials earlier in the year and the aqueduct had finally been completed, but not without controversy.

Pilate managed to convince the Sanhedrin to use the temple treasury funds for the construction, stating it would improve the people's lives and the people wouldn't be taxed for it. Opposed to the proposal at first, the priests finally agreed as long as Pilate kept his promise and the use of the funds secret. Somehow, the secret became known, word spread, and chaos ensued. Many who viewed the temple funds as sacred and not to be used for "worldly" purposes, gathered all around the city to protest. When Pilate sent soldiers out to control the crowds, the anti-Roman zealots seized the opportunity to vandalize sections of the aqueduct. It wasn't long before an angry mob gathered in the palace esplanade.

"Pilate! Pontius Pilate!" they shouted over and over.

Pilate was having his midday meal at the time and upon hearing the din of the crowd, asked, "What does the rabble want now?"

Liberius approached him and saluted. "Governor, we have reports that vandals have damaged several sections of the aqueduct and water is flowing out of control all over the city."

With a stern look, Pilate asked, "How did this happen?"

Liberius shook his head. "I don't know, Governor, but a man in the esplanade informed me that a rumor has circulated saying that you forced the Sanhedrin to use temple funds to build the aqueduct. He and many others want to know if this is true."

Pilate's jaw stiffened then he bellowed, "The funds were used to better these ungrateful peasants' lives!"

"Evidently, a few of the peasants didn't want their lives bettered," Liberius muttered.

Pilate growled then said, "Go out on the balcony and inform them I will hear their complaint after I have finished my meal and they stop yelling."

Liberius saluted and replied, "Yes, Governor."

Proceeding to the balcony in front of the palace overlooking the crowd, Liberius shouted, "The governor will hear your complaints as soon as he finishes his meal. However, he will not appear until you cease your howling!"

The crowd quieted down but continued milling about and grumbling.

Liberius returned to Pilate to give his report. "I informed the people you will appear shortly, Governor."

Pilate nodded and waved him away. As Liberius started to leave, Pilate shouted, "Wait!"

Liberius turned around.

Pilate narrowed his eyes and said, "See to it that all my Praetorians are put on alert and the guard is doubled at the gates. Then disperse the auxiliaries all around the esplanade in plain clothes, make sure they are not in uniform and have them armed with clubs and daggers under their cloaks. If the crowd refuses to leave or gets violent, I will give the signal for them to attack by waving my hand. Go now and arrange it."

Liberius saluted and left to carry out his orders.

Soon afterward, Pilate appeared on the balcony, flanked by Antonius and Marcus. Looking out upon the crowd he shouted, "I was told you are here because of the aqueduct that was built for you. What is your complaint?"

A spokesman stepped forward. "We were told that our sacred temple funds were used for its construction? Is this true?"

"Who told you this?" Pilate asked.

"Never mind who told us; is it true?" the spokesman brazenly asked again.

Pilate clenched his teeth at the man's impudence. "Yes, it is true."

A loud murmur went up from the crowd.

"But what were the funds used for?" Pilate shouted. "For me… for Rome? No, they were used for you, the people of Judaea. No more traveling back and forth to one well to gather your water. No more straining to carry the large pots long distances. The water now comes to you in cisterns all over the city. I don't understand why you would be unhappy about being provided with a way to make your lives easier."

"Because you provided it with money that was not to be used for this purpose!" an angry voice shouted from the crowd.

"It was either take the money from your temple treasury or increase your taxes to cover the costs? Would you have preferred that?" Pilate yelled.

"No, you have taxed us enough as it is," the spokesman replied, as the crowd angrily agreed. "What enrages us is the fact that the temple funds are not to be used for such common things. They are only supposed to be used for the building up of God's kingdom."

Pilate thought for a moment, then said, "Were they used to build your temple?"

"Yes," the spokesman answered.

"Do you provide water for the people who come to the temple?" Pilate asked.

"Yes," the spokesman replied.

"Ah!" Pilate exclaimed."You will spend money to provide water for people that go to your temple but you will not spend money to provide water for the rest. It seems to me your god is a discriminating god."

The spokesman shook his head and said, "An aqueduct does not increase one's spirituality. Our temple does. I'm sure if the temple authorities had not been pressured by you to use the funds, they would have refused. What did you tell them, Pilate? Did you threaten to destroy the temple if they didn't comply?"

Pilate was now tired of trying to reason with an apparently unreasonable mob. His anger was evident as he roared at the crowd. "Hear me now, o' people of Judaea. I try to improve your country and you shout insults rather than thanks. It is clear to me that no matter what I do to try and please you, you will find some way to complain about it. I thereby order you to disperse now and go back to your homes."

"Why don't you go back to Rome and let *us* decide how to spend our money!" a voice from the crowd shouted.

"Miserable ingrates!" Pilate shouted back. "Your own religious leaders decided that spending the money for a water system was in your best interests. Take the matter up with them, not me."

"That is like you Romans to take what we have and blame us for it!" another voice shouted.

"Go back to your homes or I will call out my troops and have them remove you," Pilate shouted.

"God will remove you, blasphemer!" the spokesman shouted as he shook his finger at Pilate.

His response was like taunting an angry cobra. Pilate decided it was time to strike. He waved his hand then nodded and sat down.

Some in the crowd perceived that he had finished with them and that it was a sign for them to leave. The auxiliaries that had gathered quietly around the crowd knew what the sign really meant. They fell on the unsuspecting crowd from all sides stabbing and clubbing. Women screamed and people knocked each other down, trampling the unfortunate ones. Soon, blood mingled with water from the broken aqueduct. When it was over, hundreds of people lay dead in the square. The auxiliaries surreptitiously returned the palace to change into their battle uniforms in case there was an unlikely retaliation by the people. Pilate, satisfied with the results, went back inside the palace as Marcus took one last look at the carnage and shook his head.

"Liberius!" Pilate shouted.

"Yes, Governor."

"Spread the word that a disturbance has occurred near the palace and that unknown assailants have killed a number of those who were present. Anyone who may have had loved ones or friends here should come and claim their bodies. Give them the rest of the day to do so. At dusk, remove the bodies that are left and dispose of them."

"Yes, Governor," Liberius replied. He saluted and left.

That afternoon, people came into the square and walked through the bodies, hoping that their missing relatives or friends were not among them. The cries of many revealed that their hope was in vain. In another part of the city, angry people demanded to speak with temple authorities and leaders of the Sanhedrin. As they complained to their own officials, Pilate's soldiers removed the few bodies that were not claimed. A cohort of soldiers remained in the square to impress upon all that any further disturbances would be dealt with by force.

Later that evening as Marcus slept, he had a dream. He stood chained between two pillars of an aqueduct. Looking up, he saw a mob of people rushing toward him carrying clubs and daggers. "Blasphemer! Blasphemer!" they shouted. He struggled to free himself, but his efforts were in vain. He pulled against the chains as hard as he could as the mob grew closer and closer. Then suddenly, the aqueduct pillars began to crumble and the contents splashed down upon him. To his horror, it was filled with blood.

"Ahhhh!" he screamed, sitting up in his bunk.

"What is it, Marcus?" Antonius asked, awakened by his cries.

Marcus took a deep breath and replied, "I had a dream about those people in the square. What Pilate did wasn't right, Antonius."

Antonius gestured for Marcus to be quiet. "There is nothing we can do about it, Marcus. Go back to sleep."

Marcus lay back down and stared at the ceiling. "I fear I've made a big mistake in joining the Guard," he thought to himself.

****

"On your feet, you lazy sloths!" Taurus bellowed as he burst into the barracks the next morning. "We return to Caesarea today. Get something to eat and be ready to march."

He was already out the door when Marcus sat up and rubbed his red eyes.

"This time, it looks like *you* had a rough night," Antonius said, as he stood up and yawned.

Looking up, Marcus said, "I couldn't stop thinking about those people who were killed by the auxiliaries."

Antonius drew near to him so that only he could hear and said, "You worry me, Marcus."

"What do you mean?" Marcus asked.

"Ever since you started visiting that old Jewish man, he has filled your head with all their moral zealotry," Antonius muttered.

Marcus wrinkled his nose. "Do you think what Pilate did was moral?"

Antonius shook his head. "It doesn't matter what I think. We are Roman soldiers and we have to follow orders."

"Even if they are morally wrong?" Marcus said louder.

Antonius looked around and said, "Guard what you say, Marcus. Talk like that could get you into serious trouble if it reached Pilate's ears."

Marcus gave Antonius a look of frustration then went to the latrine.

****

Two days later, Pilate was back in his Caesarean palace. He had all but forgotten about the incident in Jerusalem when Demosthenes approached his tribunal and announced, "There are several temple officials from Jerusalem here to see you, Excellency."

Pilate looked up from the dispatch he was reading and replied, "Temple officials?" What do they want?" he gruffly asked.

Demosthenes bowed slightly and replied, "They would not say, Excellency."

Pilate growled then said, "All right, send them in."

Demosthenes bowed again then left. He returned shortly with five members of the Sanhedrin, led by Caiaphas.

"What is it now, priest?" Pilate asked in a condescending tone.

Caiaphas lifted his head slightly and replied, "We wish to know why your men slaughtered our people three days ago in the palace esplanade."

"My men!" Pilate exclaimed. "Obviously there must have been some outsiders among the people who took issue with what *your* people said. Bloodshed erupted and before I could call out my troops to quell the disturbance, it was over."

Caiaphas gave Pilate an accusatory look and said, "Come now, Excellency, dost thou really take us for fools? We know that those men who *caused* the bloodshed were *your* soldiers. Many in the crowd who survived said they were Samarian and Syrian conscripts."

Pilate pretended innocence and said, "Just because I have Samarians and Syrians in my ranks, doesn't mean they were the ones causing the disturbance. There are many Syrians and Samarians living in the city who aren't conscripts. Besides, if they were my men, they would have been in uniform and used swords rather than clubs and daggers."

Now the temple leader smiled. "I don't recall mentioning anything about clubs and daggers being used."

Pilate's expression was unchanged as he replied, "The Centurion in charge of disposing the bodies informed me that many had wounds resulting from dagger thrusts and being clubbed." Holding up his hands, he said, "What else could I deduce, Priest?"

Caiaphas could see Pilate was not going to admit to the massacre. Giving him a pious look, Caiaphas spoke brazenly. "Thou canst kill our people and blaspheme our God, but even the ruler of Judaea shall pay for his sins. Your day of thy reckoning will come."

Pilate narrowed his eyes and leaned forward. "Is that a threat, Priest?"

Caiaphas replied in a huff, "Thou hast nothing to fear from me. But thou wouldst be a fool not to fear the God of Moses." He then whirled about and began to leave.

"Stop!" Pilate shouted. "I did not dismiss you!"

Caiaphas and the other priests kept walking toward the entrance.

This incensed Pilate even more. He stood up and pointed to them yelling, "Stop those priests!"

Two Praetorians standing on either side of the entrance crossed their spears to block the priests' exit.

Turning around, the priests glared at Pilate. Their eyes fixed on his as if they were burning holes in his head.

Pilate clenched his teeth and glared back. Finally, he waved them away, snarling, "Now, you may go." He nodded to the guards and they uncrossed their spears.

Caiaphas furled his cape and stormed out, followed by the other priests.

****

While tempers sizzled in Judaea, the summer day sizzled in Aletium. As Sergius toiled in the field, Camilla hung her family's clothes out to dry. Looking over at him as he worked on clearing a patch of tall grass around the house, she wished he would find it in his heart to forgive Marcus for leaving. She knew, however, that was unlikely. Sergius, for the most part, was good to her and the children but when he held a grudge he would not let go of it. His last words to Marcus telling him not to return, still stung her memory.

As the heat became more intense, sweat poured from his body as he swung his scythe back and forth to clear the tall grass. Suddenly, he felt an excruciating pain in his chest. Throwing the scythe down, he winced as he felt the pain travel down his left arm. He looked up and tried to call out to Camilla, but all he could do was gasp. Out of the corner of her eye, she saw him slump over then fall to the ground. She let out an alarmed cry and ran toward him shouting, "Sergius! Sergius!"

Arriving where he lay, she knelt down and propped his head in her lap. "Breathe, Sergius," she cried, putting her hand under his nose. But she could feel no breath. Laying her head down on his, she kept saying the words, "Don't go, Sergius… don't go." When she finally realized he would not awaken from his deathly sleep, she gently laid his head down on the ground. It was a ground that was as unforgiving as he was. It was a ground he had struggled with so many years to plant and cultivate. It was a ground that had finally killed him and would now claim his body.

Octavia was in the front watering some flowers when she saw Camilla running down the hill toward her.

"Camilla! What is the matter?" Octavia asked, when she saw tears flowing down Camilla's face as she drew nearer.

Stopping an arm's length away, out of breath, Camilla replied, "Sergius… Sergius…!" was all she could say.

"What happened?" Octavia asked.

"He just keeled over… while clearing some brush," Camilla sobbed.

Hearing Camilla's loud exclamation, Galerius and Decimus came over from their inspection of the vineyard.

"Did I hear you say Sergius fell?" Galerius asked.

Taking a moment to control herself, Camilla replied, "He collapsed… while cutting some weeds… near the house."

"I'll go and see if there is anything I can do. Perhaps he just fainted from the heat," Galerius stated.

Camilla shook her head and said, "I couldn't feel his heart… and he's not breathing."

"Galerius, take a water flask and see if you can revive him," Octavia suggested.

"A good idea," Galerius agreed.

A moment later he and Decimus went running up the hill with the flask, hoping he wasn't too late.

"Where are the children?" Octavia asked.

"I told them to wait... in the house... until I return," Camilla replied between breaths.

"Come in out of the sun until Galerius comes back. We don't want you to faint from the heat," Octavia suggested, putting her arm around her friend.

As they went inside, Camilla said, "What will we do, if Sergius is gone?"

Octavia embraced her tenderly and said, "Don't give up hope, Camilla. Perhaps Galerius is right and Sergius just fainted."

Camilla hoped Octavia was right, but in her heart she was afraid Octavia wasn't.

When Galerius and Decimus returned, the look on their faces indicated that Sergius had indeed crossed the realm between life and death.

"I'm sorry," Galerius said as he approached Camilla, "we tried to revive him but nothing we did worked. We took Sergius inside your house and put him on the bed in your room. I hope that was all right."

Camilla nodded and sobbed.

The next day, Galerius and Decimus buried Sergius under a large cypress tree, a short distance from the Flavius' house. After a brief ceremony, the children placed flowers on the mound of dirt that covered his body. While Camilla and her family lingered at the grave, Octavia and Augustina went back to the house and prepared food for the family.

After the meal, Camilla sat on her couch with Octavia's arm around her. Wiping the tears from her eyes, Camilla said, "I wish Marcus was here."

"I wish both our sons were here," Octavia said, gazing out the window.

Galerius, sitting across from them, rubbed his chin. "Perhaps I can make that happen."

"How?" Octavia asked.

Galerius stood up. "I can't promise anything, but I have an idea that may work."

The next day, he dressed in his Tribune's uniform and saddled Mercury. He knew he could ask Sejanus for a favor, but Rome was seven days away and he didn't want to wait that long.

"Where are you going?" Octavia asked.

"To Hydruntum. I'll return tomorrow," he replied.

"You are not going back into the Guard, are you Galerius?" she asked, holding her breath.

He smiled and said, "Only for today, Octavia." He then mounted up and galloped off.

As he rode away, Octavia wished her husband would not keep her in the dark as much as he did. But alas, that was his way.

That evening, Galerius arrived in Hydruntum and walked into the small army garrison there. Entering the commander's office, he approached the Centurion sitting at his desk and barked, "Centurion!"

The Centurion came to attention and saluted. "Yes, Tribune!

"I need to send a dispatch to Governor Pilate in Judaea immediately," Galerius declared officiously.

"I will get my scribe and you can dictate it to him," the Centurion offered.

Galerius waved his hand and said, "No, that won't be necessary. It is a confidential message that I must write myself."

"It must be very important," the centurion stated.

"Important enough," Galerius replied.

The Centurion raised his eyebrows. "I'll get you some writing implements immediately, Tribune. What is your name?"

"Licinius," Galerius curtly replied.

****

A month later, Taurus stopped Antonius in the hallway. "You and Flavius report to the palace Prefect. He just received a dispatch ordering both of you home."

"Ordering us to return home? Why?" Antonius asked.

Taurus gave him an unsure look and said, "It didn't indicate any reason. Go see Liberius and he can give you more details."

"All right, I'll get Marcus," Antonius said, as worry slowly crept inside his head.

A moment later, both young men stood before the palace prefect with worried looks.

After saluting, Antonius asked, "Centurion Taurus told me a dispatch arrived ordering us home. Can you tell us anything about it?"

Liberius shook his head. "No, only that Tribune Galerius Licinius sent it and ordered you to return home for two weeks."

"Then our leave is not permanent?" Marcus asked.

"No. When your two weeks there are up, you are to return to Caesarea and resume your duties. That is all I know. Go pack your things; a trireme will take you back to Italia."

While Marcus looked down in disappointment, Antonius said, "Thank you, Prefect."

They saluted and were about to leave when Liberius said, "Galerius is your father, isn't he Licinius?"

"Uh, yes," Antonius replied.

Liberius nodded and said, "That's all."

Marcus gave Antonius a puzzled look as they marched back to the barracks. "I thought your father was retired from the military. How can he order us home?"

Antonius shook his head. "He wouldn't rejoin just for that. Something has happened." He pinched the skin at his throat and added, "I fear it's something bad."

The next day, they boarded the trireme that would take them home. The ship cast off and slowly moved away from the dock, carrying supplies for the journey and two concerned Praetorians.

Marcus thought about his father's last words telling him not to return. That wasn't going to stop him from seeing his mother and siblings. He would pay them a visit and hope the confrontation with his father wouldn't be too bad. His worries were for nought, however.

****

A week later, as the trireme plowed through the sea's dark water, Marcus's brother, Matthias, plowed through their farm's dark earth. The exertion taxed his every muscle, but the large field had to be planted. Camilla watched in admiration from the garden as he struggled to keep the plow straight.

Stopping to rest, he bent over to catch his breath. A moment later, he heard his mother say, "You have worked hard, my son. Why don't you take a break."

Looking up, he saw her standing next to him. "Come, let's find your brother and sisters and go visit your father's grave," she said.

He nodded, and dropped the reins, happy for the respite.

After gathering her children, Camilla led them to Sergius' grave.

Threatening clouds began to form and a sudden rain beat down upon them, mixing raindrops with tears. Reaching the large Cyprus tree that stood over the grave like an umbrella, they stared at the rough-hewn stone Camilla had purchased to mark Sergius's grave. Rubbing her hand on the cold headstone, she hoped she didn't wind up like Sergius's mother–dying from some serious malady and leaving her children to fend for themselves in a harsh world.

"Matthias, unhitch the horse and take him to the barn. You've plowed enough for today. The rest of us will return to the house before we become ill. I'll prepare supper."

Matthias gratefully nodded.

They ate a simple meal that night and went to their rooms saying little to one another. Camilla sat in front of her bedroom window and watched the raindrops indiscriminately splatter on the puddles of water outside until the hour grew late. She sat there until the rain finally stopped. Then she went to the barn, took the horse out into the field and hitched it up to the plow. She would finish plowing the section Matthias had started. The ground was wet now and easier to till.

****

A few weeks later, Priscilla and her younger sister, Prisca, were picking vegetables for dinner from their garden when they saw a lone rider appear at the crest of the hill in front of their house. He paused a moment then started down. Priscilla noticed him first.

"Someone is coming," she said.

Prisca looked up. "Who is it?"

Priscilla watched the rider for a moment then shouted, "It's MARCUS!"

Prisca jumped up and cried, "Marcus?"

Priscilla yelled back to the house, "Mother! Marcus is here!"

Matthias and Milo came running up from the plowed field as Camilla walked slowly out of the house, thinking perhaps her children were playing a prank on her. Upon seeing her son riding up, she put her hand to her mouth.

Marcus reined his horse to a halt and dismounted. His brothers and sisters practically knocked him over as they all ran to embrace him at the same time. After taking inventory and hugging each one, he walked over to his mother. Looking around, he asked, "Where's Father?"

Tears formed in her eyes as she threw her arms around him. She managed to choke out, "He's gone, Marcus. He's gone."

"He left?" Marcus asked in disbelief.

"No, Marcus," she replied as the tears flowed down her cheeks, "he's dead."

Across the hill another lone rider approached his home. As he tied his horse to the hitching post, he looked over at a sliver of sun disappearing behind the hills. Brushing the dust from his tunic, he was about to go inside when he heard a familiar voice shout, "Antonius!"

He turned to see his mother come running from the vineyard. He smiled and said, "Mother!"

Giving him a tight hug, she said, "It is so good to see you."

248

"You as well. Where is Father?" he asked.

"Inside," she said. "Come, I'm sure he is anxious to know you arrived safely."

"He's not back in the Guard, is he, Mother?"

Octavia smiled. "Oh, no. He just had to pretend he was in order to bring you and Marcus home."

Antonius gave her a confused look. "Why did he do that?"

With a pained expression, Octavia replied, "Antonius... Marcus' father died. Galerius thought it would be good for him to spend a few weeks with his family right now. Of course, if we brought Marcus home, we had to bring you home as well."

Antonius nodded and said, "I'm glad you did."

At the Flavius house, Camilla capped off the supper she prepared with two jars of her best apricots. Although Marcus's siblings were happy to see their brother again, his presence brought back the pain of losing their father. The meal was a relatively quiet one.

"Come, girls," Camilla finally exclaimed. "Let's clear the table and clean up so your brother can rest. He's had a long journey."

"Actually, I'll help with the clean-up tonight," Marcus offered, wanting to be alone with his mother so they could talk.

"But you must be tired," Camilla stated.

"I'm fine, I just need to talk... I miss our talks."

Camilla smiled and said, "I miss them too."

"Can I see your sword?" Milo asked.

"It's called a gladius," Marcus corrected him. Taking the scabbard off his belt, he handed it to him and said, "Be careful, it's very sharp."

Milo nodded with a serious expression then quickly ran out the door with a Praetorian's gladius and a smile on his face. He had some barbaric weeds to conquer.

"Milo! Do not run with that!" Camilla called out to him.

He slowed down... just a little.

The girls happily left to play with their hand-made dolls while Matthias went outside to practice with his father's bow.

As mother and son worked together to clear the table and wash the dishes, Camilla said, "Are you sure you don't want to rest, Marcus? I can handle the clean up."

"I'm really not that tired," he assured her.

Noticing her son's pained expression, Camilla asked, "What troubles you, my son?"

He could only shake his head.

"It is about your father, isn't it?" she asked.

Marcus hesitated then blurted out, "If I hadn't joined the Guard, father would still be alive. I'm to blame for his death and the hardship it has placed on you and the family. I'm sorry… I'm so sorry, I wasn't thinking," he cried, burying his face on her shoulder.

Camilla ran her fingers through his dark blonde hair and said softly, "You must not blame yourself, my son. The gods determined your father's destiny, not you."

"But I should have stayed home," he said, shaking his head.

Camilla pulled him close to her and said, "That was not your destiny, You chose to be where you are now. You cannot change the past."

"But I'm afraid I made the wrong choice," he said. "Now you have no one to do the difficult work that is needed here on the farm."

"We will manage," Camilla stated. "Matthias has been doing more, and Galerius's hired hand occasionally comes and helps us as well. Now that you are here, perhaps you can do a few things before you have to leave."

"I'll do whatever you ask of me," Marcus said, drying his eyes. "Where did you bury Father?"

"Under the big Cypress tree. We'll go down tomorrow at first light," she replied.

Marcus nodded and embraced her. They held each other for a while, not wanting to let go.

****

Early the next day, Marcus and his family had their morning meal then went to the gravesite. Looking at the inscription on the headstone that read only "Sergius Flavius" and the date, Marcus touched the cold surface and felt a shiver run through him. He thought of the words he had heard spoken from Jesus about the afterlife.

"Do you think we will see Father again?" Marcus asked his mother.

"What do you mean?" she asked.

"Do you think after we die we will be able to see him again?"

Camilla looked off in the distance and replied, "I don't know, Marcus. Why do you ask?"

Marcus half shrugged and said, "I just thought it would be comforting to you if we could."

Camilla nodded, then said, "The wind is picking up; we should go back to the house."

"You go, Mother, I want to stay a little longer. Then I think I'll go and visit the Licinius'."

Camilla smiled. "You mean Augustina?"

Marcus blushed.

Grasping his arm, Camilla said, "Tell them to come and have supper with us this evening. I owe them so much for all they've done, especially Galerius for bringing you home."

"I will," Marcus replied, as she returned to the house with his siblings.

Kneeling down he stared at the blemished, gray stone leaning slightly forward in the ground and thought how similar his father was to it. His body, weathered and bent during his final years from the hard labor required on the farm and his hair grayed from age and stress. As tears formed in his eyes, he spoke softly. "Father, I know my choice to become a Praetorian was a disappointment to you, and I know we had bitter words before I left... but if you can hear me, wherever you are, I am sorry. I hope you can forgive me for leaving and not being here when you needed me." Standing up, he brushed himself off and said, "Maybe someday, I'll be able to tell you this in person." After wiping his eyes, he headed for the vineyard and the young girl he was fond of.

Galerius and Antonius were checking the grapes with Decimus-the new hired hand when Marcus saw them in one of the rows and walked over to them.

"Marcus!" Galerius shouted with a smile. Clasping his arm, he said, "I'm glad you're home."

"I just wanted to tell you that I appreciate what you did," Marcus replied. "I just hope you didn't have to rejoin the Guard to do it."

"Oh, no, I just pretended to... but we'll keep this our little secret," Galerius said, winking.

Marcus smiled.

Galerius put his hand on Marcus's shoulder and said, "We were all sad to learn of your father's passing, Marcus. His death came as a shock to us as I'm sure it came to you."

Marcus looked down and nodded.

Pointing to Decimus, Galerius said, "Marcus, this is Decimus Faustus. He is the man I hired to help around the vineyard."

Decimus clasped arms with Marcus and said, "I too, am sorry about your father."

"Thank you," Marcus replied.

"Have you eaten yet?" Galerius asked. "I can have Octavia fix you something if you're hungry."

"Thank you but I've eaten," Marcus replied. "I just came over to thank you for bringing us home. Is... Augustina around?"

Galerius smiled at Marcus' real reason for stopping by. "She's in the house," he said, tilting his head in that direction.

Marcus walked toward the house and stopped at the door. He turned and looked at Galerius who motioned for him to go in. Opening the door slightly, he peered in and shouted, "Hello!"

Augustina came out of the kitchen holding her breath. "Marcus!" she squealed. Running over, she threw her arms around him. After a moment, she stood back, blushing and said, "I've... missed you."

Marcus smiled. "I've missed you as well."

Octavia heard his name mentioned and came in from the other room.

"Marcus, it is so good to see you!" She walked over and embraced him for a moment. "I am terribly sorry about your father, Marcus. Our sympathies are with you and your family."

"Thank you," Marcus replied.

Octavia frowned and said, "Antonius told us you could only stay for a couple of weeks."

"Yes, unfortunately that is all the time they gave us," Marcus stated, lowering his head.

Augustina frowned and said. "Two weeks will hardly give us any time at all. I have so much to tell you."

Marcus rubbed the back of his neck and replied, "I wish we had more time, but I have to follow orders."

"Are you hungry? I can fix you something," Augustina offered.

"No, I just wanted to come over and thank you all for the help you gave mother after father..." he gave a hard swallow and paused.

Breaking the awkward silence, Octavia said, "We were happy to help. After all, there was a time when your mother gave me a lot of help when I was learning to cook. I'm just repaying her for it."

"Speaking of cooking," Marcus stated, "Mother wanted me to invite you over for supper this evening as a way of saying thanks."

Octavia shook her head. "No, Marcus. You tell your mother I want all of you to come here for supper instead. She deserves a rest."

Surprised at Octavia's firm resolve, he nodded quickly and said, "All right, I'll tell her." His focus quickly shifted to Augustina. "You've really changed since I saw you last, Augustina."

"I hope the changes are to your liking," she replied with a coy smile.

Marcus looked her over and said, "Oh, yes, the changes are... good."

Before he became thoroughly lost in her eyes, he turned to Octavia. "I should return to the house now and tell Mother about your invitation."

"Make sure you tell her I insist," Octavia said firmly.

"I will," Marcus assured her, raising his eyebrows. He started toward the door when Augustina said, "I'll walk you back." Realizing she may have presumed too much, she turned to Octavia. "May I, Mother?"

"Yes, but come right back; we have work to do," Octavia replied.

Augustina smiled and took Marcus's hand then they hurried out the door.

As they walked up the grassy hill, she could tell Marcus appeared sad and attributed it to the death of his father.

"I am sorry about your father, Marcus," she said, hoping to cheer him up.

Marcus shook his head. "If I had only been here to help, my father might still be alive. It is my fault he is dead."

Augustina stopped and faced him, grabbing both of his hands. "You must not think that, Marcus. Eventually we all die. We cannot blame ourselves for the time the gods give to others. We can only appreciate the time they allow us to spend with those we love. Mother taught me a poem called *The Dance* which helped me to realize only the gods determine how long we will live."

"How does it go?" Marcus asked.

Augustina glanced up as if trying to remember then said:

> *"The dance's length, no one can tell,*
> *So strum the kithara and ring the bell.*
> *And while we hope the dance extends,*
> *Musicians choose when the music ends.*

The gods are the musicians and we are the dancers, Marcus."

Marcus gazed at her and could see the empathy in her eyes. "Thank you, Augustina."

"Thank you for what?" she asked

He gave her hand a light squeeze and said, "For trying to make me feel better."

Augustina smiled and swung his arm. She noticed the brand on his arm and asked, "What is that, Marcus?"

Marcus made a face of dismissal and said, "Just a mark that every soldier must have."

Augustina lifted her head slightly and said, "Oh, yes, my father has one of those. Did it hurt much?"

"A little, but the pain didn't last long," Marcus replied, with a smirk.

Augustina nodded.

Upon arriving at Marcus's house, she said, "I am so glad you are safe. I have prayed to the gods at our shrine for your safety every night."

"The gods must have heard your prayers," Marcus mentioned.

"I just wish you could stay longer," she said with a pout.

Marcus smirked and said, "Unfortunately, I'm a Praetorian now and I have to do what they tell me."

Augustina put on a pouty face and said, "I don't think I like you being a Praetorian."

Marcus smirked again. "I don't think I like being one either. Someday I won't be and we can spend more time together."

"When will that someday be?" Augustina asked with hopeful eyes.

"Soon, I hope," Marcus replied, just as hopeful.

"Until then, remember this." She leaned and gave him a quick kiss then ran away. She stopped at the top of the hill and shouted, "I will see you this evening, Marcus Flavius." Then, with a rosey-faced smile, she disappeared over the hill.

When she was out of sight, Marcus touched his lips where she had kissed him. It was their first kiss and he felt a stirring inside that filled him with a strong desire for more.

****

That evening Octavia fixed a grand feast with Augustina's help. The main topics of conversation naturally centered around the exploits of their two Praetorians in Judaea. After the meal, Camilla helped clean up. Octavia made a fuss, but Camilla refused to give in. While the women performed their tasks, Marcus asked Galerius if he could speak with him in private while Antonius engaged Decimus in conversation.

As Galerius strolled out into the vineyard with Marcus, he could tell something heavy was weighing on his mind. "What is it, Marcus?" he asked.

Marcus took a deep breath then turned and faced Galerius. "What would happen if I didn't go back?"

Galerius slowly shook his head and replied, "That would be foolish, Marcus. They would come after you and cut off your hand then put you in prison where you would eventually starve to death. Besides that, it would bring great shame upon your family."

Marcus sighed, then asked, "What if I went back and explained to Pilate that my family wouldn't be able to survive without me?"

"First, you would have to ask Macro, the Praetorian Prefect. I must tell you that others who have tried to get out of their commitment for reasons similar to yours were all denied. I know, because they came to me when I was still in the Guard. Are there any other reasons why you want to leave?"

Marcus looked down. "It is mostly due to my family's situation... but something happened in Judaea that made me think perhaps I made the wrong decision to become a Praetorian."

"Go on," Galerius stated.

Marcus took in a big breath then let it out and said, "A few months ago, a crowd of people in Jerusalem gathered in the palace courtyard. Pilate had used money from their temple treasury to build an aqueduct and they were unhappy about it. When Pilate grew tired of their complaints, he sent his conscripts throughout the crowd with clubs and daggers. On his signal, they slaughtered the people like animals. What he did wasn't right."

Galerius nodded then paused slightly. "Right or wrong, I'm afraid you will have to live with the decisions that your leaders make, Marcus. When crowds refuse to disperse, force is sometimes needed."

"But Pilate didn't give the people a chance to leave!" Marcus exclaimed.

Galerius sighed then said, "What Pilate did may seem distasteful to you, but being the governor of a far-off province is not an easy task. He did what he probably felt was necessary to maintain order."

"Can you maintain order by causing the people to hate you more?" Marcus fired back.

Galerius gave him an austere look and said, "Remember who you are, Marcus and who you've sworn to protect."

Marcus bowed his head and nodded. "I know, I will just have to deal with it. My greatest worry is what will happen to the farm while I'm away. I won't be here to do the hard labor that my father did."

"Don't worry about that," Galerius assured him. "Decimus and I can help your mother when hard tasks are required. You just do your duty. Remember, it will end someday."

Marcus looked up and said, "But someday is so far away."

Galerius smiled. "Time passes quickly. You will be back in no time."

Marcus gave Galerius a nod and said, "Thank you for hearing my concerns. Please don't tell Antonius about our talk."

Galerius put his hand on Marcus' shoulder. "Come to me any time, Marcus, and I promise not to mention what you've said to anyone."

Marcus gave a slight smile.

They returned to the house and found the women had just finished cleaning up. Marcus and his family thanked their hosts and returned home.

The next day, Marcus was busy splitting logs into planks when Antonius appeared.

"What are you doing," he asked Marcus.

Marcus gave him a look out of the corner of his eye and smiled. "Killing trees," he replied.

Antonius also smiled, remembering Marcus' same reply when they first met. Marcus was shooting at a tree with his bow then.

"Actually, I'm making planks to repair the rotted ones on the barn. What are you doing?" Marcus asked.

Antonius shrugged his shoulders. "I came to help."

Marcus stopped and asked, "Shouldn't you be helping your father on the vineyard while you're here?"

"No, he said Decimus can handle the tasks for today so he ordered me to come over and help you."

"Well then, don't just stand there, you hyena, start carrying the planks over to the barn."

Antonius grinned and said, "Yes, Centurion Taurus."

****

The days passed by and the time soon arrived for Antonius and Marcus to leave. The moment both families had dreaded came too quickly. Augustina was especially downcast. She knew it would probably be years before she saw Marcus again so she was angry at Rome, angry at the Praetorian Guard and angry at Marcus for committing 16 years of his life away from her.

That morning while washing dishes with her mother, she asked a question that Octavia had asked herself many years earlier. "Mother, do you think a girl is a fool for falling in love with someone whom she might not see again for a long time?"

Octavia smiled. "There was a day when I thought that about your father. I wouldn't see him for months sometime when he was in the field. Then he would come home. Love is a funny thing, my child. You'd think that time, distance and loneliness would destroy it. But if your love is strong, none of those things matter. Men make sacrifices when they serve their country; women make sacrifices when they serve their men. If you truly love a man, you will make the sacrifice."

Augustina gave her mother a nod.

As the day ended, Marcus pulled his mother aside. "Would you mind if I went over and said goodbye to the Licinius'?"

"Not at all. Only be back before it gets too dark," she stated.

"I will," he replied, anxious to see Augustina one last time.

Leaving his house, he sprinted down the hill until he arrived in front of the Licinius house. After catching his breath, he knocked on the door. As he had hoped, Augustina answered it.

"Marcus! I am so glad you came," she exclaimed, embracing him. "I was worried you might leave without saying goodbye. Come in."

As Marcus entered, he noticed Galerius and Octavia sitting on a sofa.

"Antonius says you two are leaving tomorrow," Galerius said.

"Yes. Our ship sails just after midday," Marcus replied.

Octavia stood up and embraced him. "Have a safe journey and don't run into any pirates this time."

Marcus smiled at Antonius, who was reclining on another couch. "We'll try not to. Well, I should be getting back home and pack."

"May I walk Marcus back to his house?" Augustina asked.

"It is late," Octavia replied, essentially saying 'No.' Then she saw the disappointed look in Augustina's eyes and said, "Why don't you just go for a quick walk in the vineyard?"

Augustina sighed and said, "Come, Marcus, before my parents have us say our goodbyes right here."

"All right," he replied with a grin.

Augustina took his hand and they quickly walked out the door

After they left, Galerius turned to Octavia. "Do you think I should keep an eye on them?"

"No," she replied. "Let's allow them some time alone. Antonius can go and check on them if the walk takes too long."

"Not me, I'm too comfortable," Antonius retorted, putting his hands behind his head.

The warm evening gave two sweethearts a balmy caress as they strolled along the rows of grapes. The only thing both of them could think about was when they would share their next kiss.

"Can't you stay longer?" Augustina pleaded.

"I wish I could, but if Antonius and I don't return as ordered we could be severely punished, your father told me," Marcus replied.

Augustina scrunched her face and said, "Oh, I don't care about Antonius. Just you."

Marcus smiled.

"How much longer do you think you'll be in Judaea?" she asked looking at the ground.

"Tribune Falconius told us we would be stationed there for two years," he replied.

"Oh," Augustina stated with a frown. "Where will they send you after that?"

Marcus pursed his lips then replied, "It could be anywhere, but Antonius thinks we'll be assigned to Rome."

Augustina raised her eyebrows. "That wouldn't be so bad. At least I could see you occasionally."

There was a slight pause, then Marcus asked, "Will you wait for me, Augustina?"

Her heart leapt within her. "You mean... you don't want me to marry another until... you and I can?" she asked.

He took both of her hands and looked her in the eyes. "Yes."

Feeling a stirring rise inside of her, she kissed him passionately. Her boldness surprised him.

As they continued to kiss, he forgot his feelings of guilt, sorrow and anxiety while he held her in his arms. He didn't want to stop, but knew his feelings for her were too strong. Lingering would only make their parting more difficult. He put his finger to her lips then said only, "I should go."

"Must you? Couldn't you stay longer?" she pleaded.

"Believe me, I want to, but I still have to pack and get ready. Antonius and I have a long ride to Hydruntum, so we'll have to leave early in order to catch our ship. Come, I'll walk you back."

Gazing lovingly into each other's eyes along the way, they reached the house and embraced once more. After sharing a last kiss, Marcus let go of her outstretched arms and said, "I'll be thinking of you."

"I'll be waiting for you," she promised.

He smiled and ran off.

Augustina turned and walked toward her front door, hardly feeling the ground beneath her feet.

Returning to his house, Marcus peeked in to say good night to his mother and sisters, who were already in bed. He then went to the room he shared with his brothers and packed his bag while they asked him question after question about being a Praetorian. They talked until they could no longer keep their eyes open. After they were sound asleep, Marcus walked out onto the porch to look at the farm one last time. As he gazed about, he was pleased with what he and Antonius had been able to accomplish in two weeks. Sitting down on the edge of the porch, he looked up at the full moon and thought of Augustina. He wished he had more time to spend with her. He yawned and was about to go back inside when he heard footsteps approaching.

"Who's there?" he called out.

A voice in the darkness replied, "Someone who loves you."

Looking in the direction of the voice, he saw a shapely silhouette. As the person came out of the shadow of the trees, Marcus could see that his wish had been granted.

"Augustina?" he said, hardly believing his eyes.

"Please don't be mad," Augustina pleaded. "I couldn't sleep without seeing you one more time. I wanted to make sure you know that I love you, Marcus Flavius." She put her arms around him and kissed him passionately. When the kiss ended, they looked into each other's eyes. Without another word, he picked her up and carried her into the barn.

CHAPTER XVII-Babies and Battles

The next day, Marcus awoke from a sound sleep, thanks to Milo piling onto him. "Get up, you lazy Praetorian!" Milo shouted.

Marcus pushed him off and said, "You're lucky I don't have my gladius."

"Aw, you wouldn't know how to use it anyway," Milo contended.

Marcus laughed and sat up on his bed, rubbing his eyes. He was only able to get a few hours sleep after Augustina left. He thought of his night with her and smiled. He walked over to Matthias, who was still pretending to be asleep, and pushed him.

"Don't you have chores to do?" Marcus teased.

"Go away," Matthias mumbled into his pillow.

Marcus shrugged.

Walking into the room, Camilla said, "I thought you all would be awake when I heard all the commotion. Get dressed and come to the table. I've prepared a special meal so don't dawdle or it will get cold."

Marcus leaned over and shouted, "Did you hear that, Matthias? Your meal will be cold if you don't get up now!"

Matthias turned over, yawned then stood up and stretched. Giving Marcus a look that wouldn't be confused with brotherly love, he said, "I'm up."

After a filling meal of apricots, eggs, and biscuits, Marcus helped his mother clean up. He heard a horse approaching, so he walked over to the door and opened it.

"All ready to go?" Antonius asked, reining in his horse.

"Almost," Marcus replied. "I just need to say goodbye to my family."

Antonius nodded.

As Marcus walked back inside, Camilla embraced him with tears in her eyes and said, "Come back home when you can, Son."

"I will," he assured her. "Oh, I almost forgot." He handed her a pouch of money and said, "Here is some money I brought with me. I'll be getting more but I wanted to give this to you to help with expenses."

Feeling a lump in her throat, Camilla said, "Won't you need this for your own expenses?"

"Naw," he replied. "I don't have a lot of needs and most of them are taken care of since I'm a Praetorian." He then gave each of his brothers and sisters an embrace. Picking up his knapsack, he headed out the door, his family following him. Fastening his belongings securely onto his horse, he climbed into the saddle and waved goodbye.

"You both be safe," Camilla said as tears rolled down her cheeks.

Marcus and Antonius nodded.

Giving their horses a kick, the two young Praetorians rode off to catch their ship.

As they trotted down the road, Marcus asked, "Did Augustina say anything to you about me when you left?"

Antonius lifted his head slightly and replied, "She told me to make sure you don't stab yourself with your gladius." He then gave Marcus a sideward glance for his reaction.

Marcus just shook his head and sighed.

****

The weeks at sea passed by uneventfully and while Marcus dreaded returning, Antonius was eager to get back. Arriving at the palace in the morning, they found that nothing much had changed since their departure. Seeing that they had returned, Taurus assigned their watches for the next day.

Marcus' father's death still weighed heavy on his mind and, since he had the rest of the day to himself, he thought he would visit Jacob and ask him more questions about his religious beliefs.

"What do you want to do today?" Antonius asked him as they sat on their bunks.

"I have some more questions I want to ask the Jewish man about his religion," Marcus replied. "I think I'll go visit him again."

"Are you becoming a Jew?" Antonius asked with a furrowed brow.

"No," Marcus chuckled, "I just want to know more about his beliefs in the afterlife."

"Remember what the centurion said, we should be more concerned about this life than what may or may not happen afterwards," Antonius reminded him.

"I know," Marcus said, "but what Jacob has told me so far doesn't seem that hard to believe. It doesn't hurt to know more."

"Well, just don't let it interfere with your duties," Antonius cautioned.

Marcus smiled and said, "You worry too much," as he left.

A short while later, he arrived at the familiar flat and knocked on the door.

A feeble voice inside said, "Enter."

As Marcus pushed the door open, he found Jacob lying on his bed. The once enthusiastic and illuminated old face was now dark and gaunt, and his thin frame seemed even spindlier.

Pointing to a stool near the bed, Jacob muttered, "Marcus, it is good to see you. Please, sit down."

Marcus gazed into Jacob's tired eyes as he took the stool. "Jacob! You don't appear well."

The old man managed a weak smile. "I knew you would come. My time is growing short, but I wanted to see you again before I left this world."

"Should I go and get a physician?" Marcus asked, the panic showing in his voice.

"No, a physician cannot help me now," Jacob replied feebily. "My end is near... I'm afraid. Tell me the reason you came."

Marcus suddenly felt foolish for asking a personal question to a man who appeared to be dying. He wrestled with the thought in his mind for a moment.

Jacob must have sensed his feelings and asked, "Is there something you wish to ask, Marcus? It's all right, you can ask me."

Marcus took in a breath and said, "I have always wondered about the afterlife. My father recently died. Do you think I will see him after I die?"

"Only your actions can determine that," Jacob replied with labored breath.

Marcus furrowed his brow in perplexity and asked, "My actions?"

Jacob felt a jolt of renewed strength and spoke slowly and clearly. "God rewards those who have faith and make sacrifices for the good of others. I'm afraid I cannot give you the answer you seek, Marcus; you will just have to wait and see." He then took a few shallow breaths. "I want you to know how much your visits have meant to me. Even though God took away my only son, Enoch, He allowed you to come into my life. As a parent, I had to make many sacrifices for Enoch. In the end, he made the greatest sacrifice for me." He paused to catch his breath. "One day, we were walking down the road when a group of soldiers on horseback approached us from behind. I turned and realized as they galloped toward us that they weren't going to stop. My son pushed me out of the way in time, but the soldier's horses ran him down. As I held his lifeless, broken body, I cursed them and swore revenge." Jacob paused again. "A man who saw what happened approached me and spoke of forgiveness. When I asked him how I could forgive someone for killing my son, he said these words, 'Waste not your time seeking vengeance on those who took thy son from thee. Vengeance is like poison unto the soul. Drink not from that bitter cup; it shall only bring thee unhappiness. Dost thou not know greater love hath no man than he lay down his life for another? Think of this great love that thy son had for thee and thee for him then thy heart shall have no room for hate. God will hold those responsible for his death accountable for their actions, either in this life or the next. Have faith. Another son will come to thee.' I didn't know it at the time, but the man who spoke to me was Jesus. His words were like a soothing balm placed on an open wound." Jacob took a few more shallow breaths. "When he mentioned another son would come into my life, I thought nothing of it. My wife was dead, and I had no plans to marry again. Then it came to me one night as I was saying my prayers. Marcus, you are the son Jesus prophesied would come into my life. Now, it is customary in our culture for the father to give his sons a blessing before he dies. Would you mind if I gave you a blessing in place of my real son?"

"No, I would be honored," Marcus said solemly.

"Please, sit me up," Jacob asked, struggling to rise.

Marcus gently lifted him to a sitting position.

Jacob closed his eyes and put his hands together. "God of our fathers, I, Jacob your servant, thank Thee for the blessings Thou hast given to me in my life. Now, as my spirit prepares to leave this mortal body, I wish to give a blessing upon Marcus before I go. Although he is not the son of my flesh, he has been like a son unto me. Please bless him that he will come to believe in Thee and have the faith that he will see his father again. Bless him with peace when it is his time to leave this world. And be with him when he is called upon to make his sacrifice..." he stopped for a moment and looked up. "Oh," he exclaimed, extending both arms into the air. "Enoch! My son!" He exhaled one last time and slumped over.

"Jacob! Jacob!" Marcus cried.

****

Two months went by in Aletium and Augustina awoke late one night and felt nauseous. She lay in bed for a while hoping it would pass. When it didn't, she ran for the washbasin. Another month went by, and the cause of her nausea was painfully evident. She was pregnant. Octavia had suspected it and decided to have a talk with her daughter one night after supper. Augustina was in her room resting when Octavia came in.

"Augustina, we need to talk. Your father and I have been concerned about this mysterious illness you've had for the past few weeks. Is there anything you want to tell me?"

"No," Augustina replied with wide eyes.

"Augustina, did you and Marcus have intimate relations before he returned to Judaea?"

Augustina looked down. Her heart began to beat rapidly. Tears formed in her eyes as she blurted out, "Yes!"

Octavia looked up then back at her daughter and said, "You are pregnant."

Augustina knew what she meant and began to cry. "I have brought shame upon my family," she sobbed.

"When did this happen?" Octavia asked.

"The night before Marcus had to leave," Augustina admitted. "I went to see him one last time and..." her voice trailed off.

"Was that the only time you had relations with him?" Octavia asked.

"Yes, just that one time," Augustina sobbed.

Octavia put her hand to her head. "Sometimes one time is all it takes."

"I'm so sorry for what I've done, Mother!" Augustina cried.

Octavia put her arm around her penitent daughter as she buried her face in her mother's bosom. Stroking Augustina's hair, Octavia said, "You cannot change what has already been consummated. But now you must face the consequences of your actions. You must tell your father what you've done."

"No, please, I can't!" Augustina pleaded.

"Augustina, you are beginning to show! Your father will soon notice it."

"But he will be so angry. He might even hate me for what I have done."

"He may be disappointed in you as I am," Octavia remarked, "but he will never hate you. Marcus on the other hand..." she paused, "it is hard to say how he will react to him."

"You don't think he would kill Marcus, do you?" Augustina asked with fear in her eyes.

"Kill the father of your child?" Octavia shook her head. "I don't see him going to that extreme, but he may not welcome him with open arms the next time he sees him. Still, you must tell your father. I will call him in. It is best to get it over with than to wait and continue to worry."

"Please stay with me when I tell him," she pleaded, grabbing the sleeve of Octavia's tunica.

"I will," Octavia promised, as she left the room.

While Augustina waited in agony, she imagined Galerius turning against her the way Marcus's father turned against him. Just when her mind's fears could get no worse, Galerius walked into the room and, with a concerned look, said, "Your mother mentioned there is something you wish to tell me."

Octavia came in and sat down on her daughter's bed, putting her arm around Augustina.

Augustina felt her heart pounding so hard in her breast she thought it would leap out. Quietly, she stated, "I have disgraced you, Father."

"What?" he asked, not sure he heard her right.

Augustina started to cry and blurted, "I am with child."

Galerius gave her a look of disbelief. "You are pregnant?"

She nodded.

"When did this happen?" Galerius asked, raising his voice.

"It happened when Marcus was home on his leave," Octavia replied.

"Marcus is the father?" Galerius said, raising his voice even more.

"Galerius, you know there has been no one else in her life she has been interested in," Octavia replied.

Galerius narrowed his eyes and glared at Augustina. "Did Marcus force himself on you?"

Augustina looked up with tears in her eyes and replied, "No, Father... the fault was mine. I went to see him on the last night he was home to tell him that I loved him. He asked me not to marry until he could return. We kissed then..." she paused, afraid to say anymore.

Galerius shook his head. "You can't marry! Only officers are allowed to marry in the Praetorian Guard."

Augustina began to cry again.

Octavia hugged her and said, "Perhaps he will become an officer quickly. For now, Augustina must tell Camilla what has happened. She is going to notice Augustina is with child sooner or later, and she has a right to know since Marcus is the father."

"Must I?" Augustina asked. "I'm afraid she will hate the baby or me."

Octavia shook her head and said, "I don't see Camilla reacting that way at all, Augustina. Come, I will go with you. We shall tell her together."

"Do you think we should tell Marcus about the baby?" Augustina asked.

"No!" Galerius shouted. In a quieter tone he said, "He might do something foolish like leaving Judaea without authorization. They would hang him if he did that."

Octavia turned to her daughter and said, "We'll advise Camilla not to tell him as well. Do you want to come with us, Galerius?"

"No... I need time to think," he replied.

Octavia would have preferred he accompany them, but she knew her husband needed some time to cool down.

As mother and daughter started toward the Flavius' farm, Augustina clutched Octavia's hand tightly. Walking as though Octavia was leading her to the gallows, she said, "I don't even know what to say to her."

"The words will come," Octavia assured her.

"What if she becomes angry and doesn't want anything to do with me or the baby?"

"I think I know Camilla well enough to say she will not feel that way," Octavia replied. "Besides, you must take responsibility for your actions. Part of that responsibility is notifying those who have a right to know."

"I didn't realize that having a child would be this hard," Augustina said, kicking a pebble out of her way.

Octavia smirked. "If you think it is hard now, wait until after the baby is born."

As they neared the house, they saw Camilla working in her garden.

"Camilla!" Octavia shouted.

Camilla stood up and turned, flexing her back. "Octavia... Augustina. Hello. I didn't hear you walk up."

Octavia turned toward her daughter and said, "Augustina has something she must tell you."

"Yes, Augustina, what is it?" Camilla asked, wiping the dirt from her hands.

Augustina hesitated then said, "I'm going to have a baby."

Camilla's eyes opened wide.

"And... Marcus is the father," she added in the bravest voice she could muster. Tears flowed down her cheeks again as she clung to her mother.

Camilla looked at them in horror, afraid that her son had just destroyed their friendship. "Octavia, I am so sorry for what Marcus has done. He told me he and Augustina were quite fond of each other and I have always felt they would possibly marry someday, but I didn't think..."

Octavia put up her hand. "Camilla, we did not come here to condemn you or your son. Augustina told me she was mostly to blame. Both of them will have to accept the responsibility for what happened. But you have a right to know since Marcus is the father. Our feelings toward you and your family haven't changed. What happened should not pull us apart, but bring us closer together."

Camilla's eyes became misty as she walked over and embraced both Augustina and Octavia. "Does Marcus know about the baby?" she asked.

Octavia shook her head. "No, and he must not know right now. Galerius said if he tried to come home without permission they would hang him."

Camilla's eyes widened and she nodded. Turning to Augustina, she said, "I appreciate you coming to tell me, Augustina. I know it took courage for you to do that. Don't worry, you and your baby will be welcome in our home any time."

Camilla embraced Augustina again and said, "I can't believe that I'm going to be a grandmother! When is the baby due?"

Augustina looked at her mother.

"Six maybe seven months," Octavia replied.

"Please let me know what I can do to help when the time comes," Camilla offered.

"Thank you, Camilla," Octavia said with a smile. "We would love to have your help when the baby comes."

Tears rolled down Camilla's cheeks as she hugged Octavia then Augustina. "I am fortunate to have such good friends. Someday I will repay you for your generosity."

Octavia smiled and said, "Just love your daughter-in-law and your grandchild. That will be payment enough."

****

While life was developing in Aletium, death was well under way in Creta. The Roman governor's palace in Gortyn had been under siege for three days by local factions. It all began with an incident involving Darius. One of the town's favorite sons was leaving an inn with his wife when he accidentally bumped into him one evening.

"Oh, excuse me," the young man apologized.

"I don't excuse Cretan dogs who are paying more attention to their whores than where they're going," Darius snarled.

"There is no cause to speak like that," the young man said, turning red in the face. "This woman happens to be my wife, you Roman pig. I demand an apology!"

"Here is your apology," Darius said, drawing his gladius. In a blur, he slashed the side of the young man's neck.

With a look of horror, the young man crumpled to the ground. His wife screamed and held him as Darius and Cornelius walked away as though nothing had happened.

The next day, the young widow, supported by her family and town officials, petitioned the Roman governor for an audience.

"What is your grievance?" the governor asked when they appeared before him.

The father of the dead young man, who also happened to be one of the town officials, approached. "My name is Kyros Nikodemos, Excellency. Last night, my son was viciously murdered by one of your soldiers as he and my daughter-in-law came out of the Inn of Pamphilos. I demand that you punish the man responsible."

"Can she identify him?" the governor asked.

"Yes," the young woman replied. "He had a breastplate with scorpions on it, and he was very muscular."

"You're describing one of my Praetorians. You're sure it was one of them and not a regular soldier?"

The young woman nodded and said, "I distinctly remember the scorpions."

"You are the wife I take it?"the Roman governor asked.

"Yes," she replied, as tears lined her cheeks.

"What is your name?" the governor asked.

"Aletheia," she replied.

The governor leaned toward her and said, "Tell me what happened, Aletheia."

After regaining her composure, the young woman said, "Herakles and I were just leaving the inn when he accidentally bumped into the soldier. He apologized, but the soldier called me a whore. When my husband asked him to apologize, the soldier struck Herakles with his sword. Then my husband fell, and..." The woman began to cry again.

"Did your husband make any attempt to attack the Praetorian?" the governor asked.

"No, I swear he didn't," she sobbed.

The governor turned to his aide. "Have all the Praetorians assemble in the hall immediately."

The aide bowed. A short while later, every Praetorian in the compound stood before him.

"Do you see the man?" the governor asked Aletheia.

Her eyes went right to Darius. Pointing to him, she said, "That is the animal who killed my husband."

"You're sure?" the governor asked.

"Yes," Aletheia replied, clenching her teeth, "I will never forget his face."

The governor glared at Darius. "Centurion, this woman accuses you of murdering her husband. Is this true?"

"No, Governor," Darius replied coldly. "The woman lies. Her husband took offense when I called her a whore, since many happen to reside there..."

Laughter erupted from the Praetorian ranks.

"Silence!" the governor shouted. "Continue, Centurion."

"He drew a dagger, and I defended myself."

"That is a lie!" Aletheia screamed. "He made no attempt to attack you! You murdered him when he demanded an apology!"

Darius calmly replied, "My companion, Praetorian Cornelius, was with me. He can verify what happened."

"Praetorian Cornelius, step forward!" the governor barked.

Cornelius came forward.

"Can you verify what your Centurion has said?"

"It happened exactly as the Centurion described, Governor. The man drew his dagger and was about to strike him."

"You both lie!" Aletheia screamed.

"Were there any other witnesses to the incident?" the governor asked.

The silence was only interrupted by the young widow's sobbing.

"Since it is the word of two against one, I have no choice but to rule in the Praetorian's favor. That is my judgment. I sympathize with the loss of your husband, young woman, but there is nothing more I can do for you."

Aletheia fell sobbing into her father's arms.

Turning bright red in the face, the father of the dead young man roared, "This is an outrage! Aletheia has always told the truth! There is no doubt in my mind that this man is a murderer. If Roman justice won't punish him for his crime then Cretan justice will."

"What are you saying?" the governor asked, leaning forward.

"We'll see what the people of Creta have to say about this injustice," he declared then stormed off.

After they had departed, the governor stood up and faced his Praetorian Guards. "No Praetorian will be allowed to leave the palace until this matter dies down. Is that understood?"

"Yes, Governor!" they shouted.

"Dismissed!" the governor shouted angrily.

News of the deadly altercation spread, and soon a crowd of people assembled at the Praetorium demanding that the governor hand Darius over to them. Naturally, he refused. The crowd eventually turned into a small army that surrounded the praetorium and laid siege to it. The governor quickly realized his only hope of survival was for one of his men to sneak out, commandeer a ship, then sail to the nearest Roman outpost on the mainland for reinforcements. The Cretan insurgents lobbed his head over the palace wall.

The fighting became so intense that Darius and Cornelius were the last two Praetorians left alive along with a handful of conscripts. Most of the conscripted soldiers stationed there also died in the fighting or deserted and joined the Cretans.

During a lull in the battle, the two lone Praetorians left, knelt down behind their assigned parapet.

"Perhaps killing that man at the inn wasn't a good idea," Cornelius remarked to Darius.

Darius glowered. "The man called me a pig. I'm not about to let that go unpunished. He deserved what he got. We have to show these people who their masters are."

"Masters who are about to die," Cornelius predicted.

"At least we'll die in battle," Darius proudly declared. "How are your wounds?"

Cornelius looked himself over and replied, "Not bad. And yours?"

"Just scratches," Darius snorted. "The Cretan dogs fight about as well as the pirates did."

"That was a good battle," Cornelius said, as a stone slung by an onager went whooshing over their heads.

"What are they up to now?" Darius asked.

Cornelius turned and looked over the wall. "They are forming into several groups and bringing more ladders..."

Just then, Darius heard a smacking sound. Falling backwards, Cornelius hit the stone footing with a "whump!" An arrow had struck him in the forehead and blood streamed down the mortal wound.

Darius looked his dead comrade in disbelief. The disbelief quickly turned to rage. Smearing Cornelius's blood onto his face, Darius grabbed his shield and climbed up onto the rampart. Holding his gladius high, he shouted, "Come to me, you vomitus swine! Come to me, and I will cut out your hearts and feast on them!"

Several arrows flew at him, but he deflected them easily with his shield. Then, as every attacker breached the wall near his position, Darius quickly slew them. One after another fell, until their bodies surrounded him on the parapet in great pools of blood. Daunted by Darius's ferocity, the attackers retreated. Slumping to a sitting position, he breathed heavily in and out. When he managed to catch his breath, he stared at all the dead lying all around him and spat on the ground. He had killed many, but there were still many left. He knew it was only a matter of time before the praetorium fell. Only a handful of defenders remained, strung out along the battlements. He wrapped his neckerchief around a cut on his forearm and used his teeth to tie it. The next wave would probably claim him. Trumpets blared. "The final charge," he thought.

As he arose to make his last stand, he realized the trumpets were Roman. Looking out, he saw a cohort of Roman army regulars routing what was left of the attackers. Exhausted, he sat down and began to laugh. The battle was over, and he had only minor wounds to show for it. With the uprising at an end, the Roman reinforcements marched triumphantly into the palace. Searching the parapets for wounded, they found Darius resting his head on the pommel of his bloody gladius as he knelt by the dead body of his friend. A tribune came up to him and shouted, "Centurion!"

Darius slowly stood up and gave a tired salute.

"Great Jupiter, man!" the tribune exclaimed, as he looked at Darius's face. "Your face is covered in blood!"

"It is the blood of my friend," Darius replied.

"What is your name, Praetorian?" the tribune asked.

"Darius Aurelius."

The tribune looked at the pile of slain Cretans around Aurelius and asked, "You slew all these men?"

"Yes, Tribune," Darius replied, with the few ounces of strength he had left.

"There must be over fifty dead here. I will see that this gets back to the Prefect. You may have single-handedly prevented the praetorium from being overrun. You are fortunate a sympathizer here informed us as to what was happening. The gods certainly smiled on you today." The tribune shook his head and walked away.

"The gods had nothing to do with it," Darius mumbled. "I was just the better man."

A few weeks later, the ship carrying Darius reached Portus Augusti. He reported to the Castra Praetoria and handed the tribune's report to Sejanus.

After looking it over, Sejanus said, "It says here that you likely prevented the Cretans from taking the fort at Gortyn single-handedly. It also says you killed over fifty of the Cretans."

"The actual number I counted was a hundred and one," Darius lied.

Sejanus raised his eyebrows then said, "Heroic deeds in the Praetorian Guard do not go unrewarded. I'm assigning you to head my personal body-guard detail and seeing that you get the Hasta Pura[59]."

Darius smiled. He would be the new hero of the Praetorian Guard and Galerius Magnus would soon be forgotten.

---

59 *A decoration for valour*

CHAPTER XVIII-Plots and Betrayals

The year 31 A.D. began quietly enough, but as it progressed, events took place that would cause such an upheaval in Rome that plebian and patrician alike would be affected.

Sejanus had asked to marry Tiberius's daughter-in-law once before and Tiberius turned him down. Sejanus thought that now would be a good time to ask him again. He would appeal to Tiberius's sense of moral imperative since he had saved the emperor's life during a cave-in at the town of Sperlonga the previous year.

At the time, Sejanus had received an invitation from Tiberius to attend a dinner party located at a grotto near the sea. The owner had converted it into a banquet hall, and Tiberius loved to hold occasional dinner parties there. Natural rock formations created the enclosure to the grotto and the interior contained various statues and pieces of art. It was a unique blend of natural and man-made decor, expertly arranged and constructed. Tiberius invited only those he held in high regard.

At the appointed hour, the guests arrived and took their seats. Sejanus sat in his usual place, on Tiberius's right. When it appeared that all the dignitaries were present, Tiberius stood up. "Distinguished guests I bid you welcome. I am pleased you were able to dine with me this evening and..."

A rumbling sound interrupted his greeting. Tiberius paused then said, "It appears that the goddess Fauna may have some indigestion. I certainly hope it was not from the food served here."

The guests laughed, but quickly stopped when the rumbling grew louder. Suddenly, pieces of the ceiling began to fall in large chunks. Screams echoed through the grotto as desperate people raced toward the entrance. Some escaped, some didn't. An advisor to Tiberius who made it out safely, looked around and asked, "Where is the emperor?"

A woman gasped, as she and others who escaped the mayhem realized Tiberius was still inside. A handful of Praetorians stationed outside the grotto rushed to the now obstructed opening and began clearing the rocks away. Once the hole was large enough, they scrambled in. Those lucky enough to escape the calamity waited with dreaded anticipation as they heard screams of pain coming from inside. Just when all feared the worst, a bloodied Tiberius appeared, escorted by an equally bloodied Praetorian Prefect. The crowd cheered, but Tiberius only nodded as his Praetorian escort quickly took him up the hill to the villa for medical attention.

After the physician carefully examined the emperor, he found the injuries were not life-threatening, only a few cuts, scrapes, and bruises. Tiberius asked to be helped to a sitting position then called for his surviving guests to enter the room. After they had gathered around him, he said, "Thanks to Prefect Sejanus, my injuries are not serious. When the rocks crashed down upon us, Lucius threw his body over mine while the rest of you ran for your lives. Many have accused him of being a danger to not only Rome but myself as well. If this were true, then why did he risk his life to save mine? He has proven himself to me, and I will hear no more baseless accusations regarding his loyalty to the throne." He then grasped Sejanus's hand. "You are my true protector."

Sejanus forced a smile. "I am happy you are alive, Your Highness."

Tiberius drew Sejanus nearer. "I've been thinking about your suggestion to leave Rome and take up residence on Capreae, Lucius. I think perhaps now is a good time. As soon as I am well enough to travel, escort me to the Villa Jovis and see to it my personal effects are transferred from the palace."

"I will do as you ask, Highness," Sejanus replied, feeling elated inside that he would now have total control over Rome.

After being treated for superficial wounds he received and released, Sejanus walked back to his room, flanked by his two speculatores.

"How are your wounds, Prefect?" Julius asked.

"Fortunately, they are minor. It's a good thing I stationed you two outside. You might not have been as fortunate as I was."

His two speculatores nodded, then Julius said, "You are a hero for saving the emperor, Prefect."

Sejanus smiled and said, "Yes, it is strange how the right circumstances can make one a hero or a goat. I lunged to get out of the way of some debris and happened to fall upon Tiberius just as it hit where I was sitting. I was lucky that only minor debris fell where the emperor was sitting and hit me."

As they continued to walk down the corridor, Sejanus thought of what might have happened had Tiberius been killed in the cave-in. The senate would certainly have chosen someone of royal blood to assume the throne. They may have even picked another to become Prefect because of their dislike for him. Fate certainly smiled on him that day.

****

Sejanus finished recalling the incident as he and his speculatores boarded a trireme at Portus Augusti. "To Capreae!" he ordered the trierarch.

That evening, musicians were entertaining Tiberius when the captain of the guard approached him. "Your Majesty, Prefect Sejanus is here and desires an audience with you."

Tiberius's eyes brightened. "Sejanus! Good! Send him in." He waved the musicians away and sat up in his throne.

Sejanus strode confidently into the room and saluted, greeting Tiberius with the customary, "Hail, Caesar!"

Tiberius raised his hand in reply. "Lucius, it is good to see you. Is everything well in Rome?"

"It is, Your Majesty. I have tried to manage her as I know you would," Sejanus replied.

Tiberius smiled and nodded. "What brings you to the Villa Jovis, dear Lucius?"

"A personal matter, Highness. Once before, I petitioned you for the hand of Livilla. I stand before you once again asking for your permission to marry her. Our love for each other has deepened and both of us are tired of being alone. We, therefore, humbly ask for your blessing to be wed."

Tiberius nodded several times slowly. Finally, he said, "I do not doubt that your love for each other is strong, Lucius, but what you propose goes against tradition. What would members of the senatorial class think if I allowed a marriage between one of our own and an equestrian?"

Sejanus tilted his head back and stated strongly, "You are the emperor, Your Majesty. Why should you care what members of the senatorial class think about what you allow or do not allow? If the senate had their way, they would even do away with the position of emperor altogether and rule Rome themselves. People change. Traditions should change with them. It only takes a person with the authority to declare that it *has* changed. I have proven my devotion to you by saving your life, and ask only this small favor-allow me to marry the woman I love."

Tiberius put his hand to his chin and said, "You make a good point, Lucius. Although civilization can only progress if its people follow the rules, sometimes the rules themselves must be altered to bring about progress. But change can be hard for many and change just for the sake of change isn't always advantageous. I must give this some careful thought, and weigh all the circumstances. Stay the night and you shall have my decision in the morning." Tiberius waved his hand, dismissing Sejanus.

Sejanus bowed and said, "Thank you, Your Highness. As usual, your wisdom in these matters surpasses all others." He saluted and departed.

Early the next morning, an aide appeared at Sejanus's door.

Felix and Julius were still asleep in the adjacent room.

When Sejanus answered it, the aide bowed and said, "The emperor will see you now, Prefect."

"I'll dress and be right there," Sejanus replied.

A short while later, he stood at attention before Tiberius. He maintained a stoic expression, but horses galloped inside his stomach.

Tiberius arose from his throne and began to pace while rubbing his chin. "Lucius, I have been contemplating your request all night and have come to a decision. As you know, most decisions I make are difficult."

Sejanus held his breath.

Tiberius stopped pacing and looked directly at Sejanus. "I have decided to... allow the marriage."

A relieved smile spread across the prefect's face. "Thank you, Your Highness," Sejanus replied with a head bow. "Naturally, you are invited to the wedding, Highness. Now with your permission, I shall go and tell Livilla immediately. I'm sure she will be quite pleased."

"I'm sure she will be," Tiberius stated with a slight smile.

Sejanus was about to salute and hurry out, but he realized Tiberius had not dismissed him yet. Giving the emperor a serious look, he asked, "Before I return to Rome, is there anything you require of me, Highness?"

Tiberius sat down on his throne and put his hand to his chin. He then raised one finger in the air and said, "I would be greatly pleased if you had your wedding on Capreae. Several villas here could hold all your guests, and I would prefer not traveling to Rome."

Sejanus responded with a single nod. "I accept your kind offer, Highness."

"Very well. Go now and give Livilla my love," Tiberius said, then held out his hand with the royal ring.

Sejanus walked over and kissed it then turned and hurried away. When he was outside, he wiped his mouth and, as he passed his speculatores who waited outside the chamber, he said, "We leave for Rome!"

The three hurried down the hill to a waiting trireme where Sejanus instructed the trierarch to make good time back to Portus Augusti. He was anxious to give Livilla the good news.

****

Livilla could have remained in the palace on the Palatine Hill when Drusus died, but it was too cold and empty for her taste. Shortly after his demise, she relocated to a less opulent but spacious villa nearby. Besides, she didn't want to continue living in the place where death had dwelt and she wanted more privacy to continue her relationship with Sejanus.

Walking up to the front entry of her villa that evening, Sejanus opened the door without knocking and hurried in, shouting, "Livilla! Livilla!"

A servant approached him with a surprised look, and said, "Oh, Master Sejanus. I'm sorry, I didn't hear you knock. I will go and get the mistress immediately. Please, come in."

Sejanus took off his helmet then walked into the atrium.

A moment later, Livilla entered appearing slightly embarrassed.

"Lucius. I didn't expect you," she remarked, fussing with her hair.

Sejanus walked over and warmly embraced her. "My love, I have good news. Walk with me in the garden."

"What is it, Lucius?" she asked with a puzzled look.

"I will tell you when we're alone," he said with a smug grin.

Taking her by the hand, he led her out of the house and into the garden. Looking around to make sure no prying ears would be close enough to hear, he took both her hands into his.

With a smile, he said, "Tiberius has given us his blessing to marry."

She gave him a disbelieving look. "Lucius, this is not some joke you're playing on me, is it?"

He shook his head. "I would never joke about this, my love."

A smile slowly made its way onto her lips. She threw her arms around him exclaiming, "I never thought he would allow it! Do you think he might even make you a member of the senatorial class?"

"Hmph! I seriously doubt it," Sejanus replied. "Tiberius is only playing a game to keep me in suspense so that I'll come whenever he calls and bark whenever he commands. I'm tired of being his obedient dog. The throne is almost within our grasp, my love; we just have to be patient a little longer. Soon I will be the emperor, and you will be my empress."

She threw her head back and closed her eyes. "Empress! I have long dreamed of it."

He held her closely until she suddenly pulled back.

"Lucius! We have so much to plan. The date, who to invite, the place..."

His look grew serious. "We should marry as soon as possible before Tiberius changes his mind. I'll leave that up to you as to who should come, but I do have a few friends I would like to invite. Tiberius has asked that we marry on Capreae."

Livilla scrunched her face. "I would rather we marry here in Rome."

Sejanus gave her a consoling look and said, "We only have to humor the old goat awhile longer, dearest. After we're married, I'll do away with him and claim the throne. The senate won't dare object."

Livilla smiled then pulled Sejanus toward her and rewarded him with a seductive kiss.

The next morning she awoke, excited to begin the plans for her wedding. It soon turned to dread, however, when she realized she would have to tell her mother, Antonia. She had never approved of Sejanus, mainly because he was an equestrian, but also because she simply didn't like him. To some, like Antonius's parents, class was not that important. To Antonia, it was everything. Equestrians were meant to serve the senatorial class and marriage between them was an abomination in her mind.

Livilla could have avoided telling her mother altogether, but she wanted to see her face when she gave her the news. She knew exactly how her mother would react and couldn't wait to gloat when Antonia realized she was powerless to stop it.

During the carriage ride to Antonia's villa, Livilla went over in her mind what she was going to say. Upon arrival, she took a deep breath then left the carriage and walked over to the door and knocked.

A servant quickly answered.

"Mistress Livilla, please come in," the servant entreated, with a bow. After Livilla stepped into the vestibule, the servant said, "Please make yourself comfortable in the atrium while I get your mother."

Livilla walked into the atrium and glanced around. She noticed that her mother had added some new tapestries, furniture and statues since her last visit. Antonia's insatiable desire for material possessions was only matched by her desire to be considered the grande dame of the senatorial class.

"Livilla. What brings you here?" Antonia asked coldly as she walked in.

She and her daughter had been estranged ever since she learned that Sejanus had asked for Livilla's hand the first time. Consequently, she made sure that Tiberius was aware of her disapproval and convinced him to disallow the marriage. She had made no secret of this to Livilla.

With a haughty smile, Livilla said, "Mother, you are the first to know. Lucius and I shall be married. The emperor has given us his blessing."

Antonia studied her for a moment then replied with a pompous laugh. "That is impossible! Tiberius would never allow an equestrian to marry into the senatorial class."

"But I'm afraid he did," Livilla said with a gratified smile. "The emperor has grown very fond of Lucius, especially after he saved his life at Sperlonga. You remember the incident. You were there. Tiberius may even make Lucius a senator," she added, rubbing salt in the wound.

Antonia curled her lip and snarled, "I will stop this gross abomination before it starts."

Livilla gazed up in the air with an uncaring expression. "Do what you will, but know this, Mother, times have changed. The formal class structure is less important than it was in *your* day. You may as well resolve yourself to the fact that Lucius will be your son-in-law whether you like it or not." Giving her mother a look from under her eyebrows, she added, "Most likely he may even be your ruler some day as well."

Livilla's last sentence made Antonia shudder. As enamored with Sejanus as Tiberius seemed to be, there was probably little she could do. What made her more infuriated was the fact that Sejanus had nullified her influence with the emperor.

She narrowed her eyes and replied sharply. "Go ahead and marry this equestrian, but I shall not attend your wedding. As far as I am concerned, you are no longer my daughter. Do not come here again. You have disgraced me." Antonia turned brusquely and walked out of the room.

This response didn't surprise Livilla. Antonia had scarcely shown any affection toward her throughout her life and was more interested in functions and parties than her children. Livilla had closer relationships with the servants, who essentially raised her, than her mother.

Almost laughingly, Livilla cried, "Do you suppose your scorn wounds me, Mother? What you think no longer matters." Livilla hastened out the door beaming with great relief and satisfaction.

In the next room, Antonia stared out her window with clenched teeth and muttered, "Rome will never be the same."

****

Two months later, the marriage took place on Capreae. Dignitaries, tribunes, senators and other officials, mostly those favored by Sejanus, attended. After the customary wedding vows and reading of the entrails, an enormous feast ensued. Dancers danced, musicians played and wine flowed freely, provided by Galerius as a wedding present. Sejanus had not given up on his friend returning to the Guard, and the invitation allowed him to keep the lines of communication open.

Of course, Tiberius was the guest of honor. During the feast, Sejanus seated the emperor at the head of the main table, while Galerius and Octavia sat across from where he and Livilla sat.

Still bothered by Galerius leaving the Guard so abruptly, Tiberius leaned toward Sejanus and muttered, "Do my eyes deceive me, Lucius, or is that Tribune Licinius sitting at our table?"

"It is, Your Highness," Sejanus acknowledged. "He was kind enough to come all the way from Aletium and graciously donate the wine for this evening's festivities."

"Ah," Tiberius replied. "I thought the wine tasted... different." He wrinkled his face slightly. Turning to Galerius, he asked, "Tribune Licinius. Any regrets about leaving the Guard and following a less prestigious path?"

"No, Caesar. I am content to run my vineyard," Galerius replied, ignoring the intended insult.

Seeing that Galerius would not be provoked by his initial remark, Tiberius continued his denigration. "The soil must be different in the southern regions. The wine is not as satisfying to the palate as those nectars made from our fine Roman vineyards."

"I'm sorry if the wine is not to your liking, Caesar. I have been successful in providing it to many merchants in the area. Perhaps they have just acquired a taste for it," Galerius shrewdly replied.

"Perhaps. It does have a somewhat different flavor, though," Tiberius added.

Sejanus, unable to indulge Tiberius's insulting tirade any longer, exclaimed, "I'm just glad Galerius could attend. Livilla and I are grateful for his generous gift." Raising his cup, he said. "A toast to Galerius!"

Everyone at the table slowly raised their cups as they fixed their eyes on Tiberius.

After a brief hesitation, Tiberius smiled and raised his cup. He then held it out and said, "To Galerius Magnus."

Everyone echoed, "To Galerius Magnus," then took a sip.

Tiberius, however, put his cup back on the table without drinking.

After the festivities had concluded, the wine incident was the main topic of conversation among those leaving the villa.

As the newly married couple entered their honeymoon villa a short distance away from the Villa Jovis, Livilla said, "That was a dangerous move with Tiberius this evening, my love."

"What? The wine?" Sejanus replied with an annoyed look. "I had to show Galerius I was willing to support him if I expect him to return to the Guard and support me."

"But, judging from Galerius's conversation this evening, he seems to have no intention of returning to the Guard. Even his wife seems quite content to stay on the vineyard."

"Yes, unfortunately, that is the case," Sejanus agreed. "I just need to find a reason for him to leave."

"How are you going to do that?" Livilla asked.

Sejanus thought for a moment, then said, "Obviously, the emperor was intentionally trying to insult Galerius this evening. Perhaps I can use that."

"In what way?" Livilla asked.

Sejanus put his hand to his chin and said, "I'll draw up an order to seize Galerius' property and have him arrested."

Livilla's head jerked back. "Have him arrested? I thought you wanted him to join you?"

Sejanus smiled. "No, don't you see? I can tell him that Tiberius went mad and ordered the arrest. If he helps me overthrow him, I will see that he gets his vineyard back. Then he will have no choice but to assist me."

"Can you trust him?" Livilla asked.

"He is like a brother to me. The only person I trust more is you, my love," Sejanus replied, as they embraced.

****

The following week, Sejanus was back at the Castra Praetoria, planning his next move. His timing would have to be perfect for it to succeed. He would first need to smooth the emperor's ruffled feathers about the wine incident. It might take some convincing, but Sejanus was confident he could do it. Once he was back in good standing with Tiberius, he would seize the vineyard and have Galerius arrested. Only then could he put the rest of his plan in motion.

"Thaddeus!" he shouted.

"Yes, Prefect?" his aide asked, coming into his office.

"I'm going to Capreae. I should be back on the morrow."

Thaddeus saluted and said, "Very good, sir."

That afternoon, Sejanus was on his way with his two bodyguards. After arriving at the Villa Jovis later that day, Tiberius granted him an audience.

"Hail, Caesar," Sejanus saluted.

"Prefect," Tiberius replied coldly. Normally, he called Sejanus by his first name. It was an indication that he still felt offended by Sejanus's actions at the wedding feast.

Sejanus looked down then shook his head. "Your Majesty, something has troubled me ever since the wedding. I am here to beg your forgiveness in the matter of the wine."

"The wine?" Tiberius replied as though he was unsure of Sejanus's meaning. He then lifted his head and waved his hand. "A matter of little consequence. I had forgotten about that."

Sejanus smiled inside, but outwardly he feigned remorse. "I should have had the finest wines from Rome provided for you. Galerius offered his wine for the wedding, and I didn't want to insult him. I agree his wine does not compare to the great vineyards of Rome. In the future, I will be more sensitive to your preferences, Your Majesty."

Tiberius smiled. "You need not be concerned over such a trivial matter, Lucius. Perhaps I was a bit harsh on Tribune Licinius. After all, at one time he was a valuable member of the Guard. I'm sure he's just trying to make the best living he can."

Sejanus bowed deeply. "In any case, please accept my apology."

"Done," Tiberius replied. "Was there anything else?"

"No, your highness. Livilla and I both express our appreciation for the use of the villas here on the island for our wedding party. We were particularly overwhelmed by your gift of making me co-consul[60]."

Tiberius reacted with a gratified smile. "A small token of my appreciation for your loyal service, Lucius."

Sejanus bowed again.

Tiberius then looked down his nose at Sejanus and said, "Continue to serve me well and much greater reward could be yours."

"I shall, Your Highness," Sejanus stated. "With your permission, I will return to my duties in Rome now."

Tiberius nodded.

Sejanus kissed the royal ring, saluted and marched out. He smiled at Tiberius's hint of making him his successor. He knew it was merely an act to make him wag his tail like a good little dog.

****

The next day, as Sejanus went over his messages for the day in his office, he heard a knock on his door.

"Yes? What is it?" he called out.

Thaddeus opened the door and announced, "Senator Secundus is here to see you, Prefect."

Sejanus was about to have his aide tell Secundus he was too busy, then

---

60 *Consuls were the highest ranking elected political official. Each year, two consuls were chosen for a one year term.*

thought the portly senator might have something important to tell him. He expelled an irritated sigh, and said, "Very well, send him in."

Secundus quickly appeared with a larger than normal smile. "Emperor Sejanus, so good of you to see me," he said, closing the door.

"Quiet, you fool!" Sejanus snarled. "If that kind of talk reaches the emperor's ears, you and I will both be on the Gemonian Stairs[61]. What is it that you want?"

"I apologize, uh, Prefect," Secundus faltered. "I just wanted to see if there was anything I could do for you since you haven't asked for my reports for awhile. And incidentally, congratulations on your marriage. I would have been there but my invitation must have been sent to the wrong villa."

"I didn't send you one," Sejanus retorted. "Now if you don't mind Secundus, I'm busy."

Not willing to be dismissed so easily, Secundus offered a conciliatory bow then said, "Actually, I was wondering what one, who has been so instrumental in keeping you informed of those who oppose you in the senate, can expect when things in Rome... change?"

Secundus had been useful as a spy, but Sejanus also found him repulsive and willing to do anything for money. "Yes, Satrius, you *have* been instrumental in identifying my enemies. But you have also shown that you will betray your associates. I'm afraid if I keep you too close, someday I may find your dagger in *my* back. I think it much wiser to keep you beyond arm's length. There will be a monetary reward for your loyalty once this matter is resolved. As I recall, you said your interest was in wealth. Do not hope for anything more."

Secundus felt like Sejanus had just plunged a dagger into his back.

"But... Prefect," he sputtered, "my loyalty deserves more than just a monetary reward. I know I may have given you the impression that wealth was my only interest, but wealth without power is like a magnificent scabbard that holds no gladius."

Sejanus glared at him. "It is for that reason I cannot offer you what you seek, Satrius. The desire for power sometimes blurs the line between loyalty and betrayal. I know that only too well. By Jupiter, man, you are a senator! You have more power than most men ever have in their lifetime! Be content with that which you already have. Now, please leave me. I have more important matters to attend to." Sejanus then dismissed him with a wave of his hand.

Secundus stood there for a moment, his face pale and confused looking.

61 *Also called the Stairs of Mourning; bodies of the condemned were thrown down these stairs for display and left to rot until eventually being thrown into the Tiber River.*

He had counted on a powerful position once Sejanus took the throne, like a consulship. Instead, his reward would most likely be a small amount of silver or gold. He felt like a toy cast off by a disinterested child. As he turned to leave, Sejanus delivered one last thrust of his rhetorical dagger.

"Before you go, Senator..." Sejanus leaned over his table and clasped his hands. "If the thought even enters your head about warning Tiberius, I will have it cut off. I control who sees the emperor and even the dispatches he gets. If I learn you have tried to contact him, you will receive a reprisal instead of a reward. Is my meaning clear?"

Secundus cleared his throat and said, "Quite clear." He then lumbered out of the office with an upset stomach.

Sejanus then called his aide and told him to send for Varius and Aquila.

The surreptitious senator was not the type to accept defeat easily, however. Sejanus had ruined his aspirations, so he would ruin Sejanus's. Clearly, he could not contact Tiberius. Perhaps someone he knew that was close to the emperor could. But who? "Of course," he thought, "Antonia, Livilla's mother. She was close to Tiberius, and her disdain for the Praetorian Prefect was widely known. She even refused to attend her estranged daughter's wedding to Sejanus. If he told her of Sejanus's plot, she could convey it to the emperor. Most likely, he would receive a handsome reward, perhaps even the consulship. His mood went from depression to euphoria. But he must see her immediately. Sejanus would soon have his henchmen observing his every move. Quickly leaving the Castra Praetoria, he went straight to Antonia's colossal villa, being careful not to be followed. After identifying himself to the servant, he entered and waited for Antonia in the tablinum. He gazed about at the magnificent furnishings and decorations that adorned the room, comparing them to his own lavish villa.

"Senator Secundus," she said as she walked into the room, "my servant said you were here."

"Lady Drusus, thank you for seeing me," he greeted her with a bow. "You look as radiant as ever," he added, admiring her Grecian beauty.

She smiled and gestured to a nearby couch. "Please sit down, Senator. What is on your mind?"

After Antonia had reclined on a sofa, he sat down and furrowed his brow. "Madam, I know you are close to the emperor and thought you might be interested to know that I've discovered an assassination plot against him."

"There are always ill-conceived plots to kill the emperor," she replied, "but I can assure you, he is well guarded."

"But, Milady, the plot originates with the Praetorian Prefect himself, Lucius Sejanus."

Antonia looked at him for a moment in surprised silence. "Are you quite serious?"

"I'm deadly serious, Milady," he assured her.

"How do you know this?" she pressed.

Secundus took a deep breath and unfolded his story.

"I know an informer deep in Sejanus's camp. He said the Prefect has been systematically eliminating all those who would challenge his bid for the throne. He has not only arrested senators and officials who oppose him, but members of the royal bloodline as well. Julians, Milady. Surely you noticed this?"

Antonia's look turned serious. "I must admit it has alarmed me to see Sejanus wielding such power, but I assumed Tiberius ordered the arrests for whatever personal reasons he had. Are you sure about this, Senator?"

"I can assure you the informant speaks the truth. He didn't realize the magnitude of Sejanus's plan until the Prefect revealed it to him only recently. The informant, however, is loyal to Tiberius and does not wish to be a part of any coup directed toward him."

Antonia stood up and began to pace. Her daughter's remark about Sejanus becoming emperor some day now made sense.

"This is madness," she declared. "Rome cannot afford to have Sejanus as emperor. We must warn the emperor immediately."

Secundus gave her a pained expression and said, "I'm afraid you'll have to warn him, Lady Drusus."

With a puzzled look, she asked, "Won't you accompany me and tell him this in person?"

Secundus hesitated then stood up. "Perhaps I should clarify; I am the informant, Lady Drusus. I dare not go to the emperor because Sejanus would assume my only reason would be to warn him. Before I could even travel to Capreae he would have me killed. However, you can inform the emperor of Sejanus's plot without suspicion. He trusts you implicitly. But you must hurry. Sejanus plans on carrying out this treacherous deed soon."

"Yes," Antonia replied, turning away in thought. "I will leave immediately." Turning back to Secundus, she said, "Thank you for your loyalty to the emperor, Senator. If I can warn him in time, I'm sure he will be most grateful to you."

Secundus smiled. "I am only happy to serve the one true emperor. Thank you for hearing me out, Lady Drusus." Secundus followed his remarks with a deep bow.

Antonia gave him a nod and said, "Good day, Senator."

"Good day, Lady Drusus."

A short while later, Secundus arrived at his residence. Two Praetorian speculatores in plain tunics watched him enter.

****

The following evening, Antonia arrived at the Villa Jovis. As she entered the reception hall, Tiberius greeted her warmly. "Lady Drusus! What a pleasure to see you."

"It has been too long since our last visit, your majesty," she said, walking over and kissing his ring. "I needed a respite from Rome and thought I would come and visit."

Tiberius gave her a pleased nod and said, "I welcome your company, Antonia. The journey from Rome must have been tiring for you, though; would you care to rest before we talk?"

"I'm fine, Your Majesty," she stated. "I would, however, prefer to see your magnificent gardens here at the Villa Jovis again, if you wouldn't mind accompanying me. As I recall, they were quite breathtaking."

"Certainly," Tiberius replied, stepping down from his throne.

As they proceeded outside, his Germanic bodyguards followed a few steps behind.

Antonia began with small talk. "I certainly miss your son. Drusus was such a fine boy and would have been a worthy successor to you."

"Yes, he would have been," Tiberius agreed, showing little emotion.

Looking back at the guards, Antonia asked, "Would it be possible for us to speak in greater privacy without your watchdogs nipping at my heels, Your Majesty?"

Turning to his bodyguards, he said, "Wait here. We will remain in sight."

They saluted and stood their ground.

After walking a short distance, she moved closer to him and whispered, "Your Majesty, I came to warn you about a plot against your life."

Tiberius smiled and shook his head. "I can assure you I am quite safe here, Antonia. My guards are always near, and the Prefect is careful about who comes and goes."

"That is exactly my point, Your Highness. The very forces that protect you threaten your life. Your enemy is Lucius Sejanus. He is planning a coup to kill you and take the throne."

Tiberius could tell she was serious. "Who told you this?"

"A confidant of Sejanus, who swears loyalty to you. Sejanus has been arresting prominent members of the royal bloodline and senators opposed to him in order to eliminate opposition. Unfortunately, I fear Livilla is probably involved as well."

Tiberius turned to her with a shocked look. "If what you say is true, you have just condemned your daughter as well as Sejanus."

"Despite the cost, an empire must be ruled by its elite, not by its peasants or it will cease to exist," Antonia coldly replied.

"Who is this confidant?" Tiberius asked.

"Satrius Secundus of the senate," she replied.

"He would swear to this?" Tiberius asked.

"Yes. He would have warned you himself, but he was afraid Sejanus would become suspicious and have him killed. Evidently, he is one of Sejanus's spies."

"I see." Tiberius said, stroking his chin. "Sejanus. The one person whom I trust implicitly turns out to be a traitor. Thank you for bringing this to my attention, Antonia. I know your decision wasn't easy. Please stay another day and rest from your travel. We shall talk about more pleasant things on the morrow. I'll have the captain of the guard escort you to the guests' quarters."

Curtsying, Antonia said, "Thank you, Your Highness. I look forward to your company."

Tiberius beckoned to the captain of the guard. "Centurion, escort Lady Drusus to the guest quarters reserved for aristocrats. When you have finished, have my scribe report to me. I must send a dispatch to Prefect Macro in Rome. I haven't received a report on how the Vigiles are doing for some time now. I think an accounting is past due."

"It shall be done, Highness," the Centurion replied.

****

The next day, a courier delivered Tiberius's dispatch to the Vigiles office. Although Macro was the Prefect over the Vigiles Praetorians, Sejanus regarded him as his subordinate. After reading the dispatch, Macro shook his head. He would have to call in his Centurions and have them submit their reports. He was used to reporting to Tiberius when the emperor resided in Rome. However, this was the first time he was asked to report since Tiberius relocated to Capreae. He assumed the reclusive emperor didn't care anymore. The dispatch was an indication that perhaps he did.

A few days later he arrived on Capreae. A centurion immediately ushered him out to the balcony adjoining the emperor's main quarters. Tiberius was gazing out upon the breathtaking view of the bay from the steep cliffs that descended to the sea when he heard the balcony doors open. Turning quickly, he smiled.

Macro walked over and saluted. "Hail, Caesar! I have the report you wanted, Highness."

Tiberius gestured to the centurion at the door and said, "You may leave us now and close the doors."

After the centurion closed the doors, Tiberius beckoned Macro to come closer and said in a low voice, "I called you here for another reason, Quintus. There is something I want you to verify for me if you would."

"What is it, Your Majesty?" Macro replied.

"It has been brought to my attention that Prefect Sejanus has arrested prominent Julians and members of the senatorial class in the past few months, charging them with treason. What do you know about this?"

Macro gave him an innocent look and said, "I assumed you ordered the arrests, Caesar."

Tiberius sat down on the bench near the railing. He had ordered no more arrests since Agrippina and her sons and had not been informed of any.

Tiberius rubbed his chin and said, "Quintus, you have been in charge of the Vigiles now for how long?"

"Several years, Caesar," came the reply.

"Do you enjoy your position?" Tiberius continued.

"Yes, Your Majesty." Macro replied, fearing he may be in some kind of trouble that he wasn't aware of.

Tiberius's next question turned his uneasiness into relief. "How would you like to take Sejanus's place?"

Macro reacted with raised eyebrows and said, "I... would be honored, Caesar. Does this mean Prefect Sejanus is retiring?" he asked innocently.

Tiberius studied him for a moment then smiled. "By your words, you have just absolved yourself of any complicity in Sejanus's plot. He plans to murder me and take the throne. Can I trust you, Quintus?"

Macro's mouth dropped open then his expression became earnest. "Of course, Your Majesty. What would you have me do?"

"First, I want you to make a list of Sejanus's friends and relatives; include any officers in the Guard, senators or officials who received preferential treatment. Also include those who regularly paid salutatio[62] to him. I want it

---

[62] *A time set aside each morning when the patron would hold court in the atrium of his house. During this time, he would conduct unofficial business, grant favors, line up political support and give monetary handouts to those who performed favors.*

done quickly and quietly without Sejanus becoming aware of it. When you have the list, deliver it to me personally. I also want you to transfer a third of Sejanus's men to the Vigiles. I will draw up the order and give you more instructions later. I must warn you, Prefect. If what I have confided in you finds its way to Sejanus, you will die a painful death along with him. I still have factions loyal to me who will be watching you. This is your chance for prominence and promotion. Prove your loyalty to me, and you will be the next Prefect of the Praetorian Guard."

"I will carry out your instructions to the letter, Your Highness," Macro replied with a stern look.

"That is all then. Return to Rome and do as I ask." Tiberius then waved him away.

Macro was about to leave, then turned back and asked, "Do you still want the Vigiles reports, Caesar?"

Tiberius shook his head. "No, I trust they are in order."

"They are," Macro replied, saluting and departing. As he left the villa, he knew a great purge was about to take place, which would make him the second most powerful man in the empire. He had waited a long time for this.

****

A month later, Macro arrived in Capreae and presented the list of names to Tiberius his men had compiled of those associated with Sejanus.

Tiberius looked it over and said, "Good work, Quintus. Good work indeed. Any trouble transferring Sejanus's men to your command?"

"No, Caesar. I told Sejanus that you felt more fire and police presence were needed in the city. He seemed satisfied with the reason."

"Good. Now I have an imperial order to write. I am not sure how long it will take, so I want you to remain here until I have finished it. I will send for you when it is ready. That is all for now."

"Yes, Caesar." Macro saluted and departed.

Tiberius ordered his aide to bring a stylus and wax tablet to him then began working on the declaration that would take him the rest of the day to compose. Finally after many drafts, he was satisfied with the result. Summoning the captain of the guard, he said, "Have Prefect Macro come to my bed chamber."

The Centurion saluted and departed.

When Macro arrived a short while later, the Praetorian sentries nodded in recognition as he knocked on the door.

"Enter!" Tiberius called out.

Macro's "Hail, Caesar!" was met with "Close the door."

Tiberius dismissed his servants then beckoned to Macro.

Feeling uncomfortable, Macro walked over to the reclining emperor.

Tiberius sat up and handed the tablet to him. Then he whispered, "Here is the order I want you to read to the senate. Send notices to all the senators commanding them to congregate at the Temple of Apollo on the thirteenth. On that day, go to Sejanus and tell him he is to report there and hear a new decree from the emperor. He will think I am recommending him to be my successor. After he leaves to hear the decree, gather all the Praetorians in the Castra and tell them they will receive ten aurei each if they will renew their allegiance to me and follow your orders implicitly. Afterward, take this proclamation to the temple and read it. Do not let it out of your sight between now and then. Immediately after you read it, arrest Sejanus and take him to the prison gallows. There you will hang him and put his body on the Gemonian stairs. Then go and arrest his wife, Livilla, and do the same with her. When you have carried out your orders, report back to me."

"What about Livilla's son, Gemellus?"

Tiberius smiled then whispered instructions to him.

As Macro walked out of the emperor's bedchamber, the two Praetorian sentries stationed outside raised their eyebrows. When he was out of hearing range, one whispered to the other, "I knew the emperor had a delight for various perversions, but with the Prefect of the Vigiles?"

The other sentry smiled and shook his head.

Macro boarded his trireme and sailed back to Rome. He smiled at the thought that soon he would be the second most powerful man in the whole of the Roman empire.

****

On the morning of the thirteenth, he walked into Sejanus's office. Sejanus sat behind his table wearing his customary toga. His uniform and weapons hung on a stand in the corner of his office.

"Quintus!" Sejanus exclaimed. "Don't tell me you need more men transferred to your command?"

"No," Macro replied. "The emperor requests your presence before the senate this morning at the Temple of Apollo. He has a proclamation he wants me to read concerning you."

"Ah, so that is why he sent for you. What does tbe proclamation say?" he asked, hoping to get a preview.

"I don't know; I haven't read it yet," Macro replied.

"When does the emperor want me to appear?" Sejanus asked.

"As soon as you are ready," Macro replied. "The senators have already gathered so they are just waiting for you."

"Very well," Sejanus stated in a chipper tone. "I'll have my speculatores escort me over."

"That won't be necessary," Macro informed him. "I have a mounted detail that will escort you to the temple. They are waiting for you outside."

Sejanus smiled then stood up and said, "I have a feeling this will be a glorious day."

Macro nodded and began to depart, but turned back. "This may be premature, but congratulations, Prefect." He left, confident he had conveyed the message Sejanus would interpret erroneously.

And he did. It appeared that Tiberius was going to recommend him as his successor after all, but would the senate approve it? Perhaps that was the reason for the proclamation. If Tiberius recommended something, the senate either listened or dealt with his Praetorian Guards. Although there was no need to kill Tiberius now, Sejanus still wanted him out of the way. Once Tiberius transferred his powers, he would order his speculatores to take care of the useless old fool. No one could stop him now.

He hurried out to where the detail of Macro's Praetorians were waiting and asked, "Are you my escort?"

"Yes, Prefect," the centurion in charge replied with a salute.

Sejanus climbed up on his horse they held for him and said, "Proceed."

Macro watched them depart from a nearby window. He smiled and turned to carry out the emperor's next order. His men went throughout the compound informing all Praetorians to assemble on the Castra's parade ground. A short while later, a few thousand men stood in formation.

Clearing his throat, Macro shouted, "Praetorians! I have been ordered by Caesar to inform you that he has declared Prefect Lucius Sejanus a traitor."

A murmur went up among the men.

Macro continued. "I know this may come as a shock, but the emperor has learned of a plot by the Prefect to murder him and take the throne. Tiberius has instructed me that if you reaffirm your sworn allegiance to him and denounce Sejanus you will each receive ten aurei. Those who choose not to, will meet the same fate as Sejanus. I need not remind you that the emperor still commands all the legions of the army."

The Praetorians gave each other somber looks.

"Those who pledge their loyalty to Tiberius, raise your hand!" Macro shouted as loud as he could.

Most of the Praetorians on the field had no incentive to side with Sejanus. They hadn't received favors or bribes from him, which almost exclusively went to the officers. The officers, realizing they would be in the minority if they sided with Sejanus, knew they had only one choice. All the men raised their hands including Sejanus's speculatores.

In the meantime, Sejanus arrived at the temple, eager to hear the reading of Tiberius's declaration. The senators, puzzled by the emperor's request, talked among themselves wondering why they had been summoned. Normally, they met on the first or fifteenth day of the month, so they assumed this meeting would be important. A short while later, Macro arrived and stood before them.

"Senators, the emperor has asked me to read this proclamation to you concerning Prefect Sejanus and has appointed me quaestor[63] for this purpose."

Sejanus felt a twinge of disappointment that Tiberius would not be reading it personally, but the only thing that mattered was its content. He smiled smugly as Macro began to read.

"In the past, his royal highness, Tiberius Caesar, has commended and praised his loyal and trusted friend, Prefect Lucius Sejanus for performing such varied and difficult duties for and in behalf of the emperor during his absence from Rome. Prefect Sejanus has aspired to become emperor, so now, it is Caesar's desire that he receive his just reward and become emperor."

Macro looked up at the senators who appeared visibly disturbed.

Sejanus smiled, as Macro continued.

"But he shall not become the emperor of Rome. He shall instead become the emperor of worms. His reward for plotting to murder the true emperor and take the throne is that he shall join the worms and rule in their kingdom below the earth."

A collective gasp went up from the senators. The blood drained from Sejanus's face as he tried to stand. Two large Praetorians stationed on either side of him pushed him back down in his chair as Macro continued reading the proclamation.

"Let it be known to all others who think to betray their emperor: you shall become the subjects of Prefect Sejanus in his new kingdom. Caesar, therefore, asks the senators of Rome to decree that Lucius Aelius Sejanus be put to death for his intended treasonous actions.

---

63 *Designated legal official*

Signed, His imperial highness, Tiberius Julius Caesar Augustus, Emperor of Rome." He lowered the proclamation then gazed back and forth at the senators. "How do you vote on the emperor's request?" he shouted.

For a moment, no one spoke. Then slowly, one by one, they began to quietly reply, "Death!" "Death!" "Death!" with each senator responding louder and louder until they were shouting.

Macro smiled then said to his men, "Take him to the prison where we will carry out his sentence."

In silence, the senators watched the condemned man fume who had executed many of their colleagues.

Macro's men started to bind Sejanus's hands when he broke away then rushed to the front of the assemblage and cried, "That proclamation is a fraud! The emperor would not do this to me! We are like brothers. It is a trick by Macro to take my place!"

Macro held the tablet up as his men took hold of Sejanus by both arms and said, "I will leave the proclamation here with the emperor's seal for you to inspect if you care to, senators."

Sejanus struggled to free himself, but Macro's men held him fast. As they forced him past the congregation, he glared at them. "You're all fools," he shouted. The last person he saw before leaving the room was Satrius Secundus, who smiled and gave him a thumbs-down sign. Macro's men then forced him into a covered carriage, and escorted him to the prison. Upon arrival, Macro's men pulled him out and led him to the gallows.

"Do you wish to confess your crime against the throne?" Macro asked Sejanus as they walked along.

Sejanus sneered. "What good would it do me?"

"At least you can cleanse your soul before you answer to the gods for your crimes," Macro replied.

Sejanus smiled mockingly. "I have no belief in the gods. That is for wretches who live miserable lives and need faith in non-existent deities to give them hope."

Macro shrugged his shoulders.

As Sejanus felt the rope being placed around his neck, he still didn't believe he was about to die. Even when the noose tightened against his throat, he looked around the courtyard, thinking that men loyal to him would rush in at the last moment and prevent the execution. But he heard no footsteps, no shouts, and no intervention… only the thunderous beating of his heart. Realizing his fate was sealed and he was powerless to change it, he snarled at Macro, "You'll be next."

The executioner then pulled him off his feet and watched as he slowly strangled to death.

Macro waited for his body to cease thrashing about, then drew his gladius and thrust it into Sejanus's midsection to insure he was dead. After wiping the blood from his sword onto the corpse, Macro turned to his men and said, "Two of you take the body to the Gemonian Stairs."

It didn't take long for the word to spread that Sejanus had been executed and his body was on the Stairs. Soon a mob formed of those who feared and hated him. They kicked and stomped and clubbed his corpse, venting their rage for the notorious Praetorian Prefect. A few days later, men assigned to dispose of the body threw his remains into the Tiber River.

CHAPTER XIX-THE PURGE BEGINS

Looking forward to a glorious day, Livilla Sejanus was having a light morning meal in her dining room when a servant rushed in. "Lady Sejanus, a detail of Praetorians are approaching the villa."

"What could they possibly want?" she thought.

At that moment, Macro pounded on the main entry door and yelled, "Livilla Sejanus! I have orders for your arrest from the emperor! Open the door or we'll break it down!"

Livilla's face turned pale. The cold realization set in that Tiberius had somehow discovered her husband's plot of taking the throne. Lucius was probably dead or waiting to die.

"Livilla Sejanus, I'm giving you one last chance to open the door before we break it down!" Macro shouted.

Turning to her servant, she said, "Hide Gemellus!" She then ran to the kitchen, opened a cabinet and reached for a small vial containing a dark liquid. Hesitating only a moment, she removed the cap and quickly drank its contents.

Suddenly, the front door burst open from the weight of two burly Guardsmen. Macro quickly followed them in.

"Where is she?" Macro shouted at the servant, who pointed to the dining room. Rushing in with his gladius drawn, he saw Livilla lying on the floor with the vial near her outstretched hand.

He picked it up and noticed traces of the dark colored liquid inside. "Poison," he muttered. He checked her pulse then stormed back out of the kitchen and confronted the servant. "Where is Gemellus?"

Having no time to conceal Livilla's son, the servant replied, "He is in his room, upstairs."

"Show me!" Macro snarled.

The servant proceeded to Gemellus's room and opened the door. There, in the corner, sat the trembling twelve-year-old boy.

"Tiberius Nero Gemellus?" Macro asked.

Gemellus timidly nodded his head.

Macro beckoned to him with his weaponless hand.

"Where are you taking me?" Gemellus asked, afraid to move.

With a slight grin, Macro replied, "The gods smile on you, boy. The emperor wants you to join him on Capreae. You'll be staying there with your grandfather from now on."

"What about my mother and stepfather?" Gemellus asked.

Macro paused. "A tragic accident occurred. Both of them are dead. Now, pack your things and come downstairs when you have finished."

Macro turned and went back downstairs, instructing two of his men to see that Gemellus complied with his instructions.

"What about the woman?" a Centurion asked.

"She's dead. Her body is in the dining room. Have two men take it to the Gemonian Stairs," Macro gruffly replied.

****

The next day, senators who met in the Curia Julia[64] building became embroiled over who was loyal to Sejanus and who wasn't. As they speculated over which of them might be next, Secundus could see no point in participating, so he excused himself. As his ornate carriage bounced along the cobbles to his luxurious villa, he tried to imagine what kind of reward Tiberius might give him. In a singsong manner, he chanted, "A consulship, a consulship, I shall ask for a consulship." Arriving at his villa, he entered and sat down on one of his finely crafted couches. "Perhaps I should ask for the Praetorian Prefect's position?" he muttered. He burst out laughing at the thought.

Gazing down at his marble table inlaid with gold and silver, he took a plum from the crystal bowl sitting on top and bit into its golden flesh. Just as the sweet nectar touched his palate, his servant rushed in. "Senator! Praetorians are here! They have a warrant for your arrest."

Secundus swallowed hard, almost choking, as a centurion pushed past the servant. "Satrius Secundus. His Majesty Tiberius Caesar has ordered your arrest for being an informant for the traitor Lucius Sejanus. Come with us."

"No! There must be a mistake!" Secundus pleaded. "I was the one who informed the emperor about the plot."

The centurion, unmoved, grabbed him roughly by the arm and forced him to his feet. "Lady Drusus warned the emperor. Now come along or I'll have my men drag you out!"

"But I told Lady Drusus to warn him! I am loyal to the emperor! Take me to him and let me explain!"

"The only place you'll be going to is the prison," the centurion growled.

Secundus's face turned pale; this was not supposed to happen. Dropping the half eaten plum, he muttered, "No, no..." as it rolled to a stop against his gold and silver inlaid marble table.

---

64 *The building in the Roman Forum where the Senate officially met*

Later that morning, a woman readied her son and daughter for a trip to the marketplace to purchase food. As the three along with their housemaid walked out the main door to their villa, a Praetorian centurion approached and put up his hand.

"Apicata Sejanus?" he asked.

"Yes," she replied, noticing several Praetorians behind him.

"In the name of his majesty, Tiberius Caesar, I place you and your children under arrest for treason. Please come with me."

Apicata put her arms around her children and exclaimed, "Treason? I don't understand."

The housemaid's eyes went wide and she clutched her throat.

"Lucius Sejanus was executed for plotting to take the throne. I have a list of his family and friends to arrest. Your name was on it along with the names of your children," the centurion said without emotion.

"But we have not plotted against the emperor," she pleaded. "Lucius and I were divorced."

"I have my orders," the centurion coldly stated. "Come with me now!" He then pointed to the housemaid and asked, "Who is this?"

"My housemaid," Apicata replied.

The centurion said, "You may go. I have no orders for your arrest."

The housemaid went back inside the villa and stood in the vestibule wondering what she was going to do next.

Outside, Apicata's son tugged on his mother's sleeve and asked, "What is going to happen to us, Mother?"

She kneeled down, unable to prevent the tears from welling up in her eyes. "I don't know, Capito. Your father did something bad. Don't worry, I will straighten this out. For now, we must go with these men."

"Why are you crying, Mother?" her daughter, Junilla asked on the verge of tears herself.

Apicata wiped her eyes. "It is nothing to worry about, Junilla. The sun just made my eyes water for a moment. I am fine. We must go now."

After being marched to the prison and ushered into their cell, Apicata tried to console her frightened children. When she was finally able to calm them, she thought of her ex-husband and clenched her teeth. "Damn you, Lucius!" she muttered. Somehow, she had to find a way out of their dire predicament. Finally composing herself, she remembered something that might keep her and her children from the gallows.

"Jailer!" she cried out.

"What do you want?" the jailer asked, arriving at her cell.

"I have an important message you must deliver to the emperor," she stated.

The jailer chuckled and said, "If you wish to plead for your life, everyone here wants me to deliver that message." He started to walk away when she shouted, "I was Lucius Sejanus's wife! I have information for the emperor regarding his son's death. If you take it to him, he will most likely give you a reward."

The jailer stopped. He turned around then slowly walked back to her cell. With narrowed eyes, he said, "Give it to me and I will determine whether to take it to him or not."

"I need writing materials," she demanded.

He looked at her and smiled. "Writing materials cost money."

She took a jeweled pin she had concealed in her stola and gave it to him.

"Please," she pleaded. "Take this and bring me what I ask for the sake of my children."

After examining the pin, the jailer returned with the writing materials and waited at the door of her cell as she wrote. When she had finished, he took the scroll and read it. He smiled and decided he would deliver it personally to Tiberius.

The next day, he arrived on Capreae and asked to see the emperor on a very important matter concerning his son.

A Praetorian centurion approached Tiberius and gave the customary salutation. "Hail, Caesar. There is a prison jailer from Rome outside who claims he has an important letter for you about your son's death."

"A letter? Who is it from?" Tiberius asked.

"He says it's from Sejanus's ex-wife," the centurion replied.

"Apicata? She probably just wishes to plead for mercy." Tiberius rubbed his chin. "He said it was about Drusus's death?"

"Yes, Caesar," the centurion replied.

Tiberius could not help but feel curious. He was sure Apicata was merely trying to bargain for her life, but he wanted to hear what she had to say.

"Very well. Allow him to enter," Tiberius commanded.

The centurion saluted and went to retrieve the jailer.

The jailer strode in and raised his arm. "Hail, Caesar!"

Tiberius held out his hand and said, "Well? Show me this letter!"

The jailer handed the scroll to Tiberius and stepped back.

Tiberius opened it and read:

"Your Majesty,

Before you pronounce sentence upon my family, you should know the truth of your son Drusus's death. Shortly before Lucius and I divorced, we had a bitter argument. He admitted to me that he was having an affair with Livilla and desired a divorce so that they could be together. I reminded him that she was still married to your son to which he replied that it wouldn't be for much longer. When I asked him what he meant, he replied that there were many potions that could mask a natural death. If I wanted to remain alive, I should remember that. I fear that he and Livilla poisoned your son Drusus. I would have mentioned this to you before, but I was afraid he would poison me. I am writing this in the hope you will show mercy to us. I swear before the gods, we had no part in his plot to take your throne or cause you or your son any harm.
Your loyal subject, Apicata"

Tiberius's face contorted in anger. He crumpled up the scroll and threw it down on the floor.

"Your Highness?" the jailer took a step forward. "If the letter is important to you, I was hoping you might grant..."

"Leave me!" Tiberius snarled, waving his hand.

The centurion quickly escorted the disappointed jailer out.

Tiberius sat back and put his hand on his forehead. "I should have made Sejanus suffer more. He and Livilla have already met their fates, but his ex-wife and children haven't," he thought.

"Captain of the guard!"

The Praetorian centurion approached. "Yes, Caesar?"

"Go to Rome and take Apicata Sejanus and her children to the gallows. I will draw up the execution order before you leave."

"Yes, Caesar," the centurion replied.

He saluted and was about to leave when Tiberius said, "Wait! Just hang her son and daughter. Apicata will suffer her fate at a later time."

"It shall be done." The centurion saluted again and left.

Arriving in Rome the next day, the centurion ordered the jailer to unlock Apicata's cell.

"Did the emperor read my letter?" she asked, holding her breath.

"Yes," the centurion replied, "I am here for your children."

"My children? He is just releasing my children?" she asked with a bewildered look on her face.

The centurion ignored her and pointed to Capito and Junilla. "Take them," he ordered two jailers accompanying him.

They grabbed Capito and Junilla by their arms.

"Mother!" they cried out.

"Where are you taking them?" Apicata asked, grabbing hold of her children's arms.

"It's better if you do not know," the centurion replied.

"No! Please! They have done nothing wrong!" She tried to pull her children away from the jailers, but they were too strong for her. One pushed her down then they dragged both Capito and Junilla out as they screamed for their mother to help them. Once they cleared the cell, the centurion slammed the door shut. Apicata ran to it crying, "My children are innocent! Please, show mercy on them!"

The only reply she received were her son and daughter's screams as they echoed down the dank hallway. She dropped to her knees, weeping heavily.

The next day, she heard footsteps approaching her cell. Running over to the door, she cried through the observation portal, "My children! Have you any news of my children?"

The jailer's face appeared. He had seen many taken and executed and normally would have ignored her plea. But the execution of her children touched his heart. With a sympathetic voice, he whispered, "I can only tell you they were executed on the gallows yesterday."

"NOOOO!" she cried, pressing her head against the door to her cell. Looking up, she sobbed, "But Junilla was a virgin! It is unlawful to execute a virgin!"

"Your daughter wasn't one when they executed her," the guard replied.

Apicata wailed upon hearing his response. She could only imagine the horrible suffering her daughter had to endure.

The jailer looked down the corridor then back to the sobbing woman. "I have orders to deny you food and water. If you wish to avoid the agony, I have a suicide potion that is painless. That is all I can do for you."

After a moment of reflection, Apicata wiped her eyes and said, "Give me the potion."

That same afternoon, two Praetorians arrived at the home of Antonia. Their orders were to escort a young man who was staying there temporarily to the Villa Jovis on Capreae. His name was Gaius "Caligula" Germanicus.

****

At the Castra, Sejanus's speculatores were asleep in their room when a loud knock jolted them awake.

"Who's there?" Julius yelled, as they both grabbed their swords and took a defensive stance.

They had sworn allegiance to the emperor and taken the ten gold pieces like all the other Praetorians, but someone could have informed Macro they were too close to Sejanus. It would be easy for him to assume they were also part of the plot.

"Brocchus, the Prefect's aide," the voice on the other side of the door replied. "He wants to see both of you."

Julius looked at Felix, who gave him a puzzled look.

"What does he want?" Julius asked.

"He didn't say. He just ordered you to report to him immediately."

Julius hesitated then said, "Tell the Prefect we'll be there as soon as we put on our uniforms." He went over and put his ear to the door. All he could hear was one set of footsteps leaving.

"Do you think Macro means to have us killed?" Felix whispered.

Julius narrowed his eyes. "No. If he did, several of his men would have broken down our door and taken us as we slept. He wants us for something else. Put on your uniform."

After dressing, they reported to Macro's office and stood at attention before him. Their bodies tensed as they waited to hear what he had to say.

Macro sat back in his chair and looked them over showing the slightest of smiles. He nodded and said, "Varius and Castor. You seem to be ghosts. Before Sejanus's aide met his untimely demise, he confessed that the late Prefect called on you quite frequently. I checked your records and learned you were assigned to Centurion Cominius's century. The odd thing is that Centurion Cominius swears you were never in his century. That leaves me with only one conclusion: you were Sejanus's speculatores."

Julius and Felix exchanged concerned looks then Julius spoke. "He used us as his personal bodyguards occasionally and gave us a few assignments, but that was all. We had no knowledge of his treachery and swore our allegiance to the emperor like everyone else."

Macro's smile widened. "Don't worry; Tiberius does not know about your close association with the late Prefect, and I didn't put your names on the emperor's list. It would be a waste to execute two men who were masters in their respective training classes." Macro put both hands on his desk and turned serious. "I summoned you here to give you a new assignment."

"What is it you would have us do?" Julius asked, stone-faced.

Macro threw his head back slightly and replied, "You will work for me now as my speculatores. I don't suppose that assignment will be too difficult for you to handle since you're already familiar with it."

The two men smiled.

"I have a few matters I must attend to this morning, but I will meet with you later. I'll have some arrests for you to perform. That is all for now; you are dismissed."

Julius and Felix saluted smartly and quickly left. They both felt relieved to continue as speculatores but more importantly, to still be alive.

Macro sat back in his chair with a contented smile. He was now the Prefect over all the Praetorians, but he was determined not to make the same mistakes Sejanus did. He had no aspirations of ascending to the throne. He took another look at the emperor's treason list and came to the name, "Strabo Sejanus." He would need to issue a warrant for his arrest. "What a waste," he thought. He knew Sejanus's son served in the Roman navy as a centurion and had a spotless record. More than likely, he was also proficient with a gladius. His arrest would be a good test for his speculatores.

Late that night, Brocchus entered Macro's office and opened his top cabinet drawer. He knew Macro kept a set of keys there; he just hoped one of them fit the locked drawer he had attached under his table. He tried several keys until he found the one that finally opened it. Taking out Tiberius's treason list, he smiled. Certain senators would pay a small fortune to know if their names were on it or not. Taking it to his table in the other room, he took out a stylus, ink and parchment then began to copy names.

The next evening, he approached the villa of Senator Mamercus Aemilius Scaurus, a friend. Senator Scaurus was indeed interested in knowing if his name was on the treason list. Soon, the word quietly spread in the senate that any concerned senator could learn if his name was on Tiberius's treason list for a price. Some were lucky enough to disappear before the Praetorians came for them.

****

Two days later, a Roman trireme[65] sailed just off the island of Capreae on patrol. A lookout announced to the centurion on board that a small Roman skiff was approaching carrying two Praetorians. The Centurion on the ship ordered "Oars up!" so the small boat could pull alongside. After their skiff was secured, Julius and Felix boarded the trireme and informed the young centurion on deck that they had a dispatch for the trierarch[66].

"He is at the bow," the centurion informed them.

---

65 A warship with three rows of oars on each side; one man was assigned to each oar
66 Captain of a trireme

They nodded and approached the captain. "Trierarch, we have a dispatch from Rome," Julius said, holding out the dispatch tube.

The captain opened it and unrolled the parchment. As he read the message, he shook his head. He had grown quite fond of Sejanus's son and admired his courage under fire. However, the emperor accused young Strabo of being a traitor, so he was already dead. The captain rubbed his whiskered chin then looked up at the two. "You're here to arrest him?"

"Yes," Julius replied adding, "hopefully without a fight, but if he resists we'll kill him."

The captain noticed the cold look on their faces and could tell they were merciless killers. "He is the centurion you spoke to when you came on deck."

Julius nodded and held out his hand. "The dispatch."

The captain handed it back to him and waved them off.

The two speculatores walked over to the stern where Strabo stood, then drew their swords. "Centurion Sejanus?" Julius called out.

"Yes," Strabo replied, turning toward them. Seeing the two menacing figures approaching with swords at the ready, Strabo put his hand on his gladius. "Why are your swords drawn?" he asked with a furrowed brow.

"We have orders for your arrest from the emperor," Julius shouted so all on the ship could hear. "Surrender your gladius and come along peacefully or we'll kill you where you stand."

"Why are you arresting me?" Strabo asked, clutching the grip of his gladius more tightly.

In a cold monotone, Julius replied, "Your father planned to kill Tiberius and take the throne, so he was executed. The emperor compiled a list of everyone who might be involved in the plot. Your name was on it."

"I have no knowledge of my father's plot to kill the emperor," Strabo declared. "I haven't spoken to him since the divorce of my parents."

Julius smiled and replied, "It matters not. Your name is on the list of traitors."

Strabo looked at one then the other. "Are you planning on killing me here?"

"That depends on you," Julius replied. "Surrender your weapons and there'll be no shedding of blood... for now."

Strabo thought for a moment. "If I surrender my weapons, will you take me to Rome so I can receive a fair trial?"

Julius narrowed his eyes. "The emperor has already condemned you. There will be no trial."

Strabo tried to think of a way out, but his only other option was jumping into the sea. He would probably drown before he could remove his armor and Macro's two henchmen already started to flank him.

Quickly drawing his gladius and dagger, he clenched his teeth and shouted, "I am not a traitor and neither am I a conspirator in my father's plan to take the throne! I want everyone here to know that!"

The other men on the ship watched the deadly situation unfold, daring not to interfere.

Strabo's wide eyes darted from Julius to Felix. He knew the next few moments would probably be his last, but at least he wouldn't die on the gallows like a common criminal.

Julius and Felix stood only a few paces away from him on either side and remained still.

"What are you waiting for?" Strabo cried. Just when his gaze settled on Julius, Felix shouted and feinted an attack. Turning to counter it, Strabo realized he had made a mistake. Julius's blade entered his side, penetrating a good three inches. Strabo turned back and swung his gladius, knocking Julius's blade away. As he did, Felix's blade entered his other side. His blade penetrated another three inches. Strabo turned and knocked his blade away.

The two speculatores stood back and waited for his inevitable fall.

Strabo felt the blood flowing from his wounds and took a step toward Felix, who stepped back. Tasting the blood in his mouth, Strabo began to feel light-headed. He turned back to Julius and noticed a devilish smile on his face. The smile was the last thing he saw. His body crumpled to the ship's wooden surface with his hands still clutching his weapons.

Felix walked over to the still bleeding corpse and kicked the gladius and dagger out of the dead man's hands. With a shrug, he said, "I guess he wasn't partial to being hung."

They picked up the corpse and threw it down into their skiff with a thud! Macro would certainly want to see the body.

****

Other Praetorian arrest squads went throughout Italy, knocking on the doors of the unfortunates put on the emperor's treason list. Despite some of them safely taking flight when they learned their names were on the list, the arrests continued for too many others. Glycon, the poisoner, was one who managed to disappear. After Sejanus's immediate family members had met their fate, his extended relatives and associates were next to feel the emperor's wrath. Macro's speculatores and Darius served many of the arrest warrants. Some on the list chose to resist and tragically discovered the merciless nature of Macro's enforcers.

When the shipping lanes opened, ships from every port in Italy spread the news of Sejanus, the traitor. One of the dispatches arrived in Judaea.

"Attention!" Antonius shouted as Taurus and Demosthenes entered the barracks.

Holding the message tube high in the air, Taurus shouted, "I have just received a dispatch from Rome. Prefect Sejanus was executed not long ago for attempting to take the throne from emperor Tiberius. The emperor has asked you to reaffirm your sworn allegiance to him. By doing so, you will each receive ten aurei."

Marcus and Antonius looked at each other in disbelief as murmurs spread among the men.

"Those who choose to pledge allegiance to the emperor, raise your hands," Taurus shouted.

Every Praetorian slowly raised his hand.

At a gesture from Taurus, Demosthenes distributed the promised reward to each one, which Taurus closely monitored. After Demosthenes had finished dispensing the money, Taurus shouted, "As you were." He and Demosthenes turned and departed.

Marcus turned to Antonius with a shocked look. "Sejanus is dead? How could this be?"

Antonius furrowed his brow. "I am more concerned with what it means. Perhaps Centurion Taurus will know. Let's go and ask him."

"Centurion Taurus!" Antonius called out as he walked down the hallway.

"Yes?" Taurus replied, turning around.

"Pardon us, Centurion, but we were curious about Sejanus's execution. Can you tell us when it happened?" Antonius asked.

"Three months ago, according to the dispatch," Taurus replied.

"Who took his place?" Marcus asked.

"Quintus Macro. He was the Prefect over the Vigiles Praetorians."

"What does it mean?" Antonius asked.

"It means Sejanus is dead," Taurus replied. As he walked away, he thought, "It also means I'll get no more gold from him, and I may not be able to resume my position as the head trainer. Thank you, Tiberius."

Antonius turned to his friend and said, "We're off duty until tomorrow. Let's go to the Dancing Goat. I could use a mug of wine."

"I think I could use an amphora," Marcus replied.

That night they drank wine and Antonius shared his attention with a woman who showed interest in him. When they returned to the barracks in the early morning hours, Marcus thought about his affair with Augustina. He decided to get Antonius's feelings on it without divulging particulars. "Antonius, would you marry a girl you knew intimately?" he blurted out as they lay in their bunks.

"You're not thinking of marrying one of those harlots at the Dancing Goat, are you?"

"No, no, but what if a girl was not a harlot?"

"It doesn't matter. A woman who gives herself to a man before marriage is still a harlot." Antonius stated harshly.

Without realizing it, Antonius had condemned his own sister. The inference cut Marcus to the quick. He replied more sharply than he realized. "But if a man and woman plan to marry and she gives herself only to him, is that wrong?"

"What if they don't marry, and a child comes?" Antonius argued. "Society would condemn them. The woman would bring shame not only to herself but her family as well."

"Then the man would also be a harlot, would he not?" Marcus replied, becoming red in the face.

Antonius shook his head. "It's different with a man."

"Really? How so?" Marcus asked in a challenging tone.

Antonius took in a breath then let it out and said, "Society looks differently on a man's trysts, Marcus." Why do you think there *are* harlots?"

"If two people love each other, why should it matter whether they are intimate before or after marriage?" Marcus argued.

Antonius could see that Marcus was not going to let the subject die. It was time to end it. "Look, Marcus, my mother explained this to me once. Our society has rules. We are subject to those rules and have a responsibility to obey them. If we don't, we suffer the consequences. One rule is that before a woman gives herself to a man, she should be married to that man or be branded a harlot. Those are the consequences. Whether we agree with them or not, it doesn't matter. That's how the majority of people in our society see it."

Marcus, however, was not ready to end it. "How do you know the majority feel that way?" he asked.

"I don't, but my mother does," Antonius replied firmly. "She said that if I find a woman I want to marry, I should respect her reputation by waiting until after the marriage ceremony before ending her virginity."

A tide of guilt washed over Marcus as he sat there in shame.

Antonius' last words hurt the most. "It all boils down to whether you respect the girl or not, Marcus."

Now a sea of guilt engulfed him, and Marcus felt like he was drowning in it.

****

Nine months of discomfort finally ended for Augustina. Early one morning she awoke in pain. "Mother!" she cried.

Octavia hurried in and found her daughter bent over in a soaked bed.

"I think the baby is coming!" Augustina gasped, as the pain now hit her in waves.

Octavia noticed the wet sheets and said, "Your water has broken. Let's get you a clean tunic and you can lie on the couch while I change your bedding."

Augustina nodded as Octavia helped her out of the soaked tunic then took care of the bedding.

Handing Augustina a dry blanket, Octavia said, "Remain on the couch and I will go heat some water." She then hurried out.

Augustina laid down on the couch and draped the blanket over her.

Octavia rushed to the kitchen just as Galerius walked in.

"Galerius! Augustina is about to deliver. Get Camilla!"

Galerius stood there for a moment in shock.

"NOW, GALERIUS!" she shouted.

"Yes, I'm going!" Galerius replied.

"Mother!" Augustina called out.

"Take deep breaths! I'll return when the water is ready!" Octavia replied.

An hour later, Galerius returned with Camilla and six hours later, a new baby boy entered the world.

Augustina beamed at her new son. "I knew he would be a boy. He kicked like a horse."

Octavia brushed back her daughter's moist hair as Camilla walked out to inform Galerius of his new grandson. "A boy!" she exclaimed as she took the birthing linens into the kitchen. Poking her head back out, she added, "You can go in now, Galerius."

Galerius hesitantly entered the room and stood by the door.

"Don't you want to see your grandson?" Octavia asked.

"I can see him from here," Galerius replied.

Octavia shot him a worried look then turned to her daughter. "What are you going to name the baby?"

"I have decided to name him Marcus, after his father," Augustina replied.

"I should see if we have enough barrels for our next batch of wine," Galerius said, hurrying out.

Tears welled up in Augustina's eyes. "He hates me and my son for disgracing him."

Octavia patted her arm. "No, he is just confused right now as to how he should feel. He doesn't hate you or your son, Augustina. I will speak to him."

Later that night, Octavia asked Galerius to go for a walk with her in the vineyard.

Taking him by the hand, she said, "Galerius, I know this situation with Augustina is hard for you to understand. But whether you like what has happened or not, she needs to know you don't hate her."

"I don't hate her; I just never thought she would do this to us. The more I think about it, the angrier I become. And Marcus... he could have told her to go back home instead of taking her and..."

"Yes, both of them could have done things differently, but they didn't. It happened, and we must deal with it. Galerius, you don't have to love what Augustina has *done*, but you do have to show that you love *her*."

Galerius nodded. "You are right, as usual. I will speak with her."

She leaned close, taking his arm. "You are a good man, Galerius Licinius. That is why I love you."

Augustina watched her new son sleep and jumped slightly when she heard a knock on the door.

"Yes?" she called out.

"Augustina, may I come in?" Galerius asked.

"Do you want to, Father?"

Galerius opened the door and said, "Yes, I want to."

"Come in, then."

"I'm sorry if I made you think I didn't love you," Galerius said with his head down. Looking up, he added, "This thing that happened between you and Marcus... you made a bad decision to share your love with each other before marriage. Because of that, we will all have to deal with the consequences of how others will react to what you did. But that doesn't mean I hate you; I'm just disappointed."

Augustina bowed her head in shame. Galerius could see how regretful she felt and knew he should comfort her. Walking over, he sat down on the bed and put his hand on her arm. "What's done is done. The most important thing for you to know is that I still love you."

Looking up with pleading eyes, she asked, "Little Marcus too?"

"Yes, little Marcus too. May I see him now?"
Augustina smiled and pulled back the blanket from the baby's face.
Outside the bedroom door, a tear of relief rolled down Octavia's cheek.

****

CHAPTER XX-DARIUS' REVENGE

The treason arrests continued, causing great fear to spread in the land as patrician and plebeian alike wondered who would be next.

Late one afternoon, Macro received an imperial dispatch from Tiberius instructing him to sail to Capreae for a progress report. He shook his head when he read it. Many on the list had disappeared, and he was sure the vindictive emperor wouldn't be pleased. He sighed deeply and gathered what arrest details he had. Taking a trireme to Capreae, he arrived the next afternoon and stood before Tiberius.

With a furrowed brow, Tiberius asked, "How are the arrests coming, Prefect Macro?"

Macro took in a breath and exhaled. "I have arrested most of the names on the list, Caesar."

"Most? You should have arrested them all by now. What is the delay?" Tiberius snapped.

Macro avoided Tiberius's gaze and replied, "Some probably feared they were on the list and disappeared. I have men out looking for them, but…"

"Have you arrested Galerius Licinius?" Tiberius interrupted.

With an apprehensive look, Macro replied, "No, your majesty. We have been concentrating on all those who live in or near Rome."

Tiberius's stare made Macro stop breathing for a moment. "As a close friend of Sejanus, he should have been considered a priority!" Tiberius growled. Then he shouted, "I want him and his whole family arrested immediately! Do you understand?"

"Yes, Caesar," Macro replied, cowering slightly.

"Leave now and do not fail me!" Tiberius thundered.

Macro saluted and departed feeling the blood rushing to his face. Returning to Rome that evening, he sent for his aide.

"Yes, Prefect?" Brocchus, his aide said entering the room.

"Check the records and find out what properties Galerius Licinius owns. Bring me the information."

Brocchus saluted and hurried out. A short while later he returned.

"Well, what did you find?" Macro asked.

"Licinius and his family live on their vineyard in Aletium but he owns a villa here in Rome. Those are the only two properties," Brocchus replied.

Macro nodded. "Very good. Now go and get Centurion Aurelius and have him report to me. He just returned from an arrest detail I sent him on."

Brocchus saluted and left. A short while later, he returned with Darius.

"You wish to see me, Prefect?" Darius asked, coming to attention.

"Yes, Centurion. The late Prefect once informed me that you were the best man he had with a gladius."

"I did kill one hundred and one men in the siege of the Gortyn Praetorium on Creta," Darius lied again.

Macro cleared his throat, he said, "The emperor wants Galerius Licinius and his family arrested and taken to the prison. Are you familiar with the name?"

Darius smiled. "I knew his son when we were in Praetorian training together. I'm aware of his reputation."

"I am sending you with a contubernium of men. Knowing the type of man Galerius is, I would suggest preparing yourself for resistance."

"If he resists, he will die," Darius declared confidently.

"Yes, well, it would be wise to take him before he has a gladius in his hand," Macro instructed.

"No matter, gladius or no gladius he won't be a problem," Darius boasted. "Am I to arrest his son as well?"

"Yes. You and your men should be able to handle Galerius if he resists. The same with his son. The numbers should favor you."

Darius sneered. "He does have a close friend living in the same town who also trained with us. His name is Marcus Flavius. If he is not on the list, he should be."

"I don't recall his name being on it. Why do you think he would be a threat to the emperor?"

"In my experience, Flavius and Licinius stick up for each other. When I arrest Licinius, Flavius will surely throw in his lot with his friend and try to interfere."

"Very well; I will add his name," Macro agreed.

"And his family," Darius added.

"Fine, his family as well." Macro made the notations on the list.

"Now, according to my speculatores, the Licinius family has a vineyard in Aletium and a villa here in Rome. Check the villa first and if you don't find Galerius there then go to the vineyard. Once you've arrested him and his family, I'll arrange a trireme for you to use then you can go to Judaea and arrest his son and friend."

Darius showed a slight smile. "As you wish, Prefect."

Macro handed him a scroll and said, "Here is the arrest order. I'll have the other order for his son and friend prepared by the time you are ready to leave for Judaea. Do you have any questions?"

"No, Prefect; my duty is clear," Darius said coldly.

"Very well, dismissed," Macro declared.

Darius saluted and strutted out. Walking briskly down the corridor, he smiled and thought, "Time for you and your father to die, Licinius."

****

That afternoon, Ignatius was sitting on a couch in the Licinius villa atrium when he heard a loud knock on the front door. Jumping up, he opened it and saw Darius in uniform with his hand on his sword hilt.

"Are you Galerius Licinius?" Darius asked brusquely.

"No, I am the caretaker for his villa," Ignatius replied.

Darius pushed past him and asked, "Is he here?"

"No, he is at his vineyard in Aletium with his family."

"Are you related in any way?" Darius asked, looking around.

"No! My wife and I are only the caretakers," Ignatius shakily replied.

"Is any member of his family here now?" Darius asked, raising his voice.

"No," Ignatius replied. "Why are you looking for them?"

Darius turned with a somber look and replied, "It's none of your concern. Gather your belongings and leave immediately," Darius snarled. "Do not try to contact the Licinius family about me coming here or you will be arrested as well. Is my meaning clear?"

Ignatius nodded and quickly went to find Lucia.

"Who was at the door?" she asked, as he walked in to the kitchen.

With a face as pale as his tunic, he replied, "A Praetorian centurion. We have been ordered to leave."

"Ordered to leave?" she exclaimed. "Why?"

"I think the emperor has put Galerius and his family on his treason list. More than likely all of Galerius's holdings will be seized by Tiberius."

"Oh, Ignatius. What will we do? Where shall we go?" she asked, feeling her throat tightening up.

He looked to the side and said, "I don't know, Lucia."

As she began to cry, Ignatius walked over and put his arm around her. "I know our future looks dark right now, dearest; but we have some money saved. Right now we must leave."

"What about Galerius and Octavia? Shouldn't we get word to them?" she asked, feeling helpless.

Ignatius shook his head. "No, the Praetorian warned me against it. We would be thrown into prison as well. All we can do now is hope that Galerius finds out the emperor is looking for him and disappears with his family."

"But we owe it to them!" Lucia pleaded.

Just then Darius entered the room and bellowed, "Why are you delaying? Pack your things now or I will have my men throw you out with just the clothes on your backs."

"Yes, Centurion," Ignatius replied. "I was just informing my wife."

While they hurriedly packed what they could, Darius went from room to room making sure no one else was there. During his search, an idea came to him. "This would be a perfect villa for me," he thought. "I'll have to see if the Prefect will allow me to take possession as a reward for the arrests I'll make for him. Yes… this could do nicely."

After Ignatius and Lucia left in a wagon with as many personal items they could load, Darius returned to the Castra Praetoria to make his report.

"Any trouble at the villa?" Macro asked.

"No, Prefect. Caretakers were the only ones there so I removed them without incident. I was wondering. I have wanted a villa of my own in Rome and was thinking this one would suit my needs quite nicely. Any chance you would allow me to have it for, say… services rendered?"

"Well, you are brash, I'll give you that." Macro leaned back and said, "I'll make you a promise—arrest Galerius and the deed will be yours."

"Draw up the papers," Darius replied, saluting with perfect form.

****

A week later, Galerius's recurring nightmare unfolded once more as he slept. He stood on the surreal battlefield as usual with the thick mist surrounding him. The ghostly figures appeared and began their chant— "Death to the slayer! Death to the slayer!" They charged again and just before they reached him, he noticed a hand holding a dagger, plunging toward him.

Waking with a jolt, he sat up and wiped the sweat from his brow and looked to make sure it wasn't blood. It was just the dream. But the dream had changed slightly, and it worried him.

The next morning, he climbed out of bed, dressed and went for a walk in the vineyard. He knew that Tiberius had executed Sejanus for attempting to take the throne, and he heard rumors that Praetorians had been arresting Sejanus's relations and acquaintances put on a treason list. He had seen this kind of purge before with Augustus. The thought concerned him that he might also have been put on the list, but it had been a several months since Sejanus's execution. As a close friend, Praetorians would have come for him by now if he was indeed on the list. Still, the possibility existed.

"What are you thinking about, my husband?" Octavia asked, walking up beside him.

He furrowed his brow and replied, "I am concerned about our future, Octavia."

"What concerns you?" she asked.

"Lucius's arrest and execution," he replied. "Since we were close friends, I worry that Tiberius may come after us."

"But you had nothing to do with his plot to overthrow Tiberius and we are leagues away from Rome," Octavia reasoned.

"Yes, but Tiberius might think I did. Purges often have a tendency to punish the innocent as well as the guilty," Galerius stated.

Still, Octavia was hopeful. "But it has been awhile since Lucius's execution. If Tiberius was going to arrest us, don't you think he would have done it by now?"

Galerius' face twisted in uncertainty. "It's still possible, Octavia. Every moment we remain here could be dangerous for us."

Octavia now was frightened. "Are you saying we should just pack up and leave?"

He was about to respond when he saw a number of riders approaching. As they drew closer, he swallowed hard. "Praetorians," he said, as his heart began to race.

Octavia's eyes grew wide as she turned to him.

Keeping his eyes on the approaching riders, Galerius took Octavia by the arm and said, "We had better return to the house."

Arriving at the same time that Darius and his men did, Galerius walked up and greeted them while trying to appear calm. "Good morning, Praetorians. What can I do for you?"

"Are you Galerius Licinius?" Darius asked in a formal tone.

"Yes," Galerius replied while Octavia held her breath.

Darius dismounted then unrolled a scroll and said, "By order of his Imperial Majesty, Emperor Tiberius Caesar, I am placing you and your family under arrest for treason. Your lands and properties shall be seized."

Octavia gasped and gripped Galerius's arm tightly.

Galerius gave Darius a steely stare. "If this is concerning Sejanus's plot against the emperor, we had no part in it."

Darius pointed at Galerius with the scroll and stated, "You were known acquaintances of the traitor Lucius Sejanus. The emperor has deemed that all those related or who supported him are his enemies. I was thereby ordered to arrest you and your family." Darius ended his discourse with a smug smile.

Galerius took in a deep breath. "It is true Sejanus and I were once friends in the Guard, but I have had little contact with him since."

"Perhaps enough contact to help plan a coup?" Darius insinuated.

"This is madness. I am a vineyard owner not a traitor!" Galerius roared.

Darius merely shrugged his shoulders as he rolled up the scroll.

Realizing that arguing with Darius was futile, Galerius asked, "Are you taking us to Rome?"

Darius turned and looked at his men then back at Galerius. With a deadly smile, he said, "Actually, I was going to take you to the prison there… but you resisted, so I was forced to kill you. That will be my official report."

Raising her voice, Octavia pleaded. "We are not resisting! Galerius, tell him we will surrender ourselves peacefully until this gets sorted out."

However, Galerius saw in Darius's cold, dead eyes that no appeal would be accepted. He feared that his dream from the night before was about to come true.

Turning to his wife, he tenderly took her by both arms and said, "You don't understand, Octavia. He means to kill us no matter what we do."

"But we have done nothing wrong!" she insisted, as Darius drew his gladius and smiled again.

Turning to Darius, Galerius glared at him and said, "If it is blood you want, take mine; but escort my wife and daughter to Rome where they can at least stand trial."

"I'm afraid you've already been tried. I might, however, give your women a short reprieve until I've finished with them." Darius gave Octavia a lascivious look.

Without taking his eyes off Darius, Galerius said, "Octavia, go back inside and bring me my spatha."

Octavia, still in shock, remained motionless.

"Do what I say, Octavia!" he said firmly.

"That won't be necessary," Darius forestalled her with a raised hand. Turning to his optio, he said, "Throw him your sword, Atticus."

Atticus unsheathed his sword and tossed it before Galerius.

Darius pointed at it with the tip of his gladius. "Go ahead; pick it up."

Just then, Augustina appeared at the doorway of the house, wondering what was happening. Octavia ran to her and held her close.

"Mother, what are these soldiers doing here?" Augustina asked with wide eyes, seeing her father surrounded by nine Praetorians.

Tears ran down Octavia's cheeks. "Pray for your father, Augustina. Pray for us all."

As Galerius slowly picked up the gladius on the ground, Darius's Praetorians drew their swords. Keeping his eyes on Darius, he said, "If fate allows, I will take as many of you blackguards with me as I can."

"I'm afraid you'll have to take me first, master swordsman," Darius said, mockingly. He then beckoned to Galerius and said, "Come and show me how you killed 100 men in one battle."

Galerius shouted and attacked. Back and forth the two titans battled, each having a few near misses. Slightly winded, Galerius stepped back and studied his opponent.

Darius smiled. "You look surprised, gladius master. You're probably wondering how I'm able to counter your best moves. You see I learned them all from your son when we sparred in training. You have no surprises for me, but I have a few for you."

"You trained with my son?" Galerius asked.

"Yes," Darius replied haughtily. "He and his farmer friend should never have been allowed to join in the first place. Because you were close to the late Prefect, he passed them ahead of other good soldiers who earned the right to be there."

With a slight grin, Galerius said, "If they weren't as good as the others, then how did they win Masters titles with the gladius and bow during the competitions?"

Darius clenched his teeth then motioned for Galerius to continue.

Galerius resumed his attack, but his moves had slowed with age. As he struggled to match the conditioning and tactics of his younger and quicker foe, Darius cut him superficially across the chest. Galerius winced in pain and stopped to wipe the blood away.

"Ah, the legend can bleed. You must fight harder if you wish to keep your women's virtue intact."

With newly found determination, Galerius attacked again with as much strength as he could muster. This time, he managed to graze Darius's arm. The cut was shallow, however, just enough to anger his foe. Darius wiped the blood off and smiled as Galerius once again caught his breath. With a sneer, he said, "Enjoy your small victory while you can. Soon you will be lying in the dust enjoying your last breath."

They went at each other again.

Galerius fought hard to end it quickly, but the offensive onslaught took its toll. Breathing heavily, he tried to maintain his guard, but he could barely hold his gladius.

Darius began to cut him at will. With each cut, Octavia gasped. Blood flowed from Galerius's arms and legs.

Darius finally grew tired of playing with his victim. With a look of finality, he feinted high and slashed low across Galerius's side. The cut ran deep.

Galerius dropped his gladius and fell to his knees. The dark red blood flowed through his fingers. Still conscious, he fell on his back. He knew his death was near.

Octavia screamed. Rushing over, she knelt by his side. As she held his head up, she heard him say, "Forgive me." Glaring at Darius, she cried, "May you rot in Tartarus for eternity, you murdering coward!"

Darius smiled and pulled out a dagger from behind his back. "Does this look familiar, Galerius Magnus?"

Galerius recognized his dagger and said in a weak voice, "Not only are you a disgrace to the uniform but a common thief as well."

Darius sneered. "Your son and I made a bet and he lost. The dagger was the wager. However, I do plan on returning it to him the same way I will return it to you." He then quickly plunged it in Galerius's throat as Octavia looked on in horror.

"Galerius!" she cried.

Choking on the blood in his throat, the last thing Galerius saw was his prized dagger in Darius' hand.

"Galerius!" Octavia cried out again, but his choking had ceased. Weeping bitterly, she gently placed her dead husband's head on the ground. Slowly, she stood up and clenched her teeth. Rushing toward Darius, she began beating him with her fists screaming, "Murderer! Murderer!"

At first, she felt as though someone hit her in the stomach. Then came the pain. She gasped and looked down at the blood flowing from the deep dagger wound. Taking one last glimpse at Augustina, she collapsed next to Galerius. Her blood mingled with his as she breathed her last breath.

Augustina screamed.

Darius and his men rushed her.

She tried to close the door, but two men forced it open and knocked her onto the floor. She lay there afraid to move, her eyes wide with fear. As Darius approached, his men stood back.

"Well, aren't you a pretty young thing," he said, kneeling down. She tried to turn and escape, but he grabbed her shoulder and spun her back. "Oh no, sweet girl. You are my prize."

Knowing what was about to happen, Augustina screamed again and clawed at Darius, drawing blood from his cheek. Two of his men quickly contained her.

Wiping the blood from his face, Darius tasted it then kissed her strongly on the mouth. When he had finished, she spat in his face and struggled to escape, but Darius's men held her firmly. As she lay there, out of breath, Darius smiled then ripped apart her tunic. Screams of shame and terror echoed throughout the house as he ravaged her.

When he was finished, he smoothed her hair while she wept uncontrollably. "There, there. Don't cry now," he said. "Your brother will be joining you soon."

Augustina, barely conscious, hardly registered his words.

He smiled as he took out the dagger and plunged it deep into her heart. Her eyes went wide as she tried to scream but could only release a rush of air.

When her heart pulsated its final beat, her son's cry rang out.

Darius turned toward the sound then wiped the bloody dagger onto her torn clothing. After arranging his tunic, he stood up and followed the cries until he came to a room where the infant boy lay. As he walked over to the crib, little Marcus noticed he was a stranger and began to cry louder.

Darius saw that the infant had wriggled out of his undergarment and said, "What have we here? A Licinius boy. Well, Licinius boy, your family is dead and there is no one to care for you. It would be cruel of me to leave you here to starve to death now, wouldn't it?" Darius drew the dagger again and raised it to strike the deathblow. Before plunging it into the innocent child, he stopped and said, "You might be useful to me yet. I think I'll keep you alive for now."

Sheathing the dagger, he walked out of the room. "Caius!" he yelled.

"Yes, Centurion," a soldier replied, saluting.

"There is a baby in that room. Stand watch until I decide what to do with him."

"But I know nothing about babies, Centurion," the soldier replied.

"Just watch him!" Darius ordered.

"Yes, Centurion!"

Walking back out in the yard, Darius turned to his optio. "Atticus! Search the area thoroughly to see if there are any others around."

"Yes, Centurion!"

In a small copse of nearby trees, Decimus had watched the whole shocking episode. He had been on his way back from helping Camilla with some chores and hid when he saw the fighting. As Praetorians fanned out to search the grounds, he quickly ran back to the farm to warn Camilla and her family.

After a thorough search of the area, the optio returned to Darius and reported. "There is no one else around, Centurion."

Darius nodded. "Very well. Take some men and look for the farm owned by the Flavius family. It should be nearby, according to what they told me in training. When you find it, arrest anyone there."

Atticus saluted and sent two men in each direction. By this time, Decimus reached Camilla and related the tragic events at the vineyard. Terrified, she gathered her children into the house just as two of Darius's men galloped up.

"It is too late!" Decimus cried. "We're trapped!"

The two Praetorians dismounted and pounded on the door.

"The window!" Camilla exclaimed. "Quick! Go out the back window and warn Marcus and Antonius!"

"But how? They are in Judaea!" he exclaimed.

"Go there and warn them!" she whispered loudly.

The pounding on the door grew louder. "Go now!" she cried.

Decimus nodded and crawled out the window as a soldier shouted, "Open in the name of his majesty Tiberius!"

Camilla opened the door and stood there with wide eyes.

"Is this the Flavius farm?" the Praetorian asked.

Camilla hesitated, then replied, "No. They live... over the hill to the east."

But little Prisca pulled on her tunica and said, "Why did you say that, Mother? We are the Flavius's."

Drawing their swords, the two Praetorians pushed past her.

"What do you want from us?" Camilla asked.

"The emperor has ordered your arrest," one of the Praetorians said, looking around. "Is there anyone else in the house besides you and your children?"

"No," she replied, as all the children huddled around her except for Matthias, who remained standing at the doorway to his room.

"Where is your husband?" the Praetorian snarled.

"Dead," she replied, trying hard to control her emotions.

Frightened by the Praetorian's bellicose demeanor, Camilla's youngest daughter Prisca began to cry.

"Search the house," he ordered his companion. "I'll watch them."

After going through the whole house, the Praetorian returned and shook his head.

His companion said, "Go back and inform the Centurion we have the Flavius family in custody. I'll wait here until you return."

The Praetorian nodded and left while his companion stared at Prisca, who was now crying loudly.

"If you don't calm her, I will," he said, pointing his gladius at the child.

"I'm trying. Please, stop crying, Prisca! Everything will be all right."

Matthias, now well into his sixteenth year, looked over to where his bow and arrows were hanging near the door. The Praetorian noticed it and smiled. "You want to try for your bow, boy? Let's see if I can get my gladius out of its scabbard before you can put an arrow in me." He sheathed his gladius and held both hands in the air. "Go ahead," he dared Matthias.

Everyone in the house stood deathly still. Matthias glanced back and forth from the Praetorian to his bow. Just as he was about to go for it, Camilla wrapped her arms around him and gave the man a spiteful look.

The thuggish looking soldier laughed then turned serious. "Thank your mother, boy. She just saved your life, for now."

A short while later, Darius rode up with the rest of his men, except for the guard watching Little Marcus. After informing them to wait outside, he went into the house with his optio.

"You are the mother of Marcus Flavius?" he asked with a stern look.

"Yes," she replied.

"Where is your husband?" he asked, looking from side to side.

"He died last year," she replied, struggling to hold back her emotions.

He looked at her suspiciously for a moment.

"What are you going to do with us?" she asked, trembling.

With a sneer, he replied, "Your son is wanted for treason; consequently, you will also be charged, since you are members of his family."

"But we have done nothing wrong!" she pleaded.

"The emperor thinks you have, so you will suffer the consequences!" Darius bellowed, causing Camilla to cower. He started to walk out the door then turned back. "We found an infant in the Licinius's home. Whose child is he, woman? And if I find out you're lying, I'll have him killed."

"He is alive?" Camilla asked.

"For now; who is he?" Darius pressed.

Camilla hesitated then said, "He is the son of the Licinius' daughter. My son Marcus is his father."

Darius smiled. Turning to his optio, he said, "I noticed a wagon by the barn; we'll use that to transport them. Once they're loaded, we'll pick up the infant from the vineyard. The woman can care for him while we travel. Gather some provisions from the house for the journey back to Rome."

"Yes, Centurion" Atticus said.

Decimus watched helplessly from his place of concealment as Praetorians put Camilla and her family into the wagon. After obtaining the provisions, Darius and his men mounted up and headed for the vineyard to pick up little Marcus and his guard.

Decimus ran to the top of the hill where he could see them and waited until they picked up the child and left. When they were out of sight, he hurried down the hill to determine if anyone was still alive. Running over to where Galerius and Octavia lay, he checked for signs of life. He then ran to the house and checked Augustina. When he determined that all were beyond help, he gently covered Augustina's nakedness then walked over to the front door. Enraged by the cruelty he had witnessed, he clenched his teeth then looked up in the sky and cried, "WHY?" He was about to procure a shovel to dig the graves when he heard horses approaching in the distance. Darius and a few of his men were returning.

Darting back inside, Decimus ran into the kitchen and frantically looked for a place to hide. Noticing one of the pantry doors ajar, he stepped inside and closed it just as Darius and three of his men walked through the front door.

"Find me some writing materials!" Darius barked.

Decimus peered through a narrow crack in the door panel as a Praetorian entered the room and began searching. Seeing the pantry, he walked over and reached for the handle just as a voice from the other room called out, "I found some."

The Praetorian turned and walked away.

Decimus felt his heart beating so furiously he thought the soldier would hear it and return.

After receiving the parchment, ink and stylus his men found, Darius sat down in the dining area. He thought for a moment then began to write. When he finished, he said, "There, that should bring Licinius and Flavius to me in case they happen to show up before we can arrest them." Handing it to one of his men, he said, "Take this and post it on the front door. Make sure it is secure; I don't want it blowing away."

"Yes, Centurion," the Praetorian replied.

Decimus waited until he heard them riding off again then cautiously left his hiding place and went to the front door. Opening it slightly, he peered out to make sure they were gone then he read Darius's note.

"Licinius and Flavius,

If you read this, you have escaped the emperor's justice, but you haven't escaped mine. Just so you know, your families were put on the emperor's treason list. I executed Licinius's family and took the child hostage. I then arrested Flavius's family and took them to Rome where they will be imprisoned. I will keep the child at my new villa until you come for him. You should be quite familiar with it, Licinius. It is the villa in Rome your family once owned. The terms for securing the infant's release are simple. Licinius will fight me to the death. If I win, anyone with you will also be executed. If you win, you and anyone with you shall be pardoned and go free. Surrender yourselves before the first of Septembris or the child dies. This time we shall see who the real gladius master is.

Darius Aurelius

Praetorian Centurion to his majesty, Tiberius Caesar of Rome"

After reading the message, Decimus took the note and put it in his tunic. He had to reach Antonius and Marcus before Darius did. He would go to Hydruntum and catch the next ship for Judaea. But before leaving, he had three graves to dig.

He had just finished digging when Ignatius and Lucia drove up in their wagon. Seeing them pulling up to the main living quarters, he hurried to meet them.

Not having been introduced, Decimus approached and said, "May I help you?"

Ignatius hopped down from the wagon and walked over. "We are the caretakers for the Licinius' villa in Rome. Are they here?"

Decimus hung his head and sighed.

Ignatius could tell they were too late. "Praetorians have been here already, haven't they?" he asked.

"I just finished burying the whole family, all except for Antonius," Decimus said. "I'm Decimus. The Licinius' hired me to work the vineyard."

Ignatius turned to Lucia who could see his pained expression. He didn't have to say anything. She began to weep.

"They will be going after Antonius too," Ignatius said.

"Yes, Marcus as well," Decimus added. He showed him the note Darius left. "I was going to the port in Hydruntum and catch a ship for Judaea to warn them."

"May the gods go with you," Ignatius said. He then went back to the wagon and climbed on board.

"We are too late, aren't we?" Lucia asked, drying her eyes with a linen.

"Yes," Ignatius replied.

Lucia put her head in her hand and said, "Where do we go from here?"

Ignatius snapped the reins and said, "I don't know, but we can't say here."

****

Seven days later, Darius arrived in Rome. Entering Macro's office, he saluted and came to attention.

With a slight raise of his head, Macro asked, "Since you're alive, I take it the arrest of Galerius Licinius went well. Is he at the prison?"

"He resisted so I was forced to kill him. His wife and daughter met the same fate."

"You had to kill the women? You couldn't subdue them?"

"No, they had weapons," Darius lied with a straight face.

"I see," Macro said. "What about the Flavius family?"

"They surrendered peacefully. I transported them to the prison."

Macro scratched his head. "With all the men you had I'm surprised Galerius put up a fight."

"I told him to come peacefully but he drew a sword and attacked me. I had no choice," Darius replied.

"Still your men could have subdued him," Macro remarked.

Darius furrowed his brow and said, "They were afraid of his reputation. After all, he did kill 100 men in one battle, word has it."

Macro nodded, unsure whether he believed Darius's account or not. "Well his son should be more trouble for you than his father, so make sure you take enough men to arrest him."

"A contubernium should be enough," Darius stated through half-closed eyes. "Now, you did promise me Licinius's villa if I arrested him," Darius said quickly.

"Yes… I did, didn't I? Go ahead and move your things in then report back to me when you're finished. I'll have orders waiting for you to commandeer a trireme for the voyage. Arrest the younger Licinius and his friend and bring them back to Rome for execution. That is all."

Darius saluted smartly then left.

Macro sat back in his chair as an exasperated sigh forced itself from his mouth. One of Rome's greatest warriors was dead simply because he befriended the wrong man. Macro took a quick mental inventory on the friends he had acquired and decided he was safe... for now.

CHAPTER XXI-RETURNING HOME

After moving into his newly acquired villa and transferring Marcus's infant son there under armed guard, Darius reported to Macro's office.

"My men and I are ready to depart for Judaea, Prefect."

Macro nodded. Taking out a scroll, he authorized Darius to appropriate a trireme, put a daub of wax at the end and pressed his ring on it. "Take this to the trierarch of any trireme docked at Ostia," he said, handing it to Darius. "And before you leave, tell your optio to post some men at the Licinius and Flavius houses in case Galerius's son and his friend learn their names are on the emperor's list and show up. It also wouldn't hurt to have your men occasionally check the inns and taverns in the area as well. According to my speculatores, a few whose names were on the list have disappeared."

"I'll see to it, Prefect," Darius promised.

"Good. Report to me when you return. Dismissed," Macro uttered.

Darius saluted and left. As he walked down the hall, he smiled at the thought of facing Antonius again. This time the outcome would be different.

****

One week later, a merchant ship pulled into the Caesarean harbor carrying goods and passengers. Decimus was one of the passengers. Not wanting to be without transportation in a strange land, he brought Mercury with him. After asking for directions to the palace, Decimus galloped off.

"Licinius, you have a visitor at the front gate," one of the Praetorians informed Antonius, who was sitting on his bunk cleaning his armor.

"Who is it?" Antonius asked.

"I don't know, I was just told to let you know someone is asking for you," the Praetorian replied.

Antonius put down his armor and headed for the main gate.

"Who would be asking for me?" he thought.

As he walked up to the gate, he saw Decimus and could tell he appeared uneasy. Something was wrong. "Decimus! What are you doing here?" he asked.

"I must speak to you and Marcus," Decimus replied, with a worried look.

Not wanting to remain in suspense, Antonius said, "You can tell me, and I'll tell Marcus."

"No, this is for both of you to hear in private," Decimus insisted.

"All right," Antonius said, sensing that something was terribly wrong.

"Wait here and I'll get him." He then hurried off and returned with Marcus a moment later.

"Open the gate," Antonius said to the sentry. As he and Marcus walked out, he asked, "What is this all about, Decimus?"

Decimus shook his head. "Not here."

"Is it about our families?" Marcus asked.

Decimus put up his hand and led them away until they were alone. He turned and started to say something then bowed his head and shook it slightly.

"Decimus! What happened?" Antonius demanded.

Looking back up, Decimus said, "Praetorians came to the vineyard a month ago. The centurion in charge said he was there to arrest your family for treason. He..." Decimus hesitated, not wanting to continue.

"He what?" Antonius exclaimed.

Decimus took Darius's note from his tunic and handed it to Antonius. "The centurion left this on the door."

Antonius began to read. When he finished, his hand dropped to his side, and the note slowly floated to the ground.

Marcus grabbed his arm and asked, "Antonius, what did it say?"

Antonius stood there in shock, unable to speak for a moment. Finally, he turned to Marcus and muttered, "My family is dead."

"What?" Marcus said, picking up the note. When he finished reading, all he said was, "Darius."

Marcus shook his head in disbelief and turned to Decimus. "They're not really dead are they, Decimus? This message is just a ploy of Darius's to make us surrender to him. Isn't it?"

With tear-filled eyes, Decimus said, "I saw the centurion slay them with my own eyes. I'm sorry, Antonius."

Marcus closed his eyes as Antonius stared out to sea with a dazed look on his face. "My family is dead," he kept repeating over and over in his mind. He had never thought how life would be without his family. Now, reality had rammed it down his throat. He pictured Darius's smug smile after murdering them and wanted not just to kill him but to make him suffer. He clenched his teeth then remembered something in the note that vexed him. Turning to Decimus, he asked, "Darius said he took the child. What did he mean?"

Decimus glanced at them with a furrowed brow. "Augustina had a son. He was your son, Marcus, named after you."

"What? I have a son?" Marcus exclaimed with wide eyes.

"Yes. You did not know?" Decimus asked.

Marcus shook his head.

Antonius clenched his fists. Now Marcus's questions about a man marrying a woman he had been intimate with made sense. He wasn't sure how to react to the revelation that his best friend and sister had consummated their love. The only thing he was sure of at that moment was avenging the deaths of his family. Turning to Decimus, he said, "Tell me what happened when the emperor's Praetorians came. I must know every detail."

Decimus took in a breath, then said, "I was coming back from the Flavius farm after helping with a few chores. When I neared the vineyard house, I saw some Praetorians ride up. I had a bad feeling, so I hid in the trees nearby. The centurion approached your father and mother and told them they were under arrest for treason. Then the centurion had one of his men toss his sword on the ground and forced your father to fight him. Galerius fought valiantly, but the centurion was too skilled." Decimus paused to regain his composure then continued. "Eventually, your father fell to the ground gravely wounded. He was still alive when the Centurion stabbed him in the neck with his dagger. Then your mother started to hit the Centurion..." he paused again.

"Go on, Decimus," Antonius urged, clenching his teeth once again.

"He... stabbed her as well," Decimus said quietly.

"No!" Antonius cried, turning away.

"What happened to Augustina?" Marcus asked, wanting, yet not wanting to know.

Decimus swallowed hard. "Augustina stood at the doorway of the house when all this happened. She tried to run in and close the door, but the soldiers broke through. The centurion..." he lifted up his hands as though pleading for mercy and lowered his gaze.

"What?" Marcus asked, afraid of what Decimus was about to say.

Decimus trembled. "He raped then murdered her."

Marcus hung his head and shook it, saying, "No, no." Then suddenly he looked up with terror in his eyes. "What about my family? Are they all right?"

Decimus put up his hand. "I heard the centurion say he was going to arrest them too. I ran to warn Camilla, but I was barely ahead of the soldiers he sent to find your house. When they arrived, Camilla told me to slip out of the back window and try to get word to you. I was able to escape before they arrested her and your brothers and sisters."

Marcus expelled a sigh of relief as Decimus continued.

"After I watched them ride off in the wagon, I went back over to the vineyard to see if anyone there was still alive. The centurion returned and almost caught me, but I hid. After they left, I buried Antonius's family and took the next ship to Judaea from Hydruntum."

Marcus gave Antonius a confused look and asked, "What are we going to do, Antonius?"

Still blinded by rage, thinking only of avenging his family, Antonius just silently stood there.

"Antonius! What are we going to do?" Marcus cried.

Slowly looking up, Antonius replied stoically, "We must return home. Decimus, do you have enough money left to book passage for yourself back to Italia?"

"Yes," Decimus replied. "The ship I came on is due to leave tomorrow morning. I'm sure we can take it back."

"Good." Antonius dug into his purse and pulled out several silver coins. "Here. Book passage for me and Marcus and we'll meet you there as soon as we pack our things."

Decimus nodded and left.

As Antonius put Darius's note in his tunic, Marcus asked, "What will we do when we return to Italia?"

With a determined look, Antonius replied, "Rescue your family and make Darius pay."

After returning to the barracks, they started packing their knapsacks as quietly as they could. They had almost finished when Taurus walked in. He noticed their knapsacks open and things scattered about on their bunks. "Going somewhere?" he asked.

Antonius and Marcus stood there in silence, looking like a tidal wave was about to crash down upon them.

Taurus had seen the look in an enemy's eyes before when he had nowhere to run and resistance was futile. Antonius and Marcus had that look. "You two come to my room," he ordered.

They glanced at each other, unsure as to what they should do. Finally, Antonius nodded, and they followed Taurus out.

After entering his room, Taurus closed the door and gave them a curious stare. "All right you two. What's going on?"

Marcus glanced nervously at Antonius. Antonius knew that if he told the truth, Taurus would probably arrest them on the spot. Unfortunately, their swords were back at the barracks and Taurus had his. Antonius had no choice but to be forthright and hope Taurus would by some act of grace let them go. Taking a deep breath, he said, "Do you remember Darius?"

"Of course," Taurus replied. "What about him?"

"He murdered my family and arrested Marcus' family then left us a note at the vineyard saying that if we didn't surrender to him by the first of Septembris, he would kill Marcus's son. The man my father hired came from Italia to inform us. We were going to catch a ship back with him and rescue Marcus' son."

Taurus studied them for a moment. "Your families were put on the emperor's treason list, weren't they?"

Antonius felt his heart pounding rapidly. "Yes, Centurion," he replied.

Taurus nodded, watching them closely. "Your father wasn't involved with Sejanus in the plot to overthrow the emperor was he?"

"No, that's impossible!" Antonius replied strongly. "He moved to Aletium to get as far away from Rome as he could. He was happy working his vineyard. Sejanus even visited us and tried to convince him to return to the Guard, but my father turned him down. Marcus and I told him we wanted to join so he invited us to the training camp."

Taurus looked up and nodded. "Your father was a hero to many. Sejanus was probably hoping to entice him back in the Guard to use as a recruiting tool for his side. If Tiberius put your families on his treason list, they will come for you as well."

"But Marcus and I had nothing to do with a plot against the emperor! How could we, we've been in Judaea?" Antonius exclaimed.

Taurus rubbed his chin. Protocol required that he should arrest them, but he had gone against protocol before. Besides, he was fond of these two who had no military experience but fought and clawed their way through the toughest training a soldier could endure. Not to mention their skills surpassed their peers. He couldn't see them hanged as common criminals. It took him only a moment to decide. "You two return to the barracks. I'll go to Liberius and secure furloughs for you so you're not deserters. It will cost you, though. It is customary to pay a furlough fee to your centurion."

"How much is the fee?" Antonius asked.

"I'll let you know after I clear it with Liberius. When does your ship sail?" Taurus asked.

"In the morning. We were going to pack our things and meet Decimus back at the ship," Antonius replied.

"Good. Come to my room after you finish packing. I'll go and secure your leave papers. We'll keep this business about the list between us."

"Thank you, Centurion," Antonius replied.

"Yes, thank you," Marcus added.

They saluted, and departed.

Taurus stood there for a moment trying to think. Suddenly, the gold Sejanus gave him to watch over them came to mind. If Tiberius learned about the payments and assumed he was in collusion with Sejanus, he too might be in danger. The emperor's spies were everywhere. There was only one way to be on the safe side. He would arrange a leave for himself as well and find out from a reliable source if his name was on the list. If so, his sister and her family could also be in danger. Obtaining leaves for Antonius, Marcus and himself wouldn't be easy. He would have to come up with a plausible excuse. After pacing back and forth, an idea came to him. He proceeded with haste to Liberius's office.

"What is it, Centurion?" Liberius asked.

"Prefect, I'm requesting a leave for Praetorians Licinius, Flavius, and myself."

Liberius looked up. "What? Didn't those two just have furloughs?"

"They were ordered to return home. A death in the family I believe," Taurus explained.

Liberius gave him a dubious look. "A questionable order if I say so myself. The Tribune who sent it was Licinius's father. What's so important that all three of you must leave?"

"My niece Julia, the girl who visited us last year, is getting married. She asked that we attend her wedding."

"Hmmm. I don't know..." Liberius hedged, "it might cause resentment with the other men in your unit to see Licinius and Flavius sail back to Rome again so soon."

Taurus thought quickly. Looking around to make sure no one could overhear, he said, "What if I give you the ten gold pieces I received for swearing allegiance to Tiberius?"

Liberius studied Taurus for a tense moment. Finally, he said, "Make it thirty gold pieces, ten for each of you."

"Very well, thirty," Taurus capitulated, knowing he just lost the furlough fees he was going to assess from Antonius and Marcus.

Liberius smiled greedily and said, "Bring the gold before you leave and tell your other men I sent the three of you on a dangerous mission where the chances of your survival are slim. That should avoid any jealousy."

Taurus smiled then saluted and left. Without knowing it, Liberius had just given him the real reason they were leaving to use as an excuse. And he could be right. They might not survive it.

"Licinius, Flavius," he barked as he walked into the barracks.

"Yes, Centurion?" they replied.

Speaking loud enough for everyone to hear, he said, "Liberius just gave the go-ahead on that dangerous mission I told you two about. Albertus!"

"Yes, Centurion," the large man replied, coming to attention.

"While the three of us are gone, you will be in charge of the watches until we return. Is that clear?"

"Yes, Centurion," Albertus replied. "When will you be coming back?"

Giving Albertus a grave look, he replied, "If we haven't returned in a month, we'll be dead." He then pushed Antonius and Marcus quickly out of the barracks.

Appearing confused, Marcus said, "You told him 'the three of us' will be on the mission."

Without answering, Taurus said, "I'll need the ten gold pieces each of you received for renouncing Sejanus."

"Why?" Antonius asked.

"I need them to pay Liberius so he will give us the furloughs I asked for," Taurus replied. "Now get your things together; we leave immediately. Wear tunics but no swords; we don't want to attract attention. Pack your uniforms and swords, though. When you have finished, meet me in my room and bring the gold."

"Why are you going with us, Centurion?" Marcus asked.

"I have my reasons, now hurry," Taurus said, walking away quickly.

Antonius and Marcus exchanged surprised looks then returned to the barracks and finished packing. After making sure they left nothing of importance behind, they proceeded to Taurus's room. Setting their bags down just outside his door, Antonius knocked.

Taurus opened the door slightly and motioned for them to enter. Closing the door, he asked, "Do you have the gold?"

They handed him the coins.

After putting them in a small pouch, Taurus said, "Now I need to pick up our furlough papers from Liberius. While I'm doing that, requisition three horses from the stable."

Antonius and Marcus nodded.

After paying off Liberius and securing their possessions on their horses, the three rode out of the palace gates and headed for the docks.

"Decimus should have booked passage for us by now," Antonius said as they approached the harbor.

"Then we'll have to book one more," Taurus said.

After meeting up with Decimus, Taurus booked his passage with the ship's captain then they loaded their horses and stowed their belongings. By then it was late afternoon.

"Since the ship doesn't leave until morning, I say we visit the Dancing Goat one last time," Taurus suggested.

His three companions nodded.

After drowning their melancholy in watered down wine until the wee hours of the night, the four men stumbled back to the ship to catch what sleep they could. But there would be little sleep for Antonius and Marcus. Thoughts of their families misfortune kept them awake for most of the night.

Early the next morning, the ship pulled out of the harbor as the sun glistened on the dark blue sea. The lurching of the vessel from the sails catching the gusting wind woke Taurus. Looking around, he noticed that Antonius and Marcus were gone. Shaking Decimus, he asked, "Where are Licinius and Flavius?"

Rolling over, Decimus rubbed his eyes and replied, "I don't know. Aren't they here?"

"Perhaps they went topside," Taurus mumbled. He hurried up on deck and spotted them at the railing of the ship, staring back at the port.

He sighed then walked over. "You must have risen early," he said as they turned around.

"Actually, neither of us slept much," Antonius replied.

Marcus nodded then asked, "Centurion, it is obvious why we are returning to Italia but why are you?"

"I want to check on my family to make sure they are all right," he replied. "I don't think their names are on the list, but you never can tell with these purges. I'll go to the Castra and see a Tribune who owes me a favor. He might have access to it."

"But what if your family *is* on the list? They'll be looking for you as well. Won't that be risky?" Antonius asked.

Taurus smiled. "It will be like trying to catch a falling dagger, but I don't know of anyone else I can trust."

Marcus shook his head. "I still don't understand why the emperor would think we are a threat. We are in Judaea, not Rome."

Taurus gave them an grim look and said, "Remember this lesson and remember it well, you two. When emperors learn of treachery, they eliminate all who might threaten them whether they are guilty or not. A purge is taking place now. It doesn't matter where you are; it only matters who you are. You'll have to leave Italia or meet the same fate that Sejanus did. Do you understand what I'm telling you?"

Marcus bowed his head and said, "I never thought I would have to leave my homeland and not be able to return."

Rearing his head back slightly, Taurus said, "Don't give up hope altogether, Flavius. Tiberius won't live forever. Often new rulers will abolish a previous ruler's decrees especially if it adversely affects the citizens. There's a good chance the treason list will die with Tiberius."

"Then we can only hope he dies soon," Antonius added.

****

Two days later, a Roman trireme sailing nonstop pulled into the Caesarean harbor. Darius and his men disembarked and quickly rode to the palace. On the way, Darius hoped Antonius and Marcus hadn't received news of their families yet so that he could put an end to them. Once they were in custody and on board the ship returning to Rome, he would kill them both and inform Macro they tried to escape. That would be his official report.

Upon entering the palace, Darius and his men received directions to Liberius's quarters from one of the gate guards. He would follow protocol in this instance and notify the palace Prefect of the arrests.

As they marched down the corridor, Darius instructed his men. "When we confront Licinius and Flavius be ready for a fight. If they resist, kill the fair-haired Praetorian, but leave the other to me." Arriving at Liberius's stateroom, he knocked on the door and said to his men, "Wait here."

A servant answered. "Yes?"

Darius pushed past the servant and found Liberius, reclining on a couch drinking a goblet of wine.

"What's the meaning of this intrusion?" Liberius demanded.

Darius marched over to him. "I am Centurion Darius Aurelius, here on official orders from his Majesty Tiberius. Where can I find Praetorians Licinius and Flavius?"

"I gave them furloughs to Rome along with their centurion. Why do you want to know?" Liberius asked with narrowed eyes.

Incensed that Liberius had ruined his initial plan, Darius turned his anger on him. "You let them go? Didn't it seem strange to you that all three wanted to leave at the same time?"

"No, not at all. They left to attend a wedding for the centurion's niece," Liberius replied.

"When did they leave?" Darius snarled.

"Two days ago. Why are you looking for them?" Liberius asked, becoming irritated by the junior officer's impudence.

"They are wanted for treason by the emperor. I was sent here to take them back to Rome for execution. Obviously, they learned they were on the emperor's list and made up that story to avoid arrest. When I give my report to Prefect Macro in Rome, I will tell him you were the one who let them escape. Enjoy what little time you have left, Palace Prefect." Darius sneered then abruptly turned and stormed out of the room.

"What now, Centurion?" one of Darius's men asked, as they marched briskly back to their horses.

"We'll see if we can catch up to them. Their ship is most likely a merchant ship and will be slower than a trireme. We should be able to catch it if our ship's captain makes haste. Apparently, my old training centurion might be with the two we want. That might complicate matters somewhat."

After returning to the trireme, Darius ordered the trierarch to leave immediately. Three rows of oarsmen powered the ship out of the harbor as Darius stood on deck wondering why Taurus had taken a leave with them. The possibility of facing his old training instructor was something he hadn't counted on, but one man, no matter how good he was, could not defeat a contubernium of Praetorians. All three would die. Darius would savor the perfect revenge, seeing the two he hated the most lying dead at his feet. For a moment, he wondered if they really were going to Rome to attend a wedding. "No, it's too coincidental," he thought. They were running, and the first place they would run to would be their homes. That would be his first stop.

****

Liberius sat there in shock. Earlier in the day, Pilate chastised him for giving Antonius a leave just as the racing season was about to begin. He thought his troubles could get no worse. Once Darius's report reached Tiberius, the consequences would be much worse. He went into his bedroom and took out the small pouch from a nearby chest containing the thirty pieces of gold Taurus had given him. Dumping the coins into his hand, he wished he had been stronger and denied the leave request. Because of his greed, he traded thirty pieces of gold for his life. He could wait for the inevitable arrest or disappear and start fresh somewhere else. It took him only a moment to decide. He gathered the rest of the money he had, told his servant to pack their belongings then they rode out of the palace gate past the puzzled looks of the guards.

****

Two weeks later, a lookout on Darius's ship shouted, "Ship off the port bow!"

"Where?" Darius asked, running to the bow.

The lookout pointed to a speck on the horizon. "There, Centurion."

The trierarch walked over and asked, "You think that is the ship you're looking for?"

"There is only one way to find out," Darius replied with renewed hope. "Can you have your oarsmen row faster so we can catch up to it?"

"I'll have my cadence keeper increase the speed," the trierarch stated. He then turned to the lookout and said, "Go below and tell Rufio to increase the cadence. Ramming speed until we catch the ship."

"Yes, Trierarch." The lookout replied.

A moment later, the trireme ripped through the water as three rows of oars slapped against the dark sea to the increased cadence. An hour later, the trireme pulled close to the merchant ship.

"Drop your sail!" Darius shouted at the merchant ship.

"What are your intentions?" its captain shouted back.

"I'm looking for three Praetorians who left Caesarea earlier on their way to Italia," Darius shouted.

"My ship departed from Creta; there are no Praetorians on board," the merchant captain replied.

"Have you seen another ship traveling in the same direction?" Darius asked.

"No," came the merchant captain's reply.

"Curse the gods," Darius swore to himself. Turning to the trierarch, he said, "Have your oarsmen resume speed."

The trierarch narrowed his eyes and said, "We have a good wind. The sail will carry us fast enough."

"Not fast enough for me!" Darius barked. "I'm trying to catch criminals disloyal to the emperor!"

"And I'm trying to keep my oarsmen from keeling over dead, Centurion. Oars up!" he shouted. "We sail with the wind!"

Darius growled.

****

Antonius, Marcus and Taurus stood on the port side of their ship when the lookout shouted, "Italia off the starboard bow!" They raced over to the other side as it approached the southeastern Italian peninsula.

"Hydruntum!" Antonius exclaimed as they headed toward the port.

The ship gently pulled into the dock and moored temporarily while the four guided their horses down the gangplank.

After mounting up, they made their way to the outskirts of town as the ship departed.

Taurus reined in his horse and said, "Let's stop for a moment." He dismounted, and the others followed suit. "This note that Darius left for you... do you still have it?" he asked.

Antonius nodded.

"May I see it?"

Antonius took it out and handed it to him. "Darius says that if we come to the villa and surrender ourselves, he will fight me to the death. If I win, we will all be pardoned and go free. If he wins, we all die. If we don't appear by the date indicated, he will kill Marcus's son."

Taurus shook his head. "He promises something he cannot honor. Only the emperor can pardon you. As soon as you surrender, you are dead men. Darius has no intention of letting you live."

"We can't let him kill my son!" Marcus exclaimed. "We must do something!"

"We'll confront Darius," Taurus assured him, "but not to surrender. I'll come up with a plan."

"You are going with us?" Marcus asked.

Taurus snorted. "If I don't, you two will surely get yourselves killed. But first, I must find out if my family is on the list. When I learn they're safe, we'll rescue Flavius's family. Now, there may be patrols on the main roads looking for us, so we'll need to travel cross-country. We should leave the road now before we're spotted. We'll have to obtain food and water along the way."

Antonius turned to Decimus. "Thank you, Decimus, for getting word to us about what happened. Do I owe you any money for your work on the vineyard before we go?"

Decimus took a deep breath. "I would like to accompany you and help where I can if you'll let me. I've never fought with a gladius, but I can be useful in other ways."

"There is no need for you to do that, Decimus. I'm sure you can find work elsewhere."

"Your family meant a lot to me, Antonius. There was nothing I could do when the Praetorians came, but there is something I can do now. I'm asking you to please let me help."

Taurus put his hand on Decimus's shoulder and shook his head slightly. "This isn't going to be a walk in the meadow, my friend. You understand that if you throw your lot in with us, there is a likely chance you won't survive."

"I am willing to take that chance," Decimus replied calmly. "I can think of no better cause and no better company to keep than with you three men."

Taurus shrugged his shoulders. "As long as you know the risk."

"How are we going to rescue my family?" Marcus asked.

"I'll think of something on the way to Rome," Taurus replied. "I know the prison fairly well. Don't worry Flavius, if they are still there, we'll find a way to free them."

"Do you think they are still alive?" Marcus asked.

Taurus turned to him and said, "It's hard to say. They've been imprisoned for awhile... unless Tiberius had them executed."

Marcus winced.

Realizing his remark was insensitive, Taurus turned and said, "I'm sorry, Flavius. I'm sure they're still alive."

"If they are, how are we going to get them out with so many soldiers and guards there?" Antonius asked. "There are only four of us."

Taurus sighed. "The only chance we have is to bribe the interior guards. We'll need to get past the Praetorians at the entrance to the prison first. That will be our hardest task. If we can do that, we have a chance."

"That is a chance I am willing to take," Marcus said. "I will not remain free while my family suffers in prison."

Taurus nodded slightly. "I had a feeling you would say that." Under his breath, he added, "I just hope they're still alive."

Antonius put up his hand and said, "If we're going to start new lives, I'll need to get the money my family was saving. My father hid it in the stable. I'm sure it's still there."

"Praetorians may also be there," Taurus suggested.

"That is a chance *I'm* willing to take," Antonius said, smiling at Marcus.

Taurus wanted to reject the idea, but he knew Antonius was right. The impending obstacles they faced were likely insurmountable anyway. What was one more? "How far is your home from here, Licinius?" he asked.

"If we leave now, we should arrive before daylight," Antonius replied.

Taurus nodded. "All right, let's be on our way."

The four mounted up and galloped off with high hopes.

A few hours before sunrise, they arrived at a hill overlooking the vineyard. After tying their horses to some nearby bushes, they crawled to the crest of the hill and peered over. By the pale light of a half moon, they could see four sentries around the house and four sentries around the stable.

Taurus shook his head. "I was afraid of this. It will be impossible to enter the stable without being spotted."

"What if we created a diversion?" Marcus asked. "I could go to the back of the stable and make some noise in the bushes. When they leave their posts to investigate, Antonius can slip in."

Taurus smiled. "You were paying attention during the training on diversionary tactics, weren't you, Flavius?"

Marcus grinned.

Taurus rubbed his chin. "That could work, but once you have the sentries' attention, you'll have to get out quickly without them seeing you."

Marcus nodded.

Surveying the area again, Taurus said, "Eight sentries means there are at least eight more asleep somewhere. Let's hope they're not in the stable. All right, here is the plan: The three of us will go down. Decimus, you stay here and watch the horses."

"What if something happens to you?" Decimus asked.

"Nothing will happen to us, Decimus," Taurus said firmly, shaking his head. "Now, once we're close enough to the stable, Licinius and Flavius, you take your places, and I'll wait in the middle in case we need another diversion. Flavius, I'll take your bow and arrows just in case they discover you or Licinius."

Marcus removed it from his horse and handed it to him. After Decimus had wished them luck, the three crept down the hill. Once they were close enough to the stable, Marcus quietly made his way through the bushes to the other side and waited for Antonius to position himself. When he felt that the time was right, he shook the bushes near him.

"What was that?" one of the sentries asked his counterpart.

"It sounded like there's something in the bushes near the stable," his companion replied, pointing toward the sound.

Keeping their pilums in one hand and shields in the other, they cautiously approached the area where Marcus lay. The other two sentries near the front of the stable also focused their attention in the direction of the sound and stepped away from their posts. Marcus' noisy distraction had succeeded.

Antonius scurried over to the stable and slipped inside. As the sentries came closer, Marcus turned and began to crawl through the dense foliage. Suddenly, his tunic snagged on a briar bush. He tried in vain to free himself, but the noise attracted the attention of the sentries. They headed directly toward him. Marcus froze. If he tried to move, they would surely see him. His only advantage to avoid being seen was the darkness. He closed his eyes and whispered, "God of Israel, please help me."

Seeing that Marcus was about to be discovered, Taurus drew back the arrow he had nocked and aimed at the sentry approaching him.

Just as the sentry was a few feet away from where Marcus lay, the other sentry shouted, "I found the noise!" He held up his pilum. A rabbit on the end went through the final phase of its death throes.

"It looks like we'll have rabbit stew tomorrow," his companion grinned. Turning back around, the two sentries headed back to their posts as Marcus said a silent, "Thank you."

Taurus slowly released the tension on the bow's drawstring and exhaled.

After cutting off the piece of his tunic that caught on the bush, Marcus quietly returned to Taurus's position. A moment later, Antonius appeared with the chest.

"Let's return to where Decimus is waiting and continue before they discover us," Taurus whispered.

Seeing his three companions approach, Decimus let out a relieved sigh.

Antonius opened the chest and said, "Hopefully this will last us for awhile."

Taurus's eyes opened wide at the substantial pile of money. Looking at Antonius from under his eyebrows, he said, "I think that will be ample for your needs.

After Antonius had poured the money from the chest into his knapsack, they all mounted up. Taurus turned to them and muttered, "To Rome."

Antonius looked back at the vineyard he wanted so desperately to leave before. Now, he wished he had never left.

CHAPTER XXII-FUGITIVES

As they rode along, Marcus said, "I wanted to visit my father's grave one last time, but Praetorians were probably there as well."

Antonius nodded. "I wish I could have visited my family's graves."

"Just be thankful *your* graves won't be added to them," Taurus stated, receiving tired nods from both of them.

A few hours later, dawn began its glow. Seeing they were all struggling just to stay in their saddles, Taurus brought his small troop to a halt. "All right, you three. Get off your horses before you fall off. We'll rest here until sundown."

After dismounting and tying their horses to some nearby trees, they spread out their bedrolls.

"We'll sleep during the day and travel during the night, so get as much rest as you can," Taurus informed them. He rolled his shoulders and leaned his head from side to side.

"Why are we traveling by night rather than by day?" Marcus asked stifling a yawn.

"Less chance of being spotted," Taurus replied. "I'm not tired, so I'll stand watch first. I'll wake one of you when I can't stay awake."

Decimus fell asleep quickly. Antonius and Marcus tried to get comfortable, but nagging thoughts kept them awake.

Unable to keep his disappointment hidden any longer, Antonius gave Marcus a stern look and asked, "Why didn't you tell me you and my sister were intimate?"

Marcus feared the subject would come up eventually. Now that it had, he realized what he and Augustina had done also affected their families. With a slight trembling in his voice, he said, "I'm sorry, Antonius. I should have told you, but I was afraid I would lose your friendship. You should know, I did not force myself upon Augustina. On the last night of our furlough, she unexpectedly came to the farm and our feelings were so strong for each other that it just happened. I remember what you said in Judaea about women who give themselves to men before marriage, but I want to marry Augustina and I do respect her. Please forgive me, Antonius. I didn't mean to bring shame upon our families."

Antonius nodded. "Shame is the least of our worries. If I hadn't talked you into joining, you and your family would be safe now."

"Joining was my decision, Antonius. I could have stayed on the farm, but I chose to leave. Maybe my decision is one I regret, but I'm still the one who made it, not you."

"Perhaps I should have stayed at home as well. My family might still be alive," Antonius said, feeling a twinge of regret.

"That wouldn't have changed the fact that your father and Sejanus were good friends. Chances are the emperor would still have included your family on his treason list and you'd be dead too," Marcus reminded him.

"But not your family," Antonius countered.

Marcus sighed. "We can't change that now."

Antonius nodded then turned on his back and looked up at the transitioning sky as the sun began its ascent. He couldn't fight the fatigue any longer and drifted off to sleep.

As he slept, he dreamt he was back in the vineyard, standing between the grapevines. Ahead he saw three figures walking away from him. He recognized them as his father, mother, and sister. His father wore his Praetorian armor, and his mother and sister walked on either side. He ran toward them and tried to yell, "Wait! Don't go!" but the words would not come. Finally, he caught up and ran around in front to face them. That's when he saw they were covered in blood. "NOOOOOO!" he screamed, as he awoke and popped up into a sitting position.

His cry also woke Marcus and Decimus.

"What is it?" Taurus said, running over as Marcus and Decimus sat up and looked around.

"I must have had a nightmare," Antonius replied.

"Next time, have quieter ones. Anyone a league away could have heard you," Taurus chided him.

Antonius nodded. "I'm awake now. Let me relieve you."

"All right, but if you hear anyone approaching, wake us all immediately."

"Yes, Centurion," Antonius agreed.

Taurus gave him a scowl and said, "And stop calling me 'Centurion.' We'll call each other by our first names."

"What is your first name?" Marcus asked.

Taurus gritted his teeth then blurted out, "Cicero."

His three companions snickered until they saw his eyes narrow.

"Go back to sleep!" Taurus barked at Marcus and Decimus, who quickly closed their eyes. Shaking his head, he spread out his blanket and said to Antonius, "Make sure the fire doesn't go out."

Antonius thought of the wolves attacking them on their way to Rome and replied, "Don't worry, I won't."

That night, the ship carrying Darius and his men pulled into Hydruntum's port. After unloading their horses, the nine Praetorians galloped off for Aletium. Arriving at the vineyard just as the sun was rising, Darius and his men dismounted and approached the house.

"Any signs of the criminals?" Darius asked one of the sentries.

"No sign of them, Centurion," came the reply.

"Hmmph," Darius snorted. He walked inside the house and went from room to room, yelling, "On your feet! Assemble outside!"

When all his men assembled, he addressed them.

"Did any of you see anything unusual while I was gone?"

Sixteen heads shook.

"Nothing appeared missing? You didn't hear any strange noises?" Darius queried.

Atticus stepped forward. "One of the men on sentry duty did hear a rabbit in the bushes the other night, Centurion."

"How did he know the noise was a rabbit?" Darius gruffly asked.

"Ancus speared it with his pilum," a Praetorian replied.

"Show me where this happened," Darius insisted.

Proceeding to the location, the Praetorian pointed to the area and said, "Right in here, Centurion."

Darius looked about for a moment then noticed something. Kneeling down, he removed a torn piece of tunic and held it up. "It appears rabbits are wearing tunics now. Atticus, search the entire area, including the surrounding hills. See if you can find any tracks. I'll ride over to the Flavius farm and ask the men there if they heard any 'rabbit noises.'"

"Yes, Centurion," his red-faced optio replied.

Returning a short while later with the rest of his men, Darius asked, "Did you locate any tracks, Atticus?"

"Yes, Centurion. We found an empty chest and foot and hoof prints on the hill. It looks like four riders headed north."

"Four of them?" Darius asked. "I wonder who else they recruited. An empty chest means they must have stopped to get the money that was inside. Have the men pack some food and water. We'll follow their trail until dark."

"Yes, Centurion!"

That evening, a sharp kick to their feet awoke Marcus and Decimus.

Rubbing his eyes, Marcus could see Taurus standing over him. "Did you get any sleep?" he asked.

"I don't need much sleep," Taurus replied, shaking his head. "Besides, I can sleep while I ride. Now get up. Licinius and I already saddled the horses so we are ready to leave."

"When are we going to eat?" Marcus asked as he stood up.

"A good question," Taurus replied, "we need provisions. You three know this area better than I do. Any suggestions?"

Antonius nodded. "My father and I supplied wine for the Olive Branch Inn not too far from here. I'm sure I could get provisions there."

"I'll go with him," Marcus offered.

"No, a man alone will attract less attention." Turning to Antonius, he said, "Scout the area for soldiers or Praetorians carefully before you go in. If you aren't back by the time the sun rises, I'll assume the worst. The rest of us will move on. We can't remain here for long."

"I understand," Antonius said. He looked over at Marcus, who was biting his lip and gave him a single nod then rode off.

After reaching the inn, Antonius cautiously circled it. Seeing no signs of Praetorians or other soldiers, he rode to the front entry and tied his horse to the hitching post. Taking a last look around, he walked inside. The hour was now quite late, and there was no one behind the reception counter. Antonius knew Crassus's living quarters occupied most of the downstairs area and walked over to the door. Lightly knocking on it, he put his ear to the door and heard someone stirring.

"Yes, yes, I'll be right there," Crassus mumbled.

A moment later the door opened revealing the innkeeper in his long night tunic. "Yes? You need a room?" After focusing his eyes, Crassus said, "Antonius? Is that you?"

"Yes, Crassus. I apologize for the late hour, but I need your help."

"My help?" Crassus asked, now stepping into the reception area and closing the door. "Is something wrong?"

Antonius hesitated a moment then said, "You know about Prefect Sejanus being arrested and executed for treason."

Crassus nodded. "Yes, what about it?"

"Tiberius ordered the arrests of his family and friends as well and put their names on a treason list. Since my father and the Prefect were close friends, my family and my friend's family were included. Antonius swallowed hard to hold back his anger.

"Oh, no!" Crassus said with a furrowed brow.

"That is why I am here. I learned that one of the emperor's Praetorians... killed my family and took my friend's family to the prison in Rome."

Crassus's mouth dropped open. "Killed? Oh, Antonius, I am truly sorry. Your parents were two of the best people I have ever known, especially your father. We shared many a goblet of wine together. I will greatly miss him. What can I do for you, Antonius?"

"I need provisions. I have the money to pay for them."

Crassus led him into the store room and said, "Take whatever you require; we'll settle it later."

"Perhaps I should pay for it now; there may not be a later," Antonius said.

Crassus bristled. "Antonius! If your father were here, he would be greatly disappointed to hear you talk like a defeated man."

A reddish hue colored Antonius's cheeks. "I just... don't want you to think I'm taking advantage of a favor," he stammered.

"Your father granted me many favors," Crassus stated firmly. "Consider this one in return." Crassus then handed him an empty bag and said, "Fill this with what you need. I'll return shortly."

Antonius went through the cupboards and bins filling his sack with cheese, fruit, and bread. When he estimated he had enough for the remainder of the journey back to Rome, he returned to the front reception area.

A moment later Crassus appeared. "He handed Antonius a large wineskin and said, "Here is some of your wine. Don't you and your companions drink it all in one sitting," he added with a smile. "And here is something just for you," he added, handing Antonius a gold medallion.

"What is this?" Antonius asked.

"A medallion with the goddess Vesta inscribed on it. She is the patron of hearth and home. Wherever you go, keep her with you as a reminder of your family. She'll bring you luck and see you never go hungry," Crassus replied.

Antonius' face lit up as he said, "This is beyond kindness. Thank you, Crassus." Antonius placed the medallion in his pocket and said, "Now I must join my companions. If I'm not back soon, they will leave without me."

"Then you must go! Here, I'll walk out with you," Crassus said. "Does this mean I will have to find another wine supplier?" he asked.

Antonius nodded. "I'm afraid so. I wish we could continue, but the vineyard belongs to Caesar now."

As Antonius opened the door leading outside, he came face to face with two Praetorians. "Oh! Uh, excuse me," he said. Holding his breath, he slid past them and walked toward his horse with the supplies Crassus gave him.

He took three steps when he heard, "You there! Hold!"

Antonius closed his eyes and stood still.

"What are you doing up so late?" the larger Praetorian asked.

"I'm on my way to Rome and thought I would get an early start," Antonius replied without turning around.

"You're a Praetorian!" the big Praetorian exclaimed.

Antonius's heart began to race.

Crassus turned pale.

Antonius turned around slowly to face them and asked, "What makes you think that?"

"The scabbard and gladius tied to your horse are Praetorian. Besides, civilians aren't allowed to carry weapons. What unit do you belong to?" the large Praetorian asked.

Antonius hesitated then said, "The gladius is my father's. He was a Praetorian and let me borrow it while I travel in case I should run into trouble."

The larger Praetorian narrowed his eyes and said. "We just happen to be looking for relatives of a Praetorian. I think we'll take you to our optio for questioning." He then drew his gladius and gave his companion a nod.

His younger companion understood his signal and drew his gladius as well.

Antonius could see his only alternative was to fight. He wouldn't be able to mount his horse and ride off before they would be upon him. Quickly taking out his father's gladius, he said, "My family was murdered by a Praetorian and I will not stop until I bring him to justice. I don't want to shed your blood, but I can't let you detain me."

"The only blood that will be shed will be yours. You are one of the fugitives we're looking for, aren't you?" the big Praetorian asked.

Antonius boldly proclaimed, "Yes, I am one of the Praetorians you seek. I am Antonius Licinius, son of Galerius Licinius."

The big Praetorian smiled. "Galerius Magnus's son, eh? You may be the son of a famous Praetorian, but you are still one of the criminals Centurion Aurelius told us to watch for."

"Your centurion is actually the criminal," Antonius retorted.

The big Praetorian snorted and said, "I'll give you one more chance to surrender your weapon. Unlike you, I don't mind shedding your blood. The choice is yours."

Antonius switched hands a couple of times to get the feel of his gladius, then shook his head and said, "There will be no surrender."

The larger Praetorian smiled. "You won't live to regret your decision, son of Galerius."

Then the two Praetorians began to flank Antonius. He noticed the younger one appeared to be less sure of himself. Recalling his training, he maneuvered himself, so his back was against the wall of the inn. The big Praetorian lifted his head and said, "Ah, I see you remembered your training."

As the two Praetorians flanked Antonius and inched closer, he sprang at the younger one. After a few lightning moves, he sliced the side of the Praetorian's neck open. As he fell, the larger one slashed Antonius on his back. Antonius saw it coming and tried to move, but wasn't quick enough to avoid the blade altogether. Fortunately, the wound was only superficial, and he was able to repel the rest of his adversary's initial assault. It was obvious the big Praetorian would be much harder to defeat. Seeing the blood on his gladius, the large Praetorian smiled and circled Antonius like a shark. He feinted a few times, but Antonius held his ground.

"Why don't you come at me?" the Praetorian said. "You certainly have skills, killing my companion as quickly as you did. Surely, you aren't afraid. Come at me."

Antonius kept his eyes on the big man as they shuffled from side to side, looking for an opening.

The Praetorian smirked. "We could dance like this until my relief comes. Then you'll have to deal with many. Are you confident you can ..."

Before he could finish his sentence, Antonius attacked. He had waited until his opponent paid more attention to what he was saying than keeping up his guard. The lapse in concentration was only a moment, but a moment was all Antonius needed. After a few quick moves, he ended it. Looking down at the large man lying on the ground, Antonius muttered, "It appears we both have shed blood."

Crassus ran over and threw his arms around him. "I was afraid it was all over for you, Antonius, but you fought like Mars himself! Your father would have been proud." Seeing that Antonius was bleeding, Crassus said, "You've been cut. Come in and I will dress your wound."

After quickly cleaning and bandaging the laceration, Crassus said, "That should do. You must leave now before other Praetorians come."

Antonius nodded. "When they arrive, tell them the two posted here discovered me trying to steal food. After I had defeated them, I rode off toward the coast."

Crassus's eyes filled with tears as he said, "I will miss your family, as I know you will, Antonius. May the gods protect you."

"Thank you, Crassus; be well."

"Be well, Antonius."

Antonius picked up the supplies then quickly mounted his horse and rode off. He felt bad about the two Praetorians, but he couldn't let anyone stop him until he faced Darius. Just as the sun cleared the horizon, he came galloping up to his comrades, who were just preparing to leave.

"Good, you're back. Any trouble?" Taurus asked.

Antonius expelled a deep breath. "Unfortunately, I ran into two of Darius's men who noticed my Praetorian gladius. I had to deal with them."

Taurus raised his eyebrows and asked, "Are you all right?"

"One cut me on my back but it isn't bad. The innkeeper treated it."

Taurus cursed. "Merda[67], I should have thought of that. Praetorian scabbards are too obvious. We must keep our swords wrapped and secured to our horses. Just make sure you can pull them out easily if we need to. From now on we avoid all inns and taverns until we reach Rome." Turning to Antonius, he asked, "I hope you had time to get the supplies we needed?"

Antonius pulled out the bag of food and the wineskin from his horse. "Enough until we arrive, including some wine."

"Good man," Taurus exclaimed. "We had better move to a different location. It may not be safe for us here much longer."

At midday, the four fugitives stopped and rested for a few hours then continued. Later that evening they came to a long, shallow stream glistening in the moonlight.

"We'll cross here," Taurus said.

The following day, Darius and his men reached the same stream.

At their next camp, Taurus gathered them together. "Once we arrive in Rome, we will need a place to stay. A patrol might come across us if we're out in the open. They'll be watching taverns and inns as well."

Decimus raised his finger. "My brother owns a small cottage just outside of Rome that he and his wife use whenever he goes to the city. He might let us stay there."

"Where does your brother live?" Taurus asked.

"Fregellae," Decimus replied.

Taurus smiled. "The gods are with us. Fregellae is directly on our way."

"I thought you didn't believe in the gods," Marcus remarked.

Taurus smiled. "I never said I didn't believe in them, I only remarked, *'If*

---

67 *Slang for excrement*

you believe in the gods.' I like to keep my options open."

Antonius grinned and said, "I'll take the first watch."

Taurus bristled. "Are you forgetting that I am still the centurion, and I give the orders, Licinius?"

Antonius smiled. "You said we were supposed to forget about you being a centurion."

Taurus smiled. "So I did. Very well, I'll sleep until awakened. Just don't shake me or you might get a dagger in your groin."

Marcus and Decimus winced.

"I will use the branch of a tree to awaken you then," Antonius stated.

Taurus gave a single serious nod and unrolled his blanket.

As Antonius began his watch, he sat down and scoured the landscape they had just traveled across. The sun rose above the hills, and a soft breeze began to blow. He raked his fingers through his tousled hair as Marcus walked over and sat down beside him. "You should get some sleep," Antonius advised his friend.

"I will, when I get sleepy," Marcus said, looking up in the sky. "The weather has been good for us."

"What?" Antonius asked.

"The weather… it has been good since we returned from Judaea. It looks like there are some dark clouds in the distance, though."

Antonius looked at them and said, "We may be in for some rain."

Marcus scrunched his face and said, "I can't understand why Darius didn't arrest your family like he did mine."

Antonius stared off into the distance. "Darius hated me more than he did you because my father's friendship with Sejanus enabled us to join the Guard. That's why Darius murdered him rather than arrest him. My father once told me when a soldier kills out of duty or self-defense it is acceptable. However, when a man kills for any other reason, it is murder, and they must pay the penalty for it. He called it justice. Darius didn't kill my family out of duty or self-defense. He murdered them because of a grudge he held against me. Now he must pay for their deaths."

"He will," Marcus predicted, as his eyes slowly closed. A moment later he was asleep.

As the deadly game of hide-and-seek continued, Darius and his men gained a little more ground until they were less than a league behind.

Just outside of Fregellae, the fugitives rode down a hill, crossed a small brook and entered a dense grove of trees. Their hunters appeared on the hill moments later and approached the stream. In the dark, Darius strained his eyes to follow the tracks. Reaching the brook, one of Darius's men said, "Listen! I think I heard something."

As they strained to hear what they hoped would be horses ridden by the men they were pursuing, a long growling roll of thunder echoed across the dark summer sky. Large drops of rain suddenly began to fall.

"Curse this weather! All we need now is rain," Darius grumbled. "Quick! Ennius! Marcellinus! You're my best trackers. Follow the trail of the fugitives before the rain destroys their tracks!"

The two Praetorians quickly rode forward and began tracking.

Taurus, sensing danger was near, pressed his companions to continue. Exiting the grove near a small road, he held up his hand for them to stop.

"Fregellae is a few leagues away," Decimus said. "My brother lives only a short distance from here. We must go right, down this road."

Taurus nodded. "Lead the way." As they proceeded onto the road, Taurus suddenly reined his horse to a halt. "Wait! Riders are coming. Quick! Back into the trees!"

Well hidden with swords drawn, they waited as four horses galloped down the road with their riders hunched over to keep the rain from stinging their faces.

After making sure no other riders were coming, Taurus and his companions proceeded down the road, unaware that Darius was close behind. They had barely disappeared around the bend when Darius and his men came out of the trees where they had been. The two trackers looked at the road in bewilderment. The heavy rain was quickly obscuring the numerous horse hoof impressions.

"There are tracks going in both directions," one of the trackers said.

"They must not slip through our fingers!" Darius snarled. "Give me your best guess which direction they took!"

Studying the tracks for a moment, one pointed to the right and the other to the left. Darius shook his head and angrily bellowed, "We go to the left!"

The four fugitives rode on until they reached a smaller, bisecting road that led to the house of Decimus's brother.

Decimus pointed and said, "My brother lives down this road."

"Get the key to the cottage. We'll wait for you here," Taurus said.

After a short ride, Decimus arrived at his brother's house and knocked on the door.

Opening the door, his brother squinted and asked, "Decimus? Is that you?"

"Hello, Hadrianus," Decimus said with a grin.

"Here, come in out of the rain before you drown."

"Thank you," Decimus said, brushing himself off before entering.

"What brings you here at such a late hour in this cursed weather?" his brother asked, closing the door.

"I'm sorry, I thought I could get here earlier, but circumstances prevented that from happening," Decimus explained his rehearsed answer.

"No matter. Can you stay the night?"

"No, actually I was hoping to stay at your cottage in Rome. Would it be possible for me to get the key?" Decimus asked with a pained expression.

"That's still a good ride from here and it's pouring out there," his brother mentioned. "Are you sure you don't want to stay with us and leave in the morning?"

"I do appreciate the offer," Decimus stated, "but I have pressing business for the vineyard I must take care of early tomorrow."

With a look of capitulation, Hadrianus said, "Very well, then. I'll get the key. I still think you're foolish to ride in this weather."

He disappeared for a moment then returned with a large key. "Here it is. Stop back by when you return. Marcella will fix you a grand supper."

"Thank you, brother, I will try," Decimus said, hurrying away.

As Hadrianus returned to bed, his wife Marcella asked, "Who was that?"

"Decimus. He was on his way to Rome and wanted to stay at the cottage."

"Why didn't he stay with us here?" she asked with a frown.

"He said he was in a hurry," Hadrianus replied, rolling over.

Marcella sat up and looked out the window. "He must be, if he's riding in this weather."

Returning to his companions, Decimus held up the key.

"Good," Taurus said as he pulled the hood on his tunic more over his face. "Now, let's get to the cottage before we're struck by lightning."

The heavy rain had now turned all tracks on the road into unreadable puddles. Darius realized that stumbling across their quarry now was highly unlikely. He decided to give up the chase and proceed to Rome as quickly as possible.

Late the following morning, he reported to Macro's office.

"Were you able to arrest Galerius's son and his friend?" Macro asked.

"I'm afraid not, Prefect. When I arrived in Judaea, I discovered that their palace Prefect gave them furloughs. Liberius was his name. We should add it to the list for aiding them. We should also add Centurion Taurus' name on the list as well. It appears he has joined with them."

Macro nodded but made no notations.

Darius continued. "Obviously, Licinius and Flavius learned their names were on the list and gave the Prefect in Judaea a made-up story so they could flee. Figuring they would go to the vineyard, I went there when I returned from Judaea and found they had stopped there briefly to obtain money from a chest we found. I picked up their tracks and followed them as far as Fregellae. Unfortunately, we were caught in a storm and lost them on a road just outside of town. We will have them in custody soon, however. I arranged it so they would come to me."

Macro sat back in his chair and asked, "Really? How so?"

"After I dealt with Licinius's family, I left a message at the vineyard indicating I had an infant we found there and would be bringing him to Rome to hold as hostage until they surrendered. I gave them until the first of Septembris or the child's life would be forfeit. When I sent some men to the vineyard to watch for them as you suggested, they noticed the note was gone when they arrived. I'm sure whoever took it made sure it reached our fugitives."

Macro nodded. "Do you have enough men to ensure their capture?"

"I have four contuberniums on each watch and will keep them posted until we resolve the matter."

"This infant is related to young Licinius?" Macro asked.

"Yes, it is his nephew and the son of his friend, Flavius."

"Very good. Rather than continuing to chase them all over the countryside you will force them to come to you, an excellent strategy. Anything else, centurion?"

"Yes. Another person we haven't identified yet has joined them as well. So there are four altogether."

Macro gave him a slight nod. "Four against thirty-two shouldn't present any problems for you. Keep me informed of any further developments."

"I will, Prefect," Darius said, saluting as he departed.

Macro rubbed his chin and hoped the younger Licinius and his friend would surrender. Killing an infant was distasteful to him, but he knew that Aurelius would have no qualms in doing it.

****

The next day, the fugitives arrived at the cottage. Taurus walked around the perimeter looking for an escape route, should they need it. Satisfied with his initial inspection, he turned to Decimus. "This will do. We'll take our horses around to the back."

After securing and unloading their horses, they returned to the front of the cottage. Decimus unlocked the front door and gestured for them to enter.

The quaint two-room dwelling had a couch, table and chairs in the main room and a large bed, chair and dresser in the other. An oil lamp stood on a small table by the door, and another stood on a table in the sleeping area.

Turning to his companions, he said, "It isn't large, but it was well built. There is a water pump out back."

Walking over to make sure the back shutters covering the opening on the wall were easy to get through if they needed to escape quickly, Taurus nodded. "A little cramped perhaps, once we rescue Flavius's family, but we shouldn't be here long."

"How will we transport them?" Marcus asked. "We don't have enough horses."

Taurus nodded. "We'll need a wagon."

"We can use some of my money to buy that and anything else we need," Antonius volunteered.

Taurus rubbed his chin. "We'll need food, bedding, and clothes for Flavius's family. They should be easy to find in Rome. Since someone could recognize us, Decimus should go. Would you do that, Decimus?"

"Yes, I would be happy to," he replied.

"Good. I'll make out a list. Do you have something to write with?" Taurus asked.

"I do," Marcus said, going to his knapsack.

"I'll get the money," Antonius said.

Decimus nodded as Taurus wrote down what was needed.

After finishing the list, with Marcus's help on clothing sizes for his family, Taurus handed it to Decimus.

Opening his knapsack, Antonius took out a few gold and silver coins. "This should be enough, but if it isn't, return and I'll give you more."

As Decimus took the money, Taurus said, "Spend it wisely."

"I will," he said. A moment later, he rode off.

Taurus rubbed his chin and asked, "You don't think he'll take the money and disappear, do you?"

"No," Antonius replied. "I came to know him fairly well when I was home on furlough. He will return."

Taurus narrowed his eyes and said, "I just hope he doesn't return with Praetorians. What if he thinks he could get a reward for turning us in?"

"I don't see him doing that," Antonius replied. "My parents thought very highly of him."

"Nevertheless, perhaps we should leave the cottage and wait until he returns," Taurus insisted. "We can take our horses over the hill across the way and wait. If he comes back with what we need, we'll know he can be trusted. If he brings back Praetorians, we ride off."

"I'm willing to go along with that," Marcus said.

"He won't betray us," Antonius assured him, shaking his head. "But I'll do as you suggest. I'm sure he will prove you wrong,"

Lying down on the hill overlooking the cottage, they waited.

"Of course," Taurus pointed out, "you realize if Decimus decides to turn us in for a reward and goes to Macro, we must forget about rescuing anyone and disappear."

"Then let's hope he doesn't betray us," Antonius said.

Marcus closed his eyes and said a silent prayer.

Morning turned to afternoon. Antonius and Marcus eventually succumbed to the drowsiness caused by the heat and fell asleep. Fortunately, Taurus knew how to remain alert.

"Wake up you two," he said, shaking both of them.

"What?" Antonius exclaimed, as he and Marcus awoke.

"I hear horses approaching," Taurus replied.

They waited anxiously to see if Taurus or Antonius was right about Decimus's allegiance.

Taurus shook his head. "It sounds like too many horses for just a solitary wagon. You may have been wrong about him, Licinius. Many horses mean many riders, which probably means Praetorians. We ride out now!"

"But my family!" Marcus pleaded.

"We cannot save them if we are dead!" Taurus exclaimed. "We must leave now before they discover us!"

"Wait! I think we should trust Antonius's feelings. Please, Centurion," Marcus pleaded.

Taurus raised his eyebrows and said, "Suit yourselves, but if I see one Praetorian, I am riding off as fast as I can and not looking back."

Antonius and Marcus nodded in agreement.

All three held their breath until Decimus appeared driving a wagon pulled by a team of four horses. He had tied his horse to the back along with a goat. Antonius and Marcus grinned at Taurus, who shrugged his shoulders. "It is better for a man to make sure a serpent isn't poisonous before he picks it up."

The three mounted up and rode down the hill as Decimus stepped down from the wagon.

"There you are," he said. "I was able to get this wagon and the four horses for a good price from a farmer. He even threw in a goat. I figured the goat would be good to provide milk for the infant when we rescue him. I also bought some clothes for Marcus's family, a few straw mattresses, and some food."

Handing Antonius his purse, he said proudly, "Here is the money I didn't spend."

"You did well," Antonius said, impressed with Decimus's optimism about rescuing the child.

"Yes," Taurus added, "very well."

Decimus beamed. "I'm glad you approve."

Tipping his head in the direction of the cottage door, Taurus said, "Take everything inside then we can discuss the plan to rescue Flavius's family."

After emptying the wagon and taking care of the horses and goat, they gathered around the small table and sat down. Taurus clasped his hands together and gave each a serious glance. "My family's safety is my first concern. I will contact the Tribune at the Castra Praetoria and see if he knows if their names are on the emperor's treason list. I'll also ask him to provide me with an incarceration order to get into the prison. Darius expects us at the villa, but hopefully not at the prison."

"Who is the incarceration order for?" Marcus asked.

"For you," Taurus replied. "Licinius and I will take you in as our prisoner. You'll be our reason to get inside."

"This tribune, are you sure you can trust him?" Antonius asked.

"Yes. As I mentioned before, he owes me a big favor. I don't think I'll have a problem obtaining the order."

"Who is he?" Marcus asked.

Taurus smiled. "Your old training commander, Tribune Falconius."

"You're just going to walk right into the Castra?" Antonius asked. "If your name is on the list, the gate guards might arrest you."

"Don't figure me for a fool just yet. I know another way inside. There is a storage area on the northeastern side I can access through a door on the outside of the wall. Bushes conceal it, and few know it's there. I was given a key to the inner door so I could obtain items stored there for the training camps. My key also fits the outer door. I just forgot to turn it in." He leaned back, smiling. "Once I'm in, no one is going to pay any attention to me with all the other Praetorians around. If all goes well, I'll return with the documents we need. We should be able to bribe the interior prison guards, but the guards at the main prison gate are Praetorians and will sound the alarm if we try to bribe them. They have been handpicked and threatened with death if they take a bribe and the Prefect learns of it. Besides, only the Prefect himself can authorize prisoner releases."

"Then how do we get out?" Marcus asked.

"I will think of something. Right now we need the incarceration order. This evening, Antonius and I will go to the Castra to get it."

"What about me?" Marcus asked.

"You'll stay here with Decimus. The more men we take, the more chance we'll have of being spotted.

Marcus nodded.

Taurus felt his stomach growl and said, "I don't know about you, but I could eat a camel."

"I could eat two," Marcus interjected.

Looking at Decimus, Taurus asked, "Is there any place nearby that serves food?"

"Yes. A small marketplace not too far away has a few outside eating places," Decimus replied.

"Good. Let's be off. I'm tired of eating grapes, figs, and olives; I want some roasted meat!"

After a short walk, they found a thermopolium[68], ordered their food and sat down to eat.

As Taurus bit into his chicken, Antonius said, "I still don't understand why you would join us and risk your life, centur... uh, I mean... Cicero."

Taurus swallowed his mouthful and said, "My reason is simple. I don't like Aurelius. I could tell in his training that he was a cold-blooded killer without a conscience. That works well for one on the battlefield, but not on the training field and certainly not when you're dealing with people who mean you no harm. There is no doubt in my mind that he intentionally murdered your family because of his hatred for you. I want to see him pay for what he did just as you do. Another reason is that my niece seems to think you two are special. I consider her a good judge of character. A quality she likely learned from me."

Antonius and Marcus grinned until Taurus frowned at them.

After a hearty meal, they returned to the cottage to execute the first part of their plan.

Taurus put on his uniform then he and Antonius saddled their horses.

68-A place where food was prepared and served, similar to fast food restaurants today

"Stay alert!" Taurus admonished Decimus and Marcus, as he and Antonius mounted up and left for the Castra Praetoria.

Nearing the fortress wall, illuminated by torchlight, they tied their horses to a bush. After waiting for the sentry patrolling the wall to leave, Taurus turned to Antonius. "It shouldn't take me long to obtain what we need."

"What if you can't get it?"

Taurus smiled. "You can get anything with the right attitude, my boy. Just make sure a sentry doesn't spot you. When you see me come out of the bushes, signal when the coast is clear."

"I will," Antonius said.

After one more check for sentries, Taurus ran across the open area until he reached the wall. He searched through the bushes until he found the large, rusted metal door. Removing the key fastened around his neck, he took a deep breath and tried it in the door. The lock clicked, and he gave it a push. Slowly it creaked opened. Hearing nothing, he continued pushing until he could slip inside. Tiptoeing over to the door that led to the interior of the fortress, he opened it just enough to peer out. After verifying that the coast was clear, he proceeded to the Tribune barracks. When he arrived at Falconius's room, he hesitated. He knew he was taking a big risk. Falconius could immediately have him arrested, and that would put a quick end to the rescue plans. But he had always enjoyed a good rapport with him and if all else failed, he would appeal to his conscience. Success would depend on how convincing he was. He took a deep breath and knocked on the door.

"Who's there?" Falconius asked.

"Centurion Taurus," Taurus replied in a soft voice.

Falconius opened the door with a look of surprise. "Taurus? I thought you were in Judaea."

"Recent circumstances have caused me to return to Rome," he replied.

"Come in," Falconius said, gesturing for him to take a seat. "What are you doing in Rome espcially at this late hour? You didn't desert, did you?"

"Oh, no. I'm on furlough, but I need your help, Tribune."

"What kind of help?" Falconius asked as he sat down.

Taurus took a moment to get Falconius's full attention then said quietly, "A copy of the emperor's treason list and a signed incarceration order."

Falconius looked at him as if he were joking and asked, "You don't ask for much, do you? Why do you need them?"

Taurus rubbed his forehead. "It's complicated, but I'll try and explain. I have returned to Rome with Licinius and Flavius. Do you remember them?"

"Licinius and Flavius... yes... favorites of Sejanus, assigned to Judaea with you."

"Yes. Unfortunately, they were put on the emperor's treason list. only because Licinius's father and Sejanus were friends at one time. Do you also remember Darius Aurelius?"

"Yes, he was the cocky one who killed the trainee during the gladius competition and was sent to Creta."

"Yes, well he returned to Rome evidently and was assigned to arrest the families of Licinius and Flavius. He arrested Flavius' family, but a witness saw him kill Licinius' entire family except for Flavius' son. Now he is holding the child as a hostage and threatens to kill him too if Licinius and Flavius don't surrender to him personally. That's why we're here."

Falconius nodded and said, "Aurelius. Yes, I can see him doing that. He used to be a favorite of Sejanus now he's one of Macro's henchmen. He's developed a reputation for killing first and asking questions later. If Licinius and Flavius are on the emperor's list, shouldn't you be arresting them not helping them."

"But they don't deserve to be arrested. I have come to know them well; they are good men and had nothing to do with Sejanus' plot to take the throne. How could they? They've been in Judaea with me!"

Falconius put his hand to his chin and said, "There aren't many trainees I have been fond of, but I liked those two. The world's harshness hadn't soured them on life yet. Good upbringing, I suppose. Why did Aurelius kill Licinius's family? Did they try to resist?"

Taurus shook his head. "Not according to the witness who saw the whole thing. He said Aurelius forced Galerius to fight him and after killing him, he killed the two women after raping one of them. I think Aurelius still holds a grudge against Licinius and Flavius because they were allowed in the training with no military experience and they ruined his chance to be the grand master. Killing Licinius's family and arresting Flavius's was his way of getting even."

Falconius gave an upper nod and said, "Hmm, yes, I can see that. Why do you need the incarceration order?"

"To get Flavius's family out of prison then we'll rescue the infant who's being held hostage at the villa where Aurelius is staying," Taurus replied.

Falconius shook his head. "If I assisted you and the emperor found out, I would be executed for treason."

With an earnest look, Taurus said, "Tribune, you know I would die before

I betrayed you. Besides, there was a time when you were in need of my help on the battlefield, and I was the one who gave it. Now is your chance to repay the debt."

Falconius remembered vividly Taurus's action that kept him alive during a particular battle. Wrestling with his decision for a moment, he finally said, "There is one problem in obtaining the incarceration order. I have to sign for it and my name will be on the requisition. You must not let it fall into the wrong hands, or it will become my death sentence."

"I can assure you that as soon as it is no longer needed, I will destroy it. You have my word," Taurus promised.

Falconius pursed his lips slightly, then said, "Also, you realize I can get you into the prison with the order, but I can't give you a release order for the prisoners. Only Macro can sign those."

Taurus nodded. "I'll figure a way out."

Falconius still tried to talk him out of his plan. "Even if you do manage to get Flavius's family out of prison, it is certain Aurelius will have an overwhelming force of men waiting for you when you go to rescue the infant. Your chances of survival are slim."

"I realize that," Taurus replied. "But no matter how slim, we have to try. If we do not rescue the child by the first of Septembris, Aurelius will kill him."

"You are willing to risk your life for these two young Praetorians and a child?" Falconius asked.

Taurus looked earnestly in Falconius' eyes and said, "What if the child was your nephew? What would *you* do, Tribune?"

Falconius could see Taurus could not be dissuaded and his cause was a valiant one. But he tried one last time. "I have always respected your courage and principles, Centurion Taurus, but I'm afraid what you seek to do is impossible. Are you sure about this?"

Taurus smiled and said, "The impossible only takes a little longer to accomplish, Tribune. You once taught me that."

Falconius nodded. "So I did."

"Now, what about the treason list?" Taurus asked.

Falconius scrunched his face and said, "I'm afraid I can't help you there. Macro has it but somehow others have managed to learn who is on it so he keeps it with him now. Are you worried that you might be on the list?"

Taurus shrugged his shoulders slightly and replied, "Anyone could be on it. Now, I hate to press you, but time is of the essence. Could you get the incarceration order for me now?"

Falconius gave him a look of doubt, but said, "I can try. I just hope the optio in charge of records is still there."

Falconius was about to leave when Taurus lightly grabbed his arm. With a searching look, Taurus said, "Remember, it is not just my life in your hands, but those of other innocent people. I'm trusting you, Tribune."

Falconius nodded. "I'm trusting you as well, Centurion. I will return shortly with what you need. No one should disturb you while I'm away, but keep the door bolted just in case."

Taurus gave a single nod and said, "I'll do that."

After Falconius had left, Taurus wondered if he would betray him. He sat down on the bed, took out his gladius and laid it beside him just in case.

Proceeding to the documents office, Falconius was relieved to see the man in charge of the records hadn't left yet. "Praetorian, I need an incarceration order," he declared, approaching the man behind the table.

The man stood up, handed him a parchment and said, "You're fortunate, Tribune. I was just about to leave. Sign the requisition order and I will get it for you. You'll need the arresting officer to sign the incarceration order. Who did they arrest this time, another senator?"

"No, no one that important. Just another one of Sejanus's underlings we caught up with," Falconius replied as he signed the requisition. He then took the incarceration order and quickly left.

Taurus's pulse quickened when he heard a knock on the door.

"It's Falconius. Open the door," the familiar voice announced.

Taurus opened it cautiously. When he confirmed Falconius was alone, he sheathed his gladius and let him in.

"Here is what you asked for," Falconius said, handing Taurus the order. "That's all I can do for you."

"Thank you, Tribune. I greatly appreciate your help. Rest assured; no one will know that you assisted us," Taurus said, saluting.

Falconius placed his hand on Taurus's shoulder and made one last effort to talk him out of his plan. "Are you sure you want to do this, Centurion?"

Without hesitation, Taurus replied, "Yes, I'm sure."

Falconius shook his head and said, "You always were as hard to argue with as a corpse. I just hope you're not one when this is all over with."

"Believe me, Tribune; I share your sentiment," Taurus said with raised eyebrows.

Falconius patted his shoulder and said, "Go then, and may the gods be with you."

Taurus nodded. After cracking open the door and seeing the coast was clear, he quietly slipped away.

Falconius sat back down on his bed and cradled his head in his hands. He imagined the consequences if Macro traced the document back to him. "What have I done?" he muttered.

Antonius was beginning to feel uneasy. It was getting late and Taurus had not returned. He feared the worst and debated whether to leave or not when he saw the outer door open. After observing the sentry was not present on the wall above, he beckoned for Taurus to come.

Taurus ran over to him and said, "I have what we need."

Returning to the cottage, Taurus walked in and held up the incarceration order. "Our ticket in," he announced with a grin.

"What is our next move?" Marcus asked.

"I fill it out," Taurus said, grabbing a stylus and ink. After listing the necessary information, he said, "There. Now, if our capture is inevitable, we must lose this or Falconius will join us on the gallows. I promised him that would not happen."

Antonius and Marcus gave each other serious looks.

"When do we go to the prison?" Marcus asked.

"Just before the day watch takes over. The guards will be sleepy and dull-witted then," Taurus replied. "There will only be an optio in charge, so I'll have seniority. After that, we rescue Marcus's son. We'll go for the infant right after the midday meal. Darius's men at the villa should be sluggish and sleepy around that time, so their reflexes won't be as sharp. Here is how we work the prison release. We'll take Flavius in as our prisoner. He'll have the ransom money tied around his neck under his tunic."

"You can draw what you need from the chest," Antonius offered.

"No, you have done enough with your family's money, Licinius. This time, I will take care of the ransom."

"But won't we need a lot to get them out?" Antonius asked.

Walking into the other room, Taurus returned with the large bag of nearly 600 gold coins he had received from Sejanus for watching over Antonius and Marcus. Setting it on the table, some of the coins spilled out. "We can use some of this."

"Centurion, you are a rich man," Antonius said, half-astonished, half-delighted. "Did you save all this from your pay?"

Taurus laughed out loud. "I always spent my pay quicker than I received it. No, let's just say this is money from the late Prefect for a favor

I did for him."

"Won't you need it to start a new life as well?" Marcus asked.

"Don't worry; I'm not giving all of it to the guards," Taurus assured him. "I know how much will assure their cooperation. Now, listen; this is important. After we arrive at the prison, I'll show the incarceration order to the Praetorian gate sentries for Marcus. Once we're inside, we'll go to the guard station where they keep the housing records of each prisoner. The guards there will be the ones we'll have to bribe. Once they show us where Flavius's family is, we'll secure their release and escort them out. Decimus will drive the wagon and wait nearby until we leave the prison then we'll all go to the cottage."

"But how do we get them out?" Marcus insisted. "You said we needed a release order."

"I have an idea that should work, but it is too complicated to explain. Just go along with whatever I say. If my plan goes awry, be prepared to fight."

"What if Marcus's family isn't there?" Antonius asked.

"Attitude, Licinius, attitude," Taurus declared.

Antonius smiled and nodded.

Taurus threw up his hand and said, "Now get some sleep. I'll wake you just before we need to leave for the prison."

"Why don't you let me stand watch," Decimus offered. "You three will need to be alert for the rescue."

Taurus hesitated for a moment. Then, with a stern expression, he said, "All right, but if you even smell another Praetorian, wake us immediately."

"What does a Praetorian smell like?" Decimus asked.

Marcus and Antonius replied in unison, "Piles of horse dung."

Taurus grinned and said, "We'll be in the other room."

A few hours later, Decimus woke all three up to get ready for their mission. After everyone prepared themselves, Taurus went over details of the rescue plan one last time.

"We'll ride in on horseback and Decimus will follow us in the wagon. One last thing before we go. Decimus, I need a piece of material I can tear into strips. Can you find something I can use?"

Decimus nodded and left the room. He returned with a towel.

"Will this work?" he asked.

"Yes, perfectly." Taurus tore it into two strips and stuffed it inside his uniform.

"Are you bringing those in case someone gets wounded?" Marcus asked.

"No, I have another use in mind for it. You will see when we get to the prison. Now, Decimus, when we get there, I'll show you where to wait."

Decimus nodded.

Turning to Antonius and Marcus, Taurus said, "Let me do all the talking. Do you have the money under your tunic, Flavius?"

Marcus nodded, patting the coins hanging around his neck.

"Good. I have the incarceration paper. Licinius, find something to bind Flavius's hands with," he instructed Antonius.

Antonius took the rope from his belongings and showed it to him.

"Perfect," Taurus approved. "We'll use that to tie his hands when we arrive at the prison. Is everyone ready?"

With a solemn look, Antonius replied, "We're ready."

As the four left the cottage, Antonius wondered if he would have a chance to bring Darius to justice, Marcus wondered if his family was still alive, Taurus wondered if his plan would succeed, and Decimus wondered if he would live to tell their amazing story.

Not far away, in a Roman prison located on the northeastern slope of the Capitoline Hill in Rome, Camilla wondered if she and her family would survive another day. Shivering from the dampness, she rocked back and forth trying to comfort her younger children, huddled around her for warmth. Their emaciated bodies indicated what little food they had received. Matthias stood near the door, as he had done every night. He stared out into the darkness, hoping his older brother would come down the corridor and free them. Every night, however, brought only disappointment. He looked at his mother and siblings. He knew they couldn't last much longer on the crusts of bread and watered-down soup they received. His sisters had developed coughs and he had bouts of the chills, but still he hoped Marcus would eventually come and free them. He would not have to hope much longer.

CHAPTER XXIII-RESCUE FROM TARTARUS

Wispy Cirrus clouds partially covered the night's full moon, giving it an eerie, foreboding look as four determined men passed through the main gate of the city. Just outside the prison, they stopped the wagon.

"Wait here for us," Taurus instructed Decimus. Turning to Antonius, he pointed to Marcus. "Tie his hands loosely. You can untie them when we get past the guards at the gate."

The three walked up to the prison and approached the entry gate. A Praetorian optio inside the gate saluted. "What have you here, Centurion?"

"A criminal on the emperor's list. Here is the incarceration order," Taurus replied, handing it through the bars.

After looking it over, the guard said, "This order was signed by Tribune Falconius. I don't recall ever receiving papers signed by him before."

Taurus gave him an irritated look and growled, "What difference does it make who signed it? It's official, open up!"

The guard looked at the paper again and said, "I should probably send someone to the Castra to have this verified."

Taurus turned red in the face and yelled, "Have it verified! We are trying to put a man wanted by the emperor into prison here! I have other criminals to arrest and the emperor wants no more delays! Would you like me to wake Macro and say I couldn't obey the emperor's orders in a timely manner because you had to send someone to verify an arrest?"

"No, Centurion," the optio replied sheepishly.

"Very well then! Open the gates and let us bring in the prisoner!" Taurus barked loudly.

"Yes, Centurion," the badgered guard replied, immediately opening the gate. He handed the order back to Taurus and said, "Take this to the interior guards so they can log the prisoner in."

Taurus nodded, shoving Marcus inside. After they had gone a short distance from the main gate, Marcus exhaled and said, "That was close."

Taurus grinned and said, "You just have to know how to give orders." He pointed at Marcus's hands and Antonius undid his bonds. Due to the late hour, all was quiet, providing a brief respite from the wailing cries of the miserable souls confined there. As the three rescuers proceeded down into the prison's bowels, they felt heat emanating from one of the walls. Ovens used to bake the prisoners' bread stood on the other side.

"We must be close to Tartarus," Antonius remarked as sweat trickled down his forehead.

"This is Tartarus," Taurus remarked.

"What's that smell?" Marcus asked.

"It's a combination of feces, urine and vomit," Taurus replied. "Feel fortunate you are not prisoners here. They have to smell it everyday."

Eventually they came upon two large, grimy men sitting at a table. One was bald with scars across his face and head; the other had a protruding lower jaw, having been broken from a few altercations. The men, who each weighed close to 300 pounds, sat across from each other playing cards. The scarred one looked up. "Prisoner?"

"Actually we're looking for some other prisoners," Taurus replied. "A mother and her children. They were brought here around two months ago and their name is Flavius. Which cell are they in?"

"Why do you want to know?" the scarred one asked.

"Let's just say they are important to us and we are willing to pay you well to release them into our custody and keep the matter quiet."

The guards looked at each other and smiled.

"How well?" the scarred guard asked.

Marcus reached under his tunic, pulled out the bag of gold coins and placed it on the table. "One hundred aurei," he replied.

The guard opened the bag and poured out the coins. Looking up at Marcus, he smiled and said, "Flavius was it?"

"Yes," Taurus replied.

The guard went through his book of prisoners as Marcus held his breath. After looking through several pages, he finally said, "Yes, they are still here. This way." He stood up and started down a dark, musty corridor. They followed him past several cells until the guard stopped. "You in there! Wake up!" he shouted through the observation opening.

A weak but familiar voice from inside called out from the darkness and asked, "What is it?"

"Mother?" Marcus cried.

"Marcus? Is that you?" Matthias cried. He stood up with the help of the wall and hurried over to the cell door. At the same time, Camilla and all of the other children awoke and, in one voice cried, "Marcus?"

"You're alive!" Marcus exclaimed, as he breathed a sigh of relief. He then turned to the guard and said, "Open it."

"There is only one problem," a voice from down the corridor said. "You didn't bring enough money for the rest of us."

The other guard was joined by two companions, almost as large, with swords in hand. The guard that escorted them drew his gladius, but the tip of his blade barely cleared its sheath when he felt a sharp pain from Taurus's gladius thrust into his stomach. He moaned and dropped to the ground like a large bag of grain. Picking up the guard's sword, Taurus tossed it to Marcus just as the other guards reached them. A bevy of flashing blades filled the air while Camilla and her children cowered in their cell. When the skirmish was over, all four guards lay silent on the ground. Taking the keys from the scarred guard, Marcus ran to his family's cell and unlocked the door. "Hurry, we must leave," he declared, embracing each one as they came out. Matthias was the last to leave. Embracing Marcus tightly, he said, "I knew you'd come for us."

Seeing that Camilla could hardly stand on her feet, Marcus put his arm around her and said, "Lean on me, Mother." Matthias followed his lead and along with his younger brother, put their arms around their sisters to help them out.

Taurus pulled out the two strips of cloth he had prepared back at the cottage and gave one to Antonius. "Tie this around your nose and mouth," he ordered. Antonius nodded. After he and Taurus had masked their faces, Taurus said, "Now, when we reach the gate, let me do all the talking. If this doesn't work, be prepared for a fight. Flavius, keep your gladius hidden under your tunic until we're safely out of the prison."

Looking at Camilla and her children, Taurus could only hope they had enough strength to make it out. "Can you walk?" he asked.

"We'll run if we have to," Camilla replied.

Taurus smiled. "That's the spirit! Follow me."

On their way out, they passed by the control area and Taurus noticed that the purse holding the ransom was still sitting on the table. He picked it up and threw it to Marcus. "They won't be needing this anymore. Put it back under your tunic."

As they headed for the main prison gate, Marcus looked up and whispered, "Thank you for keeping them alive." A moment later they arrived and were confronted by the same Praetorian optio who let them in. He put up his hand and asked, "Where are you taking these prisoners, and why are your faces covered?"

Taurus wiped the perspiration off his forehead and said, "Have you heard of Plasmodium Falciparum?"

"What?" the optio asked, looking somewhat confused. He turned to his companions who shrugged their shoulders. "What is that?"

"A contagious disease that spreads quickly, and these people have it," Taurus replied. "That is why our faces are covered. I've seen it many times in the slums. It starts with a fever that keeps getting worse until your blood boils and your organs burst inside of you. Have you ever seen that happen to someone, Optio?"

"No," the puzzled optio replied, as Camilla coughed.

"Well, I have. First, they begin coughing like that then their body turns red and their chest and stomach expands. Organs rupture, sometimes breaking through the skin, sending blood and flesh everywhere. Death is instantaneous, as you can no doubt imagine. These people have the first stages. If we don't get them out of the prison before it spreads then everyone here, including you, will die. A few of your interior guards must have been exposed. I found them lying dead in the corridor near the prisoners' cell. Not a pretty sight."

The Praetorians started to back away as the optio said, "I am not supposed to let them leave without release papers."

"Did you hear me, Optio?" Taurus shouted. He grabbed Marcus, still sweating profusely from the previous battle with the guards. "Look! He has already contracted it. Why don't you have him stay with you until the release papers come? Here! Take him!" Taurus exclaimed, pushing Marcus toward the unsure optio.

The optio backed up until he hit the wall. "No! No! Get them out of here! Open the gate!"

As Taurus hurried them out, the optio asked, "Where are you taking them?"

Taurus turned back, so only the optio could hear. "To the River Tiber where we'll put them to death and throw them in. I just hope we haven't contracted it ourselves." He then hurried to rejoin the rest.

As the Praetorians at the gate watched them leave, the optio said, "The poor fools. They are probably dead men." He then looked at his companions and asked, "How do you feel?"

Outside the prison, Taurus and Antonius removed the strips of cloth around their faces and eight people scurried to safety. Taurus then waved to Decimus, who quickly brought the wagon to pick them up.

"We must hurry before the guards realize we've tricked them," Taurus barked, the tension obvious in his voice. "Everyone get in, hurry now."

"Wait. I must tell you something, Marcus," Camilla said, grabbing her son by both arms. "Augustina gave birth to a child while you were away. He is your son and I have no idea where he is now. The centurion who arrested us has him somewhere."

Marcus nodded. "We know where he is, Mother. We will rescue him as soon as you are all safe. Now please, we must leave!"

Seeing Decimus, Camilla exclaimed, "Decimus! Thank the gods you found them."

"Yes, we can all thank them later," Taurus admonished her. "Now we must hurry."

Camilla watched as Marcus and Antonius helped her children into the wagon. Antonius then took her by the hand and helped her up.

"Antonius, I am so sorry about your family," she said, gently squeezing his hand.

Antonius nodded.

"There are blankets in the wagon you can wrap yourselves in," Taurus said as the wagon rolled away.

As they approached the city gate, Taurus said, "Woman, you and your children hide under the blankets until we pass through the gate. The sentries will be checking people going in not coming out, but stay hidden just to be safe."

Camilla nodded and covered herself and her children. After safely passing through, they arrived at the cottage a short while later. Decimus lit a lamp and all four men recoiled at the sight. Camilla and her children looked as though they had been raised from the dead. Numerous sores from the filthy cell covered their emaciated bodies.

"Are you hungry?" Marcus asked, as tears formed in his eyes.

Camilla looked at her children who appeared as though they would fall asleep at any moment.

"No, I think if we could just clean up a bit and rest, that would be good for now."

Marcus nodded and said, "I'll get some soap and water."

After they had washed and received clean clothes, Marcus hugged and kissed each one. Then shuffling over to the mattresses on the floor, they collapsed onto their makeshift beds. Sleep came quickly.

Marcus closed the door, wiped away the tears that had moistened his cheeks and gave out a grateful sigh. His family was safe. The adrenaline had subsided and now he felt exhausted. Then he remembered, they still had his son to rescue. No amount of physical or emotional fatigue would prevent him from accomplishing that. As he walked over to the other men, Taurus acknowledged him with a nod then said, "When the sun comes up, I will ride to my sister's villa and make sure they are safe."

"You weren't able to find out if they were on the list or not?" Antonius asked, worried that Julia might be in danger.

"No, Falconius couldn't help with that."

"What if they were put on the list and Praetorians are watching for you at their villa?" Antonius asked.

Taurus nodded. "You're right; I could be walking into a trap."

"Let me check on them," Antonius suggested. "If Praetorians are there, they won't be watching for a younger man. I could pretend to be one of Julia's suitors."

"That shouldn't be too hard," Marcus said with a smirk.

Taurus pursed his lips then said, "Yes, that could work. Strip down to your tunic and leave your gladius and dagger here. I don't want anyone to suspect that you're military. Since you won't have your weapons, you will be taking a big risk. If you don't want to do it..."

"I'll do it," Antonius stated firmly.

Taurus smiled. "Remember, we need you and your gladius for the rest of our plan to succeed so don't get stopped by Praetorians again."

"I promise I won't this time," Antonius assured him.

"Good. I'll tell you how to get to my sister's villa. If you see any Praetorians present, then I'll know her family is either in prison or dead. That will mean I'm also on the list. Before you leave, give Decimus the directions to your villa so he can scout the area and see what we're up against with Aurelius."

Antonius nodded.

After briefing Decimus and receiving directions to Julia's villa, Antonius rode off as dawn began to brighten the countryside.

A short while later, he arrived at the Cato villa in the Campus Martius off the Via Lata. Finding an inconspicuous vantage point, he climbed off his horse and observed. All seemed quiet. Vergilius came out and began to water some plants near the front entrance. Seeing no signs of Praetorians, Antonius mounted his horse and rode over. "Excuse me, is Julia at home?" he asked.

"She is still asleep," Vergilius replied. "Would you like me to give her a message?"

"Yes. Do you have something I could write with?"

Vergilius bowed and said, "Wait here and I will get it for you." A moment later, he returned with some writing implements.

Antonius went over to the small table just outside the door and wrote a short note. He then handed the folded message to Vergilius and said, "Give this only to Julia."

Vergilius gave him a curious look and asked, "Weren't you one of the Praetorians who escorted us in Judaea?"

Antonius put his finger to his lips and rode off. Returning to the cottage, Antonius walked in the door and came face to face with Taurus.

"Well?" Taurus asked, the anxiety evident on his face.

"Everything appeared to be normal. Julia was still asleep, so I left a note asking her to come here. She can tell you what their situation is when she arrives."

With a furrowed brow, Taurus raised his voice. "You left her a note? What if my sister or her husband sees it and they start asking questions?"

"I told Vergilius to give it only to Julia and wrote down directions to the cottage. I thought it would be better for her to come here rather than your sister or her husband."

"Well, if they are not on the emperor's list, I want to keep it that way. Say nothing about why we are in Rome when she comes. I will give her some excuse then send her back home. No more messages to anyone. Do all of you understand?" Taurus bellowed.

The other three nodded.

Shaking his head, he walked away muttering, "I should have kept my position as recruit trainer."

****

Later, as Decimus returned to the cottage to give his scouting report, Julia awoke to find a note under her door. After reading it, she smiled.

"Mother?" she called, walking into the atrium where Juliana was sitting.

"Yes, what is it, Julia?"

"May I take one of the horses for a ride?"

"Where are you going?" her mother asked.

"Not far, just to the west wall and back."

"Very well, but don't be gone long."

"I won't," Julia chirped. "Vergilius! Saddle my horse, please!"

She felt butterflies in her stomach as she mounted the horse Vergilius prepared. She could hardly contain the excitement to see the Praetorian who captured her heart in Judaea.

As she rode up to the cottage a short while later, Antonius stood watch at the window. "Julia is here!" he shouted.

Taurus walked over and closed the door to the room where Camilla and her children still slept. He then nodded to Antonius.

Julia looked at the note and said under her breath, "I hope this is the cottage," then dismounted.

Antonius opened the cottage door with a smile and greeted her. "Julia."

With tears in her eyes, she ran over and embraced him. "Antonius."

Seeing Taurus and Decimus over his shoulder, she pulled away and cried, "Uncle! Antonius didn't say you were with him."

"I decided to take a leave as well. Come in," he said, motioning for her to enter.

"Who is this?" she asked, tilting her head toward Decimus.

"Oh, this is Decimus. He works for my father," Antonius replied.

"Nice to meet you, Decimus," Julia said.

Decimus smiled. "You as well, Miss Julia."

Turning back to Taurus, she asked, "Why didn't you come to the house, Uncle?"

Taurus quickly thought of a plausible excuse and said, "I had a few matters to handle. Besides, I knew you and Antonius were fond of each other and thought it would be a nice surprise for you."

"Uncle, you are Cupid!" she laughed. "How long will you be here?"

"Only a day," Taurus replied.

Julia scrunched her face as Marcus walked in.

"Marcus! Are you here on leave, too?" she asked.

"Ah... yes," Marcus replied, afraid to say anything more after seeing Taurus's stern expression.

"Why don't the three of you come and have cena[69] with us?" she offered. "I'm sure my mother would love to see you, Uncle. And I know she would like to thank Antonius and Marcus personally for helping to insure my safety while I was in Judaea."

With a pained expression, Taurus said, "That is most kind of you, my dear, but we have already made plans for the day, I'm afraid."

Julia frowned. "How about vesperna[70] then?"

"I'll have to see how long our business takes," Taurus replied.

"What kind of business?" she pressed.

Taurus expelled a blast of air out of his nostrils and replied, "Important business that Licinius, Flavius and I must attend to."

Julia raised her eyebrows and said, "It sounds mysterious. Tell me more."

Deflecting her question, Taurus replied, "Licinius, why don't you take

---

69-Lunch
70-Usually a light supper

Julia for a walk, and you can ask her what she's been up to lately. I'm sure she would like that."

Antonius nodded and opened the door.

Julia gave Taurus a puzzled look as she and Antonius walked out of the cottage. As they strolled down the road, she said, "My uncle is acting very strange. What is he not telling me?"

Antonius shook his head slightly. "He just has a lot on his mind. Tell me what you've been doing."

"I attended my sister's wedding last night," she responded.

Antonius continued walking in silence.

When Julia could see he was not going to comment, she said, "I wish I would have known you three were in Rome; you could have gone to the ceremony with me."

"We came in late last night," Antonius replied tersely.

"Oh." Julia exclaimed. "Well you could have stayed at my family's villa. We have plenty of room. And why didn't my uncle let us know you were coming?"

"I think those are all questions you should ask him," Antonius replied, keeping his gaze straight ahead.

"You and Marcus will be visiting your families while you're here, won't you?" she asked.

"Why do you ask so many questions?" he snapped.

Shocked at his abruptness, Julia said, "Antonius, you're acting like there is nothing between us. Have your feelings for me changed?"

He took in a breath and shook his head. "No, Julia, my feelings for you haven't changed. My future looks a little uncertain right now; that's all."

"What do you mean?" she asked, puzzled with his evasive attitude.

"I'll explain it to you later," he said, hoping to end the discussion.

But Julia wasn't satisfied with ending it. "No, Antonius," she stated emphatically, "explain it to me now!"

Antonius hesitated then finally said, "Marcus, your uncle and I are here on a mission."

"What kind of mission?" she pressed.

Antonius sighed and said,, "I can't give you the details, but... there is a good possibility... that we may not survive. It might be well for you to find another to share your love with."

Julia stood there, stunned. Anger and confusion welled up inside of her. She released it in a scathing reprimand.

"Antonius Licinius, you know that I love you. You can't just say such things without an explanation. I deserve better than that from you!"

He shook his head. "Please, Julia. It is best that you do not know the details of why we're here. If you become involved, it could mean the end of your life."

"I would rather have my life end than live it without you, Antonius. Now, please tell me!" she insisted.

He hesitated again then decided he couldn't deceive her any longer. "You remember when I told you the reason Marcus and I were able to get into the Praetorian training camp was because my father and Prefect Sejanus were good friends?"

"Yes." Suddenly a look of horror came over Julia. "You are on the emperor's list," she said, putting her hand to her breast.

Antonius nodded. "Tiberius put my entire family on it. Marcus's too."

"How did you learn of this?" she asked, raising her eyebrows slightly.

"The man my father hired to help on the vineyard came to Judaea. He told me a Praetorian centurion I knew in training, murdered my family and arrested Marcus's family."

Julia felt a rush of overwhelming sympathy and compassion. "Oh, Antonius. It must have been horrible for you to learn that! Your whole family?"

He somberly said, "Not everyone. We learned that my sister had a baby boy. Marcus is the father. The Praetorian centurion took the child and is keeping him at the villa we used to own and holding him as a hostage."

Julia shook her head. "Now, I understand why you and my uncle were acting so strangely. The villa is here in Rome?" she asked.

"Yes. Just off the Vicus Novus south of the Circus," he replied.

"So, that is your mission. To rescue Marcus's family and recover his son."

"Yes," Antonius confirmed her assumption. "We already have Marcus's family back at the cottage. We're going for his son at midday. The centurion holding him promised to kill the boy by the first of Septembris if we didn't turn ourselves in."

"But that is only a few days from now!" Julia stated with dread in her eyes.

Antonius nodded. "That is why I told you my future is uncertain."

"Oh, Antonius," she said, embracing him as tears filled her eyes. She wanted to help somehow, but what could she do? Then an idea came to her. It was daring and dangerous, but it might save the man she loved. Releasing him from her embrace, she said, "Antonius, I must go now, but promise me you will not leave until I return."

He looked at her strangely and said, "When we leave is up to your uncle."

"Then you must convince him to wait; it is important that I see you before you leave. Promise me you will wait," she pleaded.

He looked into her beseeching eyes and said, "I promise."

They embraced and kissed again. Mounting her horse, she turned her head to give him one last confident smile then galloped away.

Arriving at her villa a short while later, Julia went directly to her father's study and quietly closed the doors. He had already left for his judicial duties, so she had to act quickly before her mother came in and asked what she was doing. Searching through her father's shelves, she found a blank arrest document with Macro's seal that was perfect for her needs. It took only a moment to cut out the seal and place it onto a scroll she composed. Then she put it in a carrying bag and was walking out of the study, when she came face to face with her mother.

"Oh, mother!" she exclaimed.

Juliana gave her a suspicious glance and said, "What are you doing in your father's study and why didn't you tell me you returned from your ride?"

Julia hesitated then said, "I was looking for a stylus to write you a note. I have an errand I must run. I won't be gone long."

"What kind of an errand?" her mother asked.

"I... need to deliver a document," she replied, holding her breath.

Juliana studied her for a moment then said, "It must be for your father. Very well, but take the carriage and have Vergilius go along with you."

Julia was about to object then realized this could work to her advantage. "I will, if it makes you feel more at ease."

Her mother gave her a firm look and said, "It does. I'll get him."

"Thank you, Mother," Julia said.

After Vergilius brought the carriage around, she gave him the directions to Antonius's villa. A short while later they arrived at the location and saw Praetorians standing at the gate and around the perimeter. "This has to be where they are keeping the child," she thought.

"Vergilius, pull up to the gate," she instructed.

"Yes, Mistress Julia."

As the carriage came to a stop, Darius's optio walked up and looked at the driver then in at Julia. "State the nature of your business, Miss!"

"Is this where you're holding the child hostage?" Julia asked.

He narrowed his eyes and asked, "Why do you want to know?"

"Prefect Macro sent me to care for him," she replied. Pulling out the prepared parchment, she handed it to him and held her breath.

After studying the document, Atticus said, "This appears to be in order."

He handed it back to her. "I will tell the centurion you are here."

"Thank you," she said, hoping to appear more poised than she felt.

Returning a moment later, he said, "The centurion will see you. Your carriage must remain at the gate, however."

"Of course," Julia replied. After telling Vergilius to wait, she exited the carriage. Atticus escorted her to the main living quarters and opened the door. Before entering, she noticed two sentries on either side of the door and two more on the inside. She walked into a large atrium with painted walls and mosaics on the floor. Darius stood in front of a couch with his arms folded and a slight smile on his face.

"You claim you were sent here by Macro?" he asked.

"Yes," she quickly replied. "I have a letter from him appointing me to care for the child until you catch the criminals you're after."

Darius's eyes narrowed. "How do you know the Prefect?"

"Through my father. He is a judge and close friend of his," Julia quickly replied.

Darius studied her for a moment. "May I see the letter?"

"Certainly." She handed it over and held her breath.

He glanced at the document then handed it back. "That's Macro's seal all right, but I'm afraid you've come here for nothing, Miss. I've already assigned a man to care for him."

Julia gave him an intended condescending glance. "I'm sure your *man* doesn't have time to care for an infant with all his other duties. Few men know how to properly care for an infant, anyway. Besides, this is a direct order from your Prefect. Do you dare disobey him?"

Darius raised his head slightly. "No need to be contentious. Very well, you can be his nursemaid."

"Thank you, Centurion. Where is he?" she asked.

Darius pointed. "In the other room. I'm sorry, your name again was…"

"Julia."

"Julia. You look familiar to me. Have we met before?" he asked.

"No, I'm sure I would have remembered. May I see the child now?" Julia asked, trying to be as haughty as she had observed the way some of her mother's aristocratic friends act.

"This way," he said, smiling politely. He led her into another room where she found little Marcus asleep in a makeshift crib. She went over and immediately felt his head. "He appears to be a little feverish."

"My man assured me he has been taking good care of him," Darius said disputing her observation.

Julia now had to put the second part of her plan into effect. "Men know little about children's ailments," she stated, pretending having experience. "I will need to take him to a physician and have him examined."

Darius shook his head. "I'm sorry, but the infant stays here. If he needs a physician, we will send for one."

Seeing that her initial plan for rescuing the child failed, Julia thought quickly. "Actually, our family physician could probably come. I have a few more errands to run and could bring him back with me later," Julia said, holding her breath.

Darius paused then finally said, "That will be satisfactory, but only you and the physician."

"Of course," Julia replied, breathing again. "Now, if you could show me around so I can become familiar with your residence. I would prefer to sleep in the child's room so I can attend to him when needed."

Darius smiled. "We can do that when you return and get settled. Besides, it will only be for a few days."

"What if these criminals attack you?" she asked, pretending alarm. "Do you have enough men to protect me?"

"I have four men inside, besides myself, four outside guarding the main entry doors and twenty-four around the villa walls. I can send for many more if needed. There are only four criminals. Are those odds good enough to make you feel secure, Miss?"

Julia nodded. "Quite secure, Centurion."

"Good. Tell me a little about yourself, Julia. Are you married?" he asked.

"Actually, I'm promised to someone," she replied.

Darius put on a pained expression and said, "What a pity. Well, you still have time to enjoy yourself before you do marry." Darius added an inviting smile that Julia did not return.

Seeing that his advance met with rejection, he asked, "How long has your father known the Prefect?"

Julia sighed with supposed impatience. "Centurion, please excuse me, but as much as I enjoy talking with you, I must make sure the physician is available and complete my errands."

"Of course, I didn't mean to detain you," Darius stated. "You may leave," he gestured dismissively.

Julia gave him a nod and said, "Thank you, and would you inform your man at the gate that I will be returning with the physician so he won't interrogate us?"

Darius smiled. "Yes, I'll notify him."

Julia started to leave, then turned back and asked, "When the criminals are captured, what will happen to the infant?"

With a condescending look, he replied, "He belongs to a criminal family. What do you think will happen?"

"He will be put to death?" Julia asked, trying to maintain her composure.

The look Darius gave made her blood run cold. "All enemies of Rome must die, no matter how big or how small."

She nodded, trying hard to conceal her disgust. "Until that time, we must keep him well," she said, thinking, "You monster!"

"When shall I expect you back?" Darius asked.

"Sometime around midday," she replied, walking out the door.

After Julia left, Darius called to one of the guards at the front door.

"Caius, tell Optio Atticus to report to me."

"Yes, Centurion," the sentry replied.

Julia passed by the guards at the gate and entered the carriage.

"You may leave now, Vergilius. I'll direct you where to go next." Clasping her hands to keep them from shaking, she felt pleased that the charade went well. Thankfully, her mother and her friends were ideal role models when it came to acting supercilious.

As Vergilius snapped the reins, he was tempted to ask what all that was about. A servant asking questions of his masters' business, however, simply wasn't done. He would leave the intrigue to them and do as he was told.

CHAPTER XXIV-Sacrifice and Redemption

Taurus sat at the table, struggling to form a rescue plan.

Suddenly, Decimus, looking out the window shouted, "A carriage just pulled up!"

Taurus, Antonius and Marcus all hurried over. "It's Julia!" Taurus exclaimed. "What is she doing back here?"

Antonius cringed. "I'm afraid she made me tell her everything."

Taurus stared at him in disbelief. "You told her why we're here?"

Antonius lifted his shoulders and with a pained expression said, "I had no choice. She dismissed every vague excuse I made and insisted I tell her the truth."

Taurus felt his head begin to throb as Julia walked up and knocked on the door.

Decimus stood by the door and glanced at Taurus.

Taurus gritted his teeth. "Let her in," he said, scowling at Antonius.

Decimus opened the door and beckoned her in.

"Hello, Decimus."

"Miss Julia," Decimus returned the greeting.

She quickly brushed past him and went right to her uncle.

"I have some information I think will help," she said as Decimus closed the door. She then noticed Camilla and her children in the other room and asked, "Is this your family, Marcus?"

"Yes," he replied, introducing them.

Walking over, she gave Camilla a hug. "I am Julia, Uncle Taurus's niece. I'm so glad they were able to free you safely."

Taurus nodded impatiently. "Yes, we are all safe, momentarily. Now what is this information you have?"

Julia turned back to him. "You were concerned about the number of soldiers inside the villa? I can tell you how many you will be up against."

"How do you know that?"

"I was just there," she replied.

"What?" Antonius almost choked. "How did you get..."

"I told the centurion I was sent by the Prefect to care for the child temporarily and took a scroll with Macro's seal from one of my father's documents. While inside, he showed me where Marcus's son is being kept and how many men are guarding him."

"Do you realize what you have done?" Antonius cried, taking her by her

376

shoulders. "You have involved yourself. Now you and your family will be added to the emperor's treason list if they find out you helped us!"

"Wait!" Taurus interrupted. "You have a paper with Macro's seal?"

"Yes," she replied, breaking free from Antonius. "I carefully removed Macro's seal from an arrest order my father had and, with a little glue, attached it to the document I composed giving me permission to care for the child."

Taurus rubbed his forehead. "Well, whether I like it or not, my girl, you are in this now and there is no turning back." He began to walk away with his hand to his head, then stopped suddenly and turned around.

"Can you compose another document for me?" he asked.

"Of course! What do you want it to say?" she remarked.

Taurus brought her over to the table and said, "I need a document stating that Licinius, Flavius and myself have been arrested and there is no need to continue with the plan to capture us. All Praetorians are to report back to the Castra for further assignments."

Julia nodded. "I understand. Give me something to write on and a sharp knife while I get my things from the carriage."

After obtaining what she needed, Julia sat down and drew up the document with Taurus' help. Then carefully cutting around the seal from the previous document, she put some glue on the bottom and attached it to the new document.

"There," she stated. "No one will be able to tell the document isn't authentic. Before I forget, let me tell you their numbers."

The men gathered close.

Looking at each one, she said, "There are two guards stationed outside, near the main door. Two more are outside the rear door and four more are inside including the centurion. I saw two near the main door on the inside, so I'm guessing that there are two more on the inside near the rear door. That adds up to eight guarding the house. There are twenty-four stationed around the outside walls of the villa."

Taurus pondered his strategy. "Hopefully with this document I can get rid of the soldiers around on the exterior. That will leave five on the inside including Aurelius. We will have to be at our best, since the men on the inside will likely be hand-picked."

"We will be," Antonius assured him.

Julia became pensive for a moment. "One thing concerns me."

"What is that?" Taurus asked.

"Once you are inside, the Centurion might try to kill Marcus's son."

"No! That must not happen!" Marcus exclaimed.

Julia grabbed his arm. "Don't worry, Marcus. I have a plan on how to protect him."

Taurus drew his head back. "Aren't you full of surprises! Go on then, tell us your plan."

"The centurion…"

"His name is Darius," Antonius informed her.

"Darius expects me to come back with a physician after midday to check on the child," she stated.

Antonius, realizing Julia intended to put herself in danger again, turned to Taurus. "You can't let her do this! It's too dangerous!"

"I don't like it any more than you do, Licinius, but let's at least hear her out. Go on, Julia."

"I will return with someone pretending to be the physician and we can secure the room where the child is being kept. When the fighting starts, we can barricade the door until it is over. I thought of using Vergilius for the physician, but the guard at the gate has already seen him as my driver. I thought perhaps your man…"

Everyone looked at Decimus.

"I'll do it," he said with a forced smile.

Taurus took him by the arm. "You will be no match for Darius or any of his Praetorians so don't try to be a hero, just barricade the door."

Decimus nodded.

Antonius, still concerned for Julia's safety, tried one last time to dissuade her. "Julia, you are putting your life at great risk!" Turning to Taurus, he said, "Why not just send Decimus in and he can tell Darius she was detained."

"No, Antonius!" she objected. "That would raise his suspicions for sure and put all of us, let alone the child, in more danger."

All nodded, except Antonius.

"I have to say, her plan sounds better than anything I have been able to think of," Taurus admitted. He turned to Julia and took her hands in his. "Once you and Decimus are inside, we will approach. Are you sure you want to go through with this?"

"Yes, Uncle, and do not worry. I have faith that all will turn out well," she replied, smiling at Antonius.

Putting his hands on her shoulders, Taurus gave her one last admonition. "You must not take any unnecessary chances once the fighting starts, Julia. Your mother would never forgive me if anything happened to you."

"I won't," she assured him.

Taurus sat down at the table with Antonius, Marcus and Decimus joining him. "All right, here is the plan. Flavius will drive the carriage with Julia and Decimus to the villa. He'll wear a hood to conceal his face. After dropping them off, he'll wait with the carriage at the front of the villa. Licinius and I will then ride to the villa with the forged document. I'll show the document to the Praetorian in charge of the outside detail and tell him they are to report back to the Castra. Licinius and I will then enter after they have left. Once inside the fight will be on. Flavius, you will then come in the front door and help Licinius and I take on the interior guards. After we defeat Darius and his men, we'll get Julia, Decimus and the child then leave through the front door. Then we return to the carriage and horses and leave as quickly as possible. Does everyone understand what they must do?"

Everyone nodded.

"I'll go to the infirmary at the Castra Praetoria and 'borrow' a physician's bag for Decimus. When I return, we go," Taurus said with a stern look.

Overhearing their plan, Matthias came out of the other room. "What about me? I can help."

Marcus smiled. "If you went with us, who would be here to guard our family? We need you here."

"But I..."

Marcus put both his hands on his Matthias' shoulders and said, "Do you want to leave them unprotected, Brother? And what if something happens to us? Only you can lead them away from here to another place that is safe."

Matthias gave a halfhearted nod.

Turning to Taurus, Marcus asked, "Centurion, may I speak with you alone?"

"Certainly. Let's go out front." Stepping outside, Taurus asked, "What is on your mind, Flavius?"

Marcus looked down then said, "We'll be fighting our brothers-in-arms. I don't know if I..."

"Look at me!" Taurus ordered, pointing to his eyes. "I don't take pleasure in this, but you have to understand something. Darius's men have orders to kill your son and whoever tries to rescue him. They will not hesitate, whether we are brothers-in-arms or not. If we don't eliminate them first, they will eliminate us. Darius has already murdered Licinius's family and I have no doubt he will do the same to your son. It is unfortunate we have to go up against fellow Praetorians, but you must think of your son now. For our plan to work, everyone must do their part. That is the only chance your son or any of us have. Will you do yours, Flavius?"

Marcus looked directly into Taurus's eyes and replied, "Yes. I will do it for my son."

Taurus nodded then said, "Go back inside now." He realized Vergilius was still standing by the carriage. "Vergilius," he muttered to himself. He sighed and walked over. "Vergilius."

"Yes, Master Cicero," Vergilius replied.

Taurus put his hand on Vergilius' shoulder and said, "We'll be going for a carriage ride today and we already have a driver. Why don't you take one of the horses over there and ride back to my sister's villa. When we're finished, we'll bring the carriage back and pick up the horse."

"If that is your wish, Master Cicero."

"It is," Taurus said. As he watched Vergilius ride away, he muttered to himself, "One matter taken care of, let's hope the rest goes as smoothly."

Inside, Antonius took Julia's hand. "Julia, come outside with me?"

"Certainly," she said.

Once outside, Antonius said, "Now, about your plan..."

Julia put her finger to his lips. "Antonius, you cannot change my mind. Please do not try to."

He took her in his arms. "If it goes bad for us, try to escape with Marcus's son. If you cannot escape..."

Julia understood his meaning. "I know what I must do, Antonius. I cannot be captured and have them learn who my family is."

"But it also means... taking care of little Marcus," he told her, hating himself for even suggesting it.

Julia put her head on his chest. "I know; it is an awful thing to think about." She raised her head and narrowed her eyes. "The plan will work, Antonius. You must believe that!"

"I believe in you," he said, as they shared a kiss.

As Taurus rode past them on his way to get the physician's bag, he yelled, "Save that for later you two!"

They both smiled and walked back to the cottage.

Camilla and her children sat together on a sofa talking with Marcus when they walked in. She smiled and said, "Marcus tells me that you and Antonius are quite fond of each other."

Julia looked at Antonius and said, "We consider each other to be above average I would say." Her remark drew a smile from him.

"Your feelings for each other must be strong to maintain a relationship across the sea," Camilla supposed.

"They are," Julia replied, "but you and your family are the ones who have

380

shown true strength.

A short while later, Taurus returned.

"Did you get the physician's bag?" Marcus asked.

"That plus another bag," Taurus replied.

Placing a cloth bag on the table, he pulled out cheese, fruit and biscuits and said, "I bought us some food."

"Oh, this looks delicious, Uncle!" Julia exclaimed. "I will dish it out." Looking through the cupboards, she found bowls, plates and cups.

"Can I help you, Julia?" Camilla asked.

"Mother, you should save your strength for the journey we will need to make after the rescue," Marcus replied.

Camilla nodded, feeling guilty she didn't have the strength to be more helpful.

After Julia dished out the food, Camilla and her children ate sparingly, since they were used to meager rations while they were confined. Taurus, Antonius and Marcus ate light as well, mainly because they knew a battle was forthcoming and eating a large meal before exertion was not a wise thing. They learned that in training.

After the meal, Taurus, Antonius, and Marcus sharpened their swords. Taurus and Antonius put on their Praetorian uniforms and Marcus donned a pull-over cloak with a hood. Giving Decimus his extra dagger, Taurus said, "You will probably be searched, so hide this in the physician's bag. If the rescue goes badly, use it on yourself. Otherwise, you'll probably be tortured and hung. The same goes for Julia and the child."

Decimus looked at Julia, who nodded. Camilla's face went pale at the thought of her grandson being killed, but she remained silent. Her worried look shifted to Marcus.

Noticing Camilla's expression, Antonius walked over and put his hand on her shoulder. "Don't worry, Camilla. I will look out for Marcus. I've gotten used to that," he said, giving Marcus a teasing grin.

Taurus cleared his throat. "When this business is over, we'll return here as quickly as we can. Julia and Decimus will take the boy in the carriage, Flavius will drive and Licinius and I will escort them. After that, we must leave Rome immediately."

"What if you don't return?" Matthias asked.

Taurus wanted to be positive and assure him they would return, but he knew the odds were against them. "If we haven't returned by dark, load the wagon and get your family as far away from Rome as you can. I have money in my bag..."

"And I have some in my knapsack," Antonius said, pointing to it.

Taurus nodded. "That should give you a new start."

Tears formed in Camilla's eyes. "I don't know where to go or what to do if you don't return."

"Don't worry, Mother," Marcus said in a calm voice. "We will return and all leave together."

Marcus then took Matthias aside so his mother wouldn't hear. "Brother, if I should not come back, I'm counting on you to take care of the family."

"You will come back," Matthias said, clutching Marcus's shoulder.

Taurus gazed into each face then with a voice betraying just a hint of uncertainty, said, "It is time. Is everyone ready?"

Four heads nodded.

"Then let's be off," Taurus ordered.

Camilla hugged them all and wished them good luck. Marcus was the last to leave, stopping to hug his siblings. When he went to embrace his mother, he saw the fear in her eyes.

"Don't worry Mother. All will be well," he said.

"Just come back to me," she pleaded.

"We are in God's hands now," Marcus replied. He kissed her goodbye and joined the others.

Decimus and Julia entered the carriage as Marcus tied an extra horse onto it then climbed on top. After Antonius and Taurus mounted up, they took the lead as Marcus snapped the reins and followed.

Inside the carriage, Julia felt like little people were doing somersaults inside her stomach.

As the five rescuers proceeded to their destination, hoping Julia's new document would fool their antagonists, another document arrived for Macro at the Castra Praetoria. After reading it, he laid it down upon his desk and said aloud, "Thank the gods."

A short distance away from the villa, Antonius said, "We should stop here." Taurus disomounted and helped Julia out then motioned for everyone to gather around. Once he was sure he had their attention, he asked, "Are all of you clear on your assignments?"

Everyone nodded.

Taurus looked into the eyes of Antonius and Marcus. He recognized the same look he saw in men going into battle when the outcome was uncertain. He needed to remind them why they were there. "A child's life depends on us. We must do our very best for his sake and for our own. Remember that a woman and her children are counting on us and you will do well. Now, let's get Flavius's son and make Aurelius pay for his murderous misdeeds."

"Huhf!" Antonius and Marcus responded.

"Flavius! Antonius and I will wait until you drop off Julia and Decimus then stay with the carriage until all the guards on the outside leave and Licinius and I are inside the villa. Then hurry inside. "We'll need your sword."

Marcus nodded.

After Decimus and Julia took their places inside the carriage, Marcus climbed on top and donned his hood.

When they were out of sight, Taurus turned to Antonius. "Once inside, we must get to Julia and Decimus as quickly as we can."

Antonius gave him a serious nod.

The carriage rumbled up to the villa and stopped at the gate letting Julia and Decimus out. After recognizing Julia and being told that Decimus was the physician, Atticus escorted them to the villa. Marcus waited.

As Julia and Decimus approached the outside sentries, one opened the door and they entered. Darius, dressed in his uniform, stood up from the couch and greeted them. "Ah, you are the physician I take it?"

"Yes," Decimus replied. "I was told a child was running a fever. I have brought some herbs and potions that will help."

"Before you see the child, my men must search you. Just a precaution," Darius said, nodding to one of his sentries.

"Certainly," Decimus said, gripping his bag tightly. A sentry walked over and patted him down for weapons, then looked at the bag. "Open it!" he ordered Decimus, who gave Julia a worried glance then smiled. "I have only my tools and medicinal items. Surely, you don't want me to spread them all out before you?"

Darius stared coldly at him and said, "Open the bag!"

Decimus hesitantly opened the bag as Julia held her breath.

The sentry rummaged around then pulled out a dagger and showed it to Darius.

Darius shook his head slightly. "That doesn't look like a physician's tool to me."

"I... use it when cutting the patient is required. It is very sharp," Decimus stammered, hoping his explanation was believable.

Julia could feel her heart pounding.

Darius stared at them for a moment. "I'm sure you won't need to cut the infant. We'll just keep the dagger here with me." Looking Decimus over, Darius asked, "You are young for a physician, aren't you?"

Decimus swallowed hard. "Yes, I am really the physician's assistant. He was... attending another patient so he sent me in his place."

Darius nodded. "I suppose we all have to learn a trade, don't we? Julia, show him where the child is being kept."

Julia and Decimus both exhaled in relief and went inside the child's room. Decimus placed his bag of physician's tools next to where Marcus's son lay. Seeing that he had been crying, Decimus said, "Well, little one. You don't look like you feel that well."

He put his hand on the child's forehead. "Yes, he is running a fever. I will give him something then I should stay awhile to observe him."

Darius showed a slight smile. "Do what you must, physician's assistant."

Taurus waited a short while then he turned to Antonius and said, "Don't try to show off your skills with a gladius, just kill Darius' men as quickly as you can."

Antonius nodded then the two galloped off and passed Marcus, giving him a nod.

As they approached the front villa gate, the guards went on alert and drew their swords.

"Hold there, and state your business!" Atticus shouted.

"I have an order from Prefect Macro," Taurus said.

"Let me see it," Atticus demanded, looking at him suspiciously. Seeing Antonius start to dismount as well, he shouted, "Only the centurion! You there, remain on your horse."

Taurus walked up and handed the forged document to him. After looking it over, Atticus said, "The fugitives we were waiting for have been arrested, eh?"

"Yes, just today. You can take your men and return to the Castra now."

"Good. I'm glad to be off this assignment anyway." He handed the document back to Taurus and instructed a Praetorian to go around the perimeter and gather the other men. When all the perimeter guards had reported to the front gate, Atticus said, "I should probably inform Centurion Aurelius we are leaving."

"I'll tell him for you," Taurus offered.

Atticus looked at him for a moment then said, "Very well. Mount up, men! We return to the Castra Praetoria."

Just as he was about to leave, Taurus called to him. "Oh, and optio... the next time a superior officer approaches, you had better salute him."

"Yes, Centurion," Atticus replied, making a face as he saluted. When all his men had assembled, he waved his hand forward and the detail departed.

Antonius dismounted and tied his horse to the hitching post just outside the gate. Julia's plan was working better than they had hoped.

Walking over to where Taurus stood, he quietly said, "They left the two guards at the front door."

"Yes," Taurus replied. "Flavius will have to take care of them otherwise we'll have them at our backs once we enter."

"Unless we bolt the door from the inside," Antonius suggested.

Taurus glance over at the guards at the front door and said, "Flavius will still have to eliminate them so we don't have to deal with two more when we leave. Did he bring his bow and arrows?"

"I saw him put them on the carriage just in case," Antonius replied.

"Good," Taurus stated. "Well, lets get this over with before the ones at the door get suspicious."

As Taurus and Antonius walked toward them, the guards at the front door tightly gripped their spears.

Stopping before them, Taurus held out the document. "The emperor's treason list has been abolished. Here, read it for yourselves."

One of the sentries nodded and said, "We trust you, centurion; enter and inform Centurion Aurelius."

As soon as Taurus and Antonius walked inside, they closed and bolted the door then drew their swords. But instead of being met with armed resistance they were met with silence. The room was empty. The guards Julia said to expect inside the main door were nowhere to be seen.

"I thought this was too easy," Taurus said, feeling the hair rise on the back of his neck.

"Julia!" Antonius called out.

A scream pierced the air from one of the rooms. Antonius and Taurus headed toward it just as Darius appeared with Julia in his grasp, holding the infant. Four of his best swordsmen stood before him with swords drawn. Darius yelled to his sentries outside the front door, "Guards! Make sure no one comes out the front entrance!"

The two sentries outside the front turned to face the door, pilums and shields at the ready. By doing so, however, they exposed their backs to Marcus, who picked up his bow nocked an arrow and fired.

One sentry fell.

Marcus quickly nocked another arrow and the second sentry fell.

A short distance away, Atticus brought his men to a halt. "This is far enough. Let's return to the villa and spring the trap."

Turning to one of his men, he added, "Ride to the Castra Praetoria and

72 *A piece of armor for the forearm*

tell the Prefect we are about to capture the rogue Praetorians we've been looking for. He may want to be present."

The soldier saluted and rode away at a hard gallop while the remaining men quickly made their way back to the villa.

Inside Darius sneered. "It appears you have fallen into my trap, Licinius. Surprised? You really didn't think I believed that Macro would send a girl to care for the child, did you? He could care less whether a criminal child lives or dies."

"Where is Decimus?" Antonius asked.

"The physician? Oh, don't worry; he is still alive. He will have a nasty bump on his head but he will live to face the gallows. And if you think your farmer friend outside will help, my perimeter guards you dismissed have probably returned by now and taken care of him as well. In a moment they will come through that door and my revenge will be complete."

"That is what this is all about, isn't it, Darius? Revenge."

Darius smiled. "Isn't that why you're here, Licinius?

Antonius thought of his father and replied, "No, Darius, I'm here to see that justice is done."

"Justice? Justice was served when your family was executed for treason against the emperor," Darius countered.

"That was not justice, that was murder and my family was innocent. You ignored procedure and killed them in cold blood."

Darius smiled. "That's not what I told Macro."

Outside, Marcus opened the front gate to the villa when he heard horses approaching. The detail of Praetorians was returning and he had to warn his companions.

Inside, Darius took out the dagger from his belt and raised it menacingly toward Julia and the child so Antonius could get a good look at it. "Do you like my new bauble, Licinius?"

Antonius clenched his teeth."You were the one who stole my father's dagger."

Darius smiled wickedly. "Come now, Licinius. A weapon this magnificent really belongs to one who deserves it; one who has earned it on the battlefield like I have."

"My father was the only one who earned it, Darius, and you aren't even deserving enough to wear his armor." He took a step toward Darius.

Darius's grip tightened on Julia's arm. "If you try anything before the rest of my men arrive, I'll kill the child and your lady friend here."

"Let them go!" Antonius shouted, keeping eyes on Darius. "It's me you want, Darius. Come and we'll settle this once and for all."

Darius merely glared at Antonius, daring him to move.

Marcus reached the front door and found it bolted. Pounding on it, he yelled, "Antonius! The other Praetorians are returning!"

Darius smiled. "Your farmer friend will soon meet his fate then you shall, Licinius.

Marcus hurried and looked for another way to get in. Peering through a small ventilation hole in the wall, he stopped and saw Darius holding Antonius and Taurus at bay using Julia and his son for a shield. Darius's men were almost upon him. At that moment, he knew what his sacrifice was that Jesus had foretold.

"Please let my aim be true," he said under his breath. Raising his bow, he let the arrow fly through the ventilation opening. He saw his arrow hit the metal vambrace[71] on Darius's wrist knocking the dagger out of his grip. He also saw the curly blonde head and pudgy face of his son just before Atticus and his men reached him.

Startled at having the dagger shot out of his hand, Darius released his grip on Julia and the infant. She quickly stepped to the side, holding tightly to little Marcus. At the same time, Antonius looked in the direction of where the arrow came from and exclaimed under his breath, "Marcus."

Seeing Darius drop the dagger, Taurus yelled, "Now, Licinius!" and sprang at the guards.

Antonius followed his lead and the battle began. The guards engaged them as Darius drew his sword and yelled, "Remember your instructions! I want the younger one alive!"

Outside, after several tries of putting their weight into it, Darius's men finally broke down the door and rushed inside.

"Behind you!" Julia shouted.

Taurus turned to face them as Antonius continued with the ones in front of him.

A moment later, Antonius turned to see his mentor cut down. However, not until he had slain three before the rest overwhelmed him.

As they stabbed him over and over, Julia cried, "Uncle!"

Facing dozens of swords that now surrounded him, Antonius looked at Julia and the child the same way his father had looked at his mother just before he died, knowing the end was near.

"Don't touch him... he's mine," Darius shouted.

Antonius clenched his teeth. For a moment the rage consumed him, but he forced himself to regain control. "Darius, if I defeat you, order your men to let us go like you promised. If you kill me, at least free Julia and the baby."

Darius pushed through his men. With a smirk, he stated, "You are in no position to make demands here, Licinius. After I kill you, we will take your girlfriend here and have her hung… of course, when I'm finished with her. Then I will have one of my men throw the child in the Tiber River. You are good when it comes to meaningless competitions where no lives are at stake. But you see, when it comes to life and death situations, I am the better man." He sliced the air a few times with his gladius then exclaimed, "Enjoy your last few breaths. In a moment, you will join your family in Tartarus."

Antonius felt his rage build as Darius attacked. They went back and forth as the other Praetorians surrounded them. Darius pressed the attack and forced Antonius back into one of the Praetorians who pushed him back into the fray. They slashed at each other for several more minutes until Darius managed to cut Antonius superficially on his upper arm. Stopping for a moment to catch their breath, Antonius said, "First blood. Congratulations."

Darius smiled. "But not the last. When I'm finished, all of yours will be on the floor."

They continued. During another exchange, Antonius slashed Darius on his arm. Darius backed off and wiped off the blood.

"Now we are even," Antonius said, feeling more confident as Darius snarled and attacked.

They parried back and forth until both found themselves out of breath again, neither with an advantage.

After resting another moment, Antonius gave Darius a piercing look and beckoned. "Come, let us finish this, Darius."

"It will be finished, when I finish you," Darius growled.

Circling each other, Darius decided to try a new tactic. "You know, Licinius, your sister was especially nice to me before she died. Who knows? Had she lived, she might have had another son."

The rage flared up once again and Antonius lunged at his foe. His rage cost him his focus, however. As quick as the strike of a cobra, Darius slashed Antonius on the wrist that held his weapon. The gladius clattered to the floor. Antonius had no feeling in his hand. Quickly picking up the gladius with his other hand, Antonius took a defensive posture.

With a smug grin, Darius asked, "Does this remind you of our final match during training, Licinius? Only now the roles are reversed. First I will cut you little by little. Then when you can no longer hold your gladius, I will cut your throat like I did your father and thrust my blade through your heart,

388

like I did your sister."

Antonius felt the surge of anger again, but this time, he heard Taurus's voice inside his head. "Stay focused." He calmed his rage and gave Darius a resolute look. "Yes, Darius, you are good at killing a man who gave up the sword a long time ago and defenseless women, but I am still the gladius master and the match isn't over yet, you putrid pile of pig dung."

Darius's smile turned into a scowl as he snarled and attacked. Much to Darius's surprise, Antonius defended himself skillfully. Darius kept pressing, looking for an opening but Antonius gave him none. Soon, fatigue became Darius's other foe.

Antonius waited for the opportune moment. Then, in a blur, he feinted high, crouched low and quickly lunged. His blade penetrated Darius's abdomen under his breastplate.

Darius's eyes went wide. With mouth agape, he dropped his gladius and crumpled to the floor. He saw the dagger with the black tourmaline handle nearby and reached for it. Before he could grasp his ill-gotten trophy, Antonius placed his foot on it.

"That belongs to my father," he said.

Feeling the searing pain of his mortal wound, Darius rolled over onto his back and with a dying rasp, said, "What are you waiting for? Go ahead! Finish it! Claim your trophy and have your revenge."

Antonius looked down at the wretched man dying at his feet and was surprised he felt no satisfaction in his victory, only pity.

"You don't understand, Darius. Lives are not trophies to be claimed. I seek no revenge, only justice."

With his last breath, Darius uttered, "Whether you call it justice or revenge, both of us are dead men anyway." Darius then let out his last breath.

Antonius knew that now he would have to face Darius's men. He took a fighting stance and slowly pivoted inside the circle from one Praetorian to the next, waiting for the inevitable charge.

The confused Praetorians turned to Atticus, awaiting the order to attack when suddenly, Macro and several Praetorians burst into the room with swords drawn.

"I was afraid of this," Macro said, as he surveyed the scene. Gesturing toward Darius, he asked, "Who killed Centurion Aurelius?"

A few Praetorians parted the circle and pointed to Antonius.

"You did this?" Macro asked Antonius.

Antonius came to attention. "Yes, Prefect."

Marcus felt himself rising in the air. He looked down and noticed his back covered in blood from the numerous stab wouds he received. The separation from his body made him realize he was no longer a mortal man. As he began to rise higher and higher into the sky, he felt the warmth of a light shining down on him from above. He found himself drawn to it with increasing eagerness and delight. Suddenly, three silhouettes appeared through a hazy mist. As he drew closer, he could tell they were Augustina, Jacob, and his father all dressed in white. Instantly, he felt at peace and thought, "There *is* an afterlife."

PALESTINE

MEDITERRANEAN SEA
SYRO-PHOENICIA
GAULANITIS
Lake Huleh
Chorazin
Acco (Ptolemais)
Capernaum
Bethsaida
Magadan
GALILEE
Sea of Galilee
Tiberias
Hippos
Cana
Sepphoris
Nazareth
Nain
DECAPOLIS
PLAIN OF SHARON
Caesarea
Pella
Salim
Aenon
SAMARIA
Sebaste
Sychar
Mt. Gerizim
Antipatris
Alexandrium
Joppa (Japho)
Arimathaea
PERAEA
Lydda
Ephraim
Philadelphia
Emmaus
Jericho
Cyprus
Betharamptha (Livias Julias)
Jamnia
Jerusalem
Qumran
Azotus
Bethany
Bethlehem
JUDAEA
Herodium
Ascalon
Dead Sea (Salt Sea)
Machaerus
Gaza
Hebron
0 Miles 20
Masada
Roads
N
Beersheba
IDUMAEA

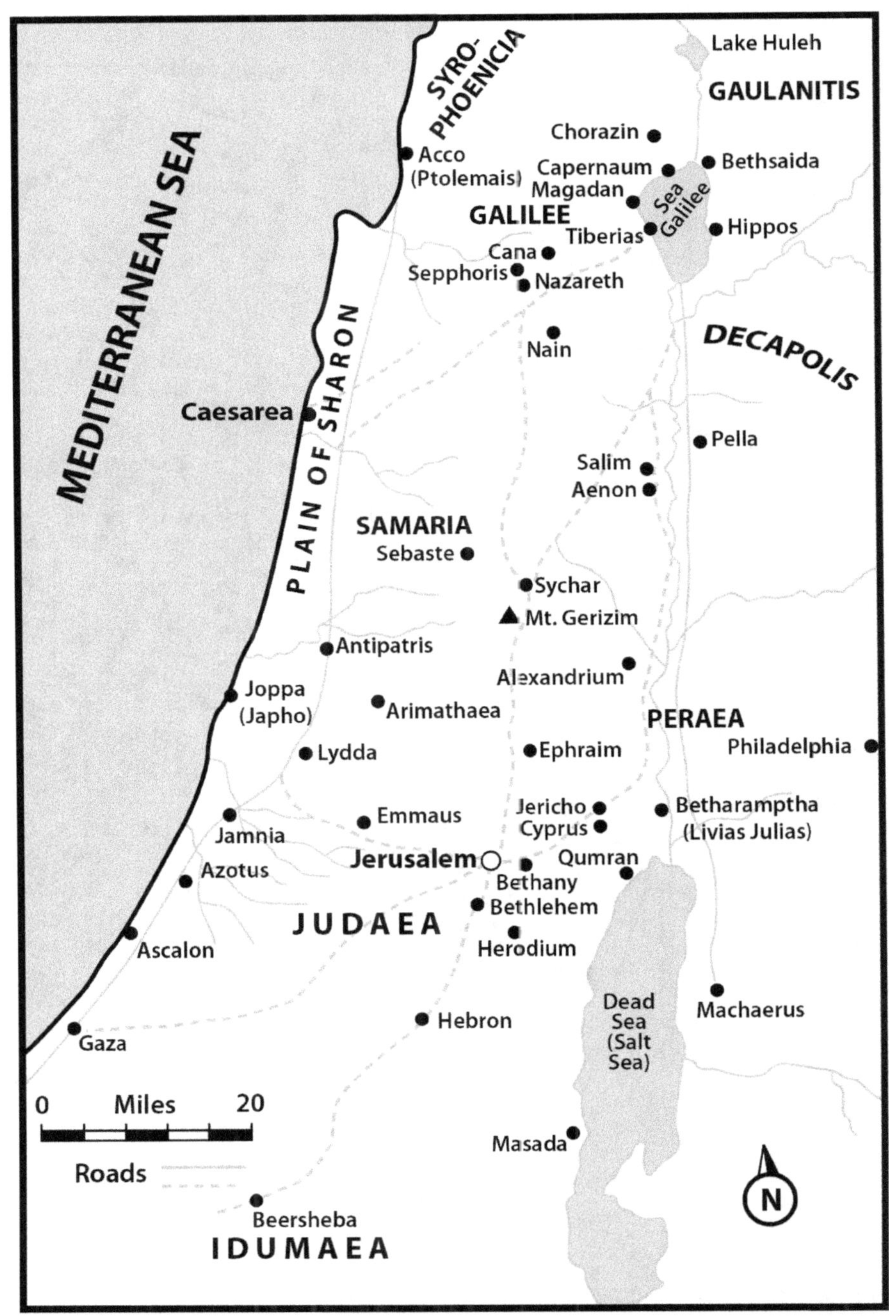

ROME
PART 1

P.ta Flaminia
Horti Domitiorum
Horti Aciliorum
P.ta Pinciana
PINCI
Naumachia Vaticana
Mausoleum Augusti
Horti Luculliani
S. Laurenti in Lucina
Castra Urbana
VII
V. TRIUMPHALIS
Mausoleum Hadriani
Porticus Vipsania
Pons Aelius
Arc. Gratiani
CAMPUS MARTIUS
IX
CAMPUS AGRIPPAE
Thermae Neronianae
Arcus Claudii
Tarentum
Stadium Domitiani
Pantheon
Saepta
VIII
Columna Traiani Forum
Odeon
Thermae Agrippae
6
Theatrum Pompeii
7
S. Marci
Circus Flaminius
P.ta Septimiana
Pons Agrippae
Theatrum Balbi
Porticus Octaviae
Capitolium
10
Horti Getae
Pons Aurelius
Pons Fabricius
8
12
Forum
Aqua Alsietina
TIBERINA I.
Pons Cestius
16
VIA AURELIA
PAGUS IANICULENSIS
Pons Sublicius
FORUM BOARIUM
XI
Circus Maximus
Naumachia Augusti?
18
19
Aqua Traiana
Pons Probi
Thermae Suranae
XIV
Horti Caesaris
Emporium
Port. Aemilia
Aventinus
Thermae Decianae
XII
P.ta Portuensis
XIII
S. Balbin.
Horti
Horrea Galbiana
(MONTE VERDE)
PONTIANI
Testaceus Mons
20
P.ta Ostiensis
Tiberis
V. OSTIENSIS

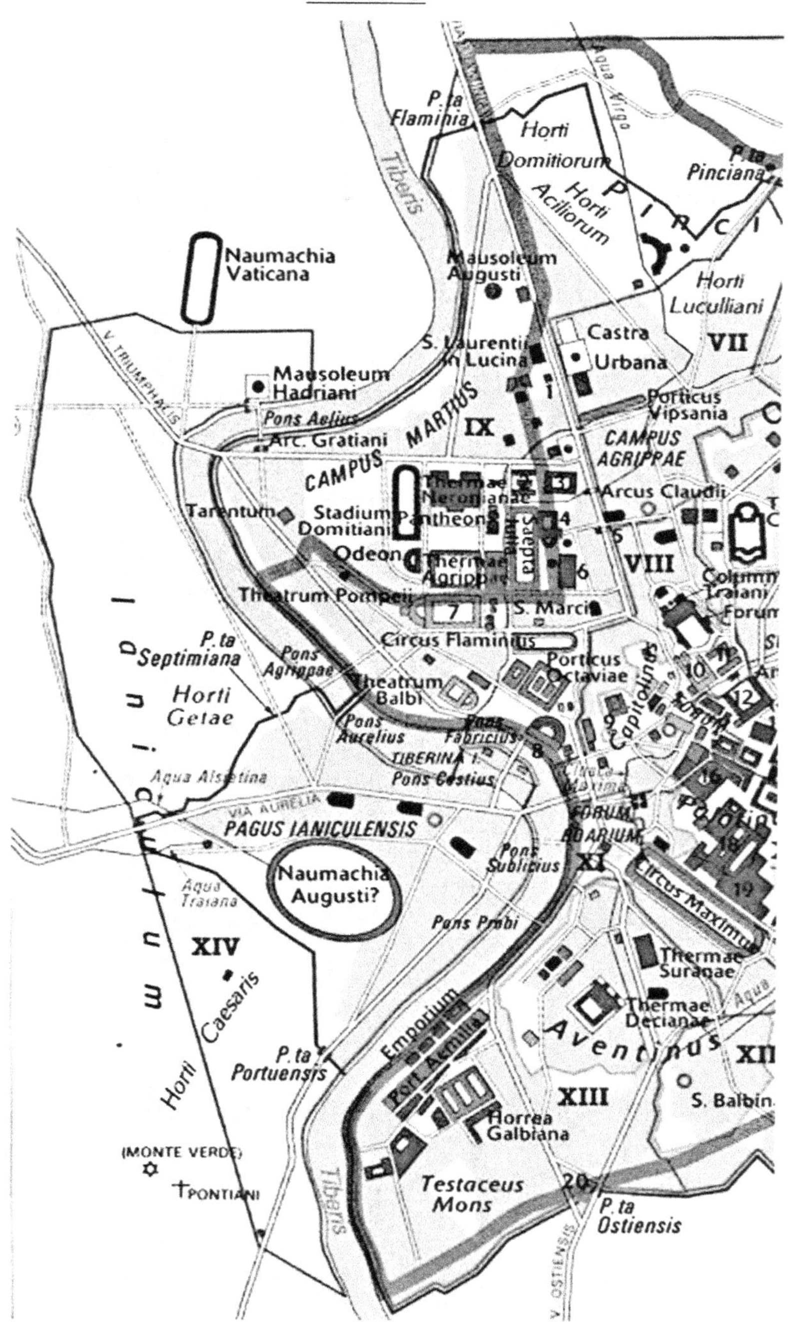

ROME
PART 2

VIA SALARIA
VIA NOMENTANA
P.ta Salaria
P.ta Nomentana
NICOMEDIS
Horti Sallustiani
Castra Praetoria
Thermae Diocletiani
V
Aqua Marcia
Quirinalis
Horti Lollani
VI
Vicus Longus
Viminalis
Thermae Constantini
Patricius
Anio Vetus
Macellum Liviae
Horti Tauriani
Horti
Hom
P.ta Tiburtina
Aqua Iulia
um Traiani
SUBURA
IV
Vicus
Esquilinus
Maecenatis
Porticus Liviae
Amphitheatrum Flavium (Colosseum)
Thermae Traiani
AURELIORUM
Horti Liciniani
P.ta Praenestina
V. PRAENES
13
14
15
III
X
Ludus Magnus
Aqua Marcia
Aqua Claudia
Thermae Helenae
Ludus
Hierusalem
Templum Divi Claudii
Caelius
Salvatoris in Laterano
P.ta Asinaria
II
Macellum
VIA TRION
P.ta Metrovia
II
S. Xysti
I
Thermae Antoninianae (Caracallae)
21
P.ta Latina
VIA LATINA
VIA APPIA
Aqua Severiana
P.ta Ardeatina
P.ta Appia

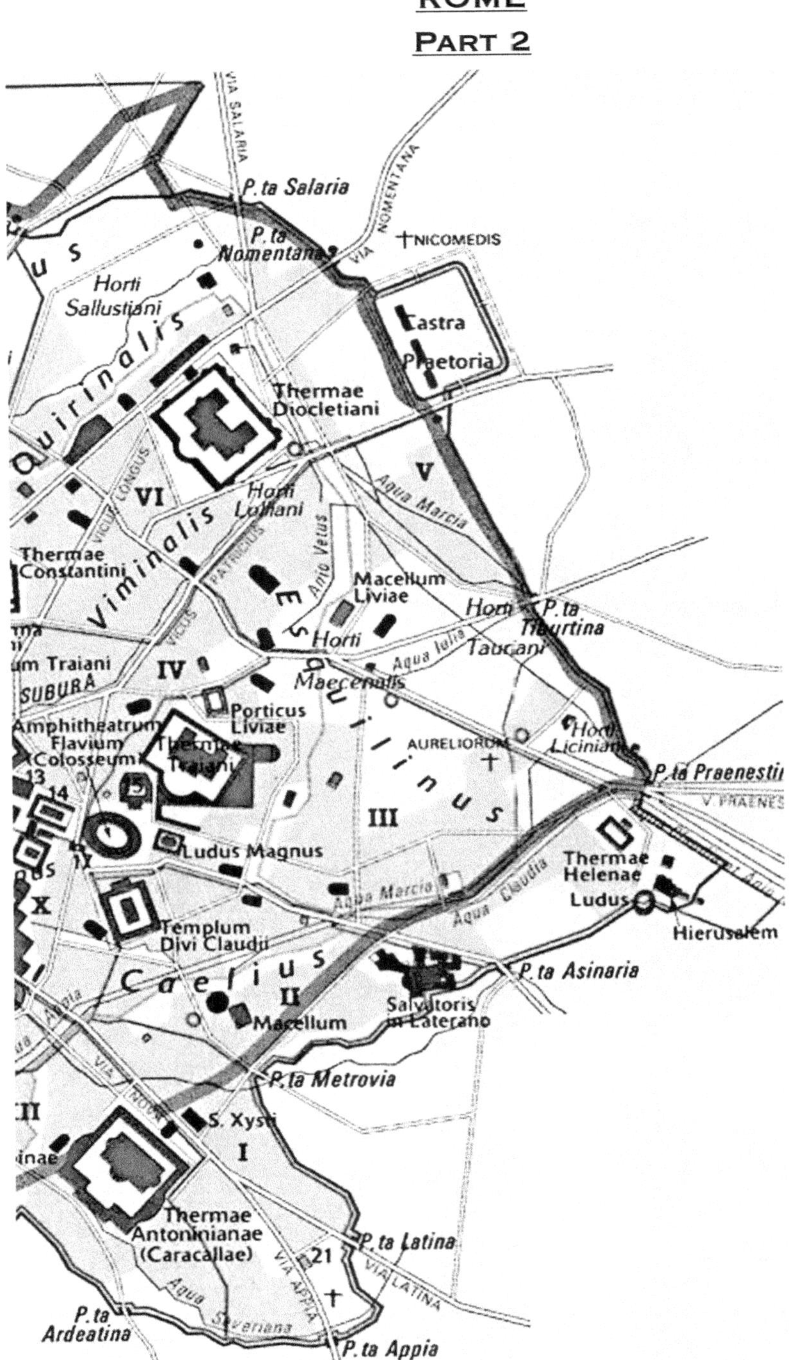

ROMAN EMPIRE

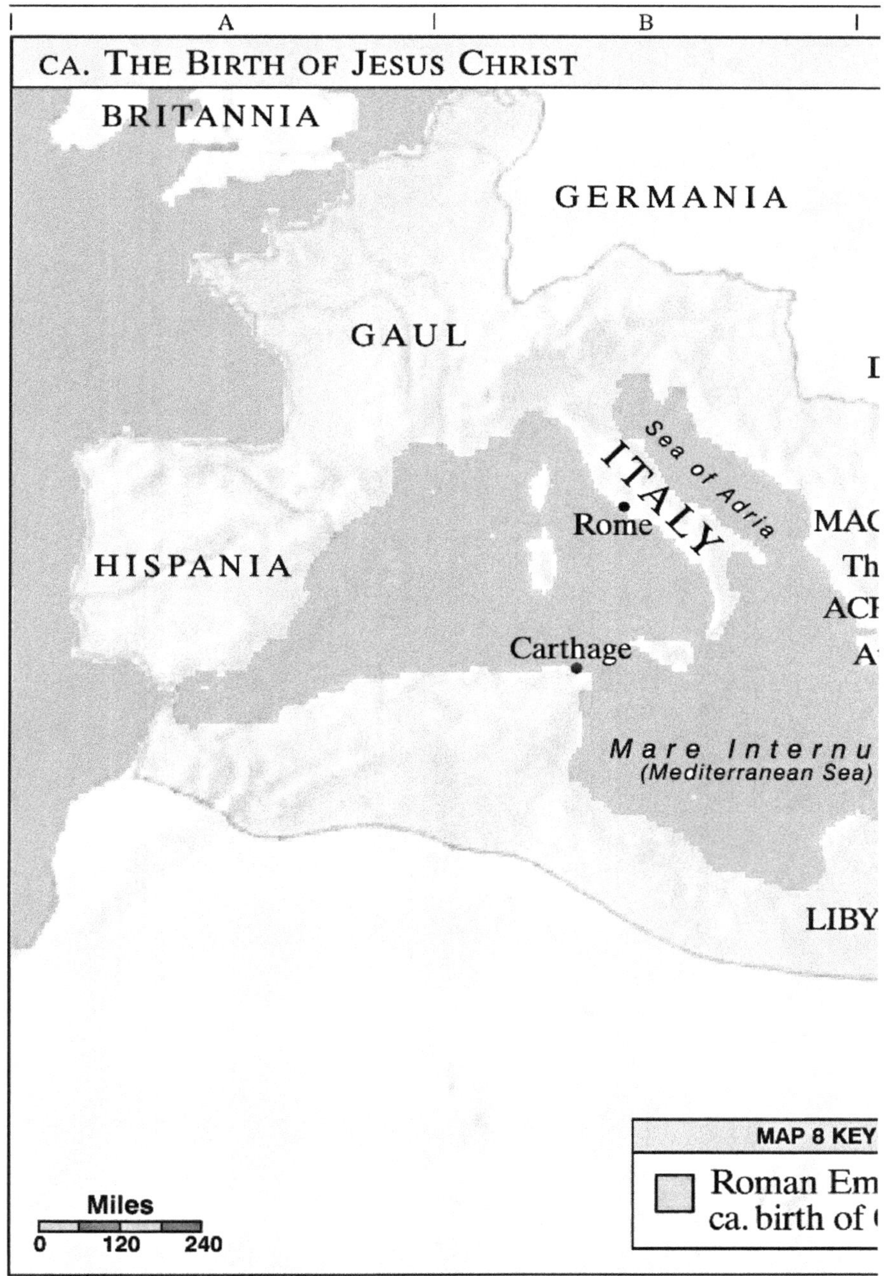

ROMAN EMPIRE

GLOSSARY OF FOOTNOTES
IN ALPHABETICAL ORDER

Amphora- A jar used for wine, usually ceramic but sometimes metal

Aramaic- A language belonging to the Semitic family that includes Hebrew and Phoenician

Atrium- Formal room where guests were received

Aureii- The plural of aureus-the largest gold coin circulated during this period

Buckler- A small, round shield used for close combat

Caligae- Classic Roman military sandals or hob-nailed boots

Circus Maximus- A large stadium in the heart of Rome used for chariot racing and large entertainment venues; could hold 150,000 spectators

Contubernium- Smallest unit of the Roman military, consisting of eight men

Creta- Crete–the largest and most populous of the Greek islands

Cubiculum- Bedroom

Cubit- A unit of length = 1.5 feet

Cucina- Kitchen

Cuirass- An armored breastplate and backplate

Curia Julia- The building in the Roman Forum where the senate officially met

Decanus- The leader of a contubernium (squad of eight) that lived in the same tent

Denarii- Plural of denarius-the largest silver coin used during this period

Equestrian- Patricians consisting of wealthy businessmen & high officials, and by extension their families; wore tunics called augusticlavi

Flagrum- A whip consisting of three leather tendrils attached to a wooden handle

Gemonian stairs- Also called "Stairs of Mourning" Bodies of the condemned were thrown down these stairs for display and left to rot in full view of the Forum, until eventually being thrown into the Tiber River

Gladius- The short sword used by Roman footsoldiers

Gravitas- A seriousness or solemnity of manner

Greaves- Leather or metal armor that protected the shin area

Hippodrome- An arena used for chariot racing, gladiator contests and other sporting events

Julians- Those people related to the first five Roman emperors

League- A unit of length = 1.379 miles

Libra- A unit of weight, roughly 3/4 of a pound

Liburnian- A small galley ship used for raiding with two rows of oars

Maestas- Treason

Magnus- "The Great"

Mappa- A large, white handkerchief used to start the race

Merda- Slang for excrement

Milite- The trained Roman foot soldier

396

Onager- A Roman siege weapon similar to a catapult

Optio- A rank similar to lieutenant; second in command of a century of men

Patrician- Considered by ancient Roman standards to be the upper class of people; nobility and wealthy landowners

Pilum- A javelin used by the Roman military

Plebeian- Considered by ancient Roman standards to be the lower class of people, from tradesmen down to the very poor

Princeps- Literally means "first citizen;" referring to the emperor

Pugio- Dagger

Quaestor- Designated legal official

Quando tu Gaius, ego Gaia- Phrase uttered by the bride to the groom during the marriage ceremony meaning: "Where you go I will follow"

Quaternio- Death squad assigned to scourge and crucify a prisoner

Salutatio- A time set aside each morning when the patron would hold court in the atrium of his house. During this time unofficial business would be conducted, favors requested, political support lined up, and monetary handouts given to those who performed favors.

Scutum- A large rectangular, concave battle shield

Sesterce- The largest brass coin used during this period

Solemnitas togae purae- A rite of passage for a Roman boy into manhood, celebrated on his fourteenth birthday

Spatha- A sword similar to a gladius, but with a longer blade; used by cavalry

Speculatore- Bodyguards, couriers, law-enforcers, and sometimes executioners

Stipes- The main wooden post used for crucifixion

Stola- A long, pleated dress; the traditional outer garment of Roman women

Subligaculum- A cloth undergarment wrapped around the groin

Tablinum- Study

Testudo- A maneuver where soldiers hold a shield wall around the sides and top of a formation

Tribune- Officer who ranked above Centurion, similar to a captain

Triclinium- Dining room

Trierarch- Captain of a Roman trireme

Trireme- A war ship with three rows of oars on each side, with one man per oar

Vambrace- A piece of armor for the forearm

Verberatio- Scourging

Vestibulum- A small entrance hall into the house

Vigiles- Firefighters and police; also acted as a night watch for the city

Villa Urbana- Living quarters for the owner and his family

Vitis- A swagger stick carried by Centurions, approximately 3' in length

Xystis- A garment charioteers wore that covered the entire body, fastened at the waist with a simple belt; also called a chiton

LIST OF MAIN CHARACTERS

Antonia Minor- mother to Claudia Livia "Livilla"

Antonius Licinius- son of Galerius and Octavia Licinius; 19 years old at the beginning of the story

Apicata Sejanus- divorced wife of Lucius Sejanus

Augustina Licinius- Antonius's sister; three years younger than Antonius

Camilla Flavius- Marcus's mother; works the farm with her husband and children; sells their extra produce in town

Cicero Taurus- training Centurion for Praetorian recruits

Claudia Livia "Livilla" Julia- wife of Drusus Julius Caesar; later became Lucius Sejanus's second wife

Crassus Varinius- innkeeper of the Olive Branch Inn at Tarrentum; retired Praetorian and friend to Galerius Licinius

Darius Aurelius- Praetorian who becomes Antonius's chief adversary

Decimus Faustus- hired hand on the Licinius vineyard

Demosthenes-Greek aide to Pontius Pilate

Domitia- matronly servant to the Cato family

Drusus Julius Caesar- Emperor Tiberius's son; married Claudia Julia Livia

Felix Castor- another speculatore/bodyguard for Lucius Sejanus

Gaius "Caligula" Germanicus- adopted grandson of Tiberius

Galerius Licinius- Antonius's father; a former Tribune in the Praetorian Guard, now owns a vineyard in Aletium, Italy where his family resides

Horatio Cornelius- Praetorian and close friend of Aurelius

Ignatio & Lucia Regulus- middle-aged husband and wife caretakers for the Licinius villa in Rome

Julia Cato- a young girl who becomes Antonius's love interest

Juliana Cato- Julia's mother

Julius Varius- a speculatore/bodyguard for Lucius Sejanus

Lucius Aelius Sejanus- Praetorian Prefect in charge of Tiberius's security; highest ranking Praetorian

Marcus Flavius- friend of Antonius who lives on a farm just over the hill from the vineyard; a year younger than Antonius

Martinus Liberius- Prefect in charge of the Roman garrison in Caesarea

Matthias, Milo, Priscilla & Prisca Flavius- Marcus's brothers and sisters

Octavia Licinius- Antonius's mother; a former senator's daughter

Pontius Pilate- Roman governor to Judaea

Procula Pilate- wife of Pontius Pilate

Quintus Sutorius Macro- Praetorian Prefect of the Vigiles-Praetorians who made up the night watch for the city, the police and the fire brigade

Satrius Secundus- senator and spy for Lucius Sejanus
Sergius Flavius- Marcus's father; has a hatred for Praetorians and Patricians
Serina Cato- Julia's older sister
Sidonius Cato- Julia's father; a praetor or judge
Strabo, Capito & Junilla- children of Lucius and Apicata Sejanus
Thracius Falconius- Tribune in charge of the Praetorian training camp
Tiberius Gemellus- son of Claudia Livia from her marriage to Drusus
Tiberius Julius Caesar Augustus- Emperor of Rome during this period

Other books by Rod Warren:

Book 2-The Praetorian and the Vipers
Book 3-The Praetorian and the Emperor's Madness

Who Let This Guy in the White House?
(Political Satire)

Pickle Beach Comics
(Surfing Comic Strips)

You can purchase them on Amazon.com or IngramSpark.com
For examples of the author's illustration work,
log onto www.rwarren.art

400